- To Lisa, my wife, and my children, Alex, Nicolle, Gill and Danielle For helping me off the island.

He loved the darkness. Being able to sneak around without a soul aware was a power he enjoyed. It gave him a sense of being and almost Godliness. Not being there one minute and then there the next, like he had invisibility or powers of teleportation. He was more than those he was hunting. Just like the man he now stalked.

The dim offices of Reynolds & Hoffman were a maze of cubicles and walkways. Nestled in one of the executive skyscrapers within Exchange Place, the law office on the 11th floor was almost empty. Save for a Douglas Martin, working late for one of the partners on an upcoming trial. He saw the lone light burning from the street below, knowing that it was Douglas's. Who else would be in the building at 3am on a Sunday morning? Trying desperately to impress the partners and make himself known to those above him. All a waste, though, he thought. Poor Doug would only be a page eight article.

He stood proudly in the dark hall, to the side, watching Doug rummage through the filing cabinet in the small filing room on the East wing. Doug searched for the one file that would help him make a difference in the case. He watched on. There was such light and determination in Doug. It almost made him sad to do what he was there to do. But then again, watching Doug for the entire week made him sad for the poor guy.

He had followed Doug, learning his routine, watching his habits, and getting into Doug's head. Doug lived in a brownstone in Hoboken, NJ where he managed to hang out with the few friends he gained, working at the law office. Not too bad looking, Doug still was not a ladies man.

He had not brought home any women in the time that he was watching. Wondering if his tastes ran the other way, he broke into the house and found a box of heterosexual porn. This answered his question.

Doug closed the one drawer and opened the one below that, continuing his search for the one folder. He crept into the doorway and remained still. He was waiting for the right moment to strike. Seconds later, Doug found his folder and yanked it out of the drawer.

"Yes! Got it. Douglas, you are the man!" Douglas laughed to himself, slamming the drawer close. As he did, something fluttered in the corner of his eye. Doug spun around, expecting to see one of the night cleaners watching him. But when he did, there was no one in the doorway. Doug breathed a sigh of relief. Now that he had found the folder his work for the night was done.

Douglas returned to his desk, the uneasy feeling returning to him. Was someone here? He looked around and listened. There was no sound other than the whirl of the computer's internal fan. He waved it off, thinking it was the exhaustion kicking in. He had put in quite a few hours for his boss, hoping to nail the robber that they were prosecuting. It was your typical 'guy robs a liquor store and beats employee for fun' case. The one catch was what he had been searching for. The criminal had a habit that was clear on the tape but only if you were looking for it. And that was the slamming of the door. Case closed, Doug thought. Once this was all finished, he could return to the case that he was working on previously.

He gathered the papers and the folder and placed it into his briefcase. It was time to go home. A quick twelve minute drive back to his place, a nice cold shower to ward off the August heat and then straight to bed for a few hours. That was his weekend. But Doug didn't mind. He was doing his part in keeping the streets safe.

The air outside the building was muggy, giving him the slimy workout feeling that most humid August days in the Tri-State area gave. Doug walked to his car and got in. The night silence was a bit unnerving, considering the area around Exchange Place was a bit slum-like. But he guessed, even criminals had to sleep sometime.

Doug checked his backseat and then started the car. He drove away, satisfied by the quality of work he had completed. Once he arrived home, he was happy to find the parking spot he left hours ago was still there. Parking in Hoboken, New Jersey was about as easy as finding a needle in a mile high haystack. But the life of the bustling city was something he loved. And the line of bars on Washington Street was an added bonus.

He walked into his studio apartment and placed the briefcase on the kitchen table. He walked over and opened the fridge, pulling out a bottle of water. Closing the fridge, he nearly dropped the bottle and screamed. A man stood in front of him, dressed in black nylon, wearing plastic surgical gloves.

"Whoa! Hold on! You can have anything you want in the place, just leave me alone." He told the intruder.

"The only thing I want from you, Doug, is your blood." The man replied, before throwing Doug across the room. Doug crashed into the kitchen table and knocked it over. He jumped to his feet, ready to run for the door. But the intruder grabbed him by the shoulder and brought the steak knife he had taken from the kitchen drawer and stabbed Doug in the chest. The air left Doug's lungs as the pain shot through his body. The intruder did not stop. He stabbed Doug over and over.

Doug tried to cry out but the pain clenched his vocal cords, preventing anything than a muttered breath out of his mouth. The world around him darkened and he crumbled to the floor, the blood creeping out of his wounds and gathering beneath him.

The intruder smiled, his plan coming to completion. He dropped the knife on the floor next to Doug Martin and removed the glove from his right hand. He then gently dipped his thumb into the blood puddle and walked over to the couch, where the briefcase had landed. Placing his thumb on the briefcase, he held it there for a few seconds. He stood up and returned the glove to his hand. Returning to his silent mode, he opened the front door and left the apartment. Evil begets chaos, he thought. And, oh what chaos was to come for an innocent man.

ONE

THE EVIDENCE

1

Craig Waterford woke that morning to the aroma of French Vanilla coffee brewing. The breaking sun peeked through the blinds and lay across his legs. Without moving he sensed that Jacqueline was not lying beside him. Craig turned slightly and saw the rustled sheet had been thrown aside and the other side of the bed was empty. She was always more of a morning person than he was. But ever since the inheritance, he had no choice but to make the change.

He sat up and placed his bare feet on the new plush carpet that Jacqueline had convinced him to put down. She was, again, right when she had told him that it would be more comforting than placing feet on a cold hardwood floor first thing in the morning. Glancing at the clock, he saw that it was a few minutes after 5 a.m. There was enough time to jump in the shower and head down Washington Street to work.

Craig walked out of the bedroom and headed down the short hall to the kitchen first. Coffee first, then shower he thought. Jacqueline was there, cooking eggs and toast for breakfast. She stood barefoot, wearing a long t-shirt and soft cotton shorts. Her long dark brown hair covered her face as she worked on the scrambled eggs. Seeing her like that cemented the fact that his life was pretty darn good.

"Morning," he muttered, wrapping his arms around her waist. He kissed her neck softly, below her ear, just where she loved it.

"Good morning scruffy bear," she replied. She turned around and rubbed the stubble on his cheek. He smiled and pulled her close. Her soft lips fit perfectly around his own as his hand slowly made it's way down her back. She stopped it midway and smiled at him.

"Now now, we don't have much time for that. You need to get ready. We are going to have quite the day ahead of us and you'll need to look your best." Jacqueline reached across the counter and handed him a fresh cup of coffee that she had poured for him. Craig took a drink of it and nodded to her, returning back to the hall and into the bathroom.

It was going to be a typical Monday for them. Mondays were always busy down at Tony's Deli. It had been named after his grandfather, Anthony Waterford, back when he first opened it in Hoboken 47 years ago. When Anthony learned that he was dying of lung cancer, he passed it on to his son, Craig's father, Harry Waterford. Harry and Pauline, Craig's mother, continued to run the business with the same success. A year and a half ago, Harry came to Craig and asked if he would like to take over the business.

"What about school?" Craig asked. Craig had gone back to college to obtain a business degree and still had a year left before he would receive his masters.

"Well, your mother and I can wait another year before we retire if you're willing."

Craig had known that this day would come. Harry was a bit of an old time traditionalist. Passing the business on through the family was important to him as his father had done the same. Craig knew that if he said no, Harry would respect his decision but still be disappointed. The business would then have to be sold and Tony's Deli would be no more.

"I'd be more than happy to take over for you once school is done," Craig had told him. Harry's face lit up and he placed his hand on Craig's shoulder.

"I know the store will be successful under your supervision." And so, once Craig had earned his Master's degree in business, Harry and Pauline retired and handed the deed to the deli over to Craig and Jacqueline. It was now three months later and profit for the deli had increased by two percent.

Once Craig had showered and dressed for the day, he returned to the kitchen. Jacqueline had finished making breakfast and was watching the Channel 11 news. Craig helped himself to the eggs and toast and sat down next to her.

"Don't forget we have to call Sunrise and order some more chicken for next week's special," he reminded her.

"I'll call them right before lunch," she told him. Her attention was taken by the graphics on the screen. Then the anchor woman popped up with some grim news.

"The body of a lawyer was found in his Hoboken apartment yesterday evening. Evidence at the scene has led police to believe it was a homicide. 28 year old Douglas Martin was found by neighbors of the brownstone apartment when they noticed a strange smell and the apartment door open. Police suspect that robbery was the motive and that Martin had walked in on the robber. No word of any suspects at this time but Hoboken police are currently working on several leads."

"That scares me," Jacqueline told Craig.

"I'll install a stronger lock on the door."

"It's not that," Jacqueline explained, "It scares me because what about when we have a baby. We'll be bringing it into this." She pointed at the screen.

"Sweetheart, we were brought into this world and look how we turned out. When the time comes, we'll be prepared to teach our child to be prepared and cautious about this." He placed his hand on hers and rubbed it gently, soothing her worry. She looked over at him and smiled. He loved her smile and the way it brighten the room and his soul.

"Well, let's say for argument's sake, we did have a child. Do you think it would cause problems for the deli? I'd have to take time off and we'd be down one worker."

"Jacqueline, if we had a baby I'd make adjustments at the deli ahead of time. We can hire another person. And we have Jon, Mike and Connie to help out already. The deli will be fine."

"You're right, I'm just being silly." Craig squinted his eyes at her. She was acting rather strange and it made him wonder.

"Why the sudden worry? When we decide to have a baby, we'll be prepared. It's not like you'll be having a baby on a mysterious island in the middle of nowhere with the Others chasing you."

"Well, that's why. I was thinking last night that I'm late and I thought about getting a test this morning."

"But you said you're only late by a couple of days."

"I know but I just got this feeling and figured I'd check to make sure."

Craig put the fork down and looked at her. She was playing her poker face and he wasn't sure where she was going with this. He leaned forward and held her hand.

"And?"

Jacqueline lifted her other hand and held up the pregnancy test that she had taken while Craig still slept. Craig saw the plus sign and his mouth dropped open.

"Hi, daddy," Jacqueline said with a smile.

2

Hoboken Homicide detective Brett Foster and his partner Josh Raghetti pulled up to the brownstone. The first officers on the scene had already cordoned off the area with yellow tape and appeared to be interviewing the other occupants of the building. The worst part was the small crowd that had already gathered and was slowly growing. They were the part of the job that Brett didn't like. It displayed the morbid curiosity that society was finding suitable. Luckily, no reporters had yet showed.

"Twenty bucks says it's a lovers' spat gone wrong," Josh tempted Brett. Brett just looked at him and rolled his eyes. He made the motion of getting out of the vehicle but stopped and shook the hand that Josh held out for the bet.

"I say it's your typical robbery gone wrong."

"You're on," Josh replied. His eyes sparkled with the happiness knowing that he would be twenty bucks richer in the next thirty minutes.

The detectives walked over and ducked under the tape and over to the officer speaking to one of the witnesses. The officer was surprisingly older than the two detectives. Brett knew that he would have to take it easier on the officer out of respect. The officer turned to the approaching men and nodded. His face was worn from the years on the job and portrayed the definition of sullen.

"Detectives Foster and Raghetti," Brett told the officer, flashing the badge he wore on his belt. "Are you the first officer on the scene?"

"Yes, I was," the older man explained, "Officer Dean Palmer." He held his hand out. Brett shook it and asked for the details as they walked up the front steps.

"Neighbor above the victim called it in. Woman by the name of Adrienne Evers. The victim's name is Doug Martin, a lawyer. She reported the horrible smell coming from the apartment and went downstairs to say something. That's when she saw the door was ajar. She got a little nosy and peeked inside. She saw the body on the floor and rushed upstairs to call us."

"What did you see?" Josh asked impatiently. Palmer threw Brett a puzzled look and Brett shrugged.

"Upon entering the apartment, the smell of the body was pretty strong. The apartment itself is quite the mess. Definite signs of struggle and I noticed the lack of some typical household items. My opinion is that the victim walked in on a home robbery. Robber got freaked out and attacked. Weapon was left behind next to the body. Steak knife from the apartment." Brett smirked at Josh. Josh frowned and shook his head.

"It's not definite yet," was all he said.

"Has the examiner arrived?" Brett asked Palmer.

"No, but he should be here rather quickly. They were notified ten minutes ago."

The three entered the apartment and Brett immediately covered his nose with his shirt sleeve. The August humidity in the New Jersey and New York City area was pretty thick and it had caused the body to slightly speed up the decaying process. The heat the body gathered had caused the organs to expel the gases built up throughout any pores and orifices.

The apartment was indeed a mess. The kitchen table was destroyed, counters were clear while their items rested broken on the floor. Desk drawers were torn out and thrown to the floor as well. This did appear to be a robbery homicide. But Brett knew better than to take things at their surface. He didn't work his way up to homicide by guessing. He pulled on a pair of thin plastic gloves that he had kept in his pants pocket and sifted through the mess. Josh walked over to the couch and looked around there. He examined the photos on the coffee table and noticed some were of the victim with a few women, each in their own separate photos. As they were searching for clues, the medical examiner arrived. Like Officer Palmer, the examiner's appearance surprised Brett.

The young medical examiner had short black hair, tanned skin and wore a white lab coat over a red t shirt. Over the excessive gum chewing, Brett could hear the ipod's headphones spit out some 70s disco music. And he noticed on the right wrist of the examiner was the Chinese symbol for life.

"Hey, you Homicide?" he asked Brett.

"Brett Foster," Brett replied. Then he pointed to Josh, "That's Josh Raghetti."

"I'm Dave. Dave Francis. Let's have a look at the body before the smell gets to me." Brett motioned him over to the body and Dave went to work.

"We've got multiple stab wounds. From the pattern of the marks, I'd say the killer is Left handed. The edges of the wounds are smooth, not ragged, that says that the killer wasn't in a rage when he did this. He was calm but from the amount of wounds, he enjoyed it."

"Who would enjoy something like this?" Brett thought out loud.

"That's what you guys are here for," Dave answered.

"Thanks, I wasn't sure about that," Brett sarcastically muttered.

"Hey Brett, I'm going to run out and grab the print kit. We've got a nice bloody print here on Martin's briefcase. Looks like a thumb." Josh pointed down to the briefcase at his feet. Brett walked over and squatted down to examine it. Josh was right. The print was perfect. But looking around, he didn't see any other blood splatter except for around the body, which was a good fifteen to twenty feet away. The brief case was opened and the papers were strewn around. Something didn't sit right in Brett's stomach but a lead was a lead.

"Maybe this will be closed faster than we thought."

It was midnight, five hours later, when Brett gave up waiting for an answer to the identity of the thumbprint. The computer tech, Melvin, did him a favor and jumped his print to the head of the line. But only for a price.

"You're awesome," Melvin praised Brett. Brett had made it important to know everyone's weakness in the tech lab. Thus he could use it to his advantage when looking for fast results. Melvin's was a certain food.

Melvin dug into the White Castle bag and pulled out a Slider, the infamous tiny square burger that was made popular from that comedy film, Harold and Kumar. The first of seven was devoured in two bites.

"So you can get this done first?" Brett asked him.

"I can scan the print into the system now. That will only take a few minutes and then let the machine run while I take care of the other cases. You're lucky we don't have any other prints to check. And please don't mention this to Wogle, he'll have my ass for it if he finds out."

Michael Wogle was the head of the Hoboken Crime Analysis Lab. He was very by the book and unleashed a rage that only a boss could if corners were cut and favorites were made with the investigative detectives.

"Don't worry, I won't say a word. How long will it take to find a match?"

"Normally, checking both criminal and civilian databases, it takes about two to three hours. But. They're currently upgrading the system, so that's going to push it back another three hours if it works on the first try."

"Of course, it is," Brett sighed, "Just give me a call on my cell phone when you find something.

Melvin finished the White Castle treat and then scanned the thumbprint into the IAFIS database, which stood for Integrated Automated Fingerprint Identification System, a network used by local and state police, FBI and CIA to match fingerprints.

Brett drove home to his little apartment on Grand Street two blocks from St Mary's Hospital. He was not too far from where he grew up in Jersey City, the next town over. After graduating from the police academy, he had found a spot on the Jersey City Police force. It was there, he had learned what he needed to be the best detective he could be.

His mentor, Officer Shawn Locke, told stories for hours during their shifts together. It was to get him familiar with what he would one day take over. As Brett would drive, Shawn would explain the people and events of that which surrounded them.

"See that homeless lady over there?" Shawn had pointed out one night, "That's Lady Sandy. First thing you should know about her is she's not homeless. Her real name's Sandra Dolci. She heads the citizens patrol in this neighborhood. Does herself up like a homeless person because no one cares about the homeless so she can watch without being bothered."

Shawn got out of the vehicle and Brett followed. They walked up to Lady Sandy and Shawn began talking to her.

"Hey Sandy, anything going on tonight?"

"Not tonight officer," she explained, "All's quiet on the streets."

"Good to hear," he replied. Shawn pulled a protein bar from his pocket and handed it to her.

"Bless your soul, Shawn Locke. People here should be glad to have you watching them."

"Thanks Sandy. Stay safe."

"With the Lord on my side, I'm always safe," she smiled. Her teeth appeared yellow but Shawn later explained that it was due to the yellow food coloring she put on them before going out. At the end of the night, the two officers returned to the station. As they got out of the car, Shawn stopped him.

"What was the lesson of the night?"

"Lady Sandy's a good guy?" Brett guessed.

"No," Shawn explained, "Never judge a book by it's cover. If it looks like a duck and quacks like a duck, it doesn't mean that it's actually a duck. Always look deeper because sometimes the innocent-looking can actually the guilty ones."

Brett had always remembered the lessons that Shawn Locke passed on to him. Years later, the move to Hoboken had earned him the detective position, which he has held well since.

Brett entered the apartment and turned on the television. The background noise made the apartment feel more of a home. Jimmy Kimmel interviewed some current star on their new movie as Brett opened the fridge and pulled a beer from it. He sat down in his lounger and tried to relax. Yet he couldn't help but flashback to the apartment of Doug Martin. The fingerprint bothered him. It was too simple, as if the owner of it wanted them to see it. But why?

Brett fell asleep shortly after still asking himself that question.

3

Melvin handed his Police Lab co-worker, Lucky, the folder that he was working on at the time. The two technicians had worked hard over the nightshift. The AFIS upgrade didn't affect the rest of the cases but Melvin kept an eye on it for Brett. Once the upgrade was fully complete at 3 a.m. he scanned the print into the system and began the search for a match. Then he and Lucky continued working on the other cases that appeared.

Lucky was working on a gang related murder while Melvin had taken the evidence for a club fight that turned into a death. Detective Lyndsay Moskin was assigned to that case. Ten suspects and only one medium sized hand crease on the victim's throat. She had to print the suspects' entire right hand and use that to match up to the mark on the neck.

"Hey can I use your computer to scan in these palms while you work on the blood analysis?" Melvin asked.

"Yah, sure," the short stocky technician replied.

Melvin opened the scanner and placed the first palm in. Twenty minutes later, he had finished and the two were visited by examiner, Dave Francis. He held up his hand, which held the small vial of red liquid. He smiled at the two and pulled the earphones out of his ears.

"Evening, gents. How goes the witching twins?"

"Hey Dave, is that for me?" Melvin asked.

"Yep, here's the blood for the Martin case. Sorry it's late but we're up to our necks in bodies down there. Friggin' August is always busy."

16

"It's due to the heat," Lucky explained to Dave, "The humidity makes everyone cranky and that leads to all the deaths."

"Well, next year I think I'll take my vacation in August. Let the boss man, Pretterick, do the dirty work." Christopher Pretterrick was the head of the Morgue Squad. He assigned the autopsies and oversaw the big important John Doe cases that came into the Hoboken Morgue. He had been working the morgue for nine years and had helped work on some of the bigger cases, such as the Reese murders, where killer Edward Reese had faked his death in order to continue killing without having the police on his trail. North Bergen detective Colin Jacobs had closed the case on that one with the help of Pretterrick.

"Good idea," Melvin said, taking the blood sample and walking back to the counter with the tools covering it. Melvin had asked Dave to deliver a small does of Doug Martin's blood to compare it to the blood on the print. Brett believed that they were the same but they had to make sure. If the killer had cut himself, it would give them stronger evidence to arrest a suspect.

"Oh and I found something of interest on Martin's upper right arm. I emailed you a photo of a bruise in the shape of a hand. Pretty big hand too. Like a gorilla. Looks like the killer grabbed him pretty freakin' hard while he was stabbing him." Dave pointed out.

"Cool, that'll help. Thanks Dave."

"Any time, boys. I'm going to grab some coffee. Oh and nice Dharma shirt, Lucky. Talk to you later." Dave left the lab and the two returned to their work. Melvin sat down at his computer station and opened the email from Ernest. It contained an attachment of two .jpeg files. He opened the first file and saw that it was a photo of Doug Martin's front right bicep. The second file was of the back of the right bicep. Melvin placed the two photos together to get the wraparound shot. It showed the finger impressions of the killer's grip. Any bruising at the time of the murder would only become more prominent once the blood in the body stopped flowing through the veins.

Melvin got the idea to use the scan of the thumbprint and compare it to the shape of the bruising. He opened the thumb print and turned it ninety degrees clockwise. He then maneuvered the print over what looked like the thumb of the grip. The print fit into the bruise of the thumb almost perfectly.

"Hey Lucky, what do you think?" he asked. Lucky walked over to the screen and looked closely. He turned his head slightly and then nodded.

"Looks good. I'd say it was from the same person."

"Yeah me, too. Looks like this will be an open and shut case once we find a match for the print."

"As long as the right guy pays for the crime, that's what matters," Lucky said.

"That's what we're here for." Melvin returned back to the other case of the club murder. An hour later, the two were interrupted by an electronic ding from Melvin's computer. Melvin wheeled his chair over to read the results of the print search. The screen flashed 98% MATCH at him.

"Winner, winner, chicken dinner!" Melvin said excited. He threw his arms in the air and accidently knocked over his Hurley figure from his desk. He then clicked the mouse. Lucky walked over and looked over Melvin's shoulder. The screen changed to show the face of the thumbprint's owner. The two lab technicians stared into the eyes of the young male that appeared.

"That's him? He doesn't look like a killer," Lucky thought out loud.

"Sometimes they don't," Melvin responded as he read over the information on the side of the picture.

"Hmmm, this is something Foster's going to want to see." Melvin reached for the phone and dialed.

4

Brett woke up on his couch to the sound of the ring tone on his cell phone. He glanced around, wondering what he had done with his phone. The ring directed him to the floor in front of the couch and he picked it up before the call went through to his voice mail. The screen on the phone read LAB. Flipping the phone open, he answered the call.

"Foster, it's Melvin. Sorry for waking you but you wanted to know when I found a match."

"It's ok, Melvin," Brett answered. He looked up at the clock and saw that it was only 6:30 in the morning. The sun was just beginning to peek into his windows, over the giant skyscrapers of New York City. "What did you find?"

"Well, we've got a match. But I thought you'd want to come in and take a look at this."

"Why? Is there something strange?"

"Not really, but you should still come in and take a look."

"Okay, fine. Give me twenty minutes." Brett hung up and then made another call to Josh. After seven rings, Josh finally picked up.

"Hey, Princess," Brett said, "Get dressed. We've got a match."

"Are you kidding? I've got a pounding headache."

"Listen, drink some coffee, kick the girl out of your bed, get dressed and meet me at the crime lab."

"Listen, you don't kick a lady like this out of your bed," Josh muttered into the phone.

"I don't want to hear it. Meet me in twenty minutes." Brett hung up

19

and jumped in the shower. Twenty five minutes later, Josh arrived at the crime lab steps. Brett handed him a cup of coffee from the coffee shop a block away.

"Aw, you wonderful man, you." Josh took the coffee and drank half of it before he even walked through the door.

The two detectives headed up to the second floor of the building where Melvin and Lucky were just finishing the night shift. The lab was not as neat as it appeared when Brett stopped in last night. There were several empty liter bottles of Pepsi, an empty pizza box, two bags of potato chips and a candy wrapper.

"Wow," Josh mentioned, "This looks like my old dorm room."

"Excuse the mess, it's hard work staying in the zone on a midnight shift," Melvin explained.

"Don't worry about it, Melvin," Brett told him, "What do you have for us?" Melvin directed them to his computer for what he found.

"So finally, I got into AFIS at three this morning and ran a search for a match in both Criminal and Civilian systems, just to be thorough. A half hour ago, it came back with this." Melvin hit the space bar on the keyboard and the file on the thumbprint's owner appeared on the sleeping monitor.

Brett looked at the picture of 18-year-old Craig Waterford and read his information. The date of birth placed Craig Waterford at 38 years old now. Then Brett's eyes lowered on the screen and saw what Melvin had wanted him to see.

"Wow, nice criminal record."

"Yeah, that's what caught my eye also. So I did a little further searching. Here's what I found." Melvin hit a couple of keys and more information appeared on Craig Waterford. Brett and Josh read it through and Brett knew that they had their man.

"Do we have any information on where he lives?" Josh asked.

"He's got an apartment on Shipyard Lane. And he now owns Tony's Deli on Washington."

"I know that place," Lucky added, "They make some delicious subs."

Josh looked over at Lucky and rolled his eyes. "What? They do."

"Good work, Melvin. Thanks." Brett said, grabbing the printout of the information on the man that left behind his bloody thumbprint.

"Let's go," Brett told Josh.

"Where to first?"

"Let's try his home. It's only 7 in the morning. We can probably catch him getting ready for work."

"Great, let's get the criminal with his pants down."

"Well, it'll help to keep him from running."

The two detectives left the lab and returned to the street outside. Josh's cell phone began ringing before they could reach Brett's car. Brett knew the ringer before Raghetti could answer. Josh looked at the phone's screen and moaned in annoyance. He gritted his teeth and still answered.

"What do you want now, Angie?" he mumbled into the phone.

Angelica Fernandez was Josh's ex-wife and the mother to his 4 year old daughter, Tamara. The two had married young and a year after Tamara was born, Josh felt trapped and watched life pass him by. So he left her. But it had cost him a lot in alimony. Brett was hoping some day to get him to be more responsible with Tamara. One day, he would succeed, but not today.

Josh shut his eyes and rubbed his forehead. "I didn't forget to pick her up. I was on the way over. I just had to stop over at headquarters first." Josh then made yapping motions with his hand. "Yeah, yeah. I'll be right over. Okay. Okaaaay. Goodbye."

"You forgot Tamara again didn't you?" Brett asked.

"Hey, I just got it from Angie, I don't need it from you too. We're going to have to make a pit stop first before we visit Waterford."

"Fine, just get in."

Brett pulled up to Angie's home and found her and Tamara waiting patiently outside on the steps. He double parked and Josh got out to hug Tamara.

"Nice," Angie started in, "I'm going to be late for work. That's the second time this month."

"I heard you the first time," Josh said. Angie then noticed Brett in the driver seat. She walked over to say hello.

"Hey Brett, how are you?" Angie smiled at him from the window of the passenger side.

"Good Angie, sorry to keep Josh, we're working on something."

"Not a problem. Hey you still single? There's a new girl at the diner and she's real nice. Want me to hook you up with her?"

Brett smiled at her. This wasn't the first time she had tried to set him up with her friends. She had even tried to introduce him to her cousin who couldn't speak a word of English.

"That's very nice of you, Angie, but I'm not looking for Mrs. Foster right now. Work keeps me busy."

"You should really give yourself some 'me' time. All this detecting is going to affect your brain and you'll end up being the old guy down the block who lives by himself with some old dog. That's a sad ending for such a fine strapping middle-aged man like yourself."

"I thought you were running late?" Josh interfered.

"Mind your business, I'm trying to help your partner," she spat at Josh. Then she turned back to Brett, "Remember that and call me when you're ready." Angie winked and then gave Tamara a hug and kiss.

Josh buckled Tamara in the back seat and climbed into the front. Brett said good bye to Angie and pulled away.

"You're trying to hook up with my ex now?" Josh asked him.

"No, I'm not trying to sleep with Angie. But it wouldn't hurt to be civil to her in front of your daughter."

"This coming from Mr. Celibate of the Decade."

"That has nothing to do with you being a douchebag to your ex."

"I've not having this conversation with you again," Josh said, getting angry.

"Daddy?" a tiny voice spoke from the back seat.

"Yes, sweetie, what do you need?"

"I don't think you're a douchebag."

"See?" he said to Brett, "She's smarter than you."

5

Craig and Jacqueline entered the deli at their usual time. Their morning employees were already there and waiting. Connie Tenson, Wanda Stokes and Mike Robbins had started working at Tony's Deli under his father and were proud to see Craig take over the business for him. Craig felt the group that his father had working for him was another thing that made it easy for him to say yes on taking over the deli. There was Connie and her happy and joking attitude that made everyone laugh. Wanda's short stature didn't represent the size of her heart and dedication to her job. And Mike was professional and pleasant to the last customer. And the afternoon ladies were just as great and important. There was Terri Height who helped run things when Craig and Jackie were tiring from the morning and Shannon Hershey who played the motherly role to the group.

"Good morning all," Craig said, "I'd like to have a little meeting before we begin our day, please."

Puzzled by Craig's straight tone, the three employees looked at each other and moved in closer for the meeting.

"Thanks, now as you know, we've been improving in sales and I want to thank you all for the help and stepping up to the increase of customers. We're slowly putting Monte Cristo's Deli out of business." This brought smiles to the trio.

"And to show my appreciation, I've decided to give you all pay increases. It won't be a huge one but it's still one. I did the numbers for last week and compared to this time last year, we've increased sales eleven percent. So give yourselves a round of applause.

"The final thing I have to report is that Jackie and I are announcing that we are having a baby. Well, Jackie's having the baby, I've just helped get it started."

"I can baby sit for you," joked Connie.

"I don't know if that's a good idea, I think there's a rule about not letting infants watch Titanic over and over," Craig joked.

"There's nothing wrong about watching a good romantic movie," Connie retorted.

"Doesn't everyone except for Rose die in the end?" Wanda added.

"Yes, but she lived thanks to Jack saving her life! I'd like to see a man today be as chivalrous as Jack."

"Okay, enough of the talk, let's get this place filled with customers." Craig said, feeling proud and happy of how his life was turning for the better.

"Here you are, Mrs. Christenson, two pounds of regular chicken breast sliced just the way your little boy likes it," Jackie said, handing the customer her package of sliced meat.

"Forgive me for asking, but you look different today. Did you do something with your hair?"

"Actually, I just found out this morning that I'm pregnant."

"Oh my God, congratulations! That is so wonderful!"

Craig smiled at the amount of happiness the customers showed Jackie. Even though Hoboken had it's crime and grime, there was still a feeling of togetherness in the neighborhood.

"I honestly don't think the world is ready for Craig Waterford to be breeding," someone said from behind the customers. Craig frowned and leaned over the counter, looking for a face to the voice. From behind Mrs. Christenson appeared someone that Craig had not seen in a few months.

"Jacob Scott, I thought you had been eaten alive by the system."

"Lucky for me, I have harder skin than they thought. Unlucky for you, I need some coffee to keep me awake for the rest of the day."

"It's only 8:30a.m."

"Yeah, for you. For me it's lunch time. There's no rest for the wicked."

"If anyone knows that, it'd be you," Craig joked.

Jacob Scott was an old high school friend of Craig's. They had both grown up in the same neighborhood their entire childhood. After they had graduated, Jacob sought his dream of being a lawyer and worked night and day for it. Even after high school, they had still kept in touch through emails and get-togethers. Yet lately, since Jacob had finished law school and found an internship at a nearby law firm, the contact had been few and far between.

"So how's things going here?" Jacob asked.

"Deli's running great, how are you?"

"Being pulled thin, but that's to be expected for someone in my line of work. Hours are long and the personal life is non-existent but I'm making a difference."

"How's that blonde you were seeing, Penny?"

"Ah, she dumped me for some Australian hippie named Desmond," Jacob replied.

"Sorry to hear. You should stop over one night for dinner," Craig offered.

"Sounds like a good idea. I'll have to get back to you on it after I look at my schedule."

"You won't charge me by the hour will you?"

"Yeah, but I'll give you the family discount."

"Better than nothing. So I'll give you a call?"

"Here," Jacob handed him his card. Craig read it out loud.

"Jacob Scott, attorney. Reynolds and Hoffman. Pretty fancy."

"Only the best stock used for that card. Gotta look good for the ladies."

"So that means you've finally decided to go straight?"

"Very funny, Waterford. Still the same lame humor, I see."

"Only for my best customers."

"I might have to consider revoking that family discount if that's what I'm going to have to deal with."

"It would be good to have you visit. Never know when I'll need a lawyer after Monte Cristo's sues me for stealing all their customers."

"Just email me on what day is good and I'll make room for you."

"Good to see you again and here. Coffee's free today."

"Thanks, Craig. Take it easy."

"You too." Jacob turned and made his way out between the small crowd of people. As Craig watched him leave, Mike approached him.

"Craig, the misters in the case are acting up again."

Craig sighed, "I knew today was too good to be true. Let's see what we can do to fix it," he laughed.

6

The two detectives exited the thin elevator onto the third floor of the apartment building where Craig Waterford lived. The hallway covered in greenish tiles and green paint walls, was empty and silent. It was something out of a 70's television show. Brett turned to the left and walked over to the also green door with the numbers 301 on it.

"This is the place," Brett said. Josh looked left and right as a precaution and then Brett knocked on the door. He waited half a minute and received no response. He knocked again, harder this time and added a call with it.

"Craig Waterford? This is Hoboken police."

Josh placed his hand on the butt of his weapon, ready for anything wrong that may happen. Yet there was still no response.

"You wanna check out the deli? Maybe he gets there early," Josh asked.

"Yeah, there's no fire escape by his windows so if he is in there, he's either hiding or he jumped out the third floor window onto some small bushes."

Brett turned and headed back to press the elevator call button when a door behind them opened. Josh turned around quickly and found a rather large woman in a flowery housecoat poke her head out of her own apartment.

"Are you really with the police?"

"Yes, ma'am, Detective Foster and this is Detective Raghetti. Do you know if Mr. Waterford is home?"

"Oh no, he and Jacqueline left already. You can find them at the Deli downtown." The neighbor looked them over as she talked. Her eyes stopping for a second on the guns they had. Josh couldn't help but stare at the smudge that looked like mayo on the edge of her mouth, wanting to wipe it off for her.

"Thank you," Brett said, starting to turn away and back to the elevator.

"He's not in any trouble, is he?"

"No, we just want to ask him a few questions about a case."

"Oh, that's exciting. Is he going to help you break the case? I could see that. He's a good soul, helping his father with the store. And that wife of his is a sweetheart. She's so funny."

"Has he ever shown any signs of anger or malice?" Josh threw out there.

"Lord, no. He's an angel. Why, last week he helped me with my kitchen sink. If he didn't, I'd still be waiting for the landlord today! Now you want to talk anger and malice, our landlord is the man you're looking for. He's never around, raising the rent so he can pay off his Mercedes."

"Thank you, Miss. You've been a big help," Brett said, hoping to end the conversation.

"Yes, a BIG help," Josh had to add.

"Oh, anytime, anytime, detectives. You need any information about the residents here, you come ask me. I'll tell you everything you want to know."

"I'll keep that in mind," Brett thanked her again and pressed the elevator call button. He and Josh entered into the elevator while she continued on and sighed relief when the doors closed and they began descending.

"So, Waterford's an angel, huh?" Josh wondered.

"It's always the neighbors that are the last to know." Brett replied.

7

Craig enjoyed the slower hours between breakfast and lunch. It allowed him to take care of the business side of the deli. He walked back into the office and turned the monitor on. The screen flickered on and he sat back in his office chair as the background photo appeared on the 17inch screen. The photo was of a waterfall that Jackie had taken when they vacationed in Upstate New York for an autumn week with friends. It was the place where he had decided to pop the question to her. The setting was romantic. The trees and ground were covered in colorful leaves, the air was crisp yet warmed by the shining sun and their morning had begun with some playful lovemaking.

The nostalgic photo warmed his heart and brought his thoughts back to their baby. He was going to be a father. The idea was incredible to him. He had always wanted to be a father one day and having the idea dropped on his lap did not scare him in the least. He was excited to watch Jackie's flat stomach take shape and curve outward in the upcoming months.

"Hey boss," Jackie called, "You're excited aren't you?" She walked into the office and wrapped her arms around his neck and shoulders from behind.

"I'm that obvious?"

"The big smile on your face gave it away."

"I can't help it. I'm so happy now." Jackie smiled back at him and kissed him passionately.

"What if we went away for a day next weekend? Just the two of us. We can sleep late and have a little fun as well," she said to him.

"Sounds like a good idea. I'll ask Mike and Terri if they can handle the open and close shifts for us."

"I think I can convince them," she winked with a smile.

"With that look, you can convince me that I have blue skin."

"Poof, you're a Smurf." He laughed and they kissed again.

"You know, if you two are going to keep that up, she's going to end up pregnant," Connie teased from the doorway.

"What's up?" Craig asked.

"There's two men here asking for you."

"Sales guys?"

"I don't think so. They look too serious to be salesmen."

Craig raised his eyebrows at Jackie and walked out to the front of the store. He noticed the two men right away. They were in business casual suits and the shiny gold badges on their belts were prominent. The taller one had an annoyed look on his face and the glasses he wore didn't hide the look of seriousness in his eyes. The other and shorter man spoke up.

"Mister Craig Waterford?" he asked. Craig nodded and held out his hand. The shorter man shook it firmly and introduced himself.

"I'm Detective Brett Foster and this is Detective Josh Raghetti. We have some questions for you, do you have an hour?"

"Is something wrong?"

"We just want to ask you a few questions and would like if you could do so at our headquarters." Craig was getting concerned. This was not normal. The police have never visited or spoken to him except for that one time when he was younger.

"Can I ask what this is about?"

"We just want to know what you know about a Douglas Martin."

"I've never heard of him. Is he upset about the service here?"

"Mr. Martin is dead, sir."

"Oh. Well, I'm sorry but what does his death have to do with me?"

"That's why we like to question you downtown, please. Once we can clear everything up, you'll be back here in time for the lunch rush." Detective Foster was very polite and it relaxed Craig a little but he was still confused by their appearance.

"Okay, I'll come with you," Craig told them. He turned to Jackie and smiled, "I'll be right back, I'm sure this is all just a misunderstanding."

"Are you sure?" Jackie asked. She looked up at the detectives, looking for some reassurance and understanding. Raghetti squinted at her and couldn't help but stare at her for a minute. Craig broke the stare when he walked back to the detectives.

"I'm sure this is a misunderstanding as well, Mrs. Waterford. We just want to clear a few things up on our case," Brett reassured her.

"I'll be okay," Craig said to her before he left with the detectives. Yet he was having a hard time convincing himself of that.

8

Jacob walked out of the elevator and into the firm, headed for his office. He noticed right away, the floor was not bustling as it normally was on a Monday morning. He looked around and saw the faces on the other lawyers and paralegals. They were talking low about something and Jacob had no idea what it was. Did someone get fired?

He got to his office where his assistant, Robin Masters, sat at her desk and spoke into the phone on it. Robin looked beautiful as she always did. Her short blonde hair was pulled back by a black hair clip and she looked up with her sparkling blue eyes when she noticed him approach.

"I'll stop over in a few minutes. Okay, bye." She said into the phone. When she hung up, she stood and greeted Jacob.

"What's going on? Did Hoffman can someone again?" he asked her.

"You didn't hear?"

"Hear what?"

"Doug was murdered over the weekend."

"What?"

"Yeah, there's an email that went out early this morning. Reynolds is supposed to speak to everyone later this morning. Kristie is a mess."

Kristie Marks was Doug's assistant. The two had worked together when Doug was brought in to the firm a year ago. Kristie showed promise and was working hard on studying for the bar in hopes of being recognized as an equal.

"I can't believe it. I got a text from him Saturday. Everything was fine. What happened?"

"I've only heard that he walked in on a robber and there was a fight. But Kyla in accounting is going to ask Alexa about it when she gets in."

Jacob was in shock. Doug Martin and he were in the same law class together at Fordham in New York City. Working together, they quickly became good friends and were in the top ten of their class. They were happy when Reynolds and Hoffman decided to hire the both of them. Both Jacob and Doug had worked hard to make an impression on the partners. Doug had gotten lucky when Reynolds had taken a liking to him. Hoffman, on the other hand, was very old school and acted as if he didn't like any of them in the office, including his poor assistant, Alisha.

"Wow. That's insane. What time is the meeting with Reynolds?"

"Everyone is to be in the Conference room at 9a.m." Jacob checked his watch. It was only 8:15. He had time to settle in and gather his thoughts.

"Okay good. Do you have the files for the Greenwood case?"

"I'm on my way over to the filing room to grab them. Did you want some coffee while I'm over there?"

"Yes please. And call Ms. Greenwood and ask her if it's okay to move the meeting for her case back to noon."

"Got it." Robin said. She paused for a moment and looked at Jacob. She placed a soft hand on his arm. "Are you going to be okay?"

"Yeah, I'm just still taking it in. Thank you." He smiled at her and she smiled back.

Jacob had felt something for Robin but due to the professional relationship had not played on it. She was kind, sweet, and caring, always going out of her way to help others first even though she was worried about her own life and future at the same time. He found her endearing and was caught staring at her from time to time. But he knew the partners would frown on it and pushed it out of his mind.

Robin walked away to the other side of the floor where the filing room was located. She walked past Doug's office and he stopped and stared at the closed door. He couldn't believe that his friend and co-worker was no longer going to stop over to say hello and talk about last night's baseball game.

At 9 a.m., Jacob walked past Hoffman's office and over to the large conference room that separated Reynolds' and Hoffman's offices on either side of the East wall of the floor. The offices and conference room overlooked the Hudson River and New York City skyline. The conference room was used mostly for meetings with the lawyers and major cases. The large oak table in the center sat sixteen chairs comfortably. The chairs were plush and cushioned with back support.

The room was already packed with the entire office. Mark Reynolds and Allan Hoffman stood at the head of the table, waiting for the talk to quiet down. Mark Reynolds stood tall next to Allan Hoffman. Where Allan was shorter and had slump shoulders, Reynolds stood firm and straight. Where Allan had thinning silver grey hair, Reynolds had wavy dark brown hair. Both partners, though, had an air of intimidation about them.

"I believe that's everyone. Thank you all for attending, this will only take a few minutes," Reynolds said loudly.

"As you may have already heard, Doug Martin was murdered late Saturday night by an intruder in his home. From the detectives on the case, he received numerous stab wounds and died from them. There will be an email about the time and date of his wake when it is scheduled so anyone who wishes to attend, can. Allan and I both thought of Doug as strong willed and filled with such potential. We were honored to have him as part of this firm. He was a good man and a great defender. He will be missed.

"Now, for the business part of it. Doug was currently working on a few cases. I'd like to spread them out amongst you all so that his clients can feel taken care of and remain Reynolds and Hoffman clients. Graves, I'd like you to take the Sandford case. Delgado, you've already got the Rosenvelt case, if you can also take the Patterson divorce case as well. And Scott, I'm going to assign the Grabenstein case. Ms. Marks will provide you with all of Doug's notes and files on the cases as needed and if you can please let me know when each case is done. Doug's office will remain off limits and unavailable for the time being out of respect to him. Any questions?" The room remained silent while heads shook no. "Very well, let's get back to work and make Doug proud."

As the firm dispersed from the conference room, Jacob managed to make his way over to Kristie. Her eyes were slightly puffy and red but she walked with a purpose.

"Hey, how are you holding up?" Jacob asked her.

"I'm ok," Kristie replied, "Just still a little shocked by the news."

"Well, if you need anything, I'm here to help."

"Thanks Jacob. I'll stop by in an hour once I have the files for the Rosenvelt case."

"Which case is that?" Jacob asked.

"It was the liquor store robbery that he was working on. Rosenvelt Liquors over on 12th. Defendant's name is Maurice Devito. Devito said that he went in for beer and left but video in the back room shows him returning to hold the store up at gunpoint. Weird thing is that Doug emailed me Saturday night from here saying that he found a loophole for Devito. He didn't say what but it sounded like he was going to get Devito off the hook for the charge."

"I'll come by to grab them after lunch. Worry about the others first."

"Okay, I'm sure Delgado is already waiting for his files."

"Impatient prick."

"Jacob? Thanks again." Kristie smiled.

"You're welcome." Jacob returned to his office where Robin was already on the phone with Deena Greenwood. He paused for a moment as he walked past her desk and then dismissed the thought and continued to his desk where he continued his work.

9

Thank you for coming in with us, Mr. Waterford," Brett told Craig,
"We're just going to bring you to one of our interview rooms and
we can talk there."

Craig had an odd feeling about the two detectives. Something was
up yet they weren't letting him know what. He couldn't think of meeting
anyone named Doug Martin nor could he figure out what he had to do with
the man's death. Could they think that he killed this Doug Martin?

Craig and the two detectives walked into the lobby of the police
precinct. He immediately noticed that it was rather quiet for mid-morning,
nothing like what he saw on TV cop shows. The large counter sat in the
center of the lobby with several small desks behind it. A woman with thin
glasses halfway down her nose sat at the closest desk. She glanced up from
her computer so see who was walking in. Noticing Josh and Brett, she
returned her eyes back to her monitor.

Josh and Brett led Craig behind the counter and down the small hall
on the right side of the lobby. The rooms were numbered and each door
had a small window to peer inside. The detectives stopped at Room #3 and
opened the door. Inside a small table sat. Two chairs were placed on one
side and one lone chair sat on the opposite side.

"We'll just have you sit in here. Detective Raghetti and I are going to
get some coffee and water. Would you like some?" Brett asked Craig.

"Water is fine, thank you," Craig replied. Brett and Josh left the room,
leaving Craig alone and in silence. He noticed that there was no one way
mirror for them to watch him from behind. But there was a video camera

in the far corner of the room, directed at him. He glanced up at it and then looked away, ashamed that he was here in this room, feeling like a criminal instead of a witness.

Craig stared at the table thinking of why he was here. Was it someone he knew that had committed the murder? Was Doug Martin an old family member that he knew nothing of? Who was Doug Martin anyway? Craig thought back to college and even high school. He could not remember having known anyone with that name.

Craig looked up at the small window wondering when the detectives were going to return.

"You're awfully quiet," Brett mentioned to Josh. Josh had seemed distant on the way back to the precinct. Brett had seen that look on his partner before. He was thinking and calculating about the case. Something bothered him and he was trying to figure it out.

"Something about the apartment. I remember something that may help with the questioning."

"What? Another clue to nail Waterford?"

"Possibly. Hang on, I'll be right back." Josh walked away and over to Moskin's desk. There Lyndsay and, her partner, Alicia Bowman, talked over the case they were working on.

"I'm telling you Vinny knows something about that missing girl," Alicia said, excited.

"Yeah but his alibi holds up. How do you explain that?" Lyndsay retorted.

"Morning ladies," Raghetti said, smiling. He tried the charm even though it never worked with the female detectives. They looked at Josh with man hating eyes.

"What do you want, Raghetti?" Alicia asked, annoyed.

"What, I can't just greet my fellow co-workers with a good morning?"

"The last time you greeted us with a smile was that office party last Christmas when you were drunk and tried hitting on me," Lyndsay said.

"Can I help if you looked gorgeous outside of your detective clothes?"

Lyndsay rolled her eyes, "Like she said, what do you want?"

"Listen, I just need some help. I've got our suspect for the Martin case and I need you to run back to his apartment and grab something."

"What, a clue? Some evidence? Some gel for that greasy hair of yours?" Alicia joked.

"I don't use gel," Josh said, matter-of-factly, "I'm not a reject from the Jersey Shore."

"If you were, they'd called you the Accident." Alicia laughed and high-fived Lyndsay.

"Look, are you going to help or not?"

"Fine, what are you needing?"

Josh explained what he thought would help him and Brett with the interview. After hearing him out, the women nodded and agreed to help grab the evidence for him.

"But you'll owe us for this," Lyndsay told him.

"Hey, if you can help us nail this guy to the wall, I'll do anything to pay you back."

"Be careful what you say, I can be very creative," Alicia replied.

Brett waited for Josh by going over to his desk and grabbing the small tape recorder that he kept in the bottom drawer of his desk. He took the used tape out of the recorder and walked over to the supplies cabinet for a fresh new one. As he was sifting through one of the shelves, he was surprised by a voice from behind.

"Morning Foster."

Brett turned around to find his boss, Chief Christine Black, standing there with a cup of coffee in her hand. Christine Black was one of the youngest to make chief at age thirty-nine. Her history on the Hoboken Police force helped break female discrimination in the town. At age twenty-two, she was added to the force with exceptional testing scores. Her career skyrocketed when she was asked to help out with the Fernandez drug raid. She had managed to catch and arrest Danny Fernandez, the head of the drug family, after he had escaped from the head of the task force. She had made detective in less than two years and had impressed the mayor that he had handed her the position of Hoboken Chief of Police.

This, of course, bothered the old timers of the force and rumors soon spread that she had slept her way to the top. But Christine knew the truth and to her, that was all that mattered. She had proven her worth and eventually even the old timers began to respect her.

"Oh hey Chief, you got me there."

"How's the Martin case going?"

"Good," Brett answered, "Melvin found a match to the print this morning and we've already got the suspect in Room 3. We're just about to question him. Did you want to sit in?"

"No, I've got a meeting with the mayor this morning that I have to get ready for. Does this suspect seem like he did it?"

"Actually no, he's just some regular guy. Owns the deli by Johnny Rockets'. But the evidence says he was at least there when it happened. So maybe we can either get a confession or at least a point in the right direction to who did."

"Good. You and Raghetti should see me when the questioning is over. Let me know what you find."

"Absolutely, chief."

"Hey Chief, how's it going?" Josh said, walking over to the two.

"Not now, Raghetti, it's too early." Black told him. She turned and headed to her office, sipping the coffee as she did.

"What, are all the women in here having 'that' time of the month?"

"I wouldn't ask that question today," Brett said. "Are you ready?"

"Yeah, I've got Moskin and Bowman working on something for us."

"What?"

Josh explained his thoughts as they walked back to the interview room. Brett understood finally and agreed with him. He opened the door to Room 3 and found Craig sitting quietly at the table.

"I apologize for the wait, Mr. Waterford. Here's your water." Josh held out the bottle and Craig took it, thanking him.

"Now," Brett began to speak, "if it is okay with you, I'd like to tape this conversation. So we can get the details correct. Are you fine with that?"

"Yes, it's fine. I just want to know what I have to do with this man's death."

"Well, I can understand that. First, why don't you tell us what you know about Doug Martin?"

10

That's what I've been trying to tell you. I've never heard of Doug Martin. I have no idea who he is. Why are you asking me this?"

"Let me inform you then, Mr. Waterford. Do you mind if I call you Craig?" Brett interjected.

"Yes, that's fine."

"Great. Craig, Doug Martin is a lawyer who lives in Hoboken here. Detective Raghetti and I were called to his apartment yesterday. We found him dead. Stabbed several times. Now I'm sure you, like everyone else in America, watch CSI, correct?"

"My wife and I watch it sometimes."

"Of course, it's a good show. I watch it too. Anyway, we had our forensic unit going over the room with a fine tooth comb. Out of the entire apartment, we found one thumbprint. It was covered in Doug's blood."

"So?" Craig asked, still unsure of what Foster was getting at.

"Craig, the thumbprint found at the crime scene matches yours."

The statement hit Craig like a sledge hammer. He knew he heard Foster tell him but the statement was too surreal to be true. Craig sat back, his mouth open and he brought up his hand to cover it.

"How-how is that possible? How could my thumbprint be there if I never was?"

"That's what we'd like to know. Did you perhaps run into him and have a fight on the street? Did he maybe cut you off and you followed him?"

"No, no way. I'm not an angry person. I don't get road rage and I don't get into fights. Everyone I know will tell you I'm pretty laid back."

"Craig, listen," Josh said, "The thumbprint, **your** thumbprint was found on Doug Martin's briefcase. In his blood. It's obvious that you were there either during or after the fact. Now if you tell us what happened and why, we can work with you. We can help you."

"Exactly," Brett added, "Everyone has their bad moments. I'm sure running that deli there can get pretty stressful. We've all been there. Did he maybe come in and act all unruly?"

"But I don't even know what this guy looks like?" Craig tried to explain.

Josh nodded and opened up the folder and slid it across the table to in front of Craig. Craig looked down and at the photo. It was a shot of Doug Martin lying on the floor of his apartment. The blood soaking his shirt, tie and the floor around the body. Craig felt his stomach lurch upward at the sight. He had never seen a murdered body before. He turned his face and body away, shutting his eyes tight, fighting to keep himself from vomiting what breakfast he had.

"Take a deep breath," Brett instructed.

"I don't know this man," Craig stated again.

"Then how did your thumbprint get there?"

"I don't know."

Moskin and Bowman arrived at Doug's brownstone and pulled up in front of the building. Lyndsay placed the car in park and they got out, looking up to the window of the dead lawyer's apartment as they did.

"This better be good," Alicia muttered.

"Raghetti may be a pig of a man, but he knows his detecting," Lyndsay debated.

"If you say so. What are we looking for anyway?"

The females walked into the tiny entrance of the building and pushed the superintendant's button. They waited a minute and after no response, they pushed it again. Finally a voice came out of the speaker.

"Yeah who is it?"

"Hoboken Police," Lyndsay said.

"Now what do you want?" the grumpy voice asked.

"We need to get into Doug Martin's apartment, now open up." Bowman replied annoyed. Lyndsay smiled at her partner's lack of patience.

It had worked as the lock buzzed open and Lyndsay pushed the door open. They headed up to the second floor where Doug Martin's apartment was. The yellow police tape had been left undisturbed across the front door. Moskin put on the plastic gloves and tore the tape off the entrance. Alicia entered behind her and they looked over the living room area.

"Did he say where we're supposed to find them?" Alicia asked.

"He said they were on the entertainment unit in the corner." Lyndsay walked over to the unit with the rather large TV and examined it.

"You know what they say about guys with giant TVs," Alicia joked.

"They're blind?" Lyndsay joked back. Alicia held her fingers up, leaving an inch between them. Lyndsay laughed. She had to admit, her partner was more like a sister. Regardless of the short time they had been partnered, they became close immediately. Alicia had been there for her when Lyndsay's sister had passed away from breast cancer. She had never forgotten that and would always appreciate it.

"Here," Lyndsay said, picking up a framed photo featuring Doug Martin and a female standing on the riverfront, the New York skyline behind them.

"That's it?"

"That's what Raghetti asked for."

"Good, this place is giving me the creeps. Let's go give it to him."

"Unless you have a clone that we don't know about, there's only one explanation on how your thumbprint got left at the scene, Craig." Josh mocked their suspect.

"Detectives, you have to believe me, I don't know Doug Martin, nor was I ever in his apartment, let alone on the night you think I killed him."

"Craig, really," Brett said to him, "It's been reported that no two people have the same fingerprints. Now if the match was only 50% alike, I would understand. But it was a 98% match. This is not looking good. The evidence is there. There's no way out of it. The thumbprint places you there. If you admit to that, then we can help out with how much time you do for the murder."

"Time? But I haven't killed him. You can't send me to jail."

"Fingerprints are admissible in a court of law. With the evidence, any jury wouldn't think twice about your participation."

"Oh God, how can this be happening?" Craig held his head in his hands and leaned forward onto the table. Brett noticed the slight shake that Craig's hands had. He knew that their suspect would be breaking soon. Then they would have their confession.

"Cut the crap, Waterford," Josh said, fed up over the amount of time it was taking, "There's no getting out of this. Just tell us what happened and we can end it here."

"I can't tell you what happened to Doug Martin because I don't know. I spent Saturday night having dinner with my parents and wife. Then Jackie and I came home, watched a little TV and went to sleep."

"That's not what the print says."

"Detectives, I've never killed or even harmed another person in my life," Craig pleaded.

"Oh really?" Josh asked, now standing up, "That's not what your file says."

"What?" Craig asked.

"Why don't you tell us about the manslaughter charge?"

11

B ut that was an accident," Craig told them. The memories of when he was nineteen came rushing back into his mind, bringing the horror of the accident with it. It had been almost twenty years since and he had pushed it to the back of his mind for fear of it haunting him for the rest of his life. The flashing red lights, the hum of the street lights and the car engines, the slight coppery smell in the night air and the rain drops on his skin felt real, even though he knew that he was still in the police station. It was the trauma being relived all over again.

Craig had been on his way home from a party at the end of his freshman year in college. Being the designated driver, he had agreed to first drive home his three friends. First he had dropped off Anthony, which he had considered a good thing as Anthony vomited all over his front lawn after getting out of Craig's car. Then he had dropped off Greg and finally Jimmy. "Hey, thanks man," Jimmy said.

"Anytime," Craig yawned.

"Are you going to be okay going home?"

"Yeah, just tired. I'm going to sleep till Sunday."

"Well, try listening to the hard rock station, it'll keep you from falling asleep till you get home."

"Good idea, Have a good night," Craig waved.

"I've already have!" Jimmy shouted as Craig drove away.

Craig glanced at the clock on the dashboard. It read 1:08 a.m. *Wow,* he thought, *it's later than I thought.* He decided to take Jimmy's advice and changed the radio to the rock channel and turned the volume up a little.

He focused on the road more than normal as he felt the exhaustion of the night's fun begin to get to him.

There was only eight more blocks to his home and once there he would breathe a sigh of relief. Then he noticed the song on the radio was hypnotizing. It was almost calming. Why would the rock station play something slow?

His eyelids began to get heavy and droop. He fought back and opened them wide. But it felt like the more he fought sleep, the heavier his eyelids became. There were only 5 blocks left, he could make it if he went a little faster. He pushed down on the gas pedal slightly and drove on.

It was when he reached the block before his that sleep took over and his head dropped. And it was then that young Kimberly O'Neil was rushing home to sneak back into her house from her secret boyfriend's before her father woke for the day.

Craig remembered waking up minutes after his car had struck the tree on the opposite side of the intersection. Blood trickled down his forehead and into his eyes. Smoke spewed from the crushed radiator. And the police were just arriving onto the scene. He crawled out of the car and stood on his feet. He remembered his body having no feeling whatsoever. And then he turned his eyes onto the red mass of flesh in the center of the intersection. At that moment, the world went black.

He woke two days later in the hospital. His father sat at his bedside from the moment he arrived until he awoke. The police questioned him and after he was released he was charged with murder. A year later, the trial put him and his family through hard times yet when everything was done, the charge was lowered to manslaughter. His life was turned upside down over a night of fun. He found himself lucky when he met Jacqueline. She had helped him move on and things had been looking good for him once again.

But now things were plummeting downward again. He was going to be charged with a murder that he had nothing to do with, but no one was believing him. He wished he knew how his fingerprint had gotten there. If he knew that, he would have been walking out of the police precinct right now.

"Nice story," Josh said, mocking, "I love the happy ending. The one problem I have with that is the lack of evidence that it was an accident. What, did this girl dump you? She tell everyone you have a mini Winnie? Or was she disgusted by the sick twisted mind of yours?"

"Listen Craig, honestly, this is not looking good," Brett interrupted,

"There's no getting around the thumbprint. You are our one and only suspect in Doug Martin's murder. The evidence is there. I'm sorry, but we are going to have to hold you until we find out otherwise."

"Please, you have to believe me. I did not murder Doug Martin."

"Was it an accident?"

"No, I was never there. I know it sounds stupid, but I swear I never met him and I never laid a foot in his apartment."

Brett was about to say something but was stopped when a knock on the door broke the conversation. The three looked up and over at the window in the door. Lyndsay Moskin waved Josh over and Josh got up and left the room.

"You find it?" he asked excited.

"Yeah, are you going to tell me what this is all about?"

"Only if you go out with me," he said with his Burt Reynolds smile.

"Forget it, I'll read about it in the report later," She handed him the framed photo and walked back to her desk.

"Suit yourself," he said and then returned to the room. He held the photo at his side, as if he were hiding it for now.

"Are you done?" Brett asked.

"Just getting started," Josh answered, "So Craig, you say you don't know Doug Martin, right?"

"No, that's what I've been telling you the whole time," Craig pleaded.

"Does that also apply to your hottie of a wife?"

"What?" both Craig and Brett asked.

"Did Jacqueline Waterford know Doug?"

"Why, why would you ask me that?"

"Cause I've just figured out your motive in killing Doug Martin!"

"What are you talking about?" Brett asked, annoyed about being left in the dark by his partner.

Josh brought the framed photo up and placed in face up on the table between them. Craig looked down and his mouth dropped open. In the photo was Doug Martin alive and smiling. And in his arms, was an equally smiling Jacqueline Waterford.

12

Craig was shocked. He couldn't believe all this was actually happening. It had to have been a dream. Not only was he being accused of murder but he was seeing proof of his wife having an affair. Did Jackie know Doug? The thought of it made him queasy.

"No, this isn't real, what are you trying to do to me?" he asked the two detectives.

"Let me know if I've got it right. I've seen this before so I'm pretty sure I will," Josh began, "You marry this gorgeous gal, you're happy, sex is awesome. Then one day you find out that Dougie boy is stuffing your wife with his sausage. Now I don't know about you but that would put me over the fuckin' edge. So you go visit Doug and plan on telling him to stay away from her. But he refuses and in anger, you grab a nearby knife and let loose."

"Are you insane?" Craig said loudly.

"Craig, calm down," Brett told him, standing up. This was turning ugly and he did not want Craig to be overcome with rage, attacking them in the small room.

"No, I will not. You can't just start making this up to get me to confess to something I never did."

"We're not making this up. This is all hard evidence."

"This!?!" Craig picked up the photo of Jackie and Doug and shook it at the detectives, "I refuse to believe this is my wife with this man. She doesn't even own this sweater."

"Maybe he bought it for her for being such a good lay," Josh offered.

Brett gripped Josh's shoulder. It was his way of telling Josh that he was pushing it. But Brett felt it was too late for that. He could see the anger and frustration in Craig's eyes.

"That's not true!" Craig yelled. He stood up and slammed his fist on the table.

"Craig, calm down," Brett said, trying to soothe their suspect, "He didn't mean anything by that."

"I know when I'm trying to be pushed, detective. And your partner here is the bad cop in this scenario. I'm not playing your mind games. And I'm no longer talking to you until I have a lawyer present."

13

Okay, Craig," Brett told him, "If that's what you want then we will get you a lawyer. But until we can get him here, we'll have to place you in a holding cell. It's police procedure, alright?"

"I want my phone call too," Craig said, now calming down.

"Okay, we can get you that as well. But you'll have to give us a few minutes."

"You want a pony with that too?" Josh muttered. Brett gritted his teeth and pointed at the door. Josh looked at Brett and without saying a word, argued his demand. Brett refused to give and continued staring at Josh in the eyes. Josh frowned and walked out of the interview room.

"Look, Detective Raghetti can go a little overboard some times."

"Overboard? He called my wife a slut!"

"I know and I'm sorry. But the evidence is too strong against you right now and it's only going to get worse if you attack a cop. Understand?"

"I understand." Craig's situation sunk back into reality and he sank back into his chair. Placing his hands on the table, outstretched, he took a deep breath. He still felt numb from the shock of what was happening to him.

"I feel so exhausted and it's not even lunch, is it?"

"No, Craig, it's only 10 a.m. Did you want more water?"

"No thank you. I just want my phone call and a lawyer."

"Okay, I'll get to work on that right now. I'm going to have one of the uniformed officers bring you down to the holding cells. I will personally make sure that he takes care of you while you're down there."

"Thank you, detective."

"You're welcome." Brett left the door and closed the door firmly behind him. Josh stood there, leaning on the opposite wall, silently fuming. Brett didn't give him a moment to speak. He got in close to Josh's face and stuck his finger out in it.

"What the fuck was that in there?" he asked Raghetti.

"That was you making me look like a fuckin' tool," Josh said, pushing back at his partner.

"Why didn't you tell me that you knew his wife was with Martin?"

"I didn't know until I realized where I had seen her before meeting her at the deli! And I didn't want to stop the interrogation because I knew this guy would pull the lawyer card." Brett knew that Josh had a point. Once the suspect demands a lawyer, a confession was near impossible.

"Well your plan backfired, now what, genius?"

"Now we nail him on what we have," Josh said confidently, "We've got evidence that he was there when Martin was murdered, we've got proof of a connection between the two of them *and* we now have motive. He found out the wife was riding another pony and he killed him for it."

"The thumbprint is never going to hold up," Brett explained, "Yes, it proves he was there but doesn't prove that he actually murdered Doug Martin. There were no prints on the murder weapon nor was there any of Waterford's DNA on Martin's body. The best we could get him on is Accessory to murder."

"You getting soft on me?" Josh asked.

"No, I'm getting realistic. Ask Black, I'm sure she'll agree."

"Fine, hey Loomis, take this guy in here down to the holding cells until we can get him a phone call," Raghetti asked one of the passing patrolmen. He nodded to the detective and Brett and Josh walked over to Chief Black's office.

Brett knocked on the door and they were given permission to enter. Christine Black looked up and frowned the moment she saw it was them.

"Now what?"

Black sat back, waiting to hear what the detectives had in store for her. Her short brown hair bobbed around her face and the frown marks were beginning to show around her mouth.

"Waterford lawyered up."

"What the hell happened?"

"We found a photo at Martin's apartment of him and Waterford's wife cuddling. It freaked him out and he clammed up, demanding a lawyer."

"Why would you show him a photo that you found?" Black asked, disappointed.

"I thought it would make him break," Raghetti answered.

"Nice job, Raghetti. Looks like it worked perfectly." She sighed and thought about their next step. The evidence they had was too light for a conviction. If Craig Waterford did murder Doug Martin, they were going to need more in order to make the charge stick in court.

"We're going to need more evidence to pin it on him. I suggest you talk to the wife about her relationship with Martin, then go back to his apartment and look to see if you missed anything. I'm going to call Clark and see if he has any advice," the chief told them.

Guy Clark was the Assistant District Attorney of Hudson County. He had known and helped Christine Black when she was beginning to make a name for herself. Guy had teamed with her in convicting mass murderer, Charles Lee Barlowe, several years back. Of course, after the trial was over and Barlowe was sent to prison for life without parole, he celebrated by slapping Black on her rear. One threat to his manhood later, he apologized and didn't attempt touching her again.

"Got it, chief, we'll let you know if anything comes up." Brett followed Josh out of the office and down into the lobby. They stepped out into the warming summer air and Brett stopped short before they had reached the vehicle. Josh turned to look back at him and wondered what was wrong.

"There something you want to tell me?" Brett asked his partner.

"I've got nothing to say. Should I?"

"You haven't seemed like your normal self today. I'm just thinking that something happened between you and Angie this morning."

"Well aren't you the mind reader?" Josh replied with sarcasm.

"Look, I'm sorry I blew up at you inside, but it was a bonehead move. If you're distracted, I can deal with the wife while you take care of things."

"There's nothing to take care of, now drop it. Ok?"

"Sure thing." Brett held his hand out, waiting for Raghetti to lead the way to the car. Josh walked forward and got into the driver seat. Brett slid into the passenger seat and they drove off to speak to Jacqueline Waterford.

14

The TV gave off the only light in the room. Pete Rogers found that his eyes were sensitive when he came down from a meth high. He squinted at the television hoping that something good would be on so that he wouldn't think about the low that came with the loss of the smooth feeling that he loved.

Pete didn't notice the smell of rank body odor that permeated from his sweaty skin. Nor did he notice that the apartment was in shambles around him. His focus was mainly on the screen that sat two feet from his face.

He pressed the channel button again, changing from the trippy kids cartoon about a talking mouse and tiny white dog to a news report. The New Jersey Network logo appeared on the bottom right of the screen while a middle-aged reporter stood outside a townhouse on Hudson Street. Pete leaned forward, interested on the house behind the reporter.

"Police are asking that anyone who may have some information on the murder of attorney Douglas Martin, to please contact them at the number below. Your identity will remain confidential. Back to you in the studio, LuAnn."

Pete leaned forward until his nose was barely touching the screen. He had a memory that was trying to escape the cloud in his brain but it was having a hard time coming to the surface. The house. He had seen the house before, he thought. But he didn't know from where. What did he do to remember? Oh yeah, he thought.

Pete stood up from his rotting couch and headed into the bathroom. He turned the water on in the bathtub and filled it. Once it was half full, he tore his clothes off and got in. The water surrounded him and clogged his ears.

Remember.

He stretched his fingers out in the water and tightened his muscles, letting the water seep into his pores.

Remember.

He closed his eyes and breathed out of his nose in long deep breathes.

Remember.

The image of the townhouse pushed through the fog in his brain and he collected everything around it that he could see in his mind's eye.

He remembered.

Pete's eyes opened in shock and he leapt from the bathtub. He had to do something! He rushed out back into the living room, water dripping from his naked body all over the old shaggy carpet. He stumbled over the table and fell over.

"Oh, fuck, fuck, fuck!" he mumbled, searching for the one thing that would help him.

The phone was lying next to the couch on the floor and he grabbed it up with both hands. He tried to dial the number on the television but he could not remember it nor was it on the screen any longer.

"What is it? What is it?" He decided instead to just dial 911. He then brought the phone to his ear and waited for a response.

"911, what is your emergency?"

"I know who killed that lawyer guy on the TV!"

15

Alicia dreaded typing out the paperwork. But she and Lyndsay had an agreement that they would trade up with every other case. Unfortunately, this time it was her turn.

"I still say that we should have assistants or secretaries to do this for us." Alicia hit the Tab button and moved to the next page. Lyndsay sat back at her desk and took a sip of her coffee.

"But then we would only end up with pay cuts in order to pay the secretaries. We're screwed either way," Lyndsay rationalized.

"It still sucks," Alicia pouted. Lyndsay's phone intercom buzzed to life.

"Moskin, who's in charge of the Martin murder case?" It was the desk sergeant, Mac Mendez.

"That's Foster and Raghetti, why?"

"I've got a caller with some info on the murder. Are they still here?"

"I don't think so," Lyndsay replied.

"No," Alicia told her, "I saw them just leave."

"Then can you take this call? I'll tell you now, this guy doesn't sound sane. But that's my opinion."

"Yeah, Mac, send him on through." Lyndsay waited a moment for the call to be transferred. When her phone rang, she picked it up, "Homicide, this is Detective Moskin, how can I help you?"

"You the one working on the lawyer murder?" the caller asked.

"No, the detectives on that case are out at the moment but any information you have I can take down for you and give it to them."

"Okay, but do I get a reward for it?"

Lyndsay then knew that this call was most likely bogus. Just another person looking to make a quick buck. "It depends on whether or not the information you have provides an arrest."

"I know who did it," the caller told her, "I saw him leave the place."

"Can you give me a description of what he looked like?" Lyndsay could tell from the tone in the caller's voice that he was either drunk or high on something. She smirked at Alicia, who had stopped typing to listen in on her side of the call.

"No way. Not over the phone. You want it, you have to meet me."

Lyndsay sighed quietly. It was another lunatic who thought the government was tapping all the phones and we out to get him.

"Where?"

"Meet me at Stevens Park. In an hour. No, make it two instead."

"And how will I know you?"

"What are you wearing?"

"Excuse me?"

"I'm not telling you what I look like but I'll come to you when I know it's safe."

"That's fine. I'm wearing a burgundy blouse and black pants. And I have glasses."

"Fine. I'll see you at 1p.m." And with that, the caller hung up.

"Okay, goodbye," Lyndsay said sarcastically.

"Thank you for your time, Chief Black. The attention your men are giving to this case is admirable." Mark Reynolds walked out of Chief Black's office with Christine following him.

"It's just our job, Mr. Reynolds."

"My firm will be happy to hear that the case is closing in on an arrest. Douglas was an asset to our firm and he will definitely be missed." Reynolds had stopped into the police station in hopes of any updates on the search for Doug's killer. Christine gave him what she could without giving away too much information on the case.

"When my detectives provide me with any information, I'll be sure to call you. Let me walk you out." Christine followed him past Lyndsay and Alicia.

"Chief," Lyndsay called out. Christine turned around and Reynolds stopped as well, startled by the shout.

"What is it?" Black asked.

"We just had someone call with information on the Martin case."

"Does it sound like a good lead?"

Lyndsay started to tell Black about the call but paused, looking at Reynolds. Christine noticed her hesitation was directed at Reynolds and she nodded.

"It's ok, this is Mark Reynolds, Doug Martin's boss."

"Well, I'm not sure yet. He sounded a little loony toons. But he said that he saw the killer leave Martin's place."

"Did he give a description?"

"No, he refused to do it over the phone but he wanted to meet at 1 at Church Square."

"Fine, you two will take care of this meeting, I'll get some officers to accompany you there. Try to bring him in and see if we can get him to pick Waterford out of a lineup."

"You got it Chief," Lyndsay replied.

"So this is good?" Reynolds piped up.

"Could be. If our suspect gets picked out of a lineup it'll only build a stronger case for you lawyers."

"Excellent. Well, I'll let you get back to what you do best. Thank you again Chief Black." Reynolds left the police station and Lyndsay and Alicia finished up their paperwork so they could prepare for the meet with the mysterious witness.

16

Kristie Marks stacked the small pile of file folders on the edge of the desk. She was almost finished with the transferring of case files to the other lawyers in the firm. She stared at the empty chair behind Doug's desk and paused, thinking of Doug's excitement of the case he was working and how he was convinced that the defendant was innocent. Now, he was dead. His polite smile no longer there to cheer her up on a stressful day.

But now his death brought more stress on her. With no lawyer to assist, would the firm just release her? The current market out there for jobs was scarce and rare. And being a single mother made life hard enough. Kristie's life was her son, Connor. His father had left her shortly before Connor was born, telling her in a letter that he was afraid that he couldn't be a good enough father for the baby. Rather than trying, he decided it was better for all of them that he vanish forever.

Reynolds and Hoffman had been more than helpful with her schedule. Not many other employers would be as lenient as they had been with her. Especially with her studying on her free time for the bar. Reynolds had told her that if she passed the bar, the firm would reimburse her and hire her on the spot. But the bar was still months away. She just hoped that they would allow her to remain until she could take it.

She picked up the pile from the edge of the desk and walked down the hall to Chris Delgado's office. On the way, she met up with Robin. Robin smiled at her and gave her a quick hug. Kristie had been silently envious of Robin, her short blonde hair, slim and curvy figure and the smile that melted any man that laid eyes on it. Kristie was also attractive with her long curly brown hair, nicely toned legs and sexy secretary look. But the moment her son came into the conversation, her dates turned tail and ran the opposite way.

"How are you doing?" Robin asked.

"Just keeping myself busy. I'm on my way to deliver these cases to Delgado. It's kinda weird. Handing over the hard work that Doug and I did, only to have someone else take the credit."

"Yeah but you will get the credit. Without your notes and Doug's thoughts, Delgado wouldn't be able to help the defendants as well if someone else were to have worked on it."

"Yeah you're right."

"So will you be staying with the firm?"

"If they'll have me. No one's said anything about if I'm still going to have a job now that Doug is gone."

"How about I get Jacob to put in a good word to Hoffman for you? Between you and me, I know that Hoffman is fond of Jacob."

"Thank you, that would be fantastic. You are so awesome," Kristie smiled.

"Some people are born that way," Robin joked.

"So speaking of Jacob, what's going on with the two of you? It's been a while since we've talked."

"Ugh, I don't know. I mean, he's a great guy but I do work for him. And I don't want to jeopardize his position here, but God he has a nice tight butt."

"I hear you, sister!" Robin and Kristie laughed. They reached Delgado's office and Kristie met with his assistant, Maura Auburn. Maura was a tiny woman with wavy black hair and a cheerful demeanor. It made Kristie always wonder how a woman like her could work for a grumpy self-centered man like Delgado. She guessed that Maura was able to see through the crabby exterior.

"Hi Maura, I've got the files for Chris."

"Good morning! I'll let him know that you're here." Maura buzzed Delgado and explained that Kristie was here with Doug's case files. Delgado took a minute and then walked out into the reception area. He held out his hands and Kristie gave over the files.

"Is this top one the last case he was given?"

"Yes it is. It's the liquor robbery case. I think his last notes are in there also. I know he texted me on Saturday telling me that he figured the one clue that the police missed that cleared the defendant. He never told me what it was but I'm pretty sure that he included that in his notes."

"Fine," Delgado sighed, "I'll just have Maura go through it again."

Kristie looked over at Maura, "If you need any help, just give me a call."

"Thanks, Kristie, I will."

"That all?" Delgado asked her. Kristie nodded and he turned back quickly and returned to his office, closing the door behind him.

"Ok then, Grumpy pants," Robin joked.

"Maura, you should be given sainthood for dealing with that man for all these years."

"I see it as God's little challenge for me," Maura replied.

"Hey," Robin asked Kristie, "What are you doing for lunch?"

"Nothing really. I just have to finish with the files and that should only take another half hour. I'm game for a trip to Johnny Rockets if you are."

"The shakes are on me!" Robin smiled.

17

Craig was finally escorted to the pay phone where he could make the one call that he was allowed. The officer who led him to a generic pay phone with the coin slot removed was short and a bit pudgy. Too many trips to the Dunkin Donuts, Craig thought.

"You've got three minutes," he told Craig, "What's the number you want to dial?"

Craig gave him the phone number to the deli and hoped that Jacqueline was still there. The officer dialed the number for him and handed over the receiver. Craig placed it to his ear and waited for someone to pick up.

"Anthony's Deli, how can I help you?" Connie asked.

"Connie, it's Craig, can you please get me Jackie?"

"Sure Craig, everything okay?"

"Not really. Please hurry."

Craig could hear Connie place the phone down and in the background, he heard the customers and his staff interacting. Even though he had been there only an hour ago, he missed it.

"Hi, sweetie, what's going on?"

"I've been arrested for murder," Craig said, laying it all on the table for her.

"What?"

"They think I killed some lawyer. Do you know a Doug Martin?"

"Doug Martin? No, should I?"

Craig paused. Was she being truthful, he thought. Did she have an affair with Doug Martin? And if so, could the baby she was now carrying be his? The paranoia was setting in and he had to believe that Jackie wouldn't cheat on him. He pushed the questions out of his mind and answered her.

"I don't know, but they're saying that my prints were at the scene of his murder. I've never heard of the guy nor have I killed anyone."

"This must be some kind of mistake," she said, "What should I do?"

"Find the card that Jacob Scott left me this morning and give him a call. Tell him everything and have him meet me here at the station on Hudson."

"Okay, I'll do that right now. Are you sure you're okay? They haven't hurt you?"

"No, I'm fine but I need to take care of this quickly. I love you."

"I love you too."

"Time's up, Waterford," the officer told him.

"I have to go. I'll see you soon." He hung up and the officer returned him to the holding cell until the detectives returned.

"Oh my God," Jackie said, covering her mouth. Her legs felt weak and her hands began shaking. She tried to understand what Craig had just told her but it felt as if she was in the middle of a nightmare. Craig was not a killer but how could his fingerprints be there if he wasn't?

She leaned back on the counter and gripped the edge, keeping herself from collapsing to the floor. She turned around so that no one could see the tears welling up in here eyes. This could not be happening. This was not real. This was all a bad joke.

"Hey Jackie, where is the Provolone?" Mike asked.

"It's, it's in the back fridge. Under the Swiss on the shelf." Her voice cracked as she said it. Mike picked up on the unraveling tone of her voice.

"Everything okay?"

"Yes, I just need a minute. Thank you." Mike waited a moment, then headed into the back for the Provolone.

Jackie then remembered what Craig had asked of her. The card. He wanted her to find Jacob's card and call him. She wiped the tears from her cheeks and looked over the counter. There was no card around. She took a deep breath and turned to the meat counter and looked over by the register. Next to it was the card that read: Jacob Scott, attorney-at-law. She quickly scooped it up and hurried into the back where Craig's office was located. She picked up the phone and dialed the number listed. It rang once.

"Good morning, Reynolds and Hoffman, Jacob Scott's office," said the female voice.

"Hi, my name is Jacqueline Waterford and I was hoping to speak to Mr. Scott if possible please."

"Mr. Scott is in a meeting with a client right now. Could I take a message and have him call you when he's available?"

"Please, it's very important. He was in our deli this morning and he left his card with my husband, Craig. Something's happened to Craig and now he needs help."

"Is this in regards to an arrest?"

"Yes, I'm sorry, everything is hitting me right now. My husband Craig has been arrested for murder but I know he didn't do it. He told me to call Jacob Scott as they were old friends."

"Okay, let me take all your information and I'll pass it to Jacob the moment he returns."

Jacqueline gave as much information as she knew. The secretary asked her a few questions and wrote down everything she was told. Jackie felt somewhat relieved to talk about it and the woman at the office was very sincere to her problem.

"Ok, Mrs. Waterford, I will let him know. And my name is Robin, by the way."

"Thank you, Robin." Jackie hung up and sat there quietly, thinking of what else she could do for Craig. She had to get out and see him. She had to make sure that he was alright. She took off the apron that she wore while working and placed it over the chair and headed back to the front of the store. Connie was finishing with a customer and Jackie waited for her to be free.

"Hey, what's going on?" Connie asked.

"I have to go out for a short while. Can you handle everything for now?"

"Absolutely. But not until you tell me what's wrong. Is Craig okay?"

"I don't know. He's been arrested for murder."

"What? Craig? Saying Craig murdered someone is like saying John Travolta isn't gorgeous." The comment made Jackie smile. Connie was always good at cheering people up when they were down.

"I have go down to the police station and see what I can do."

"Do what you have to, don't worry about the deli, Mike, Jonathan and I will take care of it."

"Thank you so much, Connie. You're an angel."

"An angel with a little devil in her," she joked again.

Jackie walked around the counter and headed for the door when two men walked into the deli. She looked and saw that it was the two detectives that had taken Craig to the police station for questions.

"Going somewhere, Mrs. Waterford?"

18

What do you two want?" Jackie said. The two detectives stood before her, blocking her way out of the deli in the event that she tried running. Brett watched her nostrils flare, showing that she was not happy to see them nor hiding that she knew what they had done to her husband. Brett knew that it might be to their advantage that she was angry. People normally made mistakes when angry. He thought that this would be a good thing if they were going to get anywhere with the case.

"We just were hoping to ask you a few questions, Mrs. Waterford. Do you have a few minutes?" Brett said calmly.

"Why so you can arrest me like my husband? I have nothing to say to you."

"You can answer them here or we can take you in for questioning. You decide," Josh explained. Jackie looked at the detectives, thinking of what to do. Foster counted to five in his head and she answered as he thought she would.

"Can we at least take this to the office in the back?" she asked them.

"Absolutely," Brett replied. They followed her into the back office while customers and workers alike watched the three of them disappear. Foster looked around the small office. Pictures of workers and family spotted the walls along with older awards from the town as well as local magazines. The desk, slightly cluttered, sat in the far right corner with four filing cabinets on the left side of the office. Two cushioned chairs sat in front of the desk while a larger office chair was placed behind it.

Jacqueline Waterford held her hand out, pointed to the chairs, giving the detectives the option to sit while she stood behind the desk. Brett saw it as a defensive mechanism. They were the big bad policemen and she was the helpless victim in her eyes. He found it ironic considering there was evidence that she was involved in this web.

"Mrs. Waterford, we just want to clear up some questions we have about the involvement we believe your husband had in the murder of Doug Martin."

"We don't know a Doug Martin, nor did Craig kill him. I know my husband and he's not a killer. He's a good man."

"I'm sure you believe that but evidence shows he was there and other evidence shows that you knew Doug."

Jackie's eyes squinted at the last comment. Her face was covered in confusion. "I've never known anyone named Doug."

"Maybe he gave you a different name?" Josh threw out into the air.

"Are you implying that I've cheated on my husband?"

"We're just trying to understand what happened to Mr. Martin. You have to understand our situation. We found him dead and the evidence leads to your husband."

"Then the evidence is wrong. Craig didn't kill anyone."

"Well, let's just say then, that you're right. The evidence is wrong. Then why is it leading us to Craig?"

"I don't know. Isn't that your job to find out?"

Brett was beginning to get frustrated. It was clear that Craig was involved in Doug's murder but without a confession it was hard to pin it to him. They were going to need a little luck on their side to find more to make the conviction stick.

"Are you expecting?" Josh asked her, "I only ask because I've noticed you holding your stomach." Jackie was surprised by her subconscious protecting and Raghetti's sharp eyes.

"Yes, I just found out on Sunday. I told Craig this morning."

"Congratulations," Brett said to her.

"Thank you. He was very happy as we've been trying to conceive for some time now."

"If you don't mind me asking, how are the profits with the deli here?"

"Craig had gone to college for a Master in Business and since his father turned the deli over to him, sales have increased 5%."

"Very impressive. So the new addition to the family won't add financial stress?"

"No, we would be fine financially."

"Does Craig have any anger issues? Does he get jealous of men talking to you?"

"No, Craig is very laid back and friendly to everyone. He's never hurt anyone since I've known him."

"Has he ever told you about the girl he ran over with his car back in college?" Josh asked the question, hoping to get some surprise out of her. It worked because Jackie stopped short and her mouth dropped open. Brett almost smiled at the revelation.

"I'm sorry, what?" she asked.

"He never told you about the young girl he killed with his car back when he was in college?"

"No. No, he didn't."

"It's true," Brett added, "Stated that he fell asleep at the wheel late one night and never saw her crossing."

"Makes you wonder if he kept anything else from you," Josh said, planting the seed in Jackie's head. She thought to herself, *Is Craig capable of murder?*

19

Jacob returned to his office a few minutes early after the Greenwood meeting. Robin was filing some paperwork and she turned her head once she heard him enter.

"Can you pencil Miss Greenwood in for another meeting later this month and let her know when? She still has some finalizing to do and I'm waiting for the documents to come back from the state."

"Sure, boss. Oh and there was a message for you while you were gone. A Mrs. Waterford called. She said it was very important that you knew that her husband, Craig, was arrested for murder. She said you were old friends with him."

"She said Craig Waterford?"

"Yeah, why?"

"I just ran into him this morning. Did she leave a number?"

"Yep," Robin said, grabbing the message off her desk and handing it to him. Jacob looked at the message and headed for his desk.

"Please hold my calls until I find out what's going on," he asked her. He closed the door behind him before she could respond.

It was twenty-five minutes later when Jacob walked into the lobby of the Hoboken police station, ready to free Craig. He approached the front desk and gently placed his briefcase on the floor. The desk sergeant, Mendez, looked up from his desk behind the counter and got up.

"What can I do for you?" he asked.

"I'm attorney Jacob Scott, here to see my client, Craig Waterford, please." Jacob took a card from his jacket pocket and handed it to Mendez. Mendez took the card and looked it over, as if waiting for something to pop out at him. He shrugged and picked up the phone. Mendez then dialed the extension he needed and waited for someone to pick up.

"Belanger, it's Mac. Can you grab Craig Waterford in the holding cells and bring him up to Interrogation room number 2? His lawyer's here to talk to him. Great, thanks." Mendez hung up. "He'll be in room number 2. The officer will be standing outside the door, keeping guard. Hey, Valentine, can you bring Mr. Scott back to Room 2 to see his client?"

Vice Detective Eric Valentine paused as he walked into the lobby and looked at Mendez and then Jacob. Valentine was of medium build, his muscular biceps tight under his short sleeve shirt while the goatee on his face gave him a thin, gaunt look. He tilted his head in the direction he was going and Jacob picked up his briefcase to follow him.

Heading into the back through the large room of desks where the detectives were, Jacob's mind was going over the little details that he had gotten from Jacqueline, Craig's wife. Craig was not yet charged but he was a main suspect due to his fingerprints at the scene of the crime. The police had nothing to hold him on. Fingerprints on the weapon or body gave the police a strong case but from what he understood, Craig's print was not near the body or weapon. The detectives' only lead was the one they had brought on her at the last minute with the photo of her and the victim. That was when she dropped the shock on him. Until that point he did not know that the murder Craig was going to be charged with was Jacob's friend, Doug Martin. He couldn't believe Craig would be able to kill another man. But what was his print doing there? He would need to get the truth from Craig in order to help him.

Valentine pointed him to a door with the number 2 on it. The guard and Craig were not yet there, so Jacob opened the door and placed his briefcase down on the table in the center of the room. He opened it up and picked out a pad and a ball point pen. Jacob jotted down Craig's name and the date at the top of the first page and then waited for his friend to arrive.

Two minutes later, the guard with the name Belanger escorted Craig into the room and explained to Jacob that he would stand outside for privacy and make sure Craig did not try to escape. He then closed the door, leaving them alone.

"Thank you so much for coming to help," Craig said to him.

"What the hell is going on?"

"They think I killed someone."

"I know that. Jackie told me everything. How did your fingerprints get in Doug's apartment? And what's with the picture of Jackie and him? Does she really know him?"

"You know about the photo?" Craig asked, puzzled by Jacob's amount of knowledge.

"The detectives on the case asked her about it. They just left the deli looking for more answers."

"They talked to her?"

"Yes, but I need you to be straight with me. I need to know the truth if I'm going to help you with this. Did you do it?"

"NO!," Craig said, shocked, "How could you ask me that?"

"Were you in the apartment when it happened?"

"No, I honestly don't know the guy. I have no idea how my fingerprint got there or why this Doug Martin guy was killed in the first place."

"I'll let you know now, this will be a little rough for me because I worked with Doug. We're both with the same firm. But I will help you because you're a friend and I believe you didn't do it. But we're going to need answers in order to get you freed of the suspicion."

"Thank you. Where do we start?"

"First, they don't have enough on you to keep you here. We're getting you out but that won't be enough for them to stop hounding everyone you know. We have to find out how your fingerprint got there. Then we have to find out where that photo of your wife and Doug came from."

"Was he seeing someone?" Craig wondered.

"Um, not to my knowledge. Doug was more focused on climbing up the corporate ladder than dating anyone. He had a girlfriend a couple of months ago, but I met her. She was a blonde and it didn't go far as she wanted more time than he could give her. But he wasn't one to easily make enemies."

"Yet someone killed him so he had to have one enemy."

"True, but if I've learned anything about criminals, they always hit those they know and places they frequent."

"Well, that removes me then."

"I think I may have an idea as to where to begin. But I have to get you out of here first. Wait right here." Jacob went to the entrance of the room and knocked on the door. Belanger opened it and looked at the lawyer.

"Hey there, I need to speak to the detectives on my client's case."

"They're not here at the moment," Belanger told him.

"Then please direct me to the chief of police."

Belanger pointed to the chief's office and Jacob walked over by himself. He knocked on the door and waited a moment, hearing someone on the phone. When he heard the invitation in, he opened the door and held out his hand to Chief Black.

"Jacob Scott, I'm defending Craig Waterford."

"Hello Mr. Scott, what can I do for you?" she asked.

"For one, I'd like you to release my client. Unless that is, you plan on finding something immediately to charge him with."

"We do have his prints at the scene," Christine said. She knew that it wasn't enough but she tried to bluff him anyway.

"His prints at the scene don't prove that he killed anyone. It only proves that he was there after the murder."

"It's in the blood of the victim."

"He could have gotten blood on him when he checked his pulse. He could have been trying to save him. There's no other DNA evidence that proves my client murdered the victim. And without better proof, you have no choice to let him go."

Christine Black gritted her teeth. The lawyer was good. But she wasn't chief of police by letting things go. He may have won this round, but the war was not over. Not yet.

"Fine, but he is still considered a suspect. He leaves town and we will consider him running and will bring him in immediately."

"Understood. Thank you very much for your time, Chief Black." He smiled back at her.

"Don't try to slap my ass too, Mr. Scott. Take your client and get out."

"Got it." Jacob hurried out of the office before he bit off more than he could chew.

20

Gerald Healy had just finished a set of 50 situps when the phone rang. The red light on the phone lit up the darkness of the room. Heavy drapes covered the main window and the room, itself, had the main essentials. One 37-inch television, a recliner, small table and one sole chair. He stood up and checked the caller ID. He saw who it was and was concerned that they were contacting him again. They shouldn't be calling him now. This meant something was wrong.

"We've got a problem," the caller said immediately.

"We've got a problem? Or is it you that has the problem?"

"Someone saw you leaving Martin's home."

Healy absorbed the statement. He closed his eyes and thought back to the night. He remembered leaving and making sure that no one was around to see him. Besides, he wore a hooded sweatshirt that protected his face. He wasn't an amateur.

"They won't be able to identify me."

"You sure you want to take that chance? I don't."

Healy took all possibilities into account in his head. Worst case scenario, someone did see him. Then everything they had done would be for nothing. He couldn't bear to let it be his fault.

"Give me the details."

21

Have a seat," Jacob said to Craig. Craig sat back on the small couch in Jacob's office. He thought it was best to have Craig come there so they could begin going over the case right away. Craig examined the room as Jacob spoke to his assistant, Robin. Jacob had done well for himself. The office was about the size of the front of the deli. The couch he sat on was as comfortable as his new bed. Craig was even astonished with the private bathroom.

"Can you order some lunch for us?" Jacob asked Robin.

"Sure, what did you want?"

"Grab us some Italian from that restaurant over by Newport Mall. I'll take some of their lasagna, Craig what would you like to eat?"

"Um, I'll have the ravioli," Craig answered.

"Okay, and order whatever you would like as well. Oh and let me know when the faxes from the Hoboken police arrives."

"No problem," Robin replied. She began to walk out of the office and back to her desk when Jacob called out to her again.

"Robin, thank you." He smiled at her and Craig caught the look he gave her. He had seen it before when he was interested in a girl back in high school.

"Anytime, boss," Robin said back. She left and closed the door. The moment she disappeared from sight, Jacob returned back to work.

"Okay, we need to come up with a defense as to why your print was there in his blood. Were you a client?"

"Jacob, I've never met him before. Ever."

"That's not going to do, Craig. There has to be a reason why your fingerprint was on his briefcase *and in his blood*."

"If I knew that, I wouldn't be worried out of my mind. How could it have even gotten there if I wasn't?"

"That's what we need to figure out. Without that, your case is shit."

Craig ran his hands through his short cut hair. Glancing at the clock on the wall, he couldn't believe it was only 1p.m. It had only been 7 hours since he woke up to find out he was a father-to-be. Now he was going to charged with a murder that he never committed. What would Richard Kimble do in his shoes? Find the truth. That was what he'd do.

"Maybe it was the one armed man," Craig wondered out loud. Jacob looked up at him.

"What was that?"

"Nothing, just thinking."

"No, what did you say?"

"I was just saying that maybe it was the one armed man who killed your friend."

"Maybe that's it!"

"What's it?"

"Maybe we're going in the wrong direction. Maybe it didn't have to do with Doug. It has to do with you."

"Me? Why me?"

"Maybe that's the 64,000 dollar question. It's your print that's at the crime scene. Not someone else's. What have you done to have someone frame a murder on you? Have you wronged anyone?"

"No, you know me, I don't get into arguments. It's all bad Karma."

"Well, I don't know about you but I'd say that being framed for murder is pretty bad karma. But let's write down what we know for now." Jacob got up from his desk and opened his closet. Reaching inside, he pulled out a blackboard on wheels.

"Are you going to teach now?" Craig asked.

"It helps me think when I write everything down," Jacob explained with a smile, "Now, what do we have?"

"Dead lawyer, framed deli store owner, planted fingerprint," Craig spoke out. Jacob jotted it down quickly.

"Okay so as of right now, the only thing linking you to Doug is the fingerprint." Jacob circled the word fingerprint and drew arrows from it to Doug and Craig's name on the board. "Now, the fingerprint can mean two things: the killer wants you to take the fall or the killer wants to direct the police away from him. Either way, the killer knows the both of you." Jacob wrote the word 'killer' under everything. Then he drew a line in a circle around the words.

"So I know the killer?"

"It's the only explanation I can think of considering you and Doug have no link. It must be the middleman who is the link."

"But who do I know that also knows Doug?"

"The same person that is in one of Doug Martin's photos and is also having your baby."

22

Lyndsay called Brett's cell phone from the station before she and Alicia left to meet with the witness on Foster's and Raghetti's case. Alicia grabbed her coat and Lyndsay placed her jacket on her chair while waiting for the call to answer. Her partner took a moment to pull back her long dark brown hair into a ponytail in order to keep it out of her face.

"Foster," Brett answered.

"Hey, it's Lyndsay, we're on our way over to Stevens Park. Someone called in on the Martin case, saying that they saw someone leaving the house. It may not help considering the doped-up voice of the caller but if you want to join us and help question them, we'll be there at 2."

"Sounds good. We're at Martin's house right now and that's only two blocks away. We'll meet you there."

"Okay." Lyndsay hung up and the two female detectives headed out of the station.

Brett told Josh of the phone call. They had returned to Doug Martin's place to see if there was something they missed the first time. The apartment had not yet been visited by the cleanup crew and thanks to the August heat, the smell of death was becoming overwhelming. Josh had kept some hospital masks in the trunk of the unmarked they were assigned and handed one to Brett.

Walking into the main room of the apartment, they split up and began looking for more clues left behind. Josh searched the bedroom of anything that may help with the case. He saw that Doug Martin was tidy with his bedroom. The clothes in a hamper, an aroma-therapy candle on each side of the King-sized bed. The dresser and closet door made of a dark stained oak. And the thin drapes allowed the light from the side street to shine through but not too brightly. Josh checked the side tables for any sign of sexual conquest but only found an empty box of Trojans. He smiled at Martin's achievements. Then he began searching the dresser drawers. The top drawer contained socks and men's underwear. There was a frilly thong bunched into a ball in the far corner of the drawer. Raghetti wondered if it was a souvenir left behind. The other drawers showed no signs of any evidence.

He headed to the closet next and looked through the pockets of the suits that hung neatly and orderly. There was also nothing of interest in the closet. He was not finding anything helpful. His bedroom was too clean for a man. Was it the touch of a woman left behind? Josh tried one more spot, under the bed. Sure enough, there was a shoe box under the bed.

Josh pulled out the shoe box and placed it on the bed. He opened it and searched through the papers inside. There were bank account statements, credit card statements and a few more "personal" photos of Doug and a couple of attractive women. None of the women were familiar. Josh looked over the credit card statements and noticed a high amount charged at the Newport Mall Jewelers a month ago. The bank statement also showed an amount of $200,000 deposited into his bank account and then withdrawn the following day. Josh's detecting mind thought of money laundering or perhaps blackmail and made note of it for later.

As Josh searched through the bedroom, Brett entered the kitchen area and examined the notes on the refrigerator door as well as the wall calendar. The papers were nothing but the regular bills and little personal notes. He read the birthday card given to him by his assistant, Kristie Marks. Other than that, there was nothing of interest. The wall calendar was a different story. Martin had jotted down meetings and times on the calendar. Brett read over the notes and stopped on one that had been crossed out. It was on the fourth, a week and a half before Doug's murder, and read: FIELDS & REYNOLDS 11.A.M.

Brett remembered that Doug worked for a Reynolds & Hoffman law firm. That would explain who Reynolds was but could Fields be a client of Doug's? And if so, why was that crossed out?

Then he saw something that made him smile. In two days from now, Martin had scheduled a lunch with "J.W." Jacqueline Waterford.

23

Robin brought in the faxes that the Hoboken Police sent over. She walked across the office to the desk where Jacob sat. As she did, she looked over at Craig who was sitting on the couch eating his lunch. She wondered if Jacob's mind was clouded over by the old friendship that he and Craig Waterford had over a decade ago. She knew that people changed over the years. Craig may have been a good kid but he was no longer a kid. She didn't trust him, but she was just Jacob's assistant. No one would listen to her. No one but Kristie.

"The police reports arrived," Robin told Jacob. He looked up from the papers covering his desk and smiled at her. His mouth was full of pasta and there was a smudge of sauce on the side of his mouth. Robin took one of the tissues and wiped the sauce off.

"Thank you," Jacob said. He held her stare a little longer than normal. Lately, he found himself lost in her smile. It was innocent yet sultry. Her blue eyes sparkled in the light like sapphires. She felt herself blushing and turned away, looking back to Craig.

"Do you two need anything else?" she asked.

"Craig, are you good?" Jacob added.

"I'm fine, thank you."

"Thanks Robin," Jacob said to her. Then he returned to lawyer mode. "Okay Craig, let's look this over. Maybe we can find something in this to help you." Craig carried his ravioli over to Jacob's desk and they huddled over the report.

Robin left and returned to her own desk where she had some filing to do and some scheduling to rearrange. She grabbed the schedule agenda and opened it to this week, looking over the rare unfilled spaces on the calendar. She had memorized the trial dates for the cases he was working on and kept that in mind. As she moved his meetings around, Kristie walked in and leaned on her desk.

"I'm in desperate need of a drink," she said, laughing after the comment. Robin looked up and smiled back.

"I am right there with you, sister," she said, "But I may be here late. Jacob just took over another case. Friend of his."

"Wonderful," Kristie said, rolling her eyes. "What's the charge?"

"Um, if I tell you, please promise that you'll keep it to yourself. He asked me to keep it quiet."

"What is it, a mafia boss? Drug kingpin? I know, it's Jensen Ackles!"

"Who?" Robin asked, confused.

"He's that hot guy from the TV show, Supernatural," Kristie explained.

"Oh! Yeah, he is pretty hot. But he's no Anderson Cooper."

"So what is the case about?"

"You have to promise."

"Alright, I promise not to say anything. So who's the client?"

Robin paused, hoping that Jacob wouldn't find out that she was spilling the beans to Kristie. "It's Craig Waterford. The man that the police think killed Doug."

Jacob and Craig read over the interview transcript that Craig relived again. Jacob was going over the revelation of the photo of Doug and Jacqueline. He asked Craig if she had even shown signs of being bored with their marriage or if she was having an affair. Before Craig could answer, Kristie Marks burst into the office and stomped up to the edge of the desk.

"Is this him?" she asked Jacob. Jacob looked up in surprise and noticed Robin rushing in after Kristie. He shook his head and stood.

"Craig Waterford, meet Kristie Marks. She was Doug Martin's assistant." He pushed the glasses up the bridge of his nose and tightened his lips together. He did this when he was frustrated. Robin thought it was cute but not at the moment.

"You're the sole suspect?" Kristie asked Craig. Then she looked over at

Jacob, "And you're representing him? I'm sure Doug is doing cartwheels on his morgue shelf right now, knowing that."

"Kristie, you're blowing this out of proportion. If you'd let me explain."

"I'm sorry," Craig threw out into the conversation, "but the police have it wrong, I'm innocent. I never killed your boss."

"Oh please, explain. This should be as entertaining as Delgado's bat story."

"Look, I know Craig. If he says he didn't murder Doug, then I believe that he didn't. But then that makes the police wrong in accusing him and I believe Doug would want me to find his true killer."

"And what if the police are right? What if he did kill Doug and you're wrong?"

"What if I'm not? Then Doug's killer goes free and another innocent man goes to jail. Would you feel good about yourself if that happened? Doug took you under his wing and helped you with studying for the bar. He was your friend and he was also mine. Trust me just this once. Let me show you that my gut is right on this."

Kristie looked Jacob in the eyes. Then she looked over at Craig. His eyes showed compassion and sorrow. She didn't want to be swayed to feel otherwise but the mother in her, felt sorry for him.

"If I did, how would you prove it to me?" she asked Jacob.

"Well, I would need your help. You're the only one in this room that knew Doug better than anyone else. You can give us his perspective." Kristie stood over Craig and chewed her bottom lip. She wanted to do right by Doug for being her mentor.

"Fine. Prove it to me."

"Great," Jacob said, smiling once more, "Robin, why don't you forward the calls into here and join us. Four heads are better than three."

Robin looked at him and saw him wink and give her a tiny side smile. She was surprised that he was not angry with telling Kristie about Waterford. But then again, maybe he expected her to. 'You sly man, Mr. Scott', she thought to herself and went out to her desk to do what she was told.

24

What time is it?" Alicia asked, "It's sweltering and I feel like I'm melting."

Moskin and Bowman arrived at the park ten minutes early. They took surveillance first of those already in the park, hoping that the witness was already there, looking out for them. They couldn't find anyone that fit the voice of the caller. So they decided to leave the vehicle and head into the park.

The covering of trees in the park did not help cool the female detectives. The humidity in the air gave it a sticky and slimy feel to everyone who braved to leave the air conditioned insides. Even the dogs in the small dog park were too overheated to enjoy their small freedom from the leashes.

"Let's just walk around for a few minutes and then we'll leave," Lyndsay said.

"Fine, but if he doesn't show, we're stopping back at my place so I can shower off the sweat."

"Only if I can dip into your cookie jar while I wait."

"Sure, I just made some new peanut butter cookies." Alicia had a habit of baking in order to unwind after a stressful day. Lately, she had a string of stressful days concerning the club murder case that they were on. Lyndsay loved when she came in the next morning with a plateful of goodies, but after the third day in a row, she was feeling that she would need to spend the entire weekend at the gym working the calories off.

"I really hope this is a legit eyewitness," Lyndsay said to Alicia.

"We won't know until we meet him."

They walked into the center of the park and over to the children's playground in the back of the park. The park was the size of one city block and sat in the front of one of the Stevens' Tech buildings. On the opposite side of Hudson Street was the church that the park was named after. It was only one of two parks in all of Hoboken. And even though the other park was closer to a number of schools, kids and their parents frequent Church Square every day. This day, though, the park was rather empty compared to a normal summer day.

As they approached the other side of the park, Alicia noticed a man near the Mr. Softee ice cream truck, studying the detectives. She nudged Lyndsay and tilted her head in the direction of the man. Lyndsay caught sight of the man and looked him over. He was dressed in a faded Halo T-shirt and jeans with holes in the knees. His hair was a tattered mess and his eyes were covered up with old sunglasses. He saw Lyndsay and waved his hand over to the park bench near him.

"Yeah, that's him," Lyndsay confirmed. They walked over to the scruffy man and Lyndsay flashed her badge at him, showing him that she was the one he was waiting for.

"Right on time," he said, "Not bad for a cop."

"Detective Moskin and this is Detective Bowman. Are you the man who called about the Martin murder?"

"That the lawyer who got killed?"

"That's the one. Can you describe what you saw?"

"Sure can. Got a sharp eye. Like an eagle's. But I wanna know if there's a reward first. I'm a bit on hard times. You know, being in a recession and all."

"Well, the reward depends on how good the information is. If it leads to an arrest, then we can talk about a reward."

"Promise me you'll call me when you nail the guy?"

"I'll do what I can," Lyndsay told him.

"Okay, okay. Fair enough. I just want to do my duty to my country and help out."

"And this is a great way to go about that. Now can you describe what you saw?"

"I saw the guy. That night the lawyer was killed, I couldn't sleep so I walked around the streets. The fresh air helps my lungs. Makes me sleepy."

"Okay so do you know around what time, you passed the victim's home?"

"The victim?" he asked.

"The lawyer guy," she clarified.

"Oh yeah, him. So it was like, three in the morning. Yeah cause by the time I got back to my place, Who's the Boss was just starting and that is always on at 4a.m."

"Are you normally awake at that time?"

"Yeah, I work the night shift at the BP gas station at the entrance to town. I like to watch a little TV when I get home."

"Okay, so what did you see when you passed the lawyer's house?"

"I saw this guy, he was kinda short. Not like midget short, but shorter than normal height."

"Compared to your height, how tall would you say he was?" Lyndsay had taken out her notepad and began writing the information down. As she did, neither she nor Alicia noticed the hunched homeless man pushing a shopping cart through the park and towards them. He noticed the women and the man and approached them.

"Excuse me, ladies and gentlemen," the homeless man coughed at them, "Could you help a man down on his luck?"

Lyndsay and Alicia looked up at him and saw the filth on his face and the beaten down look in his eyes. But Lyndsay looked back to the witness, hoping not to lose him with the distraction. She believed that he may actually have something for them. She knew Brett and Josh needed more to make a conviction in regards to Craig Waterford.

Pete Rogers, on the other hand, believed in helping out others in order to get back good things in life. He dug into his pants pocket and pulled out a couple of crumpled up dollar bills to hand the homeless guy something.

The homeless man saw Pete digging for something and shuffled over to him. Alicia stood up and flashed her badge. She thought the same as Lyndsay and didn't want the witness to lose his train of thought.

"Hoboken police, I'm sorry but I'm going to have to ask you to keep moving," Alicia said to the homeless man.

"Oh, thank you. God bless your soul," the homeless man ignored Alicia, in hopes of getting Pete's money. He took the money from Pete's hand and then held his hand out to shake it. Pete shook the homeless man's hand by habit.

The next few seconds seemed to occur in the blink of an eye. The homeless man, while shaking Pete's hand, brought his other hand up with abnormal speed and tapped Pete's neck several times. The homeless man then released his grip on Pete's hand and stepped back. Pete paused for a second and then his eyes went wide in panic.

Lyndsay was unsure of what occurred just then. But when Pete Rogers' throat spat like a sprinkler, her body jolted into action. She leapt forward and clamped her hands around Pete's neck, hoping to keep his shooting blood inside of him. Alicia's eyes went wide at the gushing blood and reached under her armpit to grab her gun. As she did this, the homeless man ducked to the side, picking up his shopping cart of items and tossed it her way as if it weighed ten pounds. The cart came crashing onto Alicia's legs and she fell to the ground.

The homeless man shrugged off his dirty overcoat and sprinted away. Lyndsay was helpless and forced to watch. She saw the direction of the homeless man's escape and then her head shot left and right, looking for any help as her partner was trying to lift the cart off herself.

25

It's only ten after one," Brett told Josh, "Let's swing over to the park and see if Lyndsay and Alicia are still there with the witness that called in."

"I need a drink," Josh complained, "It's way too hot out here."

"You bitch like an old woman, you know that?"

"Better to bitch like one than to look like one," Josh joked back.

Brett took offense to the comment. "What the hell is that supposed to mean?"

"Nothing," Josh said, "It means nothing, saggy tits."

Brett looked at his chest and noticed that his body was showing signs of not visiting a gym in the past two weeks. Brett had been determined in a healthy body, but within the past three weeks, his motivation had taken a hit. He found himself outside of work feeling a lack of social ability. He sat in front of the television at home eating takeout. He wasn't sure of the reason behind it but with the long hours at the station, he didn't have much time to ponder it.

"Listen up, Captain Jowls. You're no Brad Pitt yourself."

"I never said I was Brad Pitt. I see myself more of a Burt Reynolds clone, only sexier."

"Still suffering from delusions of grandeur?"

"Just living in the real world," Josh smirked. They approached the park and crossed the street to enter. As they did, Foster looked and couldn't see either Lyndsay or Alicia. He checked the benches and did not see anyone.

But he noticed what appeared as a homeless man running through the park towards the far end.

"Do you see them?"

"No," Raghetti replied, "But that homeless guy doesn't look kosher."

"A running homeless man never does." Brett continued looking in the park and stopped short. He pointed slightly to his left. Josh followed his finger and saw Lyndsay and Alicia on the ground.

"Oh shit, they're down."

"Get the homeless guy!" Lyndsay shouted at them when she saw the two detectives.

"Go help them, I'll get the guy," Brett said, running off. Josh ran to the women and pulled the cart off of Alicia. She stood up and brushed herself off. Josh then pulled off his tie and helped Lyndsay by tying it around Pete Rogers' neck, hoping to stop the blood flow but not too tight to constrict air flow.

"What the hell happened?"

"Your witness here just got silenced right in front of us. Damn!" Lyndsay was angry at herself for allowing all this is happen in front of her without stopping it. She stared at her hands and was temporarily mesmerized by the blood on her skin and the fear of the diseases that she may be exposing herself to.

"This is Detective Bowman, we need an ambulance and backup sent to the Church Square pronto," Alicia shouted into her cell phone. She gave the information the operator needed and then hung up. "Was that even a homeless guy?"

"I don't think so," Lyndsay answered.

"Those are quite the stab marks." Josh looked at the spray on the tar pathways. The length from the witness' body to the farthest blood drop had to have been at least seven or eight feet. "Whoever that homeless guy was, he knew where to strike."

Lyndsay reached down and placed two fingers on the opposite side of Rogers' neck, checking for a pulse. While searching for one, she noticed his face turning pale. She moved her fingers in a circle, knowing the artery was to be there somewhere.

"I can't get a pulse."

Josh placed his hand where Lyndsay's was and felt around for a pulse. He could not find one either.

"Yeah, he has none. He's dead." Moskin and Bowman cursed in

unison. Lyndsay felt horrible, having their witness taken out right in front of them. She knew the chief would not be happy.

"Are you two okay here?" Raghetti asked them. Alicia nodded yes and Lyndsay gave a bloody thumbs up.

"We're just groovy," she joked sarcastically.

""I'm going to help out Brett."

"Catch the bastard," Alicia ordered him. Josh ran in the direction of Brett and the homeless killer. Lyndsay sat down on the bench that she had been at when she first got there. Her legs felt weak and frustration raced through her body. Her disappointment was felt by Alicia.

"Hey, no one expected that. There was nothing we could have done. This guy, whoever he is, pulled it off pretty smooth," Alicia consoled her.

"Well, at least I didn't get knocked over by a homeless man's shopping cart," Lyndsay retorted, hoping to relieve the stress of the situation.

"Yeah, I'm going to need to get some tetanus shots now." "Do you think that was Waterford?" Lyndsay threw out there.

"I don't know," Alicia said, "I never got a good look at his face."

"If it was, that was a great disguise."

"If it was, then there's a lot more to this guy than deli owner."

26

Foster pushed his legs as fast as he could. He wasn't sure if the man he was chasing wounded his fellow detectives or if they came across him attacking someone else. But whatever happened, he knew the man running away had done wrong.

"Police, freeze!" he shouted. This did not faze the criminal. He continued to run fast. Brett saw the direction he was then.

The Stevens Park was perched at the edge of the thirty foot cliff that separated Hoboken with Sinatra Drive. Sinatra Drive ran along the edge of New Jersey's side of the Hudson River. The riverside road was decorated with a newly added park, including a jogging path along the short piers.

Once the man reached the cliff, he would have to turn to the left or right and slow him down. Hopefully, it would be enough for Brett to catch up and jump him. Then he would learn what he and Josh had walked into. He wondered if it had to do with the Waterford case. He hoped not because this would then add a new twist to the case. And there were enough twists to it as it was now.

The man reached the large wire fence that ended the park and blocked people from the thirty foot drop beyond it. Got you now, Brett thought. He prepared himself to make a quick side step in the direction that the man would turn. But he was not prepared for what came next.

Instead of turning to the side and continuing to run, the man Foster was chasing leapt up and landed in the center of the fence. Once his feet found hold spots in the fence, he scrambled up the fence.

"Son of a bitch," Brett was shocked. But he kept his momentum going in hopes of grabbing the man's legs before he could swing them over the top of the fence. He couldn't let him get away. Not after losing Waterford earlier due to demanding a lawyer.

Brett hit the fence and jumped up, putting all he could into his legs. The jump pushed him up and his arms reached up. He aimed for the ankles and the fingers on his right hand brushed the fabric of the man's pant legs. But Brett was unable to grab a handful before the legs swung up and over the fence. Foster fell to the ground and scrambled up to his feet again and quickly climbed over the fence. As he did, he kept an eye on the path the man was taking.

He dropped down on the other side of the fence and pushed through the trees and bushes that sprinkled the top of the cliff. Foster looked up and watched the man drop out of sight. Brett shook his head, not sure he saw what he thought. He reached the edge of the cliff and looked down. The man was below, rolling off the roof of a parked car.

"You've got to be kidding me," he muttered. The man stood and looked up. He smiled at Brett then ran across Sinatra Drive and into the small park area at the water's edge.

"I'm not getting paid enough for this shit," Brett said to himself and then he stepped off the cliff and onto the roof of the car that the man had landed on. Brett's legs gave out and he rolled off and onto the hood, denting both. He breathed in and felt no pain in his sides. Whew, he thought, no broken ribs. He got to his feet and continued running after the man.

The man had gotten a small lead and Brett was determined to close that. He pulled out his gun and aimed at the man.

"Stop or I will shoot!" he shouted to the homeless man. The man took a moment to look back and saw the gun in Brett's hands. Then he once again took matters into his own hands and grabbed a woman who was jogging past him and pushed her into the railing. The woman stumbled into the railing and with the force of the push, flipped over the railing and into the river.

"Damn!" Brett yelled. He holstered the gun and dove into the river after the woman. The woman screamed for help and Brett wrapped his arm around her chest, keeping her afloat. She kicked her feet and made it harder to keep her stable and above the water's surface.

"Stop kicking or you'll drown us both," he tried to tell her. "Lady, I'm a cop, stop kicking."

The woman heard this and she eased up on the freaking out. Brett noticed that several people passing by had stopped and were willing to pull them up with their help. A taller skinny man had his legs held by a larger man and he learned his upper body over the edge and held his hands out to help Brett. Brett tried lifting the woman up out of the water and the skinny man managed to reach her wrist and pulled her up to safety. Once the woman was safe on solid ground, he leaned back down to pull up Brett. Foster reached out again and was grabbed by the skinny man. He was then pulled up to the park area and sat on the ground. Brett took a moment to catch his breath before he attempted to go after the homeless man again.

"Anyone see which was that homeless guy went?" he asked the crowd. The majority pointed north up Sinatra Drive. He held up his hand in thanks and got back to his feet. Then he began running again, hoping that all was not lost.

27

Raghetti sped down Washington Street north with his siren and light flashing. After seeing the direction that both the homeless man and Brett ran, he thought he would cut the homeless man off by driving around and running into the homeless guy. Unfortunately, the traffic on Washington refused to make way for him. It took several minutes that he thought were crucial to the chase. He hoped Brett was having better luck. He knew that he shouldn't have split up with him but the circumstances required it. They needed to check up on Moskin and Bowman yet make sure the killer didn't get away.

Josh knew that the witness must have been legit because having someone kill him was too much of a coincidence. This Martin case was getting bigger than any of them expected. This would be two murders and he hoped that the homeless guy had a link back to Waterford.

He finally reached the corner of 11th and Washington and made a fast right down to Sinatra Drive. Due to the cliff on the river's edge, there were very few side streets that merged with Sinatra Drive. From Stevens' Park the first side street going north was 11th Street.

Raghetti swerved another right onto Sinatra Drive and sped as fast as he could, hoping his partner was alright. He hit the curve of Sinatra Drive around Castle Point Terrace and kept an eye out for either the homeless guy or Brett.

As he finished the curve of Sinatra Drive, he caught sight of the homeless guy. The man was running as fast as he could in the street, heading right to Josh. He smiled and braced himself.

"Come to papa, assclown."

Josh swerved the car into the other lane and right into the path of the homeless man. The homeless man stopped running the minute before Josh reached him. He looked through the windshield and into Josh's eyes. Raghetti couldn't believe that this man was looking to play chicken. He wasn't going to slow down. He wanted this guy bad.

The homeless man took several steps forward and then at the last second, jumped up and curled himself into a ball. The man landed on the hood of Josh's car and rolled up into the windshield. The momentum kept him going and he continued across the roof of the car and off the trunk. He landed hard on the street and stopped himself from rolling any further. The homeless man knew that he had to act fast if he was going to make any escape possible. But he knew that he would have to stop the driver cop from following him.

Josh stopped that car and threw it into park. Then he threw the door open and pulled out his gun as he did. The homeless man's speed shocked him. He was right there when Josh was climbing out of the car. The homeless man grabbed the car door with both hands and rammed it into Josh's side. Then without taking another breath, he yanked the door open again and slammed it into Josh's side again and again. Josh yelped in pain as the metal corner of the door dug into his side, cracking a rib. He fell back inside the car sideways. The homeless man saw that he was no longer a threat and ran off, heading north once again.

Josh held his breath and gripped his injured side, pushing through the pain. He staggered out of the car and reached for his gun. It was not in his holster and he looked in the car to see his gun on the floor well of the driver's side. He dropped to his knees and reached in for the gun. As he did, Brett reached the car.

"Are you okay?" he asked.

"I think he broke a rib. Hurts like a mother when I breathe in."

"Okay, take it easy." Brett propped him up on the driver seat and leaned in to grab the police mic. "Dispatch, this is Homicide One, we've got a 10-2 just north of Sinatra Park. I repeat, 10-2 north of Sinatra Park."

"Received Homicide One," the mic squawked back. "Is this an officer down?"

"Negative Dispatch. Officer is not down, but injured in fight with fleeing criminal."

"Acknowledged Homicide One, backup is four minutes out."

91

"Acknowledged Dispatch, Homicide One out." Brett dropped the mic on the floor and leaned back on the dented car door.

"Where the hell were you?" Josh asked.

"Saving a woman who got in the way. He tossed her into the Hudson to distract me. A better question is how do you hit the damn guy and still let him get away?"

"The guy's superhuman?" Josh joked. He snickered and clinched up when the pain jolted up his wounded side.

"That'll teach you to joke around after getting your ass kicked by a homeless guy."

"That was no homeless guy. That had to be Waterford in disguise."

"You think?" Brett asked.

"I know. Who else would want that witness silenced? It makes perfect sense. He kills Martin for sleeping with his wife, then gets seen leaving the crime scene and has to kill the witness in order to make it away clean."

"Sounds perfect, but without the further evidence needed, we're short of being able to send him away for good. No lawyer is going to find it easy in getting a conviction on the little we have."

"The guy's gotta mess up some time. They always do eventually."

Brett breathed a frustrated sigh. Josh was right, if Waterford was the killer of both Doug Martin and their witness, then the best way to get him convicted was finding the murder weapon with his prints on it. He walked around to the front of the car, taking his mind off the disappointment for a moment to look at the condition of the hood and windshield.

"For a shorter guy, he sure did a number landing on the hood," Brett observed, "We should check the hood and windshield for prints. It's worth a try. Then put a call out to the hospitals around in case he decides to get any injuries checked out."

"I just want a doctor right now. Then I want to sleep for a day. Then I'll find him and return the beating."

Brett walked back over to the driver side and something in front of the front tire caught his eye. He looked down and smiled.

"Looks like Christmas came early," he said. Brett leaned down by the front tire. Josh lost sight of him behind the open car door for a few seconds.

"What is it?" he asked. Foster stood up, a long object in his left hand. He held it up for Josh to see. Josh noticed the shine of the still-fresh blood on the homemade shiv that their homeless man dropped when Josh hit him with his car.

"I'll be damned. We just won the evidence lottery!"

28

It was after 7 p.m. when Jacob had decided to call it a day. Craig had left shortly before 1 p.m. The morning had exhausted him and he needed some sleep and alone time in order to absorb everything that had happened. Jacob didn't blame him. Going from learning that he was going to be a father, to being arrested for murder, to learning that his wife may be cheating on him, it was enough for any normal man to feel overwhelmed over.

He had let Robin go home two hours ago and stayed behind in hopes of working on an opening statement for the preliminary hearing if it went that far. Right now, though, the police didn't have enough for a conviction to occur.

Yet during his last hour in the office, his mind continuously returned to Robin. He didn't know what to do with the feelings he was beginning to feel for her. The professional work relationship they had was blocking him from going through with anything.

He remembered the feelings began two months ago when he and Robin worked late on the Newton case that he had taken on. They ordered late night takeout to the office and had kicked back talking while they ate. He learned a lot about her that night. And the more he learned, the more attractive she became.

The one plus point Jacob saw was that he felt the connection coming from her as well. Yet it didn't make it any easier that he was her boss and wanted more to develop from it. He considered firing her but with the increase in unemployment, it would be hard for her to find another job. He couldn't do that to her.

He gathered his papers together and was placing them neatly into his briefcase when his phone rang. He wondered who would be calling him at this hour. It could be Craig hoping to get reassurance on the charge.

"Jacob Scott," he answered.

"Mr. Scott, this is Detective Brett Foster. Is your client with you?"

"No, Detective, he is not. Is there something I can help you with?"

"You? No. But we would like your client to perhaps take some time and come in so we can get a palm print."

"It's after seven, detective. Can't this wait until tomorrow?"

"I thought your client would sleep better if he came in now to help clear his name." Jacob was surprised to hear a change in view from the detective that blatantly accused Craig of killing Jacob's friend and co-worker this morning.

"What changed your mind about him?"

"We, uh, had an incident earlier this afternoon down at Stevens Park. As a result, we received another piece of evidence on the case. I'd like to match the palm print we have to Craig Waterford's. Due to the incident, I'm beginning to think that Waterford may not be behind this."

"That's refreshing to know. I, of course, would like to be there to represent my client when this happens."

"Of course, anything to make Waterford more comfortable." Jacob became suspicious of Brett Foster's change of heart. This was too easy. He would appear at ease when he took Craig in to let the police take a palm print, but inside he would be on all fours like a cornered animal.

"Okay," Jacob said, "I'll call him and we'll be in within the hour."

"I'll be waiting." Brett hung up and Jacob sat back in his chair, wondering what little trick the Hoboken police had up their sleeves.

Jacob showed up at Craig's house twenty minutes later. He knocked on the door of his apartment and waited for a response. Almost a minute after, he heard some shuffling inside the apartment and the door opened. Craig looked like death warmed over. His skin was pale, his face drawn low and his hair a tussled mess.

"Hey, are you okay?"

"Yeah, what's going on?" Craig asked groggy.

"No offense but you look like crap."

"Thanks," was all Craig could say.

"Listen, that Detective Foster called me. They want you to come in and provide a palm print to compare with some new evidence they just found."

"Should I?"

"Well, I think that it may be a good thing. If you haven't murdered anyone and they see that the prints don't match, you could be cleared of this."

"But what about the thumbprint of mine they found?"

"I'm not sure. But we can find out when we get down there."

"You'll come with me?"

"Sure I will, that's what defense lawyers are for, to annoy the police." Jacob smiled. Craig just looked at him. He was worried about his old friend.

"Let me change," Craig said. He opened the door wider and headed into the back where his bedroom was located. Jacob followed him in and closed the door behind him. He looked around as Craig changed his clothes. It was a happy home, filled with pictures of Craig and Jackie and Craig with family. The furniture and decorations gave off a warm feel inviting in guests. He picked up a framed photo of Craig and Jackie, standing on a beach with the ocean spread out behind them. He stared at Jackie's face and felt some déjà vu. There was something familiar about the beach photo.

"Okay, let's get this over with," Craig said, returning from the back of the apartment. Jacob lost his train of thought as he placed the photo back on the table and followed his client out of the building.

29

"Thanks for coming in," Brett said to Craig, "This will only take a few minutes and then hopefully we can remove you as a suspect." Brett smiled for better effect. Craig showed no response. Brett tried to read him but it was harder now than when they had questioned him. He wondered if it was because Craig was feeling the heat on him and was clamming up or if Craig was play acting. Either way, Foster knew he'd have answers in the next ten minutes.

"You'll have to excuse my client," Scott piped up, "He's a bit exhausted from the events of today."

"Understood," Brett played along. He motioned Craig over to the table with the ink pad on it. Craig followed him to the table and held his hand out. Brett took the ink roller and ran it across the top of Craig's left palm.

After they returned from the hospital, Brett and Josh visited the crime lab and checked on an update of the shiv they recovered from the homeless man. The detectives found Lucky scanning in the partial palm print that he was able to pull off the shiv handle.

"It's not much but it's enough to get a match," Lucky told them.

"So if we got Waterford to provide a palm print, we would be able to compare it?" Josh asked, still nursing his side.

"Absolutely. Take a look, there's plenty of specific points that we can use to compare." Lucky pointed at some spots on the print. Brett couldn't see what he was pointing to but that was Lucky's specialty.

"Lucky, if you can help us get a solid conviction on this case," Josh offered, "I will buy you the escort of your choice for the entire night."

"Well, then you better get your credit card out and ready," the short lab tech replied with a smile.

"Ok," Brett told Craig, "Just lay your hand flat on the paper and press down." Craig did as he was told and then lifted his hand up to wipe the ink off with the paper towel he was given.

"Is there a room we can wait in while you have that scanned? We'd like to get this over with as soon as possible."

"Sure," Brett told Jacob. He walked them to the cafeteria room and offered them coffee. Craig took a cup and Jacob turned the offer down.

Brett left them there and headed over to the crime lab where Lucky was waiting for the print. He took it from Brett and placed it gently into the scanner. Hitting the scan button, they watched the scanner transfer the image to the computer monitor. It felt as if an hour was slowly passing while they watched the image appear.

Brett's mind floated away while he waited. He was thinking of his personal situation. He had been alone for so long and even though he loved his job, it did have this one disadvantage. Eighty percent of his time was taken up by the job. It didn't give him a lot of time after to socialize and meet someone that he could come home to.

It was the one thing that made him jealous of Josh. He had Angie, who he knew loved Josh dearly. But he never paid attention to her. Tamara also suffered from that relationship. Josh had taken them for granted and Brett dreamed of living that life. It gave him something to live for. Yet at the age of 38, Brett felt any chance of a happy and loving life slipping from his grasp more every day.

"How do you deal with this every day?" he asked the lab tech.

"The slowness? Nothing I can do about that. It's all budget cuts."

"No, the silence. It would drive me crazy."

"That's what the iPods are for. And with everyone needing my help on their cases, I'm rarely ever alone."

"What about after your shifts? Anyone to go home to?"

"That's the best part of the day," Lucky smiled. He reached into his pocket and pulled out his wallet. Flipping it open, he retrieved a photo from inside and held it up. It was a picture of Lucky suited up and standing next to a young blonde who was almost twice his size. Her long legs tanned and curvy made Brett envious.

"Wow," he commented.

"You can say that again. Ah, ever since the CSI shows hit it big, Melvin and I are occasionally attacked by the groupies."

"No shit?"

"No shit, you should try transferring over here."

"I might consider it." Their conversation was interrupted by an electronic beep.

"Okay," Lucky said, "Now let's find a match." He typed some buttons and hit the ENTER button. The two prints appeared on the screen next to each other and the program began pinpointing certain spots of the prints. In a matter of seconds, it had finished and the answer Brett was waiting for appeared on the screen.

"Is that right?" the detective asked.

"My system is never wrong," Lucky told him.

"Ok. Then can you please print that out so I can show my suspect?"

30

Kristie was finishing her hair for her date with her new beau, Dean. She had met Dean three months ago at Frank Sinatra Park while on her Sunday jog. She saw him coming by her and her focus on running forward was taken and she ended up running into one of the benches. It was the most humiliating moment in her life. But in the end she had given him her number. Two days later, he called her for dinner. They had hit it off since.

She looked in the mirror and thought, if he plays his cards right, he just might get some. It was their fifth date and after being accepted by her son during the last date, she was happy that she had met him. Luckily, her neighbor, Kathy, agreed to watch Connor while she went on her date.

She walked across her living room and grabbed the dress that she planned on wearing. As she did, she noticed that her email program alerted her that she had received another email. The drop in her stomach worried her that it was Dean telling her that tonight was a no-go. She sat down in front of the computer and clicked on the email.

It read:

Kristie,

If you received this, then you need to get to my place and find the audio before the others find it. This is not a joke, butterfly catcher.

Doug

Kristie looked at the sending address and saw that it was Doug's work address. Who had sent this? Doug was dead and now someone was sending her sick messages. Her legs felt weak as she read it again. The second time, the magic word stood out. It had to have come from Doug.

"What the hell is going on, Doug?" she asked the screen. Unfortunately, it did not answer her.

31

You'll be free of this nightmare, in just minutes. I'm sure of it." Jacob was trying to give Craig some hope and positivity. He was worried about him as he had never seen him act this way. The trauma of being accused of murder had finally struck him and Craig was shutting down, unable to deal with the situation he was in.

"I just want to go back home and forget this day ever happened," Craig finally spoke.

"I know. But look at it this way, Jackie and you can start preparing for the baby."

"I don't know if it's even mine." Jacob knew he had a point. There was the photo of Doug and Jackie that was still unanswered. He had no advice about that problem. Inside, Jacob felt helpless with being unable to get Craig out of that problem.

"Listen, I know it's been years since we saw each other last, but if you need anything, I'm here for you. Free of charge," Jacob smiled. He hoped the joke would lighten the mood.

"That's good because I don't know if I can afford you for this."

"Don't worry about this. Consider it a favor."

"Thank you," Craig said to him.

"Don't worry about it. You can thank me the moment we walk out of this place when they see that you're innocent."

They waited a few more minutes and finally the door opened. Brett walked in with another uniformed officer. In his hand was a sheet of paper.

"Sorry for the wait," Brett said, grabbing the one chair left empty and sat down. He looked Craig in the eyes for a silent moment. The silence became awkward. Finally he spoke again. "Earlier today we spoke to a witness who saw the person who murdered Doug Martin leaving the house. Before we could get any information out of him, someone dressed as a homeless man came by and stabbed him in the throat. He died in less than a minute. The homeless guy got away but he left the shiv behind. We got a palm print off the shiv and compared it to yours."

He placed the print results on the table and slid it over to Craig. Craig looked down and read the words in the center of the page.

98.9% MATCH

"Craig Waterford, you're under arrest for the murders of Doug Martin and Pete Rogers." Brett continued giving Craig his rights as he placed the handcuffs on Craig's wrists. Jacob jumped out of his seat and grabbed the page and read it.

"This can't be right," Jacob shouted, "He's innocent!"

"The evidence is there," Brett said to the lawyer, "He did it."

TWO

FINDING THE TRUTH

32

Jacob sat at his desk staring at the email that Kristie had delivered to him. He read it once more for the fourth time, absorbing every word and possible meaning to the cryptic message. *Find the audio before the others find it.* He had no idea what audio Doug was mentioning but he knew that this had to be the reason why Doug was murdered.

"When did you get this?"

"Monday night. I thought it was a prank at first but after reading it a second time, I knew it was from him."

"How can it be from him," Robin asked, "He died four days ago."

"Maybe he's not dead?" Kristie threw out into the air.

"No," Jacob said, "He's gone. I saw the body at the wake on Tuesday. Maybe he had someone else send it for him."

"But it came from his work email. Someone had to have sent it from here, right?"

"Yeah," Jacob said, grabbing the phone from his desk and dialing an extension. Ed Field, the head of security for the building, answered.

"Security, Ed Field speaking."

"Hey Ed, this is Jacob Scott with Reynolds and Hoffman. I'm in the need of some help. Can you check to see if anyone from our firm entered the building Monday night at," he checked the time stamp on the email, "around 8:15p.m.?"

Robin knew what Jacob was up to. Their building had locks on the entrances that were activated after 6p.m. The only way into the building after that was with your assigned badge. Each badge was encoded with the specific employee number and company number that the holder was assigned. This helped prevent any vandalism or theft after hours when the building was mostly empty.

"Is there a problem, Mr. Scott?" Ed asked.

"No, I was supposed to meet one of my co-workers here Monday night and completely forgot. I was hoping that he didn't show up and wait a while for me."

"Okay," Ed replied. Jacob could hear the typing on the keyboard as Ed looked the information up. Jacob's mind was racing now, thinking of the email and how this would help Craig who was trapped in a holding cell for the last two days. This showed motive and directed the attention off of Craig as the killer. He hoped that the audio Doug had mentioned in the email had not already been found.

"Alright, let's see," Ed told him, "Around 8p.m. on Monday. For your firm, we've got Chris Delgado swiping in at 8:04p.m. He swiped out on Elevator 7 at 8:26p.m. How's that?"

"That would be my co-worker. Well at least he didn't wait too long. Thanks, Ed."

"You're welcome, Mr. Scott. Have a good day."

"You too," Jacob said before hanging up. He sat back in his chair and wrapped his fingers together around the back of his head. Robin and Kristie stood there, staring at him, waiting for an answer. Jacob spaced out for a minute before Robin tossed a paperclip at him.

"Sorry, I was thinking."

"Was someone here that night?"

"Yeah. Delgado."

"Why would Chris Delgado kill Doug?" Kristie asked.

"Whoa, hang on, Kristie," Jacob said, now standing up, "First, we don't know that Delgado had anything to do with Doug's murder. Second, he may have a good reason for being here the night that the email went out from Doug's computer."

"That's an awful hell of a coincidence," Robin added.

"That I'll give you. But we don't have any evidence that he did it."

"Why not just ask him?"

"Because if you just come out and ask him, 'hey did you send a cryptic message from our dead co-worker's computer?' he's going to get defensive, regardless if he did it or not."

"Well, you're the big time lawyer in the room, why not just con it out of him?" Robin said with a sarcastic smile. Jacob had always found that smile sexy. He smiled back.

"Touche, Miss Masters." Jacob paused, thinking once again. "Actually, that's not a bad idea. But here's what I want to do as well." Jacob went into detail about getting as much info as they could about the email.

He planned that while he was conning Delgado into revealing stuff, the women would search out the firm's IT guy, Daniel Header, and get him to check into the computer being used since Monday morning, when the firm learned that Doug was dead. He may be able to provide them with more information then they could find on their own.

"Oh and Robin," Jacob added, "Use your tricks to get as much help from Danny as you can."

"You got it, boss."

33

Delgado looked up from his desk when he heard the slight knock on his door frame. Jacob stood there and waved his hand in front of him. Delgado waved his hand back as his eyes returned to the documents in front of him.

"What can I do for you, Jacob? I'm busy working on one of Martin's cases. I'll give him this, if anything, the guy took some pretty detailed notes."

"That's actually what I'm here for. I think one of the cases that I was handed from Doug's unclosed pile is missing a page. I was hoping that you might take a look into the ones you received and see if it's in there?" Jacob walked into the office and sat down on one of the chairs that Delgado left out for clients. Delgado looked at Jacob, making himself at home without being given permission.

"Yeah, have a seat, relax."

"Thanks. So the page missing deals with an interview with the defendant's sister. Apparently, the sister's interview is holding the major piece of the puzzle that will get the defendant cleared of all charges."

"And you want me to check now? While I'm in the middle of something?"

"It shouldn't take too long. One little page." Jacob smirked at Delgado, playing him into the web of annoyance that he was constantly in. Delgado looked at him and knew that Jacob wasn't going to leave easily. Shaking his head, he dropped the papers that he held and began sifting through the top folder on his desk. Jacob wanted to keep him in the annoyed zone.

"It's an interview with a Ms. Ortiz," Jacob added. Delgado rolled his eyes up to look at him without moving his head and gave Jacob a look. Then he returned to sifting through the top folder. Jacob gave him a minute before throwing in the casual question he phrased for him.

"That reminds me, I came back to the office, Monday night and noticed your car in the parking lot. I thought you were not one to stay so late?" Jacob tried not to smile, giving away the pleasure in sliding the question out into the conversation without any awkward questioning. He knew that if Delgado stopped everything, he was guilty as all hell.

But Delgado answered the question without breaking a stride. "I wasn't working late, I just forgot the case folder that I needed for court on Tuesday morning. Monday was a little too hectic for my liking. Figures, even in death, Doug's a pain in the ass."

Jacob laughed back, showing interest in the comment. But he knew now that Delgado was not here for the email or the audio file. His reactions revealed that he was indeed here for the reason he stated. And it figured into Delgado's personality.

"You know what, take your time looking for the page. I'll stop back later to see if you found anything." Jacob stood up from the chair and leaned over the desk to pat Delgado on the shoulder. Surprised by the invasion of personal space, Delgado responded by staring at his shoulder. Jacob turned and left the office, pretending not to hear the one word comment Delgado muttered to him, but smiled still.

"Asshole."

Robin and Kristie entered the small office of the IT handler of Reynolds and Hoffman's systems. Daniel Header sat in front of his computer, typing away. He had shown no sign of acknowledging their presence nor did he tear his eyes from the twenty-inch monitor that showed Daniel's online game account info. They stood quietly while he typed in a message to a fellow Warcraft lover.

"Hey Daniel," Robin whispered into his ear. The sound caused him to jump in his chair and almost fall to the floor. Robin and Kristie laughed as Daniel picked himself up.

"Oh hello ladies, I didn't hear you come in." Daniel flicked a button on his keyboard and the online games vanished from sight.

"Hey Danny," Kristie said, "we were wondering if you could help us with Doug's computer."

"Oh, yeah sure. Let's go have a look." He stood up and followed the women over to Doug's office. As they walked, he asked them general questions.

"Is it a security issue? Or is he missing files or network links?"

"I guess you could say it's a security issue."

"Well, then I would have to say it's impossible. Our firewall is one of the best out there. The partners pay me to keep the clients' info protected."

"Oh no," Robin said, "It's not a hacking issue. We just think that, you know what? Can you keep a secret?" Robin bit down on her thumbnail slowly, waiting for his answer. She added in her innocent girl look for good measure.

"Um, yeah, of course I can," Danny stuttered.

"Good, I knew you could. We think that someone in the firm was playing with Doug's computer after he died."

"Well the day of the meeting when the partners told everyone about Doug, they had me look into his hard drive. You know, to make sure that there were no signs of criminal activity."

"Okay. But on Monday night I received an email from Doug's work address. How is that possible if he was already dead?" Kristie questioned the IT guy.

"Maybe his ghost came back to warn you of something?" He followed the joke with his infamous laugh. It was often compared to that of a cat pretending to be a hyena with a hairball in his throat.

"Oh wow," Robin said, "Do you really think he did?" Kristie fought back hard to keep from laughing at Robin's bad acting skills.

"Well, he did die in a violent way. I saw a movie once where this victim of a violent crime came back to haunt people until the killer was caught and paid for the murder. I think it's possible."

"That would be so creepy. Like he's waiting for us in his office waiting to scare the crap out of us. Danny, would you please stay with us while we're in there?" Robin touched his arm for a better effect. She could feel the goosebumps on his arm as she did.

"Oh, yeah, you don't have to worry. I wouldn't do that to you."

"Whew, thanks."

Danny sat down at Doug's computer and booted it up. He then typed his login into the computer and waited until all the programs were loaded. Kristie looked at the desktop picture of Doug's photo in Upstate New York. The fall picture showed his parents' backyard with the trees dropping colored leaves onto the ground. She remembered the day he returned from the weekend trip and he told her all about it. He was the best boss she had ever worked for. And now he was dead.

"There we are," Danny said. He began typing and opened up a DOS prompt. Danny went into the system settings and checked into the list of login times. Robin watched his fingers work and tried to make sense of what she was seeing on the screen.

"So what is it that you're doing?" she asked.

"I'm accessing the security backups on the hard drive to see when the last time was that this computer was booted. It shows here that Doug logged in on Saturday night at 11: 54 p.m. It was then shut down three hours later. That was the last time this hard drive was accessed."

"But then explain how an email was sent from Doug Martin's email account on Monday night?" said a voice behind all three. They turned around to find Jacob standing in the doorway. He walked in and over to the computer that they were huddled around.

"Well," Danny explained, "The only thing I can think of is that he had an email written but timed to be sent from the server later on. Actually, now that I think of it, I remember him asking me about that two weeks ago."

"What do you mean?" Kristie asked.

"Well, our email system has the ability to allow someone to write up an email and hold it until a specific time before it's sent out. Like sending a package that says 'do not open until Christmas'. But Doug wanted to know if he could delay the timed sending if he chose against it."

"Can you?" Jacob asked.

"Yeah, sure. The program allows you to go back in and change the scheduled time that the email's to be sent. Let me access his account and show you." Danny opened up the email program and used his administrator role to access the hard drive's saved information. Jacob saw the list of emails sent from Doug's account. Danny opened the sent folder and saw the email that was sent to Kristie on Monday night. Next to the date and time of the sending, there was a clock icon.

"So the clock there means that it was scheduled?"

"Exactly. Now the only thing I can't see is the previous time he had it scheduled for."

"So if he wanted to," Jacob thought aloud, "he could have changed the time it was scheduled to be sent out every day."

"Yep. He could have originally scheduled it for two weeks ago and kept changing it. The program only keeps the time it actually goes out, not the time it was originally written."

Jacob paused and thought. Robin knew Jacob's mannerisms through her time working for him. He normally played with his bottom lip when he was deep in thought. The one thing she never learned was reading his thoughts.

"Thanks Danny," he said to the firm's IT guy, "And if you don't mind, this is just between us. Okay?" Jacob looked at Danny with a serious concern.

"Yeah, no problem," Danny replied, looking to Robin and Kristie for some reassurance. Both women were confused by Jacob's change of demeanor as well. Jacob left Doug's office and headed back to his own. Robin and Kristie followed.

Once in his office, he shut the door behind the two assistants and locked it. Robin was getting nervous with Jacob's mysterious attitude. She watched him paced behind his desk, thinking about something. His hand, again, went to his bottom lip.

"You're beginning to scare me, Jacob. What's going on? Why did you ask Danny to be quiet about this?" Robin stood her ground. She knew what had to be done with Jacob in order to get answers.

"That email just saved Craig Waterford," Jacob muttered to no one.

"What? How?"

"Because that email proves that Doug knew he was going to die."

34

G uy Clark took the papers from the head clerk and thanked her. Then he tilted his head and smiled as she walked away. He enjoyed his job some days. Being the assistant District Attorney in Hudson County had it's advantages.

Guy was not liked by many but those in positions above him were satisfied with his record and the way he could turn the tables on the defense when it appeared the defense would come out on top. His short and blocky stature did not scare anyone on the street but when he walked into a courtroom, the defense table would most likely moan in annoyance.

He looked at the memo and read the listing of cases they had the option to prosecute. His office was on one corner of the third floor of the building in Jersey City. Skimming through the list, one caught his eye. State v. Craig Waterford. He remembered the name but couldn't figure out where he remembered it from.

"Hey, Renee," Guy spoke into his phone's intercom. Renee was Guy's head clerk who was hired strictly for her looks. He enjoyed the eye candy, even though the intelligence bugged him from time to time. She wore her red hair short in a bob style and her healthy chest size was nice whenever he dropped something over the side of his desk.

"Yes, Mr. Clark?"

"Do you remember hearing about a Craig Waterford?"

"Craig Waterford? I believe he is the one on the news about murdering the lawyer in Hoboken."

"Right! I knew I had heard the name before." Guy disconnected the intercom before Renee could reply to his comment. He grabbed a pen off his desk and circled the case. If it was already in the news, his addition to the trial would make it that bigger. He had been looking for something exciting.

He hit the speed dial on his phone and the ringing speaker connected him to the Hoboken Police Chief, Christine Black. Black had been waiting for his call.

"What is it now, Clark?" she answered.

"My favorite police chief, how are you, Christine?" Guy sat back in his ergonomics chair and threw his hands behinds his head.

"I'm not in the mood right now, Guy. Either tell me what you want or I'm hanging up."

"Now, now, is that any way to treat an old friend? Or have you already forgotten our close relationship in the past?"

"You helped us nail a cop killer 3 years ago. That's the only relationship we had."

"Oh come on, you remember the late nights in your precinct. The conversations we had."

"Good bye, Guy."

"Whoa, hold on a second. I need your precinct to send me the file you have on the Craig Waterford case."

There was a pause on the line. "You're prosecuting the case?"

"Well, a fellow lawyer's life was taken. If this Craig Waterford guy committed the crime, he deserves the strictest punishment."

"Is that justice talking or is that your wallet?" Black asked sarcastically.

"Very funny, Chief Black. Now will you be sending me the file or do I have to mention to the press that your department took way too long in apprehending Waterford?"

"Has anyone ever told you that you're a scheming little prick?"

"At least once a day. But I do my job. Now I hope you can do yours and fax the file over to my office as soon as you can." Guy hung up the phone and smiled. There was a little joy in making people miserable while he did his job.

"Hey Renee," Guy said into the intercom, "Can you please come in and take notes on a letter I need typed up?"

35

H ow about some Johnny Rockets for lunch?" Josh asked his partner,
"My treat."

"Are you sure your wallet can handle such a purchase," Brett
joked.

"Ha,ha. You missed your true calling as a comic."

"My parents always told me I'd be the next Johnny Carson. I really
disappointed them when I became a cop."

"Yeah, and now I have to suffer the bad humor. You want something
or not?"

Foster jotted down his order and handed it to Raghetti. Josh stuck
the paper into his shirt pocket and headed out of the precinct. Brett
stayed behind to help fax over the file reports on the Waterford case to
the assistant DA. Chief Black came out of her office in a bad mood after
receiving the call from Clark. He figured it best to help her out and keep
quiet or else he'd feel her wrath.

After he finished sending them over, he returned to his desk and
found the phone ringing. The caller ID stated: RAGHETTI. What did
his partner want?

"Did you forget your wallet?" Brett joked.

"Huh?" the voice on the other end said. Brett was surprised. It was
Angie, Josh's ex. He wondered what it meant that she had not changed the
name over on their phone.

"Oh hey Angie, I thought you were Josh for a minute."

"Oh," was all she said.

"Everything okay?" he asked. Being a detective gave him a sixth sense about people but he didn't need his detecting skills to know that something was troubling Angie.

"Brett, can you meet me after your shift? I need to talk to someone and I was hoping I could talk to you."

"Absolutely, what is it about?" His curiosity had the best of him.

"Life. Tamara. Josh. Mostly me."

"Alright, I can meet you around 6p.m."

"Thank you Brett. And please don't tell Josh about this."

"Mum's the word."

Angie paused for a moment. Brett could hear her smile. Then she spoke, "You're a good man. Josh could learn a lot from you."

"We're working on the 'please' and 'thank you' words this week. He's showing much potential."

"I have to go. I'll see you later." Foster said goodbye and hung up. He wondered what the call was all about. He'd keep his promise to Angie, but he'd have to see what Josh knew.

Josh returned a few minutes later with take-out from Johnny Rockets. The two detectives sat at their desks and chowed down on the food. Brett waited for the right moment before starting the conversation.

"So how are you and Angie doing with the split?"

"It's pretty bad," Josh told him, "I screwed up pretty bad."

"Yeah well, you have to remember, it's bad because you have Tamara to worry about. Kids always take this stuff the hardest."

"I've talked to Tamara about it and she's very mature for her age. She started giving me advice."

Brett laughed, "A little Angie, huh?"

"Yeah, it's really fun when they team up on me."

Brett took another bite of his bacon burger and let the conversation sit in the air. Knowing his partner, he wouldn't be able to leave it there. He sat and chewed on the bite, staring at his desk. Josh looked over and finished his mouthful before he continued the conversation.

"You know what really gets me? It's that no matter how annoying she was, I still feel something for her." Brett knew that something was bothering his partner.

"Is that why you're acting strange?"

"Yeah. Sorry about that. It's just that I don't seem like a one-woman man but I kind of miss her. And no, I'm not gay."

Brett laughed. He and Josh never had too many talks like this one but he knew that the two of them were becoming more like brothers than co-workers. That was just what happened when you work as a cop. The danger of the job brings people together. But even though he had this family, he still wanted more. He wanted something to come home to.

"Don't worry," Brett said, "I won't tell anyone you have feelings."

"Thanks, jerk."

Now, Brett thought, if Angie felt the same, he could help bring them back together and get rid of the grouch version of his partner.

36

Craig sat in his cell, thinking of what was to come. He had not seen Jacob since the day after he was arrested. The not knowing what was going on outside his cell, drove him frantic. His mind turned to thoughts of jail and being held in a prison with others unlike him. He knew if that were to come about it wouldn't take long to tear him down to nothing.

There was nothing to do other than walk back and forth from wall to wall. He needed to clear his head and figure out where everything went wrong and how he ended up where he currently was. The framing was obvious. His print was in the apartment of a man whom he had never met. The questions to answer were who put it there and why. That would set him free. But who would benefit from Craig being framed for the murder? Craig sat down and stared at the bars and ran the investigation through his head. He scanned through the people he knew that may want him sent to jail. No one in his family would want that. His friends had no motive to do so.

His thoughts then turned to Jackie. The photo was burned into his memory. He saw the smile on her face as she was being held by Doug Martin. She appeared happy. But she seemed happy with Craig as well. He wondered which smile was the lie, the one to him or the one in the photo.

The thought of the photo only ended up making him feel nauseous. Seeing the woman he loved in the arms of another man. Knowing that he slept next to her every night, unaware that she was sleeping with someone else. Why was everything falling apart around him?

His thoughts were interrupted by one of the guards. A towering man, he walked up to the cell door and knocked the keys between two bars.

"Waterford, you have a visitor to see you."

"Is it my lawyer?"

"No, your wife."

Craig's stomach clenched. He had hoped she would come to see him but the doubt of her infidelity made him second guess the thought. Yet he stood up and waited for the guard to open the door and escort him out of the cell. Anything to be free of the tiny area.

The guard walked him down the hall to the visiting room. It was similar to those seen in cop shows and movies. There were a series of booths. A thick wire-meshed piece of glass split the booth in half. And an old phone receiver allowed both sides of the booth to speak to each other. The booths were yellow. Craig guessed this was to keep those jailed in a happier mood via color emotion.

"Down in booth #2," the guard told him. Craig walked over to the second booth and looked through the glass at Jackie. He could see right away that she had been crying. Her eyes were bloodshot and the tip of her nose was slightly blushed. He melted at the sight of her. She was still home to him.

Craig sat down and instinct caused him to hold his hand to the glass. Jackie smiled and did the same. He picked the phone up and began talking.

"Hi," was all he could say that the moment.

"I miss you," she replied, "I can't stay at the apartment with you not there. It feels too empty."

"Have you talked to Jacob?"

"I spoke to him yesterday. He is doing all he can to get you bail. I've requested money out of our IRA, but it's going to take a few days."

"That's alright. Is he getting anywhere with the case?"

"He didn't say but he's got two people working with him on it. He told me that he would call with any updates."

Craig paused, looking at Jackie through the glass. Her eyes sparkled through the tears that formed. The sight of her made him smile. It only caused the tears in her eyes to trail down her cheeks.

"Please don't cry. We'll get through this."

"It's so hard without you."

"I know," he replied, "How's the deli?" He hoped to divert her attention from the situation.

"Everyone is doing everything they can to help run it. Connie's been such an angel. And Mike has been taking care of the orders and the invoicing."

"I knew that it would run fine without me. How's the mister running?"

"The repair company showed up yesterday and replaced the sprayer. It's been working fine since."

"Good."

"Craig, I…" Jackie brought her hand up to her mouth. She fought back the cries.

"Jackie, we'll be fine. This will be over soon. Jacob's a born fighter and I know he'll work harder for me."

"The police showed me this picture," she told him. Craig knew exactly what picture she was talking about.

"The picture doesn't matter," he began to tell her. She cut him off and continued.

"I never took that picture. I don't even have that sweater."

"Jackie, it's ok."

"No, Craig, it's not. I don't know who made that photo but it's a fake. That is not me. You've been the only one I've loved all these years."

"I know. Whoever created that photo, meant it to hurt me."

"Who would do that?"

"I don't know. But I'm hoping to get out of here soon so I can help Jacob figure that out."

"Is there something I can do?"

"Just keep the deli running. I'm sure if Jacob needed help, he would ask you. And try not to get too overstressed. You have to remember the baby." Jackie smiled and her hand found it's way to her belly.

"Time to go, Waterford," the guard said to him.

"I love you, Craig."

"I love you too, Jackie. I'll see you soon." Craig hung up the phone and blew her a kiss from his side of the glass. She smiled back at him and mouthed the words, '*be safe.*'

He walked back to the guard and was escorted to his tiny cell. The door was locked behind him and he was back in his little hell. But the visit from Jackie had been exactly what he needed. It had given him the energy to keep going. He felt renewed, like after having a good night's sleep. Craig felt the ability to clear his mind and stood in the center of his cell.

He then began talking aloud to himself. Going over the evidence the police had on him. He knew all of it was faked. The thing he needed to know was how it was faked. That was the first step of clearing his name. Then he could work on finding out who did it and the why would be the final piece of the puzzle.

The vision of Jackie with her hand on her belly flashed back into his mind. The soft skin on her hand touching the cotton of her hoodie sweatshirt warmed his heart. He had so much to fight for. For that he would never give up.

And then it came to him. He imagined Jackie sitting there with her hand on her belly. Then he tried to remember the photo. That was it! Jackie was right. The photo was doctored. And he knew how to prove it. He rushed to the bars and pressed his face in between them.

"Guard! Guard!" Craig called out. The guard slowly walked back over to his cell.

"What is it, Waterford?"

"My lawyer. I need to call my lawyer."

37

W hat exactly are we going to be looking for?" Kristie asked Jacob. The two had arrived at the home of Doug Martin with hopes of finding the audio file that the email had mentioned. Jacob knew that it was the main ingredient in freeing Craig. But he was still unsure of what the audio file was of. Yet the email was clear that whatever it was of, it was important enough to kill for.

"Let's check his home computer and see if there is anything there. Or maybe it's on a flash drive. I don't know. I was hoping you would have more answers about that." Jacob followed Kristie up the front steps to the front door of the building on the corner of Hudson and 7th. The neighborhood was quiet even in the middle of the day. Jacob saw why Doug lived here. It was a great place for a lawyer to crash at any time.

"Which button is for the landlord?" Jacob asked, looking over the names on the four buzzers. Kristie dug into her purse and retrieved her ring of keys. She flipped through them and found the one that she was searching for. Placing it in the lock, she turned it. The door opened wide, allowing her to walking into the lobby. She held the door open for Jacob and they headed upstairs to Doug's apartment.

"You have a key to his apartment?" Jacob asked.

"There was a time when Doug left a client's folder here and he asked me to get it while he was in the middle of a meeting. It was given only in a professional importance."

"Of course," Jacob smiled.

"Not everyone has a thing for their boss," Kristie struck. Jacob flinched at the fact that she knew about his relationship with Robin.

When they got to the door to his apartment, the police tape was still blocking the entrance. Jacob wondered why this was so. To them, the killer was already caught. Their case was closed. The tape and security sticker should have been removed. He pursed his lips in confusion but pulled a pen out of his jacket pocket. Using it, he cut the security sticker and removed the police tape from one side of the door frame. Then he tried the door and found it unlocked. With a smile, he pushed the door open and allowed Kristie to enter.

As they did, the smell of bleach hit them. Jacob looked at the wood floor and seen the cleaned area where Doug's body had lay. Better bleach than blood, he thought to himself.

"Looks like the police team cleaned the room. Let's hope they didn't take his computer."

"I'll check for his briefcase," Kristie said.

"Don't bother," Jacob told her, "It's in police lockup as evidence. That's where they found Craig's fingerprint."

"If he was hiding a flash drive, he might have kept it there."

"No, that makes no sense. The email proves that this audio file is important. No way would he have kept it in an obvious place. Did he have a hidden safe?"

"Not that I'm aware of."

"What about a safety deposit box?"

"That he did have," Kristie explained, "He kept his important documents and personal family things there. Plus some emergency money, in case he needed it."

"We should check that too. But I doubt the bank would let us anywhere near it."

"I know that his keys are in the briefcase."

"Then we're most likely going to need the police's help in this. I was hoping to avoid that." Jacob walked across the living room and noticed that even though the blood was cleaned up, the mess of the struggle was not. He picked up a chair from Doug's dining set and placed it upright. Some knives from the kitchen scattered the floor and he picked those up as well.

"Now where would he hide something important?" Kristie asked herself. She looked around the apartment and tried to find some place where Doug would consider safe. Doug was not someone who was paranoid about thieves or muggers. But Doug was not someone who would be targeted by a killer either. Kristie feared of finding something that would cause her danger as well.

She thought back to his office at the law firm and remembered where he kept all his important things. They were right out in the open, on his desk and on the shelves behind his chair. Looking around, she saw the shelves in between the windows and she went over to search them for the file.

Jacob, meanwhile, found the computer on it's side. A hole in the side of the tower gave Jacob a disappointing feeling. He looked inside and saw the motherboard completely destroyed. The plus, though, was that the hard drive was still intact. He unscrewed the back of the tower and began unplugging the hard drive from the rest of the computer. He almost knocked Doug's iPod off the monitor as he pulled the hard drive out of the computer tower.

"The motherboard is shot but the hard drive is still good," Jacob told Kristie. Kristie heard him but continued looking on the shelves for anything out of the ordinary. "I know a guy who could access the files still on it. We'll see if the file he was talking about is on here."

"I'm not finding anything here," Kristie said, "I'm trying to think like Doug would."

"What about the email? Maybe there was a clue in it. I remember him talking about a butterfly catcher. What did that mean?"

"That was his hint to me. It proved that it came from him."

"I don't understand."

"One night when we were working late, we started talking about our childhoods. I told him that one year for my birthday my parents gave me a butterfly catcher net. I spent the entire summer trying to catch as many as I can. I had jars and jars of captured butterflies that it drove my parents crazy. I never told anyone that story before. I guess he remembered that and used it to let me know that it wasn't someone else sending the email."

"Sounds like Doug," Jacob replied, "I still think we should go back and see if there's a hidden message in there."

"I know he's left it here. I don't think it would be on the hard drive. That's too obvious for Doug. He liked to be subtle about things."

"Well for now, it may help us to find out where the file is. It's all we have unless there's another clue that we're missing."

"I'd like to stay and look a little more."

"Okay. Well, I'll check for a hidden wall safe while you check the other areas," Jacob suggested. Kristie agreed and the two continued the search.

"Hey," Kristie asked her co-worker, "Do you mind me asking what's the deal with you and Robin?"

Jacob dreaded the question. He was not sure himself. There were definitely feelings but with the professional relationship they had and the frowning the partners would have on it was what was keeping him from going for it. Working the long hours with Robin had brought them closer. He even thought of himself as the David Addison character from the old TV show, Moonlighting.

"As the answer may be incriminating, as a lawyer, I plead the fifth."

"No getting out of it that easy, Scott," Kristie joked.

"She's a great woman and I consider myself pretty lucky to have her as an assistant let alone a date."

"Fair enough. Want me to put in a good word for you?"

"I don't think you have to."

"You're right, I don't."

Jacob paused and looked over at Kristie, "Really?"

"Let's just say that the feeling is mutual." Kristie smiled at him.

"Can you blame her? I get lost in those baby blues myself when I see him from across the courtroom," spoke another voice. Both Kristie and Jacob stopped everything and looked quickly at the front door of Doug's apartment. In the doorway stood Guy Clark, his hands in his pockets and a big smile on his face. Jacob's stomach dropped from the sight of the assistant DA. The prosecutor walked in and looked around the apartment.

"Not a bad place," Guy said, "tiny but nice. Is this what Reynolds and Hoffman pay you guys? Or was Martin not much of a winner in the courtroom?"

"What do you want Clark?" Jacob asked.

"Same thing you two are probably looking for. Proof. Although my proof is going to put your client away for a long time."

"Forget it, you're not going to find it. My client is innocent and I can prove it."

"Oh really? Not holding something back on me till the last minute are you?"

"Nope, new developments. As soon as I can verify them, you'll be the first to know."

"Fair enough," Guy replied, "So how's that great piece of ass you call an assistant?"

"Screw you, Clark."

"Touchy about the subject?" Guy walked over to Jacob and got in close, "C'mon, guy to guy, how is she in the sack?"

"We're not in the courtroom, Guy. Now get out of my face before you get hurt."

"You wouldn't strike a man with glasses, would you?"

"Try me."

"Okay, boys, put the rulers away and save it for the courtroom," Kristie said, walking over.

"Kristie Mahieux," Guy said, "And how are you? I see you still haven't gotten any work done. What a shame. There's always same sex relationships."

"Listen here, you little troll. I'd stop the harassment now before you regret it."

"I love women with fire. You know, I could always use another assistant. And you without a boss now, well, gotta feed the little bastard child somehow, right?"

Jacob flinched at the verbal shot. Kristie was touchy about her son. His father had not been a good man. It had been a mistake to be with him, she knew, but she kept the history between her and him to herself. She could never believe that she'd be in love with someone who could take off the moment he found out that he would be a father. Connor never knew his father and she would tell him altered stories once a week as she was tucking him into bed.

"You son of a bitch," Kristie said harshly.

Jacob stepped in and placed his hand on Guy's chest. Guy looked at him and he threw the prosecutor a look, telling him to back off. Guy took the hint and stopped attacking.

"Well, I guess I'll take my leave now. But before I go, hey Scott, what do the partners think of you defending the killer of one of their lawyers?" Jacob had nothing to say. He had wondered that himself. But he had yet to tell them that he was defending Craig Waterford. Yet he had the feeling that now that Guy knew, the partners would soon learn as well.

Guy smiled and walked out of Doug's apartment leaving the two defenders alone and still empty handed.

38

Brett left the precinct alone with Josh finishing up on paperwork from the day before. Josh didn't mind as they normally took turns. And at that moment, Josh welcomed the aloneness. He had been thinking of Angie a lot more that day since the lunch conversation with Brett. He found himself missing her more and more. And he did not want to be a deadbeat cop father to Tamara. She didn't deserve that. And he had been raised better by his Italian parents than to leave his own child high and dry without a father figure to warn her of the way boys were. He had to be there to help protect her. It was not only his job, it was his responsibility.

Lyndsay and Alicia returned from Black's office and gathered their things from their desks. Alicia noticed Raghetti still working.

"Trying for more overtime?" she asked him.

"No, just getting this done at the last minute."

"Well, we'll see you tomorrow."

"Good night ladies."

The female detectives left the precinct as the vice detectives returned from a stakeout. Detectives Eric Valentine and Moe O'Sullivan walked past Josh and over to their desks, shoulders sagging and their faces long. Josh knew they had been working the stakeout all day and were now tired from the waiting.

Hoboken had been a relatively drug free town. But the large college student population along with the string of clubs at the south end of Washington Street, made it a bed of drug-related activity. The PATH trains that led to Manhattan were also a transit that tunneled drugs back and forth. Josh knew that they were currently working on a sting that dealt with trafficking from Dover to Hoboken via the NJ Transit Train Terminal located at the south end of Hoboken. It allowed New Jersey residents to travel to the Hudson River where they could then take the PATH trains into New York City.

"How'd the stakeout go?" he asked them.

"It sucked giant donkey balls," Valentine replied.

"I have to admit though, I never knew Guatemalan flute music could drive me to drink," O'Sullivan added.

"I wish I could join you but my daughter's performance is tonight. I have to run home to get ready." Eric told his partner.

"Yeah, I'll probably grab some takeout and log some hours in Warcraft."

"Sounds like you gentlemen have fun nights ahead of you," Josh joked.

"Well, we all can't be as great as you Homicide guys," Valentine replied.

"Of course not. We need someone to sweep up the confetti after we do our jobs," Josh cracked back.

"Later Raghetti," they said to him as they both left. Josh finished up his last page of the report and printed out the form to pass along to Chief Black. When the printer finished spitting out the last page, he knocked on the door to her office and walked in.

"Here's the paperwork, Chief." Josh handed her the forms and Christine took it, placing onto the top of the Inbox pile.

"Thanks, Raghetti. Have a good night."

"You too Chief." Josh returned to his desk and grabbed his coat while his computer shut down for the night.

"Yo, Josh, good to see you're still here," said Examiner Dave Francis. He held up a manila folder and waved it in the air as he walked over to Josh.

"What's that?"

It's the report on that witness guy, Pete Rogers. Sorry it's late but we're a little backed up on the reports."

"That's fine," Josh told him, "Anything interesting?"

"Nah, pure and simple. It was the punctures to the neck that killed him. Gotta admit though, this guy knew his stuff." Josh stopped putting on his coat and looked at Dave.

"What do you mean?"

"Well, the stabs were so precise. All three puncture wounds severed the right Carotid Artery. Like right in the center of the artery. Whoever this Waterford guy is, he knew where to strike."

"Really?"

"Oh for sure. Take a look at the third photo. You'll see, the three wounds are in a nice line." Josh opened the folder and flipped to the third photo in the file. It showed the neck of Peter Rogers. The skin now, a pale blue and the three strikes that had killed him were in a side by side formation. Josh saw the stabs when they happened. It was nearly impossible to be so neat when stabbing someone in the two seconds that it seemed to take when it happened.

"So you're telling me that this is something an angry deli store owner would not be able to do?"

"Okay, let me put it this way. You're right-handed?"

"Yeah."

"Good, now take this black marker in your left hand. Hold like you would a shiv," Dave told him. Josh held the marker like a utensil. "Now, I want you to take three quick stabs to my neck and I want you to hit me all right in this spot." Dave pointed to the spot on his neck where the Carotid Artery ran beneath the skin.

"So you want me to stab you with this marker?"

"Well, don't puncture my skin but hit me so that it marks the spot."

Josh thought the M.E. was a little nuts before but this made the thought concrete. He paused and took a deep breath. Then with all the focus he could provide, he jabbed the marker at Dave's neck three times as fast as he could. When he finished, he looked at Dave's neck. Only one jab made it close to the spot that Dave pointed to. The pattern of the jabs were scattered around the spot. Josh looked down at the photo of Pete Rogers' neck. The stabs were linear and all three hit the Carotid with exact precision.

"So Craig Waterford couldn't have done it?"

"Not unless he's like a super undercover spy."

"No," Josh said, "Not this schmoe."

"Well, the facts are all there. It was done by a left handed person. Quick and effective."

"Thanks Dave."

"Anytime, Raghetti. Anyway, I've got to get going, it's my girlfriend's birthday and I love cake."

Dave left Josh sitting at his desk wondering about one thing. If the person who killed Peter Rogers was left handed, then how could Craig Waterford's palm print be on the weapon?

39

Angie was waiting for Brett on the front steps when Brett arrived to hear what she had to say. He was a little worried when he saw that she had dressed herself up and had done her hair in a way that even Brett had found her attractive. His first thought was that she was moving on from Josh and was looking to tell him so that Brett could let his partner down. It was one of the disadvantages of partnering with another cop. You were forced to become involved in the other's personal issues, like a family member.

"Your hair looks good," Brett said to her. Angie smiled in an embarrassed way.

"Can we go for a walk? I don't have much time before I have to go somewhere."

He had been right. She was on her way to a date with someone. He wanted to tell her that Josh still had feelings for her but decided to wait until she told him what she wanted to say.

"Yeah, sure." Angie began walking towards Washington Street. Brett followed alongside of her and it took her a minute before she began explaining why she had asked him to come.

"I feel strange telling you this but I'm over Josh."

"I figured as much. Being not dressed to just run to the store."

"Oh, yeah. I guess I just wanted to look good for once, instead of being casually dressed with a child in my arms."

"It looks good on you."

"Thank you," she said, blushing. Brett felt slightly blushed as well, walking with his partner's ex. He decided to keep the conversation going, preventing her from seeing his own embarrassment.

"So I take it you want me to tell Josh that it's really over?"

"Well, not really. I think I can tell him that."

"So what did you want to talk to me about?"

She paused, as if unable to speak. The words had been stuck in her throat, unable to break free until her own fear cracked beneath the stress. She took a deep breath and continued.

"Josh and I have been apart for a few months now. Ever since, I've wanted to act on my heart's feelings. I've found myself attracted to someone else."

Brett wished she would get to the point as he was not looking forward to having to tell Josh that Angie did not feel the same as he did. It would cause discomfort at work and that wasn't even the worst part. It would be the bubbling anger that he knew Josh would try hard to push down to hide. But the hiding would only last so long.

He remembered the time when Angie had had enough of Josh's late nights and irresponsibility. She had waited for him to arrive home at two in the morning. Brett had gotten the call from Lyndsay who had to drive Josh home from the bar. Angie stood on the steps, with a fury in her eye that he had never seen before. She was throwing Josh's things at him, screaming. Several of the neighbors were hanging out of their windows either watching the show or yelling back to tell Angie to quiet down. Brett was forced to step in and take Josh away back to his own place until he could get his things the next day. Since then, he had been assigned the mediator of any meeting between the two.

"Who's the lucky man?" Brett asked.

Angie leaned forward, placed her hand on the right side of Brett's face and kissed him. Brett tensed up at first, surprised by the act. But the loneliness in him fought to keep him in the moment. He felt his hand wrap around her waist and pull her closer. Feeling the warmth of her body through their clothes. Angie's mouth opened, welcoming him in. Her body melted at his touch. What was seconds felt like hours. Then the rational side of him turned on. What was he doing? This was his partner's ex-wife! But the want in him, the desire was too strong. It had felt as if he were possessed and being controlled by something else.

Minutes later, Angie pulled back, flushed. Her hair had been tussled and her lipstick worn off her lips. The desire Brett saw in her eyes was the same he felt below his waist.

"Wow," she said. The word sat in the air between them.

"Angie, you're a beautiful woman," he started to speak. The desire in her eyes faded in a blink and the humiliation showed in her face.

"I'm such an idiot," she replied.

"No, no. You're really beautiful. But you're my partner's ex-wife. You're off the available list."

"You've never felt anything for me? You didn't feel anything just now? We're both human, Brett. You can't allow your job to take over your life one hundred percent. You're a wonderful man and you deserve to be happy. Just because Josh didn't know what he had let that keep you from knowing it too."

"I'm sorry, Angie. He's like a brother to me. You can't ask me to do this."

Angie leaned in to kiss him again but Brett leaned back, fighting her urges as well as his own. He knew giving in would only cause more problems than if he didn't.

"You're right," she said, "This is a mistake. I'm sorry Brett. Have a good life." Then Angie turned and headed back to her house. Brett wasn't sure if he should chase after her or just let her go. He hated being in the middle of this. Especially with the preliminary hearing beginning tomorrow on the Waterford case. If their evidence was strong enough, he would go away for a long time. He had to be ready for his questioning on the stand.

"Dammit."

40

Robin waited for Jacob and Kristie to return back in the office. It was almost 7 p.m. when they did. She saw by the looks on their faces that they had not found the audio file that was mentioned in the email. Disappointed, she grabbed Jacob a cup of coffee, hoping to help ease the frustration.

"We searched the whole apartment and didn't find a thing. I think whoever killed Doug found it." Jacob slumped into his chair and stared at his desk. He tried to think of another saving move for Craig's sake. But with all the evidence against him and the fact that Clark was the prosecuting attorney, the chance of winning this was slowly shrinking.

"Well, do you want the good news or the bad news?" Robin asked him.

"Give me the bad news, first."

"Reynolds is looking for you. He heard about you representing Doug's killer."

"Crap," Jacob sighed. He was not looking forward to this moment. He knew it would come when he told Craig that he would help him, but he pushed it down until it was too late.

"But Craig called. He said that he has something that may help him," Robin continued, "He wouldn't tell me what but he was hoping to have you visit him at the jail."

"I'm exhausted and tomorrow is the pre-lim. And I haven't even started the opening statement. It's going to be a long night."

"I'm here to help," Kristie told him, "And I plan on doing everything I can now that Clark is who you'll be going up against."

"Are you kidding?" Robin asked Jacob, "Clark has become part of this now?"

"Yeah," Jacob described Guy's little visit to Doug's apartment to her.

"I'll call Carol and ask her to grab us some burgers," Robin said, picking up the phone. Carol Vartan was Jacob's gopher. Whenever Jacob needed something for a trial but didn't have time to go get it, Carol was called in. She had begun interning at the law firm a year and a half ago. Unfortunately, she realized that it wasn't for her. But liking Jacob, she offered to help him with any freelance assisting.

"Actually, call her and tell her I have something else for her to take care of. Let's get started on the opening and then we can work on using the evidence to our advantage."

Robin began calling Carol and Jacob looked up when he heard a knock at his office door. The door was open and he could see Jackie Waterford standing in the doorway. Her stature was sullen, her shoulders weighed down by the stress of what was happening to her husband. Jacob stood up and walked over to her, holding his hand out to greet her.

"Jackie, hey, is everything okay?"

"I'm just wearing a path into the wood floors in my apartment. I thought I'd come by and see what I could do to help with tomorrow's trial."

"Well, it's not actually a trial, it's called a preliminary hearing. We present our case to the judge to prove whether it should have a trial."

"Well is there anything I could do to help make it a strong case?"

"I don't know. I'd use you as a character reference but the photo of you and Doug Martin makes you involved and ruins anything you could say."

"Why is this happening to us?" she asked him, tears forming in her eyes again. He took her hands into his and held them, trying to relieve her of the worry and stress that this was causing.

"It's going to be alright. I wouldn't have taken this on if I didn't know for absolute sure that Craig is innocent. I would bleed if I knew that it would help him go free." Jacob looked down at her hands in his own and he drifted off into thought. He was thinking in overtime in order to create a case that would place even the tiniest bit of doubt in the mind of the judge. A little doubt would crack the steel trap that he was sure that Clark would set for him. Guy Clark was his main worry.

As he returned from deep thought, Jacob studied Jackie's hands. He noticed a long scar on her right hand that he had never noticed before. Bringing it up to his face, he looked it over with intent.

"Jackie, how long have you had this scar on your hand?"

"Since high school," she told him. The look on his face confused her and she tried to pull her hand back, self conscious of the scar.

"So you've had this for over, what fifteen years?"

"It would be about seventeen. I was playing volleyball in my Senior year and I leaped for a save. When I landed on the floor, my hand came down on a piece of glass that no one saw. It cut me pretty good."

"That's it!" Jacob shouted. He gripped Jackie's hand and pulled her over to his desk. Not letting go of her hand, he flipped open the police file folder and searched for the photo of Jackie and Doug that the police had found in Doug's home. Once he did find it he held it up to the light.

"Jacob, what is it?" Kristie asked, worried for Jackie.

"I knew it. I knew it wasn't real," Jacob turned the photo around for the three women to look at, "Look at her hand in the photo. What's missing?"

Robin leaned in and looked at Jackie's right hand in the photo. The skin was smooth and unmarked. "There's no scar on her hand."

"Exactly! That may be Jackie's face in the photo but that's definitely not her body."

41

Do you realize that when I left the precinct earlier, I left for the rest of the night? Why are you calling?" Brett asked Josh. It had only been an hour since he had kissed Angie and he was sure that Josh had not found out yet. If Josh had known what happened, he would have found Brett and dealt with it in person. But the fear of his partner knowing what he had done made him feel like a little boy getting in trouble with his father.

"We have a problem," was all Josh said.

"Define problem."

"It's about the Waterford case. I just spoke to Dave Francis. He just proved to me that it couldn't have been Waterford who killed Rogers in the park."

"Why not?"

Josh explained the experiment that Dave had made him do and that the wounds were done by a professional. Brett wondered what this did to the preliminary that was scheduled for tomorrow. He had felt in his gut that Waterford wasn't up for murdering two men, let alone one. But some of the evidence was difficult to ignore. This new revelation only brought up more questions. If Craig didn't kill Martin or Rogers, then how did his print get to the scenes? What was Craig's involvement in all this anyway?

"Why couldn't this be just a simple case of lover's revenge?" Brett muttered over the phone.

"Because God hates us," Josh replied.

"If God hated me, he would have made me look like you."

"You're just jealous that women like the Italian better than the German."

"Okay, I'm on my way back to the precinct. I'll meet you there." Brett hung up and breathed a sigh of relief that he was still free of the trouble that the kiss with Angie was sure to bring. Now there were more things to worry about.

"I'm such a tool."

Josh waited for Brett to arrive so they could look into the evidence once more and figure out what they had missed before the hearing tomorrow morning. As he did, his cell phone went off, vibrating intensely. He touched the screen and saw that Angie had sent him a text message. WE NEED TO TALK. He was unsure if that was a good thing or a bad thing. Things normally didn't work out in Josh's favor when she told him that they should talk.

He began dialing her home phone number when a man and three women barged into the precinct past the desk sergeant. The man, dressed in a nice suit, dragged one of the women with him by the hand. Mac was chasing after the women that were behind him. Josh stood up and wondered what the hell was going on.

"Are you Foster?" he asked Josh.

"No, I'm Detective Raghetti. Detective Foster is my partner. Can I help you with something?"

"Yeah, I'm Jacob Scott. I represent Craig Waterford. I need to show you something."

"Mr. Scott, you can't just walk into the precinct like that," Mac said, grabbing Jacob's free arm. Josh held his hand up, telling Mac to step down. Mac let go and stepped back a step. He did not leave in the event that Josh should need help.

"What do you need to show me?" Josh asked.

"The photo you have with Mrs. Waterford and the victim. It's a fake."

"Excuse me?" Jacob went into detail, telling Josh about the missing scar on the right hand of what appeared to be Jackie Waterford. Josh looked the photo over once again and then Jackie's actual hand.

"That's interesting," was all Josh could say. This changed things even more. Their case against Craig Waterford was slowly falling apart.

"You're damn right that's interesting," Jacob said with excitement.

"Okay, Mr. Scott, let me run the photo by our crime lab and see what they come up with. While we're waiting, my partner is on his way here. I need to explain something to you as well. Something that our medical examiner had just found."

42

Healy looked at his phone and saw that it was them again. He gritted his teeth at the annoyance that this client was. He wanted to let it go straight to voice mail but he knew that someone like them would only call back and keep calling until he picked up. So he answered it in order to get it over.

"What's your problem now?"

"I'm calling to make sure you know the plan for tomorrow."

"You didn't hire a bumbling dolt. You know that. So why the call?"

"I'm worried, okay? I want to make sure this doesn't get back to me, understand?"

"I understood that from the beginning. And I'm good at covering my tracks. The hearing for Waterford is tomorrow. Everything is going according to plan."

"For your sake I hope so."

"I explained that I would be there tomorrow to make sure that it all went according to plan. Now stop calling me and relax. You paid good money for good work. And that's all I provide."

"Good," the caller said, "Thank you."

"Don't thank me. Just make sure the funds are placed into the account. Once the job is finished I vanish and you can sit back and enjoy the result."

"That's what I like to here." Healy disconnected the call and tried to return to his meditation. But the annoyance that the caller gave him was too distracting. He would have to go for a walk and allow the fresh summer air to purge the toxins. This job was more trouble than he first thought it would be. But Craig Waterford was the perfect patsy for this. He would go to jail for the crime and his client would smile from the perfect work that Healy guaranteed.

Healy turned the dim light off and left his Hoboken apartment to help prepare his energy for tomorrow's task.

43

What Melvin can do for us, is scan the picture and allow his program to search the photo for any imperfections that doctoring may cause," Josh explained to Jacob and the women. They, now joined by Brett, walked up the stairs to the second floor where the crime lab was located. Melvin was alone this evening and he was hard at work. When he saw the group entered, he shook his head.

"No way guys, I'm totally up to my neck with work," he told them.

"I can go downstairs and get Chief Black to come up here and put us at the front of the line," Brett said, "Shall I get her on the phone?"

Melvin stood silent for a moment and then called Brett's bluff, "Yeah, you go right ahead. If she says to take care of yours first, then I'll do it. But not until she does."

Brett grabbed the phone and dialed Black's cell phone number. It rang twice and then she answered.

"Black," she said.

"Chief, it's Foster. I've got some new developments in the Waterford case and I need Melvin to scan the Jackie Waterford photo into the system to check for abnormalities."

"Define abnormalities, Foster."

"I have reason to believe that the photo was created as evidence against Waterford. But Melvin won't jump us ahead in line unless you tell him."

"Is this legitimate?"

"Yes, Chief. There's proof as it is and we need to confirm that Jackie's face was added onto the photo."

"Fine, let me talk to Melvin." Brett handed the phone to Melvin who took it and listened to Black order him. He said, "Thank you Chief. Have a good night." Then he hung up and grabbed the photo from Josh's hand.

"You don't understand the amount of headache I get if I let someone jump the line. If I have Chief Black behind me then the others keep quiet."

"Don't worry about it, Melvin. I get it."

Melvin placed the photo into the scanner neatly and pressed the scan button on the top. As it scanned, he explained to them that it would only take five minutes to run the program on it. The program would be able to identify any pixel breaks on the photo.

"Now I know that this doesn't completely absolve Craig of the crimes but it does create doubt that he may have been framed into being charged for the murder, correct?" Jacob asked the detectives. Josh didn't want to admit it but Jacob was right. Between the photo and the wound marks on Peter Rogers, enough evidence was being brought forward to make them second guess their first conclusion.

"You're right, councilor," Brett said, "This will help your case but it doesn't fully convince that your client is innocent. You will still need more to convince the judge."

"It's a start, though," Jacob said to Jackie. Jackie was relieved and couldn't wait to see Craig again to tell him the good news.

Jacob couldn't wait to call Clark and throw it in his face. Court law demanded that any new evidence in a case was to be divulged to both sides before it was covered in the trial. Although the loophole was that Jacob didn't have to tell Clark immediately. He could hold it until just before the hearing began. It would give Jacob more of an advantage. And against Clark, he would need an ace up his sleeve. Clark had already tried to get a grand jury indictment, which would have prevented the option of a preliminary hearing. But the little time that he had left, Clark was unable to get it done. Jacob had gotten lucky in that situation.

"You should tell them about the email," Kristie brought up to Jacob. Brett heard her and tilted his head towards the lawyer.

"What email?"

"Kristie received an email Monday night from Doug's work email." Jacob went into detail about the message and their findings with the delayed message sending at the firm.

"Who else knows about this email?" Josh asked.

"No one but the three of us. We tried to find it in his apartment but we didn't know what the file was on nor where he would have hidden it."

"Then we need to get over there and find it before whoever Doug was trying to keep it from gets it first."

"I need to get back to the office and get everything together for tomorrow morning," Jacob told the detectives.

"That's fine, Brett said, "We'll call you if we find it."

"Bingo!" shouted Melvin, "We have a winner!" The group looked over at Melvin who stood over the computer monitor and raised his hands in triumph. He twirled around and pointed to the screen for the group to see. A thin red flashing line outlining the left side of Jackie's face pointed out the pixel break on the documentation of the photo.

"Does that mean that someone fixed the photo?" Jackie asked.

"Yes, it does," Melvin explained, "When you photoshop someone's face onto a different body there's going to be a break in the outline of the addition. It's a security setting in the program. The outline will always be in black showing that the face is completely false from the original photo. Some people know a way to get around this but not everyone. Whoever pasted your face on this other woman's shoulders was not one of the few."

""Can you have a report stating that for us in the morning?"

"Depends on what I get out of it?" Melvin smirked. Brett dug into his pants pocket and retrieved a bag of Dipsy Doodles corn chips. He tossed it Melvin's way and the crime tech's smirk grew into a wide smile.

"That good enough?"

"I'll get to work on it right now, Detectives."

44

Reynolds was waiting for Jacob when he, Robin and Kristie returned from the Hoboken precinct. Jacob knew that he would. And he knew that it was Guy who notified him of the lawyer taking on the case. From Reynolds' look, he knew that the partner was disappointed in Hoffman's star pupil.

"I'll be right there," Jacob told the assistants, "Get started on questions and I'll be there to help finish them."

The ladies went to Jacob's office and Robin looked back at Jacob, worried that the talk would be a bad one for her boss.

"So, when were you going to let us know about defending Waterford?"

"I've been so busy with gathering the information on it as well as taking care of the two cases that you passed to me from Doug's pile. I apologize for not finding the time to, but the overtime listed will show how nonstop things have been."

"You realize that I had to hear about it from Assistant D.A. Clark?"

"I figured as much."

"Can I ask why you chose to defend Waterford?"

"I know Craig and I believe he didn't kill Doug. If I did think that he had, I would have never taken the case. Craig is innocent and if I can help bring Doug's real killer to justice, then I will do everything in my power."

"For your sake, I hope that's true. Because I've read the police report as well. And I'd say there is plenty of evidence that Waterford did commit the murder. And Clark is looking forward to tearing you to pieces in court."

"I won't let you down, sir. I'll show you that Craig really is innocent of Doug's murder."

"Right." Reynolds walked away before Jacob could finish his last word. He was puzzled by the reaction that Reynolds had given him. Was it that he was mad at Jacob for trying to save who he believed killed his star pupil? Whatever it was, Reynolds seemed biased over Craig's innocence. It bothered Jacob. To have the partner of his firm show no confidence in him was troublesome.

He returned to the office where Robin was alone and already working on the series of questions that he would have ready for the witnesses. He looked around and noticed that Kristie was missing.

"Where's Kristie?"

"She went to get some caffeine for us. How did it go with Reynolds?"

"He's pretty pissed."

"Why? Because you're helping a friend?" Robin asked, annoyed.

"I guess. I think it has to do with the fact that we are from the same firm and I should be thinking of Doug as the victim here."

"Screw that, you know Craig is innocent. Why should Doug's killer go free? What an asshat."

Jacob smiled at Robin's creativity. It was a relief after the day he had had so far. And the day was not over yet.

"Have I thanked you for everything you do?" he asked her.

"Not lately. I was getting ready to ask you for a raise but I wasn't sure."

"You've got it. 10 percent, starting tomorrow."

"Wow, I should compliment you more often," she smiled. Jacob stared at her, taking in the smile that was warming his heart. Then on the spur of the moment, he stood up and walked over to her. Taking her face in his hands, he leaned forward and kissed her passionately. She melted in his arms, leaning back into his body. The passion he gave her had been returned in kind. She felt her toes begin to tingle and was happy that what she had daydreamed about was finally happening.

The kiss continued and Robin began to run her hands down his strong chest and abs. She kept moving her hands down and felt him grow hard against her. That was when they both heard the knob of the office door turn. In unison, the two jumped back and immediately gathered themselves. Kristie walked in with three coffee cups from the kitchen.

"Okay, my boyfriend, Dean, is on his way down with some food. Have I mentioned how awesome he is? And the fact that him shirtless is enough to get me all sweaty?" She smiled at her joke and suddenly caught on to what she had walked into. She looked from Robin to Jacob and could see the blushing overcome them both. Her amused look turned to horrified.

"Oh. I should have taken longer with the coffee huh?"

45

The guard walked down the hallway once more, making sure the few that were there were getting ready for lights out. He reached the third cell with Craig and saw that he was sitting on the cot, with his head in his hands. The guard, ordered to be biased against those in the cells, felt Craig's depression. There was just something about the man in the third cell that spoke innocent.

"Hey Waterford, it's time for lights out," he said to the downed man.

"Thank you, Joe," Craig said from behind his fingers. Joe stopped at the front of the cell and contemplated saying more. Then he remembered.

"Oh, yeah, your lawyer called."

The sentence was like a bolt of lightning into Craig's body. He leapt up from the cot and rushed over to the cell bars. Joe acted fast and jumped back from the bars and brought out his nightstick. Craig saw this and stopped himself.

"I'm sorry, Joe. Did he say anything?"

"Yeah, he said to make sure that you knew about your wife's photo was faked. And that it would help with the hearing tomorrow."

"That's great! Thank you, Joe. You just made my night."

"Anytime." Joe then continued down to cell number four. Craig returned to his cot. The smile on his face felt alien to him. It had been days since he had smiled. It was when Jackie had told him that he would be a father. Now, knowing for sure that she was still true to him and that there was hope for tomorrow's hearing was the best feeling to him. He felt the weight on his shoulders lift slightly, if not completely. He knew keeping hope for the future was not in vain. Now he could lie down and rest before the next big step of getting his freedom back. Finally, since the day he was arrested, Craig Waterford slept well that night.

46

It was 9:30 a.m. that next morning and Jacob sat with his client at the defense table, ready to get things underway. The municipal court was located on the first floor of the Hoboken City Hall building. Only open three days a week, Jacob was lucky to get the hearing that week. He had not had many clients in the town of Hoboken. Most of them originated from either Jersey City or Bayonne. But he was still familiar enough with the layout of the town's city hall.

"I'm nervous," Craig told him. He had been looking around the room like a child on a field trip. He was taking it all in.

"It's normal to be nervous," Jacob explained, "You are technically on trial."

Robin sat on the far end of the table, away from the aisle that led to the front of the room. Craig was placed strategically in-between the two with Jacob, at the edge of the table, making it easy for him to stand and approach the bench.

Because it was a preliminary hearing, no jury was required to be present. The judge would decide as to whether the evidence was enough to bring the case to trial. Jacob was hoping to close this case with the hearing saving Craig the trouble of any further stress. That and he wanted to beat Clark at his own game. It would be sweet justice to drop kick an acquittal on the cocky assistant D.A.

Kristie sat in the first row of chairs just behind the defense table. She was willing to help out as much as she could. She was glad that Dean was willing to take care of Connor the night before while she helped work on today's argument. Dean had been stepping up as a man and was not scared off by the hard working single mother. His short crew cut brown hair and rugged good looks was not something common in Hudson County. The man had moved up from Texas nine years ago for work in construction and slowly integrated into the east coast culture. She felt comfortable allowing him to help give Connor a father figure. Many of her past dates had either little patience for children or complete fear of any form of commitment.

"Now remember, there may be no jury to play up to," Jacob told Craig, "But the judge is still human and can also feel sympathy for the defense. We butter you up as best as we can and we can use it to our advantage."

"Okay," Craig went along.

"Who's the judge today?" Kristie asked.

"The docket says that it's Irwin," Robin read from the sheet earlier this morning.

"Is that bad?" Craig asked.

"Oh no. This is good news." Jacob knew the female judge. Judge Germaine Irwin was known for putting her foot down when it came to bullshit in her courtroom. She had no patience for games and even smaller patience for Guy Clark. Jacob had thanked God that morning when he found out. The forty-two year old judge had practiced in New Jersey for the past five years. Her thin wire glasses and short bob curl hair gave her a younger Judge Judy look and her attitude caused the lawyers to nickname her "the Ballbuster." Jacob knew how to play this morning to his advantage.

Jacob smiled when he heard Guy walk into the courtroom behind him. He couldn't help but turn and look up at the prosecutor. Guy's sour look had meant that he just found out that Irwin was overseeing the hearing. Guy would have to change his strategy slightly to make up for Irwin's appearance.

"Morning, Guy," Jacob said as Guy pushed open the small gate. Guy scowled at the defense table and sat down on the opposite side, opening his briefcase and retrieving the files and pad needed for today. Guy's assistant, Renee, followed behind him. She wore a low cut blouse, revealing her curvy chest.

"Wow," Robin said, glancing over, "That girl has more cleavage than an issue of Penthouse."

"This should be fun," Jacob grinned.

"Don't get too confident," Robin reminded him, "Stick to the plan and we'll be fine."

"You're right," Jacob replied. It was good to have Robin there with him. She gave him strength and even though the two had not had a chance to discuss what they shared the night before, she wasn't acting strange because of it. It gave Jacob hope for another moment like it.

The bailiff and the court stenographer walked into the court from the side door and the bailiff waited for the stenographer to take her seat and prepare her typewriter for use. The bailiff may have been female but her broad shoulders and muscular physique was a message for others not to think she was easy to overtake due to her gender. Once she was ready, she nodded to the bailiff and she then checked to make sure the judge was ready to begin.

"All rise," the bailiff bellowed, "Judge Irwin presiding."

Those at the table stood up and Guy watched Germaine Irwin walk in and sit down at the bench. The look on her face told him that she was not wanting to be there at that moment. He would make use of that feeling to his advantage or his name was not Assistant District Attorney Guy Clark.

"Showtime," he said grinning.

47

"ood morning," Irwin said to the courtroom. Many replied back
with their own greetings. She glanced at the sheet in front of her
and read off the current case. "This is the preliminary hearing for
the State of New Jersey versus Craig Waterford, correct?"

Both Jacob and Guy agreed to the statement. Irwin looked up at Guy
and frowned.

"Hello again, Mr. Clark," she said with a sour tone.

"Good morning, your Honor. Looking as lovely as always," Guy
replied with a shit-eating grin.

"Shut it, Clark," Irwin told him. Then she turned to Jacob, "And Mr.
Scott, I understand that I should keep my eye on you." Jacob looked up at
the judge with a puzzled look.

"I'm sorry, your Honor?" he asked her.

"I received a call from Mr. Reynolds this morning. He was telling me
about you."

Robin and Kristie wondered what she was talking about. They both
looked at Jacob, hoping that he understood the statement from Judge
Irwin. But they could see he was just as in the dark as they were.

"Well, I'm sure it was all good, your Honor," was all Jacob could say.

"We'll see about that. Anyway, let's get the show on the road."

Craig felt scared. The judge did not seem to like Jacob any longer
and that could prove bad for him. He leaned over to ask Jacob what was
wrong, but Jacob was already writing something on his pad. He slid the
pad past Craig and over to Robin. As he did, Craig managed to read:

WHAT THE HELL WAS THAT ABOUT? Robin read it and shrugged a response back.

"Is this going to be bad?" Craig asked him.

"I'm not sure. But don't worry. I'll get to the bottom of it."

"Alright, Mr. Clark. What do you have for us today?" Judge Irwin said to the short stocky A.D.A.

"Thank you, your Honor." Guy stood up and stepped out from behind the table he was sitting at. Straightening his tie, he took a step forward to the bench. The grin had disappeared and the all-business side of him came to the forefront. "What the prosecution has,"

"Whoa hold on a minute, Mr. Clark. Can someone get your Barbie doll assistant a blanket or something? I can see the goose bumps on her breasts from here."

Several audience members behind the gate began to laugh. Slightly embarrassed, Guy took his suit jacket off and draped it over the shoulders of Renee. He pulled it forward and closed in front to cover the cleavage that was showing.

"That's better, thank you. Okay continue," Irwin said.

"Your Honor, we are here today to request that this case be brought in front of a grand jury. The defendant is charged with two accounts of murder. The small amount of evidence may not seem like much but it proves that Mr. Waterford was present at each of the murders. May I present Exhibit A and Exhibit B? These are prints from each of the scenes. Prints that the police have linked to Mr. Waterford.

"Exhibit A has been retrieved from the murder of a Mr. Doug Martin. The defendant's thumbprint was found near the body in the victim's blood. With Exhibit B, a partial palm print was taken from the weapon used to murder Mr. Peter Rogers, the witness to the first murder. This was also proven to be the defendant's." Guy approached the bench and handed Irwin the police reports. Irwin placed her glasses on and examined the reports as Guy continued.

"Next we have Exhibit C, this is a photo of Mr. Waterford's wife and the victim in a romantic embrace. Prosecution would like to submit this as the motive behind the murder of Doug Martin." He handed the original photo to the judge as well. Irwin peered at the photo and studied it closely.

"The prosecution feels this is plenty of evidence for a grand jury to indict the defendant with the crimes brought forward today. The Prosecution rests, your Honor."

Guy sat down with a smile and winked at Kristie when Jacob took a deep breath and stood up to counteract the evidence that Guy had brought forward. He had to be at his best in order to cancel out the prosecution's stand on the murders. He had to show there was enough doubt and proof to show that Craig was not the killer. Yet hearing the warning that Reynolds had given Irwin, he wondered if it was even worth trying. The call to her proved that Reynolds was not happy with him taking Craig as a client. But to attempt to sabotage the hearing was uncalled for and unprofessional.

"Mr. Scott, what do you have to say against the evidence pointed at your client?"

"Thank you, your Honor. I would first like to provide this recent police report to the court concerning Exhibit C. It states that the photo of Mrs. Waterford and Mr. Martin is a fake. Her face was clearly placed over another woman's face who originally took the photo." Irwin picked up the photo once more and brought it to her face, studying it closer than before. She took a minute, trying to see the truth behind the lie.

"I'm not an expert at photo editing but if you asked me, I'd say that this was the original," Irwin debated.

"I understand your Honor, but as the report states, Mrs. Waterford's right hand has a deep scar that she received seventeen years ago in high school. The photo clearly shows no scar. Now, I don't know about Mr. Clark's attention to detail, but Mr. Waterford has been married to his wife for four years and dated her for three years before that. I'm sure he would know that it was not his wife in the arms of another man. Which is why the defense would like to strike Exhibit C from the evidence."

Irwin continued to stare at the photo and Jacob held his breath hoping that the judge would see that the request was reasonable. The air in the courtroom was still and silent. If he could remove the photo from the evidence, he would be up one against Guy. What felt like minutes were only seconds before Irwin spoke about the request.

"I'm going to deny your request and allow the photo into evidence," she said curtly. Jacob was shocked. And even though he was looking at Judge Irwin, he knew that Guy had his big grin back.

"May I ask why, your Honor?" Jacob asked.

"Simple, if this were my husband in the photo, I'd see his face and immediately hunt him down with the biggest steak knife I could find. I wouldn't look at the photo in detail. Who's to say Mr. Waterford didn't notice the scar missing the first time he saw the photo?"

Craig knew she was right. He hadn't looked at the hands when he first laid eyes on it. The shock of seeing Jackie's face was numbing. It took him an entire day before he even thought of the scar.

"Fair enough," Jacob said. He had to keep going for Craig's sake. There were still two other items left for him to submit. He walked back to his desk and picked up the next item. "I would like to submit this police report as well as Exhibit D. It's the examination of the wounds that Mr. Peter Rogers, the witness that came forward, received when he tried to describe the killer to police. You'll notice the wounds are very precise, even though the murder occurred, in front of police I might add, in a matter of seconds. The examiner states that one would have to have some surgical knowledge in order to quickly strike and hit the right Carotid Artery straight on three times in a row. Looking into the academic past of Mr. Waterford, it shows no medical schooling whatsoever."

"Okay, I'll admit this into evidence," she told him. Jacob held in a smile and nodded. "Anything else?"

"The Defense would like to submit one more, Exhibit E. This is an email received by the victim's legal assistant, Miss Kristie Marks." Jacob handed Irwin a printed copy of the email.

"Objection!" Guy shouted, "The Prosecution has no note of this piece of evidence."

"That is because the Defense just received it late this morning. But I do have a copy for you if you'd like," Jacob explained. He walked back to the Defense table and held out another printed copy of the email to Guy. Guy stood up and had to walk over to take it from Jacob's hand. While he did, Judge Irwin read over the email. Jacob felt confident that she would admit this. After all, it did raise questions about the fact that the murder, which appeared as a botched robbery was more than that.

"Has this audio file that's mentioned in the email been recovered?"

"Not at this time, your Honor but the police are aware that it exists and are currently looking for it."

"Are you sure you want this admitted?" she asked Jacob.

"Yes, your Honor."

"And Mr. Clark, how does the Prosecution feel about this piece of evidence?"

"Prosecution will allow it was well," Guy said a little too quickly.

"Then I will allow it. But I would like to point out that this email does not say that your client was planning to murder the victim, nor does it not state that your client wasn't looking to kill the victim either."

"I am fully aware of that, your Honor. But if this does end up making it to a grand jury, my defense will show Mr. Waterford as a man who does not have the capacity to kill another human being. Once the audio file mentioned in the email is found, I'm sure that, as well, will prove it."

"So be it," Irwin said, "Is that all?"

"Yes, your Honor. The Defense rests."

Alright then. Going over the evidence provided from both sides today, I would have to say that there are too many questions left unanswered in this case. And the fingerprints are undeniable. Unless Mr. Waterford has an evil twin? Do you?"

Craig felt like a deer in the headlights of a car at that moment. He was not expecting the judge to ask him a question personally. His throat felt dry as he tried to form the one word that would answer the question she laid upon him.

"No. No I don't, your Honor."

"Well, then I would love to hear how your prints ended up at the scenes. I hereby confirm that the evidence brought forth is suitable enough for a grand jury. Selection of the jury will begin next Tuesday at 10:30a.m. sharp. Mr. Scott, are you also requesting bail for your client?"

"Yes, your Honor."

"Fine, regardless of the first offense, bail will be set at 250,000 dollars with no option for a ten percent cash bail." Irwin banged her gavel on the wood and stood to leave. Jacob hid a smile as he placed all his papers into his briefcase. Guy walked over and patted him on the back.

"Don't fret, Scott," he said, "Not everyone can be as good as me." Then Guy placed his other arm around his assistant and left the courtroom.

"So long Porkchop," Kristie muttered under her breath, although loud enough for Jacob, Robin and Craig to hear.

"What are we going to do now?" Craig asked him. The bailiff walked over and held the handcuffs out to Craig. Unsure of what to do, Craig looked to Jacob for confirmation. Jacob nodded and Craig held his hands out for the bailiff to place the cuffs on.

"First, we find a way to post bail."

"But I don't have $250,000. The Deli is doing well but not that well."

"Let me worry about that. I have a friend in the bail bond business and they owe me a favor. What you need to do is be ready to help once you're out of jail to help get you free of the murder charges."

"How can I help? I still don't know who is doing this to me."

"I have a plan," Jacob reassured him, "But let's get you bailed first."

48

Richardson Bail Professionals was located just under the viaduct that led to Jersey City on Clinton Street. The old building sat on the corner and had been recently renovated by the owner, Kathy Richardson. New siding covered the outside and the walls inside the first floor had been gutted and replaced due to a leak in the upstairs bathroom. The first floor of the building was the business while Kathy and her husband lived on the second floor since they had first opened the business ten years ago.

Jacob had first met Kathy and her husband when the law firm hosted a holiday party for the employees and associates the year he became a part of Reynolds and Hoffman. Hoffman introduced him and they began talking about Kathy's move from Georgia where she was born. After the party, she had given him her card in the event he had a client in need of a bail. And he had used the card a number of times since.

The last time he had, his client tried to run for upstate New York. The escape over the state lines broke the rules of the bail and Kathy was forced to go after him. She had found the search for the client difficult because she could not figure out where he had gone. It wasn't until Jacob remembered a conversation with the client about a friend who owned a cabin outside of Warwick, New York. He passed the information along to Kathy and later that day she had returned with the client in hand. She explained that thanks to him, the search was cut short. She gave him the option to ever ask for help to return the favor.

Jacob walked into the lobby of the bail bonds company and saw

Kathy's husband sitting behind the counter watching a racing show called Pinks. He looked over to see the lawyer entering and smiled.

"Well, well, Mr. Jacob Scott. How are you today?"

"Good and you?"

"It's summer and business is a-booming."

"Glad to hear. Is Kathy around?"

"Yeah, she's upstairs. Hang on." He grabbed a broom near him and used it to thump on the ceiling. A thump replied back and he put the broom back down. "She'll be right down."

"Thanks," Jacob replied. A minute later, Kathy appeared from the back office and held out her hand to him. He smiled back and greeted her.

"Haven't seen you in a while. What are you up to?"

"I'm working on the Craig Waterford case and I'm needing your services."

"Okay, let's sit down and talk this over." She opened the gate at the counter and invited him into the back. He walked into the back and sat down once they were in the office. The office was well decorated with plaques and family photos covering the walls. Two new desks sat on each side with comfortable office chairs for both her and their clients. In the far corner was a small cushion bed for her pet black lab named Cocoa. Cocoa could be heard walking around in the apartment upstairs.

"Okay so what's the bail amount for your client?"

"250,000 dollars."

"Whoa, what, did he kill someone?"

"Someones. But he's been framed."

"I've heard that one before," she joked.

"I know," Jacob said, "But there's something about this case that feels wrong."

"Do you need any help with that?"

"Not unless you can contact the dead."

"Well, I do know some women in Union City that say they can. But how did you want to work this bail? Did the judge give the ten percent option?"

"No, she turned down the option."

"Okay, does your client have anything they can use as collateral? It's a big price."

"I want to put my house up as collateral."

"What?" Kathy sat back, wondering if she heard right.

"I'm paying for the bail. Out of my own pocket."

"Are you sure you want to do that?"

"I believe that this guy is innocent, Kathy. And I'm willing to do this to prove it." Kathy looked Jacob in the eye and studied him. She wondered if he had gotten too close to the case and it was affecting him. But the look in his eye said otherwise. He was determined. And knowing him from the previous times they dealt with each other, she knew that once he set his mind to it, there was no stopping him.

"If you say so," she replied, opening the top drawer of her desk to retrieve the form that had to be filled out. She began taking his information and entered it into the spaces provided. Jacob hoped that Robin and Kristie were having some luck.

49

The apartment was beginning to smell musty. A thin film of dust had now covered everything that had been left behind. Robin had felt that the world inside the apartment had stopped while the world outside continued on. She and Kristie had been asked to come back to Doug's apartment and continue looking for the mystery audio file.

But Robin was too busy wondering where her relationship with Jacob was going next. She had wanted to kiss him like she did for a long time. And the actual kiss was as toe curling as she imagined it. Just to be in his arms was worth all the wondering and hesitation. She couldn't wait to do it again.

"You're thinking about him, aren't you?" Kristie asked her.

"Who?" Robin played dumb.

"Jacob, you know, the guy that you've been wanting to kiss and finally have."

"Oh God, have I looked that obvious and desperate?"

"No, but I have a knack for these things. I think it's about time you did."

"He has such soft lips," Robin smiled, "And I didn't realize that his arms were as big as they felt."

"I'm only sorry that I walked in and ruined the moment."

"I think it was best that you did. I was on the verge of taking his shirt off."

"So what now?"

"I don't know," Robin wondered, "I was hoping that he would make the next move."

"I think right now, he's concerned about Craig. If you show him that you care and are trying to help him, he'll see that and he'll know that it's right for you two to be together."

"Yeah, you're right." Robin thought about how their first time would be. It had been some time since the last time she had a boyfriend, even though she was hit on constantly by lame wanna-be Jersey Shore clones. Her last boyfriend, Vinny, was all eye candy and empty upstairs. It was a curse being an attractive woman in New Jersey, especially in Hudson County.

"I can't think of anywhere that we haven't looked already," Kristie said, changing the subject. She walked into the kitchen, racking her brain for something about Doug that would explain where the audio file was been kept hidden.

"Then clear your mind of everything," Robin explained, "Now think only of Doug and imagine him walking across the living room and follow him to where you imagine him going."

Kristie thought it was silly but she went along with it anyway. Closing her eyes, she imagined a picture of Doug, standing in his grey suit with his blue power tie. Now walk, she thought to herself. Doug walked forward in his apartment, around the couch and she watched him head into the kitchen. He stopped there and she couldn't think of where he would have gone next.

"Do you see anything?"

"I imagined him walking into the kitchen, but I don't know why?"

"Okay, did he drink a lot of coffee?"

"He did when he was stressed."

Robin took over and walked into the kitchen looking around the coffee machine that Doug had. She looked inside the area where the filters were placed and found nothing. Then she flipped the machine over and checked the seams of the bottom. There was no sign of being pried open.

"Nothing in the coffee machine. Let's try the utensil drawer." Robin then opened the drawers near the sink and shifted things around, looking for something out of the ordinary. Unfortunately, Doug's place seemed neat and usual.

"Is he always this neat?" Robin asked.

"Yes, he was a clean freak."

"What about in his closet then? A vacuum cleaner? It would have to be something that you would know about him. That's why he sent you the email instead of someone else."

Kristie knew that Robin had a point. He did let her know in the email that it was really him from the butterfly catcher reference. But there were no other clues in the email as to where it was be stored. She thought about the stories he had told her and nothing of interest came to mind. She remembered the time he told her the story of his moon-shaped scar on the back of his skull.

He had been ten at the time and was jumping on his bed. Then he fell back to lie down and had misestimated the length of the bed, slamming the back of his head into his headboard. He had received six stitches for the gash.

"Let's try his bedroom again," Kristie suggested.

"I'm a little worried," Robin said following her.

"About what?"

"What if the others that he spoke about already found the audio file?"

"Then both Jacob and Craig have already lost."

50

He hated cleaning up other people's messes. It was the main reason why he worked alone. The more involved, the bigger the chance for a mistake to be made. And he was too careful to allow any mistakes. Yet this case was different. He had not seen certain developments coming due to the additions that were brought into this.

He had sat in the courtroom and watched. He wanted to make sure that everything was working to his planned end. Sitting in one of the middle rows, he observed everything. Sitting in the front or the back rows made you too obvious. Most people sat in the middle and he was lost among them.

He tried not to smile when the prosecutor handed over the fingerprints left behind. They were perfect matches to Craig Waterford's. Of course, they were. He never did anything sloppy. It was unlike him.

Next, came the photo, which he had made an error on. He had not noticed the scar on the wife's hand. Yet it did not matter because the photo had done it's job. It still gave the court a reason to strongly believe that Waterford had motive to kill Martin. That was the whole purpose of it's creation. And thanks to him, it worked perfectly.

He did rush things with the killing of Peter Rogers but he planned that as well. He waited nearly twenty-five minutes in the hallway before he saw someone walk by. Luck was with him that Peter Rogers was an attentive person and went straight to the police after learning about the murder. The killing was too easy as well. He had learned Peter's name from the addition that was also brought into this without his knowledge. Even though it made it easier to follow him to the meeting Rogers set up with the police, the addition was still the problem that rose.

Thanks to the addition of this, his current role was clean-up. He knew this would happen when he learned of the number of people involved. Trying to expect the unexpected was nearly impossible in this and the email revelation along with the audio file that popped up had to have been made due to the addition's role in this. That's why he told him not to involve anyone else.

Now, Healy walked up the steps in front of Doug's apartment in order to find the audio file and destroy it before this escalated any further.

51

T his is going no where," Robin complained, "Why can't the audio file have a giant flashing sign saying, 'Hi I'm the magical audio file.'?"

"Well, that would be because Doug didn't want whomever getting their hands on it."

It had been an hour and a half since Robin and Kristie first began their search. They had only moved everything from it's original spot to a new one. And they were no where close to finding out what the file was on. Kristie sat down on the computer chair and looked around at the mess they had created. She was glad to see that the police had not shown up since they got there. They would have forced them to leave and then they would never be able to return to find the file.

"Hey, can you help me move this couch to search the floor underneath?" Robin asked. Kristie stood up and knocked her knee into the computer desk she was next to. The knock into it was hard enough to shake the monitor on top and cause Doug's blue iPod to fall off the top of the monitor and onto the floor.

Kristie, in pain, continued over and still helped move the couch over to the side of the living room. Robin kept looking and Kristie returned to the computer chair to rub her knee. She looked down at the floor as she did. The iPod lay next to her shoe and she noticed something on it. On the back side of the iPod was a sticker of a butterfly. The image brought her back to the email, where Doug mentioned the butterfly catcher story. The reference to the story wasn't to prove that it was actually from Doug, it was the clue they needed to find the file!

"Robin, I think I've found it," Kristie said holding up the iPod.

"What? You did?"

"Doug's iPod. He never left home without it. He put a butterfly sticker on it!"

"Thank God, I think I just broke my last nail. Let's get it back to Jacob and see what it's all about."

Curiosity got the better of Kristie. She couldn't wait to find out what the audio file was about. She wanted to know what Doug had been killed for. She pushed the center button to turn it on but the screen did not light up. She pressed it again and to no avail. The battery inside the iPod was dead. They would need to charge the iPod to full power before they could examine it.

"Battery's dead," Kristie told her.

"I have a charger for it back at the office," Robin told her, "We can charge it as soon as we get back."

"Actually," said the man at the front door, "Neither of you will be going anywhere."

52

Robin gasped at the sudden sight of the man who just appeared. The two women threw their heads in the direction of the voice. In the doorway stood a man they had never seen before. The baseball cap and wide sunglasses covered his face. Robin couldn't tell if the goatee on his face was real or also part of his disguise. He stood with medium height and the muscles of his arms and chest stretched the fabric of his windbreaker jacket. Also, in his gloved hand was a .45 automatic pistol. A silencer had been attached to the barrel. She knew that it meant he had come to Doug's apartment to kill them both. She couldn't let that happen. Jacob was counting on them to find the file and return.

"Who are you?" Kristie asked.

"Who I am is none of your concern. Giving me the iPod is. Hand it over and I'll allow you to live. Fight with me and you will die. Your bodies will never be found and I'll still win. It is your choice."

"Why are you doing this? Did you frame Craig Waterford?"

"Enough with the questions," he said abruptly, "You have a matter of seconds before you both die."

"You're going to kill us anyway, right?" Robin asked, "I mean, you wouldn't have put a silencer on your gun if you weren't planning on using it."

"Women should be seen and not heard. Now shut your mouth and hand me the iPod."

Robin felt her body stiffen in fear. She didn't want to die this way. There had to be someway out of this situation. Jacob would know how if he were here. It hit her that she would never feel his arms around her again. She would never feel the touch of his lips on her skin, his warmth surrounding her. She couldn't take her eyes away from the gun in the stranger's hand. It was the thing that she feared the most, a painful death. She had grown up in Union City and had feared being shot or raped. Once she had moved out and into Lincoln Harbor, just north of Hoboken, the fear had subsided. Now her childhood fear was back to take her.

"Please, just take the iPod and go. That's what you want, right?"

The stranger stared at Robin. He could see the fear in her eyes. And he knew the other woman had a child. He knew everything about them within a matter of hours. He had files of all of them for future use, if needed. Threats to a person were one thing, but threats to a person's loved ones were more frightening.

"Hand me the iPod," he demanded from Kristie. Kristie gripped the clue she had spent all this time searching for and did not want to let go of it. It was the one thing that kept her alive and kept Connor from being motherless.

"Give me your word you'll let us live and you can have it."

"I don't have time for your games, bitch. Give it to me or I shoot the blonde right now."

"What's to say that you won't shoot me after I give it to you?"

"Nothing. I'll get the iPod either way. But I can be merciful if you just hand it over. It's up to you how painful death will be."

"Kristie, just give him the iPod," pleaded Robin.

Kristie saw the look in Robin's eyes. Neither said a word but both knew what the other was thinking. Kristie took a deep breath and took a step forward. She held the iPod out toward the stranger. He smiled and went to grab the item from Kristie's hand. Robin noticed that he was focused on Kristie and not her.

Thinking fast, she placed her foot at the end of the one and a half foot high coffee table in Doug's living room and pushed off with all her might. The table slid across the bare wood floor and into the stranger's shin. He lost concentration and looked down at the sliding table. Kristie moved fast and dodged to the right and into the kitchen where she hoped to find something to throw at the stranger.

Once he regained his composure, he aimed the gun towards Robin but Robin was already jumping towards him. She tried to grab the gun and he ducked out of the way, faster than the legal assistant. Kristie jumped into the mix with the coffee pot gripped in her hand. Remembering lessons from her defense class, she shoved the pot straight-forward into the stranger's face. The glass pot shattered and the stranger grabbed for his face in pain.

"Run!" Robin shouted. Kristie ducked around the stranger but he swung his left arm at the sound of her steps. The gun, still in his hand, made contact with Kristie's temple. The hit caused her to fall to the floor, dropping the iPod. The stranger grabbed for Kristie's hair, pulling her up by it and landed a backhand to her face. Robin dove for the stranger's legs again and knocked him to the wood floor. The back of his head slammed into the wood. Robin stood up and pulled Kristie to her feet.

"Let's go!" she said. Kristie turned and saw the iPod on the floor next to the stranger.

"The iPod, I have to get it."

"No, we have to get out now!"

Kristie knew Robin was right. If they didn't escape now, the stranger would kill them. She followed Robin out in to the stairwell and downstairs. They threw open the front door and turned the corner, heading down to Washington Street, where the street was more populated and would help if the stranger was chasing them. Once they were a block away they stopped running and caught their breath.

Healy touched his face and felt the blood forming on the cuts from the coffee pot. He took the handkerchief from his pant's pocket and dabbed the cuts. Looking at the floor, he saw no blood had dropped. Good, no evidence left behind to link him to this. But he smiled at the sight of the iPod still on the floor. The women had left it behind for him to take. He was pleased by the iPod but was still angry by what the single mother had done to him.

He picked up the iPod and quickly left the apartment. At the front door, he looked around first, making sure the women were not still there and that the police were not around either. Seeing that it was safe, he walked out with his head down and turned right down Hudson to his vehicle. The iPod was safely tucked into his pocket. He would take care of it first and then he would visit the single mother. And then the blonde would get a visit as well. For fun.

53

Angie waited for Brett outside his place that night, waiting for him to arrive. She had made herself up again and hoped that this time, she would be able to seduce him. She used to feel that all men were alike. Then Josh had introduced her to Brett and she saw the gentleman inside the rugged exterior. He was the opposite of Josh and she had hoped, at the time, that he would rub off on Josh and help him be a better man. But after four years, she got tired of the late nights waiting for him to come home and the lack of romance. She threw Josh out and wanted nothing more to do with him. Knowing that he was flawed, Brett still helped him out by allowing Josh to stay with him until Josh could get a place of his own. She knew that Josh was trying to be better for Tamara's sake. But she had given him too many second chances and it was time for her to move on with her life.

Brett appeared at the other side of the street and noticed Angie waiting for him. She could see the surprised look on his face. She wasn't sure if it was a good or bad thing.

"Angie, look about last night," he began.

"I know it was wrong to come onto you like that," Angie interrupted him, "I just need to talk to someone understanding. Please."

Brett paused and thought of the bad consequences that a talk with his partner's ex-wife would bring. But he couldn't just turn her away. She seemed lonely and was in need of a friend. Knowing how Josh had treated her he could not do the same.

"Just to talk?"

"I promise, I won't make any advances. I just need a friend right now."

Brett knew that it was a bad thing to lead her upstairs but he couldn't abandon her like Josh had. She was all alone and even though he found her to be beautiful, she was a good person. Angie was taking care of Tamara 80% of the time. He couldn't say no to her but knew also that he couldn't say that nothing would happen if she followed him upstairs.

"Ok, fine." Brett opened the front door and led the way to his apartment on the fourth floor. He opened the door knowing that he didn't have to be embarrassed by the state of his apartment. He rarely spent any time in it other than eating, sleeping and cleaning on the nights when sleeping wasn't an option. Brett turned on the light and Angie looked the apartment over as she walked in. The living room and the kitchen were blended into one room, being separated only by the dining table. The couch was soft and often was covered by a patterned blanket. There was his 42-inch television in the corner with his blue recliner next to the coffee table.

"It's a nice place. Very quiet," she said.

"It's not much but it's home."

"Pretty clean for a bachelor cop, too."

"Thanks," he laughed. Angie wandered the room and paused. Brett watched the sway in her walk and noticed that he had been staring at her behind. He liked the little shake it made when she walked. She turned back to him and he looked up at her, hoping she didn't know where his eyes were.

"Thank you for listening. I just wanted to vent about my life. If you'd rather not hear it, you can tell me to shut up."

"No," he said, "I don't mind. It's better than hearing about things from the others at the precinct. It would be refreshing."

"You're too nice," she told him, "That's not a bad thing."

"You've obviously not talked to any of my past dates."

"Do you think I'm pretty?"

"Of course," he said.

"Then where did I go wrong with Josh? I tried to keep the sex great and he had no complaints. Did I nag him?"

"I think it was more Josh than you. Knowing him, it was the fact that he wasn't ready to settle down but he knew the good thing he had. He wants the best of both worlds."

"Well, with Tamara in the picture, that's not possible. He has to step up and be a father whether he likes it or not."

"He knows that. And he does miss you. But I think he needs time to get used to the family thing."

"It's been several years. I can't wait forever."

"I know," Brett explained, "That's why I didn't try and talk you out of it. If you give him a second chance with Tamara though, you might be surprised."

"I won't prevent him from being a part of Tamara's life. That's not right for her. But I can't invite him back home."

"I understand. And if you need me to watch her so the two of you can talk, I'm fine with it."

"Thank you, Brett." She moved forward and gave him a hug. He felt her hair brush against his face and smelled her perfume. She smelled so good. He closed his eyes and stood there for a second, fighting the urge inside him. It had been a few years since he had felt the touch of a woman. Ever since Kate. The thought of her brought him out of the trance and he stepped back from Angie.

"I'm, I'm sorry, that was wrong."

"It's fine," he replied, "I'm just....you know."

"I should go," Angie said. She picked her purse from the coffee table and headed for the door. Brett took a deep breath and watched her open the door. She looked back at him in a glance. Then she dropped her head and left the apartment.

"Dammit," he said to himself. He knew he should go after her but his legs would not move. The pain was still fresh for him but it had been a number of years since Kate had died. He looked around him and was disappointed. He knew Kate would have felt the same if she were watching.

He threw the door open and saw Angie walking down the first set of stairs. She turned at the sound of the door. Seeing him, standing in the hall made her smile.

"Please, don't leave," Brett said to her. She listened to him and returned to the apartment. Then she stayed the night.

54

The iPod in Healy's hand flipped over and over as he waited for him to answer his phone. The job was done and seeing how no audio file would be used for the trial, the evidence that was there was enough to put Waterford to jail for a good time. By the time he would be up for parole, the truth would have been buried deep and Healy would be long gone. It made him smile that he was able to cover the other's mistakes.

"Yes," a voice whispered on the other end of the line. Healy knew he had caught him at a bad time. All the better.

"I have the iPod. His mess is cleaned. Tell him to keep his mouth shut from now on. Or else it will cost you a lot more."

"Oh, well, thank you for that." The voice had returned to normal, "I'll be sure to pass the information along."

Healy hung up. It was all up to him now. As long as everything else continued running as planned, the money he was promised would arrive in his off-shore bank account and he could move on. But until then, he had to make sure all threads had been tied together. Only once Craig Waterford was charged with the murder of Doug Martin, would everything come full circle.

Healy allowed himself a smile as he stared at the iPod. Flipping it once more, it turned face up. Then it hit him. Healy turned the iPod to the back side. He remembered hearing the single mother say that the iPod had a butterfly on the back. The back of the iPod was bare. There was no butterfly on it. It could have fallen off in the fight, Healy thought.

He pressed the main button and the iPod came to life. He moved through the menu and skimmed through the files. It was all annoying pop music. There was nothing on here that a man like Doug Martin would listen to. And the audio file that he was searching for was definitely not on the iPod.

It hit Healy like a brick wall. The anger boiled inside him. He gritted his teeth and threw the iPod against his wall. The iPod hit the wall and shattered into pieces. They had played him. He knew which one had, too. The blonde. He would teach her to play games with him.

Healy walked into his bedroom. The supplies were laid out on his bed. He began gathering them and placing them into his case. It was time to take care of the women. He knew the longer they were alive, the more trouble they would cause. Then he would take care of the other. This was all his fault. He was not going down because of the other.

Healy stepped out of the W Hotel, located two blocks from the Hoboken Police Department, and went to work.

55

I can't believe you did that!" Kristie said to Robin. The two women had returned to Jacob's office after escaping the killer and explained to him what had happened.

"Are you're sure you're okay?" Jacob asked Robin. She had bruised her face when she had tackled the killer the second time. His fist had landed on her cheek when he fell to the floor. Her cheek was already starting to change color.

"I'm fine," she assured him, "What matters first is that we find out what's on the file. Or even which file it is. I need to charge this."

Robin had dropped her purse when she was fighting off the killer and her own iPod had slipped out. Thinking fast, she left her own there and scooped Doug's iPod into her purse. When they had felt that he was not following them, they returned to the law firm to tell Jacob what had happened.

Jacob tended to Kristie's bruised temple by getting some ice out of the kitchen. Robin opened her top drawer and retrieved her iPod cord. She plugged the cord into the bottom of the iPod and then plugged the other end into her computer. The battery on the iPod was completely drained. Nothing appeared on the screen. She had seen this before. All she needed to do was leave it plugged in for a little while. She found herself smiling over the way Jacob had run to her when he saw the bruise on her cheek. Little did he know, she'd had worse scratches than the ones she had just received. But it was cute how he was concerned. Perhaps something would come of this, she thought.

Jacob and Kristie returned from the kitchen and looked over the iPod. Kristie held an ice cube wrapped in a paper towel to the side of her head. Jacob stood near, his arms crossed across his chest and his eyes revealing that he was deep in thought.

"What are you thinking?" Kristie asked.

"That, unfortunately, we have to hand that over to the police."

"Can't we listen to it first? We almost got killed for it. I, for one, would like to see what was so important that my life was on the line for it." Robin looked over at Kristie, knowing that she was right.

"Kristie, it's evidence. As much as I'd like to listen to it as well, we can't play with it until we feel like giving it to the cops. It's called tampering."

"No one's really tampering with it," Robin agreed with Kristie, "We're just listening to it before the police arrive. It should still be admissible as evidence."

Jacob knew he was outmanned. He stopped and thought of some loophole that he could use to listen to it. He figured as long as he did not alter the iPod or the file itself or make copies of the file, he should be able to listen to it.

"How long will it take to get that charged?" he asked.

"About an hour," Robin shrugged.

"You have an hour to get it listened to. Then I call Detectives Foster and Raghetti."

"Have I ever told you that you're cute when you get all boy scout?" Robin winked.

Once the hour ran out, the iPod had finished charging. Robin hit the main button and watched the screen come to life. The main menu of Doug's iPod appeared. Jacob and Kristie hovered over her shoulders and watched her glide through the menu. She flipped through the main folders and looked for one that stood out at her. As she went through, Jacob gripped her shoulder and pointed.

"Wait, go back," he said. She slowly went back through the folders and then he said, "There. That one."

He pointed to a folder called 'Convo'. Robin highlighted it and clicked the main button, opening the folder. There was a single file in the folder called IMG_0001.avi. Robin clicked on the PLAY button and the video appeared on the screen. The video portion of the file was distorted. Robin and the others could hear voices but they were muffled by the static of the microphone. They were not going to get anywhere with the file without the help of the police.

"One of the voices is definitely Doug," Kristie said, "I can recognize the tones in his voice."

"But who's he talking to? Is it the killer?" Jacob wondered out loud.

"I can't hear anything when it comes to the other voice. It's too muffled."

"The police will be able to clear out the audio portion. Can you call them and have them come here?" Jacob asked Robin. She nodded and picked up the phone. After asking the desk sergeant to transfer her call to their cell phone, she handed the phone to Jacob.

"Detective Raghetti speaking," Josh answered.

"Detective, it's Jacob Scott. Remember that audio file that was mentioned in the email sent by Doug Martin? Well, we found it."

56

Moskin had returned to the precinct because she had forgotten her day planner on her desk. Alicia had gotten her into a conversation on the latest reality TV show. Lyndsay refused to watch them while Alicia lived on them.

"You don't get enough from being a cop?" Lyndsay asked her.

"It's not that, it's the voyeur aspect to it. Watching people in their most instinctual behavior is entertaining."

"You're the reason why those shows are still around."

"Gee thanks," Alicia pouted.

"Well, it's true. Reality shows are the new corny soap operas. It's all about the common man being portrayed as idiots, selling sex and products to anyone ignorant enough to watch."

"You know I do have some Midol in my top drawer. Feel free to take some if you need it."

"Nice claws," Lyndsay laughed.

"I sharpen them daily, my dear."

Lyndsay said good night and left. Now she was back and Alicia had already gone. Grabbing her planner, she headed right back out of the precinct. As she walked for the front lobby, she passed Josh who was on the phone taking notes from the call. She waved at him and kept going. Right before she reached the lobby, Josh called out her name. She winced and cursed under her breath, knowing that he was going to ask her for some help.

She turned back and looked. He waved and motioned her back to him. Cursing under her breath again, she walked over with a smile.

"What's up?"

"I need some help," He told her, "Waterford's lawyer just found the audio file that was written about in the email. I can't reach Brett on his home or cell phone. Wanna take a ride with me to pick it up for the lab to analyze?"

Lyndsay wanted to say no, but she had to admit she was curious about what was on the file. She plotted out the amount of time it would take if she had said yes. Then she looked at Josh and his face portrayed that of an orphan from those third world country commercials. She chewed on the inside of her mouth before she replied.

"Yeah, sure."

"Thanks. Let's take my vehicle." Josh and Lyndsay left the precinct and walked into the parking lot next to the precinct where their cars were. They drove out and over to Luis Munoz Marin Boulevard. The boulevard would take them over to the Harborside Financial Center where Reynolds and Hoffman's offices were located. As they drove down Luis Munoz Marin Boulevard, Josh decided to ask Lyndsay for some advice.

"Hey, mind if I ask you a hypothetical question?"

"Do I have a choice?" Lyndsay asked in a sarcastic tone.

"Well you could walk back to the precinct," Josh answered back.

"Lay it on me."

"Let's say you were married and your husband did something stupid enough for you to throw him out of the house. What would he have to do in order for you to take him back?"

"That's easy," Lyndsay said, "He'd have to crawl back on his hands and knees, kiss each and every toe and say he's sorry. In that order."

"Very funny. I'm trying to be serious here."

"Are you?" she asked him, "You want her to take you back?"

"Yeah." He looked over to her in the passenger seat to show how serious he was. She saw it in his eyes and was genuinely surprised. Lyndsay always saw Josh as a player, never wanting to settle down. When she heard that he was married with a child she bet Alicia that it would not last the year. Then she won the bet when Angie tossed him out.

Now, Josh was asking for help. She had a hard time trying to take him serious about it but the look in his eyes was the proof that he was ready to change. She wondered what it was that turned him around.

"Can I ask why you want her to take you back? I mean, you didn't seem interested in being in the relationship when you were."

"It's lonely at my apartment. The only time I enjoy it there is when Angie lets me take Tamara. It's empty and quiet and it bugs me like a bad itch."

"Okay, but what about Angie? You can't think she'll take you back just cause you want some noise in the place. Do you miss her?"

"Yeah I do. Not to sound feminine, but it was kind of nice knowing that she was there sleeping next to me. I'd wake up sometimes in the middle of the night and just watch her sleep. She has this cute look on her face when she's sleeping. It helped me relax."

"Have you told her that?"

"No, what are you crazy?"

"No, I forgot you're the crazy one. Do you not know anything? Women like to be complimented."

"I know that but how is that a compliment? It makes me sound like a stalker."

"Josh, you married her. To know that you were watching over her while she slept is romantic. And it gives her that sense of security that most women need. You have a long way to go, buddy."

Josh pulled up to the building and parked in front. He placed the police tag on the dashboard in the event security tried to have it towed. He stepped out and stood up. Looking over the roof of the car, he said to Lyndsay, "We'll talk more about this later."

"Okay," she replied and followed him into the building, wondering how he managed to catch Angie's heart in the first place.

57

Jacob met Josh and Lyndsay at the elevators. The security guard had allowed them up after they signed in and directed them to the right elevator. Jacob shook their hands and led them back to his office to talk.

"So you said that you found the audio file?" Josh asked.

"Yes, it was on Doug's iPod. But there's more." Jacob explained the situation that Kristie and Robin found themselves in. Josh listened and took notes. Then Lyndsay sat down with the women to get a description of the stranger.

"So have you listened to it yet?" Josh asked.

"Yes, but you can't make out much. There's no video because it appears that the iPod was being hidden and wherever it was muffled the voices you can hear. We can tell that one of the voices was Doug Martin but the other one is too incoherent to tell."

"Let me bring it in," Josh suggested, "our tiny crime lab could clean it up and make it clearer."

"Go ahead," Jacob said, handing over the iPod. Josh placed it into a transparent evidence bag.

"Did the killer touch it?" Josh asked.

"Not that I know." Jacob asked Robin the same question and Robin said that the killer did not have a chance to grab the iPod before she shoved the table at him.

"Okay," Lyndsay told the women, "We'll note the case with the description you gave. Unfortunately, it doesn't sound like we'll get much.

The beard was most likely a disguise and the glasses and hat covered up everything else useful. Thank you, though and take it easy with that bruise," she told Kristie.

"I have one more question," Josh asked the women, "Did you notice anyone following you?" Josh knew a man like the killer would not allow them to escape this easy.

"No, we took a lot of precautions," Kristie said.

"Okay, but if you notice anyone following you, call us immediately."

"Thank you Detective."

Josh and Lyndsay headed downstairs and back to Hoboken. Lyndsay waited for the further questions to follow about Josh and Angie but Raghetti was quiet the entire way back. It made her wonder what was he was thinking about. She could see that he wasn't there with her in the car. His mind was elsewhere. She figured that he was thinking of what he could do to get back into his ex-wife's good graces. Then when they returned to the precinct parking lot, he spoke.

"I'm a complete asshole, aren't I?"

"Well I wouldn't say a *complete* one. More like a partial asshole. You have your good moments."

"What if Craig Waterford is as innocent as he says he is?"

"Well, maybe the audio file on that iPod will confirm it."

"I was so sure that he was guilty. I tortured him with the photo of his wife and Martin. And not once did I check to see if it was real."

"Hey, we're all human too. I've screwed up before. Don't let it make you think you're an asshole. Besides, you still have a chance to make it up. If Waterford is innocent, you can investigate further and make sure that he doesn't get charged with a crime he never committed."

"True."

"Why the beating yourself up?"

"I don't know. The split is making me think about how I am and if I'll be a good father for Tamara or not."

"Teach her to be a good person. That's the most important thing a parent could teach their kid. That and don't date anyone named after a utensil."

"What? A utensil?"

"Don't ask. Maybe I'll tell you about it another day. But just don't be a douchebag to your daughter and you'll be fine."

"Thank you, supernanny."

"You're welcome. Now let's go see a man about an audio file."

"Sure, let me just try Foster again." Josh dialed the phone and listened to the ring. Once again, Brett's cell phone went to voicemail. Shaking his head, Josh said, "Hey Partner, good news. Waterford's lawyer found the audio file that was mentioned in the email Martin sent. Moskin and I are bringing it in to have Lucky play with it and see what we can get from it. Call me as soon as you get this. I'm wondering if you're okay or not. Later."

"Maybe he found himself a hottie and they're getting it on," Lyndsay wondered.

"Him? Hooking up with someone hot? That'll be the day," Josh joked. Then he followed Lyndsay back into the precinct and up to the crime lab.

58

They found Lucky hard at work. He was dancing across the room with Salsa music blaring out of the mini CD player on his desk. Josh looked over at Lyndsay with raised eyebrows. Lyndsay shrugged her shoulders, unsure of what they had walked into. Lucky didn't notice them at first because his eyes were closed, feeling the rhythm of the beat and moving likewise. Josh stood staring at the short lab tech. He was a little impressed with the moves. Then Lucky opened his eyes and stopped short at the sight of the two detectives. Josh began clapping as Lucky turned down the music.

"Practicing for your Dancing With The Stars audition?" Josh asked.

"No, my lady friend and I are taking dancing lessons. I'm not as quick a learner as she is."

"Well, it looks like you have it down," Lyndsay complimented him.

"Thanks. So what can I do for you kids tonight?"

"Got an .avi file on this iPod that needs some cleaning," Josh explained, "We can't hear anything being said and this is important to the Doug Martin murder. So we need you at your best."

"You've got me all night," Lucky said, smiling. He pulled up a chair and sat in front of the computer. Josh handed him the iPod and Lucky plugged it into his system. Once the computer found the new hardware, Lucky punched it up on the screen and opened the main folder in the iPod. Inside was a large amount of rock songs.

"Which one are we looking for?"

"The one called 'Convo'"

"Okay, found it." Lucky played the video and the three watched. The audio was nearly impossible to hear due to what sounded like the scratching of fabric against the microphone.

"Sounds like he had it in his pocket," Josh thought out loud.

"I think you're right. Which for us is good. I can remove that portion of the audio and tweak the levels so that the voices are better. It's going to take me a while but I will have it for you later tonight."

"Yeah, I've got no where to go," Josh told him, "Just call me on my cell phone when you have something."

"You got it, Raghetti."

"Thanks Lucky."

Josh and Lyndsay returned back downstairs to their desks. Lyndsay yawned and rubbed her eyes from behind her eyeglasses. Josh sat back in his chair and opened his top drawer. Inside he pulled out a paperback book.

"What do you have there?"

"Just a book that one of Vice gave me. It's about two guys who are good friends and one of them begins to change, turning into this other-worldly version and opens a portal to another world that has red skies and stuff. Pretty good so far."

"Well, I have to get out of here. I'm exhausted. We'll talk more about you tomorrow?"

"Yeah that's fine. Thanks Moskin."

"Hey, anything to help a friend," she smiled. He smiled back and she left. He was feeling better about himself thanks to Lyndsay. It gave him some confidence that he would be able to eventually win Angie back and hopefully give Tamara a better life than being shuttled between two homes. He had a friend who went through that as a kid and he had trouble trusting women. It took years of therapy before he ended up marrying his girlfriend.

Josh kicked his feet up on his desk and cracked the book open to the page that he left off on. Soon the book sucked him in and he lost track of time. It was two hours before Lucky called him back. Lucky told him to come back upstairs and see if he could help make out what was being said.

Josh jogged up the stairs and felt a little winded when he reached the top. He made a plan to join the local gym tomorrow. He entered the lab with the expectations of seeing Lucky in a tutu trying ballet moves. He was sadly disappointed.

"I did everything I could but the distance of the second voice only allowed me to get so close to a clean and crisp copy of the audio portion. Want to listen?"

"Absolutely." Lucky clicked the PLAY button and they sat staring at the monitor. The video was again useless due to the location of the iPod at the time. The two sat and listened.

"The first voice is Doug Martin," Josh told Lucky, "Jacob Scott confirmed it. They couldn't recognize the person he was talking to."

"Well you can certainly hear what the other person had to say here," Lucky pointed out and rewound the audio back a few seconds. They listened again and Josh heard the comment that the second person made.

"Did I hear that right?"

"I'm pretty sure you heard what I did. The question is what does it mean to the case?"

"I don't know but I think we need to bring Jacob Scott back down here to help us interpret this. Great job, Lucky." Josh pulled out his cell phone and called Jacob, hoping they could figure out what the hell caused Doug Martin to get killed over the recorded conversation he had on his iPod.

59

Locking the front door behind her, Jackie turned to thank Connie and Shannon for staying a half hour late to help her clean up for closing. She smiled and wondered where she would be if not for the help of Connie and Jonathan. Both were going above and beyond to help Jackie keep everything in the deli running perfectly.

"Thank you so much ladies," Jackie said to them.

"It's no problem," Shannon said with a smile, "Do you need a ride? My husband should be here any minute."

"No thank you. I'm in the mood to walk, it's a beautiful night."

"Okay, then. You have a good night."

"You too, Shannon."

"I'll walk with you if you want," Connie offered.

"Thank you, Connie. I wouldn't mind someone to chat with."

The two women walked down Washington to Jackie's home. Jackie noticed the crowd of people on the main strip. It was a bit busier out for a Thursday. But then again, the night was nice and calm. No muggy humidity and a cool breeze in the air to boot.

"So is there anything new with Craig's case?" Connie asked.

"Other than what happened this morning, no. Craig's lawyer is working on getting him out on bail but the trial begins next Tuesday. It worries me. I don't think I could manage on my own if Craig had to go to jail. The baby alone would have me a frantic mess, but to have to run the store on my own. I'd go insane."

"What about Craig's father and mother? Would they help?"

"Well, they don't really know what's going on right now. They've moved down to West Palm Beach with all their older friends. Craig asked not to get them involved."

"But if he goes to jail, they'll have to be told."

"I know, that's what I'm afraid of. It would break his mother's heart to hear that. And I'd have to be the one to tell her if it got that bad."

"Craig is a good man. I know the two of you will get out of this okay."

"We just don't know why this is happening to us. What did we do to deserve this?"

The man sitting on the steps of the apartment building that Connie and Jackie walked past knew why this was all happening to Craig. But he wasn't paid to know things unless it benefitted the work he did. In this case if the one did not come through with his part, Gerald Healy would just spill the beans in an anonymous phone call to the police. But he had more important things to take care of right now than follow Jackie Waterford home. He had to be somewhere else and he had to be there soon if he wanted to pull it off.

60

The desk sergeant had Jacob escorted up to the crime lab where Josh and Lucky sat waiting for him. The lawyer had taken the call as he was about to take Robin home. He was worried about her being alone and also wanted to talk about taking their kiss to the next step. Kristie offered to take her back to her place and sleep in the guest room. She had mentioned that they would not be alone as Dean had offered to stay over and make sure everything was alright.

"Promise me you'll call me later to make sure you are alright?" he asked Robin.

"I'll be fine, Jacob."

"Just help satisfy my nerves, please?"

"Okay," she gave in, "I'll call you later."

He leaned in and kissed her quickly. To Jacob it felt normal. He knew Robin felt the same from the little smile on her face.

"Hey, Jacob," Josh said, standing up and holding out his hand, "I'm glad you could make it. This is one of our lab techs, Lucky. He managed to work the file out to sound a lot better. But we need you to help make sense of what is being talked about. And we hope you can recognize the second person in the conversation."

"I'll do my best," Jacob said. The three sat down and Lucky once again played the file.

'Hey, do you have a minute?'

"That's Doug," Jacob confirmed once more.

'Sure, what do you need?'

Josh looked over to Jacob, waiting for a confirmation on the second person. Jacob shook his head, unsure at the moment.

'There's a problem with the case. Do you know about Exhibit 11?'

'What about it?'

'Well, looking at it closer, it's pretty obvious that,'

The volume of the audio dropped significantly. None of them could hear what the second part of the sentence was.

"What did he say?" Jacob asked.

"That's the thing," Josh explained, "We don't know. We've listened to it over and over like eight times and that's the best Lucky could get it. Did you want to try and listen again?"

"Yes please." Lucky backtracked the audio a few seconds and Jacob listened intently.

'Well, looking at it closer, it's pretty obvious that it's no good.'

'I disagree. 11 is fine and that's why it was admitted.'

Jacob knew that voice but was still having trouble pinpointing the person. Lucky paused the audio and sat back. Josh looked over at Jacob again.

"It's very vague. But from what I hear is that Doug had a problem with some piece of evidence. It sounds like he said that Exhibit 11 was no good. Whoever the other person is disagrees."

"Why would he say that the piece of evidence is no good?" Josh asked him.

"I'm not sure. It could be several different reasons. Most likely the evidence was not substantial enough for whatever case they're talking about. Was that the entire audio?"

"No there's one more piece of the conversation left," Josh said. He nodded to Lucky, who clicked on the PLAY button again to finish it.

'Are you kidding? It's a complete fabrication!'

'You're out of line, Doug. Now I won't hear of it any longer. Go do your job or you can find somewhere else to practice law.'

The last piece of the conversation hit Jacob like a punch to the gut. Is this what Doug was killed over? Doug's last comment made sense. This didn't have to do with Craig. The conversation clearly gave the motive of Doug's death. He had found something in a case that wasn't right and whoever the second voice was, tried to bury and deny it.

"Doug sounds like the evidence he found was not real."

"Are you saying that he found planted evidence?"

191

"It sounds like he's saying that. Everything is so vague, it's hard to tell."

"Any thoughts on who the other person is?"

"It's on the tip of my tongue. Can I listen to it once more?"

Lucky played back the entire audio back once again. It wasn't until the last line of the conversation that it dawned on Jacob. He did know that voice. He heard it daily at work.

"It's Reynolds," he told Josh, "The second person is Mark Reynolds."

61

Dean Williams carried the sleeping boy into his own bedroom and gently placed him into his bed, covering him with a thin sheet. The open window in the room blew the cool breeze from outside into the room and cooled it down. Dean looked down on Connor Marks, watching him sleep. He felt that he could get used to the family thing.

Ever since he had met Kristie a month earlier, he was feeling pretty happy with life. Moving to New Jersey was the best thing he had done in his life. Back home in Texas, he had a rash of bad luck, his place had burned down thanks to the neighbor's irresponsibility, he had been mugged and the girl he was dating had placed a video of her and several men 'enjoying' each others' company online. He had only been living in Hoboken a month before he met Kristie. Her laid back attitude and her motherly instincts were a welcoming feel for him. He had remembered their first date like it was yesterday. And their following dates had only gotten better.

Two weeks into the dating, she had introduced him to Connor, a rambunctious six-year-old boy. He was all about baseball and pretending to be a superspy half the day. Being a baseball fan himself, he offered to take them to a Yankees game. Connor told Kristie that it was the best day he ever had. And then he had given her his seal of approval of Dean. So she invited him over whenever he felt lonely. A few days later, he had taken her up on the offer. They had dinner together and had a good time. He could see that Kristie was relieved that he and Connor had bonded so well and that Dean was not scared off by the boy.

He closed the door to the bedroom partially. Then he returned to the couch in the living room and decided to change the channel from the Upside Down Show to the TV show Fringe. He kicked his feet up and watched as he waited for Kristie to return from the law office. She had warned him that her friend would be staying the night due to the case they were both working on. He was very concerned when she explained what had happened that afternoon and he offered to stay the night on the couch to make sure they were safe. She thanked him for the offer and planned on taking him up on it.

During the commercial break, he got up and grabbed himself a can of soda. Popping it open, he paused for a few seconds. He thought that he had heard a floorboard creak. Thinking it was Connor waking up, he walked back into the living room, checking the hall for the little boy. Dean found no one in the hall and the place was quiet again. He brushed it off as the house settling and sat back down on the couch. He took a drink of the soda and placed it on the coffee table. Then he sat back and stretched his arms out. That was when someone behind the couch leapt up and wrapped a wire around Dean's neck. The stranger pulled the wire back as hard as he could. Dean gripped the wire and tried to loosen it from his throat. But the wire was digging into his fingers like it was with his neck.

Thinking fast, he kicked off the floor in front of the couch and back. The shove pushed the couch back and pinning the stranger between the couch and the wall. The stranger loosened his grip slightly and gave Dean the chance to reach back and punch aimlessly at the stranger behind him. He missed but the punches allowed more slack in the line and Dean gripped the wire around his throat. He put all his weight into pulling forward, flipping the stranger over the couch and causing him to loose his grip on the wire. Dean stood up taking in a deep breath and turning to get the jump on the stranger.

But the stranger was already standing, brandishing a gun. Dean stopped short and raised his hands. The stranger stepped back, giving him room to prevent Dean from lunging forward to grab the gun.

"Okay, it's cool. I'm not going to do anything stupid," Dean told him.

"I'm not worried about you," the stranger said, "I'm faster, stronger and smarter than you. There's no stopping me. You will die. And then so will the boy."

Dean's mouth dropped open. He didn't know what was going on but he couldn't allow this man to kill Connor. If he had to sacrifice his life for Connor's safety, then so be it.

"Connor! Lock your bedroom door and get out! Go to Aleah's house!" Dean shouted.

"You're making a big mistake," the stranger told him.

Connor stepped out of his bedroom and rubbed his eyes. He looked up and saw Dean and the stranger with the gun. He stopped and his eyes went wide. The fear of the gun in front of him froze him in place.

"Connor, lock your door and get out the window now!" Dean said, lunging forward at the stranger. He grabbed the gun and raised it up to the ceiling, preventing the stranger to shoot anyone. The move jolted Connor back into his bedroom and through the struggle, Dean heard the click of the lock. Good boy, he thought.

The stranger kicked at Dean's knee and Dean shouted in pain. He let go of the stranger's wrist and he fell to the living room floor. The stranger brought the gun down and fired off a shot at Dean. The bullet, doctors would learn, pierced Dean's abdominal area and landed in his intestines. Dean groaned and curled up.

The stranger walked over to the hall and tried the door to Connor's room. He could leave no witnesses. The door was firmly locked. That was fine, he thought. The stranger, known to only himself as Gerald Healy, brought his foot up and kicked in the door. The first thing he saw was the open window. Walking over, he saw the fire escape outside the window and the boy was no where to be found. He was getting angrier by the minute. This was all beginning to fall apart. And it was the other's fault. He couldn't believe that the other was told in the first place. He was such a fool.

Healy thought that the boy may be still near and he left the bedroom and looked back at Dean Williams, who was still squirming on the floor in pain. Healy aimed the gun and fired at Dean's skull. Then he rushed out of the home in search of the boy.

Connor counted to one hundred after he heard the front door close before he came out of his hiding place that his mother and Dean had practiced with him. He slid out from under his bed and slowly padded out to the hall. There was no one there. But he could see Dean on the floor. Dean's blood was slowly pooling under him. Connor felt the tears rolling down his cheeks.

"Dean? Dean, are you dead?" Connor knelt down and touched Dean's shoulder. Dean did not move. "I'll go get the police, Dean. They'll take you to the doctor's. Okay? You wait right here, I'll be back. I promise, Dean. Don't die, okay?"

Connor ran down the hall and out the front door. He wiped the tears from his eyes and stood straight. He knew that Dean was counting on him to be a little man. He couldn't let Dean down. He climbed the steps slowly, making sure that the stranger who shot Dean was not still there. He looked back and forth. There was no sign of the stranger. So he began to run down the block, headed to Washington Street. He knew that the more crowded areas had security guards or police officers. They would help Dean.

He got to the corner of his block when a hand grabbed his shoulder.

62

Brett looked at his cell phone an hour after Josh had called him. It was getting late and Angie had fallen asleep, exhausted after the lustful sex they had. The guilt of her lying there in his bed beside him was overwhelming. He had done what he swore he'd never do.

Quietly, he slid off the bed and padded into the living room where he sat on his recliner and listened to the messages that Josh had left. The messages caught him up on the Waterford case. He was pleased to hear that Jacob's assistants had managed to get the audio file before the killer had. The last message told him that they learned from the audio that Mark Reynolds from Doug Martin's law firm, Reynolds and Hoffman, was somehow involved. This was big news. He wanted to go down and see what was happening next but he couldn't leave Angie alone. That would be as bad as what Josh had done to her.

He got up to get himself a beer and peered into the fridge for a snack. The sex had made him hungry. He grabbed a sandwich that he picked up from Craig's deli. He sat down at the empty dining table and took a bite of the sandwich. Not bad, he thought. He could see why the place was so busy every time he passed it.

His eyes fell on the cell phone. Then he looked up at the bedroom door. He had to tell Josh. The buried secret would only make matters worse. He hoped that this would not come between them. But the possibility of Josh flipping out was what held his hand from grabbing the phone and dialing right there.

The wondering of Josh's reaction was killing him. He had to call and talk to his partner. Besides, Angie may take it upon herself to tell him of their night together. That would make it worse than if Brett told him.

"Ah Foster, how do you get yourself into this shit anyway?" he said to himself.

Brett scooped up the cell phone and dialed Josh's cell phone number. He stared at the phone for the first ring. Then he placed it to his ear. Closing his eyes, he took a deep breath and waited for Josh to pick up. This case is about to blow open wide and you're missing it."

"I know, I'm sorry. I had my cell phone turned off."

"Yeah, Lyndsay was betting that you were having sex with some woman that you picked up."

"Heh, yeah. Like that would happen."

"That's what I told her. But you have to come down. I'm with Lucky and Jacob Scott at the precinct. We're throwing possibilities around as to what Reynolds part may be to this case."

"Yeah, I think I will come down and see what we can find. But I need to talk to you about something personal."

"What, you don't know how to get rid of her so she's not there in the morning?"

"Um, no it's not that. Well, kind of. I'd rather talk to you in person about it."

"Okay, are you alright? You sound really strange. You didn't go chubby fishing did you?"

"What?"

"You didn't bring home a fatty."

"Oh no. No I didn't."

"Is it a he/she?"

"Did you really just ask me that?"

"Well, I'm just making sure you aren't going to lay some freaky shit on me."

"Well, about that," Brett tried to say. Then he heard something going on in the background of Josh's side. He heard Jacob talking loud at someone else.

"Hang on partner," Josh told him. He heard talking and then Josh returned to the line. "We've got a problem. The killer is looking like he's trying to tie up some loose threads. Seems like he showed up at Kristie Marks' place and shot the boyfriend. Got a pen?"

"Yeah, go ahead." Josh read him off the address to Kristie Marks' home and told him that he would meet him there. Brett hung up and placed the cell phone back on the table. He was disappointed with himself in not telling Josh the situation. He walked back into the bedroom and saw that Angie was waking up.

"Who were you talking to?" she asked groggily.

"Josh. There's been another murder linked to the case we're working on."

He saw the disappointment in her eyes. She knew she would get the same from another cop but she had given Brett the benefit of the doubt. He leaned in and kissed her as passionately as he did the first time that night.

"I will be back tonight. I promise."

"I'll give you something to come back to," she said, throwing the sheet off her naked body. He smiled at the sight and made a vow to take advantage of what was waiting for him back home.

63

Kristie refused to let go of Connor. After walking up to the house and noticing Connor running down the block alone and in his pajamas, worried her. She ran after him and grabbed him up into her arms. His hands were covered in blood and she panicked, searching him for a wound. She stopped when he explained that it was Dean's blood. She passed Connor to Robin and ran into the house.

Finding him on the living room floor, she grabbed the phone and dialed 911. Robin kept Connor out of the house for now and called Jacob on his cell phone to tell him what happened. She found that Jacob was still at the precinct and he told her he was on his way with Detective Raghetti.

Inside, Kristie checked Dean's wrist. There was a faint pulse but it proved that he was still alive. Listening to the 911 operator, she placed a warm wash cloth on Dean's stomach, trying to stop any more blood from escaping his body. The wound on the side of his head was not gaping but some blood was dripping on the wood floor.

"Please Dean, stay with me," she pleaded with him, "You're a great guy and Connor loves you to pieces. I need you here, please. Don't go on me. Fight it."

She ran her free hand through his short brown hair. His peaceful look bothered her. He looked like he was sleeping but the blood told her otherwise.

Robin sat on the front steps, cradling Connor. She rocked him back and forth as he told her about what he saw.

"So did you see the man that Dean was fighting with?" she asked him.

"Yeah. He looked at me with a mean face."

"Can you tell me what he looked like? What he was wearing?"

"Uh-huh. He was a little shorter than Dean and he had yellow hair."

"Yellow like mine?" she asked pointing to her pale blonde hair.

"His was darker yellow. It was short."

"Did it look like a wig?"

"No, but he was wearing a cap and Dean knocked it off his head."

"Okay, anything else?"

"He had a mini beard."

"A mini beard? You mean only around his mouth?"

"No, it was only under his mouth," Connor explained, "Right here." The boy pointed to under his bottom lip. Robin understood it to be a soul patch. It sounded right as the goatee he was wearing when she saw him would have covered it.

"What about the rest of his face? Was there any scars?"

"He had a few boo-boos around his nose. But he didn't have any band-aids on them." A result of the glass coffee pot to the face.

"You did a good job remembering, Connor," Robin praised him.

"Is Dean going to die?"

"No, sweetie. Dean will be okay. I promise."

"Pinkie swear?" Connor held up a lone pinkie finger.

"Pinkie swear," Robin replied, wrapping her pinkie finger around his. She hoped that she wouldn't have to break the promise.

The ambulance showed up along with Josh and Jacob within five minutes. Robin directed the paramedics into the house and Kristie took over from there. She explained what she had found and what she had done to help stop the bleeding. The paramedics opened their bags and began to work on him immediately.

"He's still got a pulse," the taller paramedic told the other.

"Head wound is not deep. I can see the skull is still intact. That's a plus," the other paramedic reported.

Kristie stepped back and allowed the paramedics to do their thing. Josh Raghetti walked into the house and looked down at the paramedics working on Dean. He placed his hand on her shoulder and guided her back outside. She hesitated at first and then realized there was nothing she could do for Dean right now and gave in.

"I'm sorry this happened," Josh told her, "Detective Foster and I have several officers combing the area for this guy. Hopefully, Dean's condition will stabilize and he could give us a description."

"Connor saw the guy," Robin added.

"He did?"

"Yes." Robin gave Josh the description that Connor had given her. Josh wrote down all the info that she provided.

"This is a great description, Connor. If he's still around, we'll definitely get him now. Good job, little guy." Josh held his hand out at Connor and Connor slapped him five. It brought a smile to his face and Kristie was glad he was not completely traumatized by it.

"Can I please go back inside and change my clothes?" Kristie asked. She looked down at herself and saw Dean's blood on her arms and chest. She thought she looked like the last girl alive from a horror movie.

"I'll take her," Robin offered. She passed Connor over to Jacob and led her friend back into the house.

"Does this prove that my client is not responsible for Doug Martin's murder?" Jacob asked.

"Well, considering he's still in jail right now, I'd say it's a good piece of evidence. Unless he has the ability to teleport. It still doesn't explain how his thumbprint got on Doug's briefcase and his palm print was taking off the weapon that killed Peter Rogers."

"I'm still working on that one. But the framing motive is my best bet."

"Then the question is, why Craig? He's obviously linked to this case in some way. And what's Mr. Coffee Pot's involvement?"

Brett walked up to them and offered a partial explanation, "I'd say this killer has been hired. If the audio was between Reynolds and Martin, and it was the reason why Doug was killed, then it makes sense that Reynolds hired someone to kill Doug to keep him quiet about whatever case they were talking about."

"It's about time you showed up," Josh ribbed his partner.

"I got over here as soon as I could. How is everything?"

Josh updated Brett with the information he had received. Brett made a call out to the precinct to help with the search.

"Mac, it's Foster. I need you to send out a BOLO for the suspect on the attack on Park and 2nd." Brett read off the description to the desk sergeant. Mac read it back to be sure and Brett confirmed. He thanked Mac and hung up. "Okay, so the description's out there. Let's see if we get anything."

"What's a Bolo?" Connor asked Brett.

"It's a police code that means 'be on the lookout'," Foster explained, "It lets the other police officers know that he's a bad guy and if they see him then arrest him."

"Or shoot him, like he did to Dean," Josh added.

"We only shoot bad guys if they shoot first." Brett threw a look to Josh. Josh nodded and went over to Brett's car. He popped open the glove compartment and retrieved a shiny object. Closing the door he walked over to Connor and Jacob and placed a shiny toy badge on Connor's pajama shirt.

"Connor, as a police officer of the Hoboken Police, for your assistance in describing the bad guy, I present to you this deputy badge."

"Wow, is it real?"

"It sure is. And not many are given out. So you make sure you don't lose it."

"I won't."

The paramedics appeared at the door and they brought Dean out in a stretcher. Brett and Josh went over and helped them down the stairs. Then they placed him in the back of the ambulance and told Brett that he would be brought to the medical center. Kristie came out with Robin and walked over to Connor. She knelt down and hugged him tightly.

"Listen, sweetie, Mommy's going to go with the ambulance to the hospital to make sure Dean is okay. Robin and Jacob are going to take you to Jacob's home. You can stay over night there until school tomorrow, okay?"

"Don't worry Mommy, I'll be okay."

"I'll assign a car to sit outside the house, in case he decides to go after you too," Brett told Kristie and Jacob.

"Thank you," Jacob told him. Robin took Connor's hand and the three of them watched the ambulance pull away.

64

Connor was fast asleep by the time Jacob pulled up to the house on Willow Ave, between 11th and 12th streets. Robin looked into the back and smiled. The little boy had curled up in the seat and looked adorable.

"I'd hate to move him," Jacob said, "He looks so peaceful."

"Where are you going to put him?"

"He can have my bed."

"Ever the gentleman," she joked.

Jacob opened the back door and gently scooped Connor up in his arms. Robin closed the door for him and opened the front door of the house. Jacob walked in sideways, making sure not to wake Connor. He then walked into the bedroom and Robin pulled the sheets back to place Connor under. Once the boy was tucked in and still sleeping, Robin and Jacob went into the kitchen.

"You did a great job with Connor," Jacob told her.

"Thanks," she replied.

"Ever thought of having kids of your own?"

"Yeah, someday. I don't think I'm ready for it right now. What about you?"

"I've always wanted a son to pass the Scott legacy on to. But work right now has me too occupied."

"I'm sure he'd be as cute."

"I'd hope so." Jacob smiled at her. The silence following was deafening.

"So," she said breaking the awkwardness, "Now what?"

"With us?"

"Yeah."

"Well, I'm willing to keep a secret if you are?"

"Would it be awkward for you? For having to hide it?"

"Honestly? I thought it would be but after our moment in the office. It just feels right between us. It's not like it just happened. I've been wanting to do that for a while now."

"Well, seeing how you're being open, I kind of wanted to also." Robin smiled at him, dipping her head downward slightly. He always found her attractive when she did that.

Jacob walked up to her and wrapped an arm around her waist. She leaned up and kissed him again. Her hands placed themselves on his waist and she pushed her body into his. The warmth she felt through her clothes aroused her. He released her and began kissing her neck, slowly making his way down to her chest. His fingers gently undid her top two buttons. She sighed with pleasure. Robin knew that if she didn't stop him, they would end up naked and on the couch. But she felt uncomfortable with Kristie's son sleeping in the bedroom.

"Wait, not yet," she told him.

"Is it too fast?"

"No, I just want everything to be right when we do. With Connor in the next room and the police sitting outside, I feel like my mother's in the room."

"I get it," he said, running his hand through his hair. He went into the bathroom and brought out some blankets. He placed a few on the couch for Robin to sleep on and placed one on the love seat at the opposite side of the living room for himself.

"Do you have a t-shirt or some pajamas I can change into for now?"

"Of course." Jacob snuck into the bedroom and brought her back a loose fitting shirt and a pair of gym shorts. "Will this do?"

"Perfect." She kicked off her shoes and padded bare foot into the bathroom to change. He took off his tie and opened his shirt. Then he sat down on the love seat and kicked his feet up. It was the first time that day that he was able to relax. He hoped to have the case closed by Monday so that the grand jury was cancelled. Anything to keep Craig from having to go back to trial. He realized that he had a lot to do tomorrow and laid back on the love seat, using a throw pillow to cushion his head. Just as he was closing his eyes, he heard the bathroom door open. He opened one eye and had to sit up at the sight approaching him. Robin walked over in the clothes he had given her. Her long tanned legs poking out from the shorts and the shirt complimenting her chest brought him back to the arousing thoughts of sharing the couch with her.

"And I'm supposed to sleep with that in the same room?"

"Yep, good night." She kissed him passionately and returned to the couch.

"You are a cruel, cruel women, Miss Masters."

"And you love it, Mr. Scott." Robin covered herself with a thin blanket and turned on her side. Jacob laid there and watched her for a short while before falling asleep himself.

65

The first thing Jacob did the next morning was shower and dress quietly while Robin slept. The cute look on her face and the quiet breathing made him smile. He made some coffee for her and was joined by Connor who was refreshed and ready to play at school.

"Your mother sent me a message and said that she'll be over in a half hour to bring you some fresh clothes and take you to school."

"Thank you for taking care of me, Mr. Scott. Your house is awesome."

"Thanks Connor. And you can call me Jacob."

""Is Robin your girlfriend?" he asked curiously.

"Well, not yet but I plan on asking her later today."

"She's pretty. If you take her down by the water and hold her hand, she'll fall in love with you and then she'll be your girlfriend," Connor said.

Jacob laughed, "Yeah I think I just might do that. How about some breakfast? I make a mean Cheese Omelet."

"That's my favorite breakfast!"

"Well, then one cheese omelet coming up."

Later, Jacob pulled up to Kathy's and got out of the car. The sun was trying to poke out through the large mass of clouds coming over. Rain was on it's way for the weekend. Jacob wondered if the bad weather was a sign of things to come. Kathy's husband was sitting outside on a lawn chair, reading the morning paper. He saw Jacob and waved to the lawyer.

"Good morning Jacob," he said.

"Good morning, is Kathy in?"

"Yeah, she's on the phone right now but go on in. She's been waiting for you."

"Thanks." Jacob walked into the building and saw Kathy sitting behind the counter writing notes down on a pad that the other person on the line. Jacob stood, waiting for his turn and looked around. Her dog had curled up next to the door, chewing on a rawhide bone. He was tempted to pet it but he feared he may not have all his digits back.

"Okay, Earl, I'll talk to you later." Kathy hung up the phone and opened the gate on the counter, allowing Jacob into the back.

"Hey Kathy."

"Morning, Jacob. You look rather peppy for so early in the morning. Little late night rendezvous?"

"I wish. The case is going well. Police have a couple of leads that may pan out to proving my client innocent."

"Good! Saves me the trouble of hunting you down if he does the guilty run."

"Thanks, it makes me feel better," Jacob smirked.

"Okay, so I made a little call and got the case info. You realize that Irwin refused the 10% option?"

"Yeah, that's why I'm coming to you. We've known each other for a few years now."

"Jacob, I'm going to save you the brown nosing session you have planned on me and ask you to give it to me straight."

"My client is innocent. But I need him out of jail in order for him to help me prove his innocence. The real killer came after Doug's assistant last night. Craig Waterford is still in jail. If I can get him out, we can figure out why he's being framed for all this."

"Okay, where's the 'but' in all this?"

"I only have the 10% to give you. I'm good but not two hundred and fifty thousand dollars good."

"You want to play up that favor then?"

"If I can. I would be forever in your debt, Kathy."

"You lawyers are born to butter me up." She paused and scratched her head. Thinking for a moment, Jacob hoped to have her see his way. "Okay fine, but on one condition."

"You've got it, whatever it is."

"If your guy Waterford, turns tail, I get that nice house of yours."

"Deal," Jacob said, holding out his hand. She shook it and handed him a pen. Then she handed him the forms to fill out. He started writing in the information needed and she got up to get another cup of tea.

"Want some Earl Gray tea?"

"No thanks, I've got 2 cups of coffee in me already with another one coming. I need every ounce of caffeine I can get right now."

"Suit yourself."

After an hour of talking and filling out paperwork, Kathy handed Jacob the bail bond and he drove off to the police precinct in order to free Craig. Mac, behind the desk, directed him downstairs to the holding cells. Officer Belanger sat at his desk and greeted Jacob. Jacob handed over the bail bond and signed off on Craig's release. Then he and Belanger walked down to Craig's cell.

"Hey Waterford," Belanger said loudly, "You've made bail."

Craig stood up from his cot and saw Jacob behind the cop. He smiled and waited for Belanger to open the cell door before he could approach the bars. Then he shook his lawyer's hand.

"Thank you for all you've done so far," Craig said to him.

"We're not out of the woods yet. There's a lot to be done today. We've got three days left to solve Doug's murder. You won't stand a chance if you go up before a grand jury with those prints as evidence."

"Okay, so where do we go from here?"

"We're going back to my office. I'll update you on what's happened recently and hopefully the police can use the new lead we have to find out what your part in all this really is."

"I still have no idea how I'm linked to Doug."

"That's the missing piece of the puzzle. But I think I know where to look."

66

Gerald Healy was furious. Everything was falling apart because the other involved could not keep their mouth shut. He stood in his hotel room on the Waterfront and applied more Polysporin to the cuts on his face. The cuts were his main concern. They could identify him with them. His blonde hair was not an issue. But the cuts had to be covered.

Healy opened the small container with the spirit gum he had used before. Using the thin brush, he applied some over the cuts and then began applying the quick hardening flesh latex on each. He made the latex smooth and realistic by sculpting it with a thin tool he found in San Francisco years ago. The key was to make it seem less like a bump and more like his cheek.

It took him twenty minutes to make the cuts disappear. Once they were it was on to the hair. He knew the boy was old enough to describe him. So he would have to make himself look different. Healy took the scissors that he bought along with the cheap razors from the nearby drug store. He began cutting the hair into the bathroom sink. Once it was short enough, he used the razors to remove the rest, giving him a bald and clean look.

Once he was done, he stepped back and admired his work. The change was noticeable and made his appearance different from what they expected. All the better for him.

What was still a problem was the amount of loose ends that the other had caused with their stupidity. They had to be tied up if Healy wanted to get out of this free and not linked to this case at all. And if anyone were to get that taken care of it was him.

He sat down at the small round table placed by the window that overlooked the Hudson River and the New York Skyline. His notes on all the people involved were too much for a measly task like Doug Martin. He had to take care of them immediately before this got out of hand any further. He cursed the other and made a list of which loose ends to tie up first. And he knew just where to start.

67

The clouds darkened as the morning went on. Jacob pulled up to the front of the deli. Craig had requested that they stop so that he could see Jackie before they went to the law firm. Jacob didn't see any harm in that. It had been several days since Craig was able to walk free.

"But make sure it's not too long. I want to be back there before the detectives show up to question Reynolds."

"Who?" Craig asked.

"I'll explain it on the way there. Just go and say hi to Jackie for me."

"I will," Craig said, opening the car door. He stepped out onto Washington and looked up. He had hoped to see the sun shining down and wondered if the grey clouds were a foretelling of what was to come. He stopped thinking negatively and walked into the deli.

The jingling bell caused the talk in the deli to halt. All heads turned to look at the identity of the person entering. Craig saw Jackie right away, always behind the register, giving every customer a smile with her service. Her eyes widened at the sight of him and her mouth dropped open. She covered her mouth and ran around the counter to jump into his arms. Her arms gripped around him tight. He hugged her back, not wanting to ever let go.

"Is it over?" she asked him.

"Not yet but it's almost," he told her, "The police have some leads that may pan out from what Jacob was telling me."

"That's good, right?"

"Yes," he smiled, "It's very good. He wants me to help him back at the law offices. But I needed to see you first."

"I'm glad that you did."

Connie, Jonathan and Mike came forward and welcomed Craig back. He thanked them and followed them back behind the counter. Connie took over the cash register and Jackie went with Craig into the back office. He sat down on the couch and she cuddled up next to him.

"I can't wait for all this to be over and we can return to our normal lives."

"We're all trying to help you not have to worry about the deli while this is happening, sweetie," Jackie said to him.

"I wasn't worried. I have faith in everyone here and I know how much of a family the team here has become. I hope you're doing okay, with the baby."

"I was at the doctor's yesterday. He was telling me that the stress is not good for the baby and that I'd have to try to take some relaxing time in order to keep the baby healthy."

"I'll make you a deal, if you work on relaxing for the baby's sake, I'll work on clearing my name on this murder charge as soon as possible. Okay?"

"Deal," she said, kissing him. She hugged him again and he enjoyed the moment. To be in her arms again was the best feeling. But like Jacob had told him minutes ago, he was not out of the woods yet. And he had to do everything he could in order to find those who framed him for Doug's murder.

"I should get going. Jacob is outside waiting for me. I'll be back later this afternoon. Then we can go home together."

"That sounds great. I love you, Craig."

"I love you too, Jackie."

She walked him to the front door and led him out to Jacob's car. He opened the door and Jackie leaned in and waved to Jacob.

"You make sure he comes back to me," she told him.

"Not to worry," Jacob told her, "He's in good hands with me."

"I'll be okay," Craig said, "I promise."

"I'll hold you to that," she said, kissing him again.

Craig got into the car and Jackie watched him drive away. She wished all of this had never happened. She wished that the only problem was the lack of cooked ham in the deli. But she knew that it would only be over when the real killer was caught. And who knew when that would happen.

Jackie returned inside and Connie approached her, "We're out of coffee grounds."

"Okay, grab 20 dollars from the register and I'll go get some more from down the block," Jackie said. Connie opened the register and pulled out a 20 dollar bill, replacing it with a note stating that the funds missing went to coffee grounds. She handed Jackie the money.

"Okay, I'll be right back."

Jackie walked down the block, her mind elsewhere again. She thought nothing of being afraid until a hand clamped over her mouth from behind.

68

Brett and Josh walked into the Reynolds and Hoffman main lobby and up to the receptionist. Josh flashed his badge to the receptionist and Brett explained that they were there to speak to Mark Reynolds.

"Is Mr. Reynolds expecting you?"

"No, he's not but we have some questions regarding the Doug Martin case. It's urgent that we speak to him as soon as possible."

The receptionist looked at Josh like he requested that pigs begin flying. She dropped her eyes to the phone in front of her and dialed Reynolds' extension. She waited a minute for him to answer and responded when he did.

"Sorry to bother you, sir, but I have a Detective-?"

"Foster and Raghetti," Brett added.

"There's a Detective Foster and Raghetti here looking to speak to you. They say it's about Doug Martin. Yes sir. I will. Thank you, sir." The receptionist disconnected the call and looked up at the detectives. "Mr. Reynolds will be out in a minute. Please have a seat," she said, pointing out the waiting chairs to the left of her desk. Brett walked over to the seats and stood there, waiting for Reynolds. Josh took the invitation to sit and stretched his legs out. Brett paced back and forth slowly, taking in the layout of the lobby. The lobby had an elegant yet modern look to it. The red and black colors ran parallel from one side of the large room to the other. The clouded glass behind the front desk prevented him from seeing nothing but silhouettes of the other lawyers walking from one office to another like ants in an ant farm.

Then he looked back at Josh, who sat in the lounge chair like there was nothing wrong. But he wasn't aware of the events at Brett's home the night before. He didn't know the woman that he still loved was being loved by someone else. Brett knew this was going to go wrong but his own desires had gotten in the way. And he dreaded the moment that he would be forced to finally tell Josh what was going on. Yet now was not the time. Now was time to work.

Reynolds finally arrived and walked out from behind the clouded glass. Josh saw him and stood up casually. Reynolds was dressed to the nines. The detective guessed Armani was on the label in the jacket lining. The lawyer reminded Brett of a young Michael Douglas. His hair was dark brown and slicked back in a wave. His face was soft yet linear in shape. And his eyes shot a gaze of power into your soul when they were laid upon you.

"I apologize for the wait, detectives. There's no rest for the wicked, is there?" Reynolds smiled and held his hand out. Brett played into it and shook.

"Not for the criminals," Brett replied.

"Or those who defend the guilty," Josh muttered. Brett could see that Reynolds heard the crack and gracefully ignored it.

"So what can I do for you?'

"Is there somewhere we can go and talk?"

"Yes, absolutely. This way," Reynolds led them into the back and through the door that led into the large meeting room that was used to announce Doug's murder to the others in the firm. Josh looked around, impressed by the oak finish on the long table and leather cushions on each of the chairs.

"Please sit," Reynolds suggested to the duo. They sat and he followed them.

"Mr. Reynolds," Brett began, "Can we ask where you were on Saturday night when Doug was murdered?"

"Why, I was at home. My wife can attest to that. We catered to some friends the whole night. May I ask why you're questioning me on it?"

"What about your relationship to Doug? Did you two get along or was there some butting heads between the ways you thought?"

"Detectives, I have nothing to hide. The professional relationship between Doug Martin and I was perfect. Doug's way of thinking reminded me of myself when I was just starting out in the business. I personally thought of him as my protégé."

"So, there was never a time where you and he did not agree?"

"Well, in the beginning, Doug was wet behind the ears. He needed some guidance but we never fought over our decisions."

"And there was never a case where he disagreed with your way of thinking?"

"Where are you two going with this?" Reynolds said, defensively. Brett knew that they would need to start reaching the home stretch before Reynolds cut the questioning short.

Raghetti decided to cut to the chase and said, "We found a recording of you and Doug arguing over a case. We're just trying to see if it has anything to do with his murder."

"I'm sorry, but any case Doug and I discussed was a private conversation. Regardless of what you may think but our clients information and cases are confidential. And good luck asking a judge for a warrant on any case information." Reynolds sat back and relished in the fact that he had halted any further questioning, hiding behind legalities.

"That's fine," Brett smiled, standing up and stepping away from the table, "I think the lead we have is strong enough without any other evidence."

"I'd also like to get the original and any copies of that recording as it does breach client confidentiality and is property of Reynolds and Hoffman."

"That's fine. I hope you can bear with us and the time it takes to gather that."

"I can get a judge on the phone within two minutes that will make your policing lives hell. Your call, detectives."

"I believe we're done here," Brett said to Josh, "Thank you for your time, Mr. Reynolds."

"I'll be seeing you soon."

"You can bet on that," Josh added. Then the two detectives left the office and returned to the parking lot across from the high rise building. Brett walked back to the car and stopped before getting in.

He looked over the roof and asked, "What do you think?"

"I think that guy covered his ass with the rules. And it's going to be hard to pin this all on him. But there's no mistaking that he knew about Doug's murder before we did."

"That's what I'm afraid of," Brett said, knowing that the hardest part was yet to come.

69

Freezing in place, Jackie felt fear overcome every muscle in her body. The stench of oily sweat from the hand covering her mouth made her gag. The body of the hand's owner pressed up against her back and she clenched up, trying to create some distance from the man that was grabbing her. She felt something poke into the right side of her back.

"Don't make a move," the man said, "Don't fight, don't scream and don't make me kill you here."

The hand moved away from her mouth and Jackie kept her lips clenched tight. She did not want to move from the spot she stood in. Then the idea of turning around to see the face of the one who had created all this chaos for her and Craig popped into her head. It was help with all the questions.

"I know what you're thinking. But you have to remember the baby." Jackie felt the hot breath on her neck as the hand now went to her belly.

"Please, what is it that we've done to you?"

"You've never done anything to me."

"Then why are you doing this to us?"

"Because I can. Now you are going to shut up and come with me. Listen and do as you're told and you will be fine. Don't and you'll never see your baby born. Do you understand?"

Jackie nodded. The she was guided over to the front entrance to an apartment building that she had been passing. Once inside the front door, the man placed a cloth over her eyes. Then he took her arm and guided her back out and over to the street. She heard a car door open and then the man grabbed her head and pushed her into his car. She fell on her side and was yanked upright and buckled into the seat. She heard the door close and thought about tearing off the blindfold and looking her captor in the eye before she threw the door open and ran back to the deli. But the opening of the driver's side door kept her immobile.

Jackie heard the man sit down next to her and close the door. The clinking of the keys on the keyring told her that he was going to start it and drive away. The thoughts of where he would take her flooded her mind along with all the questions that she had. She imagined ending up in an empty warehouse where he would do unspeakable things to her and then leave her dropped on the side of a road like a piece of garbage, barely alive.

"Please, we've done nothing to you and I haven't seen your face."

"I'll admit, you've done nothing to me but you have seen my face. You just don't remember me."

She *had* seen his face? Was he someone that she met once?

"If we haven't done anything to you then why are you doing this to us?"

"I told you already. You should listen better. Now, shut your mouth and stay still. If you speak or try to move, I will gut you like a fish. And I'm sure you know how well I use a knife."

Jackie remained still for the sake of the baby in her belly. She, instead, tried to remember the number of turns and outside noises for the police. He made a left turn and made a stop. Then he turned left again. He was making a turn back uptown, she figured. Then he drove straight for several minutes and made a right turn. She imagined that he was headed for the water. After a minute, he pulled to the side and parked the car. Where were they? Was he going to take her out now? The beeps of a cell phone being dialed broke the deadly silence.

"Now remember to keep quiet until I tell you to. Do you understand?" Jackie nodded. She listened intently to the one side of the conversation.

70

The ring of Jacob's cell phone surprised Craig. They had just arrived at the building and Jacob parked the car in the lot for workers across the street. Jacob grabbed the phone from the pocket in the front of the dashboard and looked at the display screen. He made a face at the unknown number that appeared on the screen. But he answered it anyway.

"Jacob Scott."

"Mr. Scott, let me speak to Craig Waterford."

"I'm sorry, but he's not with me right now," Jacob bluffed, "Is there something I can help you with?"

"Don't play games with me, lawyer. He's there with you. Now let me speak to him or else I will be forced to hurt his wife."

Jacob froze at the threat. Then he looked over at Craig with a frightened face and held out the phone in his direction. Craig looked at the phone confused.

"What?" Craig asked.

"It's for you."

Craig took the phone and placed it to his ear. Before he could say hello, the voice on the other line began to speak.

"Hello Craig. Don't talk, just listen to what I have to say." Craig felt a shiver down his back. The voice was haunting yet very real. He could tell that it was the one who had murdered Doug Martin. He did not say a word in reply.

"Very good. Now, you will do as I say because if you don't then your family will pay the price of your disobedience. And I'll prove to you how serious I am." The phone fell silent and then another voice came through the receiver.

"Craig," Jackie pleaded, "Please do as he says. I'm okay. I love." Her voice vanished from the phone as he imagined the killer pulling the phone away from her. Then his voice returned to the line.

"Admit to the murder. Do the jail time. Ask no questions. Obey those requests and your family will be allowed to live. With good behavior, you should be out in no time. And tell your lawyer to back the fuck off. For the baby's sake."

The call was then disconnected. Craig slowly pulled the phone away from his ear and stared at it. His heart stopped short by the request. Jacob placed a hand on Craig's shoulder and spoke. But Craig was too mesmerized by the call to have heard him. The killer had just given him the ultimatum. Either give up his freedom, or his family. There was no choice.

"He told me to give myself up or else my family would be in danger."

"What?"

"I confess. I killed Doug Martin."

71

Robin poured a cup of coffee for Jacob. The lawyer and his client had made it upstairs to his office in order to go over what had just happened. Craig sat on the couch gazing off into space. Jacob sat and watched for any response from him. He was worried about Craig.

"Craig, would you like some coffee?" Robin asked him.

Craig looked up at her like one would a complete stranger and said, "No."

"Craig," Jacob called him, "You have to listen. We'll get the police to place Jackie in a safe house. You can't give up now. We're getting closer by the day."

"I can't fight anymore, Jacob. I'm not jeopardizing the life of my wife and child. I'm telling the police that I did it and I'll go to jail."

"Look, I can't say I understand how you're feeling. But I won't say that you should just give up. This is your life. You control it. Remember that."

"Look at how easy it was to grab Jackie, Jacob! I just left her minutes ago and he already had her in his hands before we could reach the lobby of your building!"

"I'll call in Foster and Raghetti and see what they can do for us."

"No, just call them in to arrest me."

"Okay. As your lawyer, I can warn you till next week but the decision is yours. I'll call them right now." Jacob picked up the phone and dialed the precinct. When the desk sergeant picked up, he asked for Brett's desk. The desk sergeant transferred him over and the phone rang again.

"Detective Foster, homicide," Brett answered.

"Detective, it's Jacob Scott. We've got a problem here."

"What's the problem?"

"My client wants to confess to the murder of Doug Martin."

"Are you kidding? I thought we just found evidence to clear him. What the hell happened?" Jacob explained the phone call and could hear Brett relaying the information to Raghetti.

"Dammit. We'll be right there. But tell your client we're not arresting him."

"I'll let him know. Thank you." Jacob hung up and looked over at Craig. Craig looked up at him, defeated. Jacob looked at the old friend and felt pity for him. No one should have to be put through what Craig was. And he vowed to himself again to not stop in finding out who was behind all this.

"They're not arresting you," Jacob said to Craig, "They know you're innocent now. Between what happened at Kristie's and listening to the audio file, their suspicion of you have changed for the better."

"This guy, whoever he is, grabbed Jackie very easily. Who's to say that he won't do it again when he finds that you won't listen and back off? And then if he kills her next time?"

"We will not allow that to happen. You have to trust me, Craig. I've never let you down. Not back in school and definitely not now. You'll get through this just fine. You just have to let me do my job. Okay?"

Craig rubbed his hands together, thinking. Staring at the floor, he thought of the pros and cons of letting Jacob take the wheel on this. On the one hand, Jacob had dealt with people like this before in his line of work. But then again, it had been a long time since Craig had seen Jacob. He was asked to place the lives of Jackie and their baby in the hands of someone that he hadn't seen in years.

"Listen, Craig, I went and bailed you out from my own pocket. If that doesn't show that I'm on your side, then I don't know what else to say."

"You paid the whole bail amount?"

"God, no, I'm not that rich. But I called in a favor and only paid 10% of it."

Craig was speechless. He did not expect Jacob to do that. To have put up twenty-five thousand dollars up for him was above the requirement for a lawyer, let alone an old friend.

"I'm sorry," Craig said softly, "I just want to know that Jackie is safe."

"And the police will make sure of it, I promise. But you have to let me keep going. I can't go over your head. You need to give me permission."

"Okay. Go for it."

"Thank you. You and Jackie are my main concern right now. So let me worry about everything."

Kristie walked into the office with a hand full of papers. She held them up and then handed them over to Jacob. Jacob looked them over as Kristie explained them.

"Okay, so I got the list of cases that he was working on and I jotted down the names of the lawyers that took them over."

Jacob skimmed through the list. He skipped the one that he was given and stopped on the two that Chris Delgado was given.

"Do you remember the info on these?"

"Partially. It depends on the case that you're asking about."

"What about the ones that Delgado got? The Rosenvelt and Patterson cases?"

"The Patterson one was a divorce case. There was nothing special about that. The Rosenvelt one was a criminal case. I'm pretty sure that it was the liquor store robbery I told you about before," Kristie said. Jacob stared down at the list and thought over the Sandford case that another lawyer, Barry Graves, had been given. He remembered hearing about that one. It was a case where the employee of shipping company was charged with embezzlement.

"Okay, let me go talk to Delgado and see if he can let me look over the notes on that case. Robin, can you please talk to Barry and see what you can find out about the Sandford case? Let's see if we can figure out what case Doug was talking to Reynolds about in the audio."

"What can I do to help?" Craig asked. Jacob looked at him, Craig's eyes gave him the look of a lost child in a shopping center.

"For now, I want you to call Jackie and see how she is doing. Make sure she's back at the deli where she's safe for now. And tell her to stay there until the detectives show up. Then I want you to relax and rest until I need your help. I'll be back in a few minutes." Jacob looked over to Robin and they left the office together.

"I'm going to get some coffee," Kristie said to Craig, "Would you like some?"

"No thank you. I'll take some water if you have any."

"I'll bring it right back."

"Thank you. And I'm sorry your family got involved in this."

"It's not your fault. You didn't get Doug involved." Kristie smiled, trying to be strong and not think of Dean and Connor

"That's true. But I still don't get the link between your boss and I."

"Maybe the only link is the killer. Seems like it's plausible right now. That's the only thing we've found so far."

"I'm going to call my wife now, if that's okay."

"I'll go get you some water then." Kristie left the office and Craig picked up the phone on Jacob's desk. He dialed the deli's number and prayed that she was alright. The phone rang twice. Then it rang a third time. He urged someone at the deli to pick the phone up. Four rings. Five rings. He pictured the deli in flames due to the killer hurting him further. Six rings. Please pick up the phone, he prayed. He just wanted to hear Jackie's voice again. He wanted to breathe, knowing that she was out of harm's way. He didn't want to break down in Jacob's office again.

"Anthony's Deli," Connie answered.

"Oh God, Connie. It's Craig, is Jackie there?"

"Yeah, Craig, she's okay. She's an emotional mess but she's not hurt."

Craig finally let out the breath that he held in since he dialed the number. "Can I speak to her please?"

72

Delgado was returning from the cafeteria when Jacob reached his office. The Cuban lawyer held his large thermos of coffee and a bagel from Dunkin Donuts that the firm supplied to the workers every day. He munched on the bagel and nodded to Jacob. Jacob allowed his co-worker to enter the office first and followed him in. Chris walked around his desk and sat down, placing his thermos on his right and gently laid out a paper towel to place the bagel on.

"What can I do for you today, Scott?" Chris asked after he swallowed his mouthful of bagel.

"I had some questions about the one case you got from Doug's stack."

"If you're looking for the Mrs. Ortiz page, I never found it. You should try his assistant, Marks."

"Oh no I found that, thanks. I wanted to know your thoughts on the Rosenvelt case."

"What about it?"

Jacob had to take it carefully. He didn't want to seem too desperate for the info. It would throw Delgado's wall up and he may go to Reynolds to complain. Jacob wanted to keep this quiet until he had enough to talk to Reynolds with. Anything sooner and Reynolds may have time to create a defense and use it to attack him.

"You think the guy did it?"

"No, not with what Doug found."

"What did he find?" Jacob was now curious.

"Well, he had gone back over all the interviews between the liquor store night staff and the police. There was a comment made that the cops missed when they took the night staff statements. The one girl swore that the robber had light green eyes when he looked at her. The police noted it as being pale eyes."

"So?"

"So, Devito is an albino. There's no way he could have green eyes unless he bought a pair of contacts, which looking into it, he never did."

"Then the case is pretty much shut."

"Yeah," Delgado said, pausing to take a bite of his bagel again, "Guess that's why Reynolds yanked him off the other case to put him on this one." Jacob stopped short. He heard Delgado's comment but had to ask him to repeat it.

"What?"

"Reynolds yanked him off some other case in order for Doug to take care of the Rosenvelt one."

"Why would he do that?"

"You've got me. Maybe Reynolds knows Devito and asked his favorite boy to take special care of the case? You know how Reynolds favored Martin."

Jacob wondered if the case Doug argued with Reynolds about was the Rosenvelt one. Could Reynolds have put Doug on this case in hopes of Doug looking the other way? Jacob would have to look into Maurice Devito and see if there was any relationship with Reynolds. He felt himself getting closer to the truth behind Doug's murder and a surge of triumph ran through his blood.

"Why the interest in this case?" Delgado asked him.

"Doug mentioned it to me the week before he was killed. I was just curious about how it was coming along," Jacob said, thinking fast.

"That's it? You bothered me on my bagel break to satisfy your own curiosity? I've got other things more important to work on, Scott. Are you done?"

"I am now. Thanks Delgado, you're a peach." Jacob left Chris' office with a smile. He had found out what he needed and had also annoyed Delgado in the process. It was turning out to be a good morning after all.

73

Judge Germaine Irwin did not like to be disturbed on her lunch break. Being one of only two judges in the city of Hoboken, a town with a population of over forty thousand, her free time was precious. And Josh Raghetti was learning this as he sat outside her chambers waiting to speak to her.

Brett and Josh had decided to look further into getting all of Doug Martin's notes for the case that he had worked on in the past three months. With that information, they were hoping to pinpoint the case that Doug had mentioned in the audio file. Knowing full well that Mark Reynolds was not going to play ball, they decided to request a warrant for the notes.

Josh had gotten the job of talking to the judge as Brett went to see the Assistant District Attorney, Guy Clark, for information about the case. He had noticed that Brett was acting strange but thought that it was just the stress of the case. He knew that Brett had taken on certain cases personally at times but he didn't know what was stressing him out about this case. Josh knew, though, that when Brett wanted to talk about it, he would come to his partner. Until then, Josh would respect his privacy.

It was fifteen minutes of sitting there before Judge Irwin called Josh into her chambers. He walked in and closed the door behind him. Irwin was sitting behind her wide desk. The wall behind her had her law diplomas surrounded by pictures of her family. Her black robe hung to the left of her on an old fashioned coat rack. She sat straight in her chair and looked up from her lunch at Raghetti.

"Afternoon, Detective. How can I help you today?"

"Hello, your Honor. I was hoping to get your assistance with a warrant today. It concerns the case that you've had earlier this week. You may remember it, the State versus Craig Waterford case?"

"I do remember it. What are you needing?"

"My partner and I have found the audio recording that was made by the victim, Doug Martin. We believe that it points the finger away from Craig Waterford and points it to one of the other cases that he was working on. We were hoping to get all the notes he had on the cases that he worked on in the last three months."

"And you asked the partners of the firm that he worked for?"

"We did. We spoke to Mark Reynolds of Reynolds and Hoffman. His voice is on the audio clip arguing with Doug Martin. He flat out declined to hand them over. Now I understand why he did so, but I firmly believe that those notes will point us in the path of Doug Martin's true killer. That's why I'm here in front of you today."

"So you want me to sign a warrant to allow you to take personal and confidential information from an esteemed, respected law firm to point the finger at one of their clients?" Irwin stood up from her chair and placed her hands flat on her desk. Her eyebrows, raised in astonish.

"If you want to put it that way, yes, your Honor."

Irwin laughed. She walked around her desk and sat on the edge of the front. Crossing her arms, she stared down at Josh. The look made Raghetti feel like a scolded child. He smiled awkwardly at her, returning the raised eyebrows back.

"Let me tell you about Mark Reynolds," she explained, "I've known him since he passed the Bar exam. He runs a tight ship over there and he has worked hard in building that firm up to being the most respectful and prominent law firm in Hudson County. To even think that he would allow someone in his firm to break the law is a joke."

"I never said that he would, your Honor. I just think that Doug Martin's murder may be linked to a case he was working on. We weren't looking at Mark Reynolds, we were only finding him to be an obstacle in closing this case."

"I know how to read between the lines, Detective Raghetti. You may not have said it, but you implied it. Let me explain something to you in case you do not know me. I hate office politics. The backstabbing, the gossip, the stepping on others to make it further up the corporate ladder. I have never once done anything cruel to further my career. And I don't plan on starting just to help you pin a murder on a dear friend of mine."

"I understand, your Honor. And I apologize for the misunderstanding. Thank you for your time." Josh promptly stood up and left Judge Irwin's chambers. When he closed the door behind him, he cursed to himself. It was just another roadblock on the path to the truth. Without the warrant, it would only make getting the evidence harder. But he and Brett would get it in the end. They were good at their jobs and he knew it.

Josh called Brett on his cell phone to see what he had found. Brett's voice mail picked up, telling him that Brett was still talking to Guy Clark. That was a good sign. Perhaps his partner was getting more than what he had received.

Josh left the Hoboken city hall and walked back to the precinct, plotting his next step in learning the identity of Doug Martin's killer.

74

I need to find out everything we can on Maurice Devito," Jacob told Robin and Kristie, "More importantly, we need to see if there's any link between him and Reynolds."

Robin and Kristie sat in Jacob's office and the three had gone over what they had found talking to Delgado and Graves. Robin's conversation brought nothing as the Sandford case was about a young adult accused of marking up a series of apartment buildings with spray paint. It was a simple case and not one that Doug would have argued over with Reynolds. So Jacob had scratched that one off the list. That left the Rosenvelt Liquors case.

"Robin, check Devito's schooling. See where he attended and if Reynolds was in the same class. Kristie, run a criminal check on him and see if there's any other charges that Devito had thrown at him. There's got to be a reason why Reynolds put Doug on that case. We find that and we'll have something to use against Reynolds."

"Do you really think Mark had something to do with Doug's murder?" Kristie asked him.

"Right now, I don't know. But he's the only other voice in the audio clip that Doug went out of his way to point you to. If Mark didn't kill Doug, he may know who did. Either way, he's our best hope in clearing Craig of the murder."

"Okay, I'll be at Doug's office working on this if you need me for anything else," Kristie told them and left the office.

Robin sat back in her chair and looked over at Jacob. His head was down in the papers as he tried to absorb the ink on the pages. She didn't know what it was about his hard work and determination but she found him sexy when he got involved in a case. Maybe it was the commitment he put into each case, she thought. He was not afraid to put all he had into something. That was something her previous boyfriends were lacking. She also found herself mesmerized at times by his hazel eyes. They almost sparkled in the sun on a clear day.

Jacob paused and looked up, noticing Robin still there looking at him. A smile slowly spread across her face. It was a smile that he looked forward to. Something that kept the day bright and cleared the clouds of work away.

"What?" he asked.

"Nothing," she replied, "Just enjoying the view before I go back to work."

"Cute," he said.

"Oh I agree."

"So what do you think about Reynolds?"

"What's to think? He seems to live business. This place is his life. He eats, breathes and sleeps this firm."

"Do you think he'd risk putting it in danger in order to keep it running?"

"You'd have to ask him."

"Yeah I think I might have to. But I need that information on Devito before I do."

"Yes, sir." Robin got up and slowly walked to the door of the office. She swayed her hips as she did. Then she stopped at the door, not turning around when she asked him, "Like what you see?"

Jacob, who had stood there and watched her walk away, had been caught admiring her body. "Yes. Yes, I do," he admitted.

"Just checking." And with that Robin left Jacob alone to work on getting information on Maurice Devito.

75

Renee, Guy Clark's assistant, greeted Brett when he walked into the spacious corner office. Seeing the assistant once again wearing a blouse that promoted breast implants, did not surprise the detective. He wondered, though, how she could sit with her back straight in her chair for so long every day.

"How can I help you?" she asked him.

"I'm here to see D.A. Clark, please. Let him know Detective Foster is here," Brett told her, showing his badge.

"Right away, Detective. Please have a seat while I let him know."

"Thanks." Brett decided to stand instead and wait for Clark. He took out his cell phone and turned it off for the time being. He didn't want to be interrupted while he was talking to Clark.

Foster didn't like hitting a wall on a case, like they did. They had a lead but no way to reach it without the notes that Reynolds was holding from them. For him to go to Clark for advice was not common for a case like this. But Brett had a feeling that, even though he had a reputation for stirring the pot, that Clark would actually help him out this one time.

Clark finally stepped out from his office after a few minutes of making Brett wait. He shook Brett's hand with a smile like a car salesman would if he saw a wad of bills in Brett's pocket.

"Detective Foster, right? How are you doing today?"

"Had better days, Mr. Clark."

"Please, call me Guy."

"Okay, Guy. Do you have a few minutes? I was hoping to ask you a few questions about a case I'm investigating."

"I've got all the time in the room for my fellow law enforcers. Please, come into my office and we'll chat." Guy led Brett back into his office and offered him a seat in front of his desk. Guy sat down and kicked his feet up on the table. "Lay it on me," he said.

"Well, I'm sure you're familiar with the Craig Waterford case?"

"Waterford? The guy who was charged with the lawyer's murder? Sure, what about it?"

"What's the one thing that is pushing him to jail permanently?"

"That's pretty obvious. It's the prints. My whole case revolves around the fact that his prints are at the scene."

"So if the prints were made inadmissible, you'd have nothing?"

"Absolutely. If Waterford left no prints behind, you'd have no proof of him ever being there. Pardon my asking, detective, but you should already know this. Why are you asking?"

"Because I'm trying to get the court aspect of it. Now if the audio left behind by Martin were to be found and pointed the finger away from Waterford and at someone of some standing in the business, would you have something to use to bring the true killer to court?"

"Depends on what the audio states. If it's of two guys yelling, the judge would toss it out in a second. Now if it was of the murder taking place, then you have gold. What's on the audio clip?"

"It's Doug Martin arguing with Mark Reynolds about a case he was assigned to."

"That's it?'

"Yeah."

"Sorry Detective but that's as important to the case as a pile of dog crap. It does nothing to point the finger away from Waterford."

"What if there were more to the audio, like evidence linked to the audio clip about the oversight of evidence on a case?"

"Detective, forgive me for being blunt, but are you asking me to help you destroy my case against Waterford? You know I can't do that. If the evidence points to Waterford, then he did it. I represent the state and will fight for it."

"But if Waterford is innocent and was framed for the murder?"

"Then he should get himself a better lawyer than that goof, Scott."

Brett gritted his teeth. He hated this man and everything he stood for. Guy Clark was a joke and did not understand why he was in this position.

But Brett had an ace up his sleeve. He would help Brett whether he liked it or not.

"You don't remember me, do you?"

"Should I? Did I have you as a witness in a court case?"

"Not quite," Brett said in a serious tone. He didn't want to do this but the life of an innocent man was on the line. He would not be able to live with himself if he didn't do all he could to help Craig Waterford. Guy picked up on the serious tone and stopped being all friendly. He, too, became serious, wondering what game Foster was playing.

"What are you getting at, Detective?"

"Do you remember what happened on Tonnelle Avenue in Jersey City, say three years ago?"

Guy paused, thinking back to anything that may have happened to him on that busy highway stretch. Then it hit him like a ton of bricks. His mouth opened slightly in surprise. Brett saw that he did remember.

"You do, don't you? A young prostitute by the name of Brittney was found in your passenger seat, all doped up with you behind the wheel, blowing a .1? Sound familiar?"

"That, that was you?"

"Fresh out of training," Brett smiled, "I remember it getting swept under the rug as well. It would be a real shame for that to get out now, especially now that you're the big Assistant District Attorney."

Guy's eyes closed into slits. He knew he was being blackmailed. His lips opened to reveal his grinding teeth. Brett saw that he was getting angry.

"What do you want?" Guy asked in a low growl.

"I want your help in clearing Craig Waterford. He is innocent."

"Let me guess, your gut told you this?"

"No, the evidence did. But for court, it's not enough."

"It's the prints. Explain how the prints got there and you've cleared your client."

"Thanks, Clark. I knew there was a reason why you're so likeable." Brett patted Guy on the shoulder and left the office. He stopped at Renee's desk, about to ask her about Guy's treatment of her, but continued walking. He had stirred the pot enough. No need to knock it off the stove, he thought.

76

Every piece of information the three of them found on Maurice Devito brought them to the same place, a dead end. Jacob sat the women down with him and they all went over the information they had found one at a time. Robin was the first to go. She explained that Devito had grown up in Bergen County in a nice and quiet town called Englewood where he attended Dwight Morrow High School and then went on to attend Fairleigh Dickinson University where he got a Masters in Accounting.

"There would have been no way that Devito would have met up with Reynolds, unless they met a party or something," she said.

"That's right," Jacob added, "Reynolds attended Seton Hall Law. That's in Newark. And Fairleigh Dickinson University is in Teaneck. What about Devito's criminal record?"

"Besides the accusation on the Rosenvelt robbery, Maurice Devito had nothing but a speeding ticket back in 2002. And he paid it without a fight. There's no criminal record of Devito anywhere in the system before this case," Kristie reported.

"Then why would Reynolds throw Doug on that case? What's so special about it?" Jacob thought out loud, "What about the witnesses on it? Is there something strange about the robbery itself?"

"I have copies of the case file." Kristie pulled a folder off the top of her small pile of papers. She handed the folder to Jacob who opened it immediately and flipped through the notes.

"What about the evidence?" Robin suggested, "The conversation that Doug taped mentioned evidence."

"There's the video cameras in the store. There's no way they could be altered. What about the weapon? Was there anything off about it?"

Jacob read the notes in the files concerning all the evidence gathered in the robbery. There were the video cameras which were down that night due to new cameras being installed. Next was the weapon, a .45 automatic pistol that was found in a garbage can two blocks from the store, in the direction of Devito's home. And then there was the ski mask that was found in the same garbage can, a strand of Devito's hair was attached to it.

"Okay," Jacob read out to the women, "The weapon had been wiped clean of fingerprints. But there was the ski mask that the night staff of the store remember the robber wearing. That was also found with the gun in the garbage can. A strand of Devito's hair was found on the ski mask."

"Was the hair planted?" Robin asked.

"Not sure, but looking at the crime photos, the ski mask was found under some other garbage in the can. But it was a public garbage can so it proves nothing. And the fact that Devito is an albino proves again that he didn't do it because the night staff remembers the robber having green eyes. Devito has pale blue eyes."

"Then what are we missing?"

"Maybe something that wasn't picked up or listed as inadmissible?"

"Perhaps one of us should visit the liquor store?" Jacob thought. If one of them went into the store with fresh eyes, they might find something that Doug did as well. Jacob was getting stir crazy sitting in the office and going over all their information over and over. He looked out the window and saw that sun was already headed west away from the New York City skyline. Most of the day was already over and still they were no where closer to the truth then they were this morning.

"Maybe you should talk to Reynolds," Kristie wondered.

"And say what? Hey, Doug taped an argument between you and him that we believe may have been the reason that he was killed. Why did you do it?" Jacob replied sarcastically.

"Well, not in such a forward way but, yes."

"She may have a good idea," Robin agreed.

"How? It's nuts."

"No," Robin offered, "If you go in and ask him about the Devito case, he may slip up and reveal something that he was actually trying to hide."

"He's never going to fall for it. He's a partner for a reason," Jacob laughed. The women thought it would be so easy. But Jacob knew better. Reynolds would never fall for something so obvious.

"Jacob, Reynolds is a man. He's proud, territorial and power hungry. If you go in there acting like you have the bigger unit, he's going to stomp and try to show you his is bigger. And then you hit him when his pants are down," Robin said. She looked him in the eye and spoke without moving her mouth. Jacob knew what she was saying. And as crazy as it sounded, he thought it just might work. Reynolds went to a great trouble pinning Doug's murder on Craig. He would be proud that the police were having such a hard time trying to find the real killer with no good leads. And if Jacob were to go in hinting that he knew about Reynolds involvement, Reynolds would prove that he didn't. And in doing so, he would reveal how he did.

"I'll be right back," Jacob said, leaving the office with his chest out.

"He's pretty hot when he gets confident," Robin snickered.

77

Melvin enjoyed the evening shifts when the majority of people in the precinct went home for the day. It allowed him to break out the Sirius Satellite Radio and switch on one of his favorite channels, The Virus. In the evening, the channel replayed the Opie and Anthony morning show. Rude and crude, the talk show hosts with their comedian co-host, Jimmy Norton, made Melvin laugh. He stood over the cases that came in that day and looked over which to go over first.

But before he could pick one from the pile, Brett and Josh walked in. He looked over at the detectives and saw that they were there for business, not a friendly visit.

"Evening gents. What can the mad scientist do for you tonight?"

"Do you have the print from the Doug Martin murder still?" Josh asked.

It was odd for them to ask for evidence that was already processed, but it was not uncommon when the cops were at a dead end. Often, they would come back to the crime lab and ask to go over the evidence once more in the event they missed something. Melvin never missed anything but a request was a request.

"I sure do," Melvin said to them, turning around. He went over to the filing cabinet and opened the second drawer. He ran his fingers through the numerous folders inside and stopped midway through. "Here we are, Doug Martin." Melvin took the folder and opened it up onto the desk between them. Brett and Josh looked over the pieces of evidence and photos they had taken. Josh found the print and held it up.

"We need you to analyze the print again. But this time we need you to analyze the substances on the print and the blood it was in."

"The substances on the print? That's a unique request."

"We want to see if there is any particles that may point out that it's not really Craig Waterford's print," Brett explained further.

"Wait," Melvin waved his hands in front of him, trying to understand what they were getting at, "Didn't we match the prints to Waterford already?"

"Yeah but we don't think Waterford put them there."

"So you think the prints were placed on the briefcase somehow?"

"Exactly."

Melvin raised his eyebrows in surprise. Then he lowered them, nodding his head. "I get it. Very interesting twist. I'll get right on it." He shook his finger at the two. "You guys, you're good."

Brett and Josh left the crime lab and headed back downstairs. Brett looked over at Josh and felt his stomach turn somersaults. It was now or never.

"Hey, let's go grab a bite to eat while we wait for Melvin to finish that. I've got to talk to you about something," Brett said.

"Yeah, sure. I'm starving and in the mood for some Italian." Josh smiled at his partner. Brett hoped that the smile was still there on his face after he told him about Angie.

78

"Come in," Mark Reynolds told the person at his office door. He was getting ready to leave for the day and was hoping that the person was not going to prevent him from doing that. Being a partner, he had had his fill of twenty-hour work days. But the fact that he was heading his own law firm with Hoffman, he had others to do that for him now. Today was different. He had been there for almost twelve hours now, working on the case he had taken over for an old friend.

Reynolds was not surprised nor was he happy to see Jacob Scott enter his office. The lawyer was beginning to become a bit of pain in his ass. Going above and beyond to clear the name of the man that had killed one of the best lawyers this firm had ever seen.

"What is it, Jacob? I'm on my way home." Reynolds soured his face at the sight of Jacob and did not hide it from the lawyer.

"I was hoping to ask for some advice on a case I'm trying."

"If it's the Waterford case, then don't bother. The police are confident that he killed Doug. I just can't understand why you would defend someone who murdered a fellow co-worker."

"Because I know that he did not murder Doug. Craig Waterford is innocent. But you already know that, don't you?"

"Excuse me?" Reynolds turned his face quickly to Jacob in shock to hear such an accusation. Jacob could see the anger beginning to boil in Reynolds' face. He hoped that this worked or cause him to scramble like he thought Mark would when he found that the police were closing in.

"The conversation that Doug recorded. I found it. I listened to it before

I handed it over to the police. Was it the Rosenvelt Liquors case that you and Doug were talking about?"

"What Doug and I were speaking about is none of your business, Jacob. Now I suggest if you know what is good for you, you drop it. Remember that I have a lot of connections in this state and the surrounding ones too."

"Did you just threaten me?"

Reynolds sat back and examined the situation. He looked Jacob up and down and thought of the chess moves that were available to him. Jacob could see in his eyes that he was sure that Jacob knew more than he should. It was dangerous for Jacob to jump in like this but he was running out of time. Once the grand jury was under way, finding a way out for Craig would diminish. He figured he'd try to see how good his poker face was.

"I expect your resignation first thing Monday morning. What you're accusing me of is ridiculous and impossible. I've already had the police in here grilling me and you, Jacob, are about as effective a lawyer as the man who does my dry cleaning."

"What I can't figure out is what's so important about the Rosenvelt case?"

"See?" Reynolds said, "That's why you'll never be anything more that a speck on the law world. You know nothing. The Rosenvelt case is a robbery. Plain and simple. There's nothing to the argument that Doug and I had. Now get out of my office."

"Fine. But I'm not done. Doug was a friend of mine and I plan on making sure that the real person who was behind his murder pays for it."

"Then let your client go to jail and be done with it."

Jacob stopped talking and walked out of the office. He returned back to his own and found Robin and Kristie waiting for him, anxious to find out what he had learned. They could tell by the look on his face that it wasn't enough.

"Did he admit anything?" Robin asked.

"No, he got angry for me accusing him of it and threw me out of his office. Oh and he wants me to hand in my papers first thing Monday."

"What? But he's guilty!" Kristie shouted, "The audio clip makes it pretty obvious that he fought with Doug."

"Yes, but it doesn't prove that he killed Doug. Besides, he's too clever to have done it himself. He'd have an alibi to cover his tracks. We know Reynolds wasn't the killer. The guy you two ran into at Doug's apartment was. We just need to link them together now."

"How do we do that without catching the killer?" Robin wondered. "That's our next step."

Mark Reynolds was furious after speaking to Jacob. How dare he accuse him of murdering Doug. Reynolds had truly thought of Doug as a son that he never had. Even though, Doug did not understand Mark's thinking, he still loved the younger lawyer's passion for the profession. Mark balled his hands into fists and slammed them onto the top of his desk. The pain in his knuckles throbbed from the punch but he was too angry to recognize it. He stepped back and thought of his next move. Something had to be done. He knew that Jacob would not back off. Jacob Scott would have to be taken care of.

Mark Reynolds picked up his private line and dialed a number that he had recently come to remember by heart.

79

S o what's been bugging you?" Josh asked, "You haven't been yourself for the last couple of days."

Brett felt tongue-tied now that he was planning to tell Josh. The secret had eaten away at him for the past two days. Knowing his partner and how he felt for his ex-wife was the one thing that kept him hesitating. But he had no choice. If he kept it from Josh any longer, it would make things only worse.

"It's about Angie," Brett sighed.

Josh paused for a moment, almost knowing what was coming. He knew his partner had spoken to Angie for him. Brett was like a brother than a partner. He was part of the family and it didn't scare him off. That's what made Josh so comfortable around Brett. He didn't mind kicking Raghetti's ass when it was needed.

"I was afraid of this," Josh said, cutting Brett off.

"Wait a minute, what did you expect?"

"She's moved on, hasn't she?"

"Yeah, she has." Brett lowered his head, stopping there instead of continuing. He decided to take his time in breaking it to him.

"That's her decision. I've made my mistakes and I can't expect her to wait for me to come to my senses."

"That's very big of you. So where's the real Josh Raghetti?"

"Kiss my ass, Foster," Josh laughed, "Just do me one favor. Did she tell you about the guy she's seeing?"

"I've seen him if that's what you're getting at."

"Is he this buff Jersey Shore looking jag-off?"

"No, definitely not," Brett said, imagining himself in the mirror and shaking his head.

"Is he better looking?"

"Am I better looking than you?"

"Hell no. That's a step down from me."

"Gee, thanks."

"Don't mention it."

The two detectives walked down Washington while the local nightclubs began opening for the warm weekend. Lines were already forming in front of some, like Bahama Mamas and Whiskey Bar. Josh glanced into one as they passed and thought of stopping in for a drink but held himself back. Brett, on the other hand, was ready to down several shots.

"Look, Josh. There's something else."

"What? Angie's into women now?"

"No, no," Brett replied, "It's about who she's seeing now?"

"What is it? Come on, don't hold out on me."

"Angie slept with me." Brett released the secret like a bullet fired from a silencer, quick and unexpected. Josh halted in the middle of the block and stood still. Brett sighed and stopped walking as well. He looked over at Josh, waiting for some kind of response to what he had told his partner. Josh remained there, staring at the cement sidewalk under his feet. Then he spoke, low and deep.

"When?"

"What?" Brett was unable to hear him.

"I asked, when?"

"Wednesday night, when that legal assistant's family was attacked."

"Two days ago. And you didn't think it was important to tell me it was my ex-wife that made you late to the call?"

"I wasn't sure how you'd react. It's not like I was waiting for you two to break up. She came to talk to me and it just happened."

"And you conveniently went along with it. Knowing how I felt about her."

"Hey, I had no intentions of coming between you two but she came on to me. She looked to me for consoling. She had given up on you before she even talked to me."

"So that's okay then? That absolves you of all your sins? You broke the code, asshole. You could have said no, that's Josh's ex. It's wrong for me to nail her. But you didn't. And after I told you that I wanted to get her back."

"This has been eating away at me since. I'm sorry that it happened, but there's nothing I can do to change her mind about taking you back. She doesn't want that life, Josh. Get over it."

Josh heard Brett's comment and had had enough. He lunged at Brett, swinging his right fist and landed a punch into Brett's jaw. Brett's head snapped to the right and he stumbled a few steps, falling onto a nearby parked car. Josh followed Brett over and kept him from recovering. He swung again, bringing his fist upwards this time and hitting his partner in the stomach. Brett coughed all the air out of his lungs and hunched over. He tried getting another breath of air before Josh hit him again but Raghetti's next punch hit Brett in the back, under his ribs and where his kidneys were located. Brett groaned in pain and collapsed to the sidewalk.

At this time, onlookers crowded around them and a few tried to step in. Josh flashed his badge and gun at the crowd and they all backed up a few steps. He then turned back around to Foster. Brett was curled up, coughing in bits of air into his lungs. Josh looked down on him and caught himself from hitting him again.

"You're a real piece of work, Foster. You know that? I'm going to Black tomorrow and requesting a new partner. Someone who doesn't feel the need to fuck my ex-wife." Josh then pushed his way through the crowd and left.

A man from the crowd stepped forward and took Brett by the arm. He helped him to his feet and looked at him.

"Hey, are you okay?" the stranger asked.

"I'm fine, thanks for asking." Brett turned away from the stranger and spit a glob of blood onto the ground.

"Do you want me to call another cop?"

"No, don't worry about it." Brett flashed his own badge at the stranger.

"Nice," someone else from the crowd complained, "Our tax dollars at work. What, you couldn't find any criminals to beat on?"

"You're welcome," Brett coughed out. He knew he had to leave the crowd and get away from the scene before someone broke out their cellphone to take pictures or try to capture it on video so they could throw it out on Youtube. As he stumbled across Washington, his cell phone buzzed. Shocked that it hadn't broken in the fight, he glanced down at the screen. The caller display showed Melvin's desk phone number. Maybe there would be something worthwhile to this night, he thought.

"Foster," he coughed.

"Detective, it's Melvin."

"I know that. Why are you calling me?"

"Because you told me to," Melvin said matter-of-factly.

"I'm in no mood for jokes. What is it?"

"I've got the analysis completed. And I have to say, you're a smart cookie for thinking of that."

"Did you find something in the blood?"

"Not quite in the blood. What I did find was traces of something on the ridges of the print itself."

"Traces of what?"

"Ammonia, a water-based dye and, get this, rubber tree sap."

"Rubber tree sap? What the hell is that doing on the murderer's fingerprint?"

"That's what I said. So I ran a search for anything that may combine the three and in seconds, bingo!"

"Melvin, cut to the chase and tell me."

"All three can be found in what's called Liquid latex. Now looking into it further, liquid latex is used around the world to create latex flesh. Latex flesh is used in all special effect or horror movies. Get it now?"

"So whoever killed Doug Martin was wearing latex flesh on their fingertips?"

"Give the man a kewpie doll! Your killer wasn't Craig Waterford. But he wanted you to think he was because he was wearing fake fingerprints that matched Waterford's."

"But why, Waterford? What's his link to all this?"

"Well, that's for you to figure out, Columbo."

80

Healy flung the cell phone into the wall with enough force so that it shattered into dozens of pieces upon contact. He couldn't believe the lack of intelligence in Reynolds. This was a high end lawyer? Reynolds was ruining everything. But Gerald Healy would not allow himself to be brought down thanks to an imbecile like Mark Reynolds.

He sat down on the floor and attempted to calm himself into a moment of meditation. Yet his mind would not allow him to, due to the racing thoughts flashing through it. Just sitting on the floor made him restless and anxious. He stood and paced the room like a cat ready to pounce.

There was only one thing to do now that the police were onto Reynolds. He had to cut that loose end before the police used Reynolds to get to him. If they found him, then it would only be minutes before they found out about the last piece to this puzzle. Then all would be revealed. He was getting too involved in this to allow Reynolds to mess it all up.

Healy stopped pacing and began preparing for his next step. Entering the bathroom, he pulled his briefcase from under the long sink and opened it wide. He checked over all its' contents and knew it was time to have some more fun.

Healy walked up to the building wearing his latest disguise. The secret to a good disguise is making it look common. One needed to make the disguise not stand out and allow the wearer to be judged as a friendly and not be remembered in detail later. The simpler the disguise, the easier it would be that no one would remember you later when the police interviewed the witnesses.

The doorman was sitting at his desk watching a portable TV with the volume down low when Healy walked into the lobby of the building. He noticed immediately that there was only one security camera in the lobby and it was pointed at the front entrance. That was okay in his eyes. The disguise still covered any recognizable features. The glasses contained normal pieces of window glass. And the short brown wig was snug and set so that it appeared to be his normal hair and not the shaved head that was hidden underneath.

"Good evening," the doorman said, standing up from his desk, "Can I help you?"

Healy flicked the badge attached to a cheap chain around his neck, pointing out the computer logo under his picture that he had taken an hour before.

"Yeah, I'm here for a," Healy paused to look at his clipboard, "Mark Reynolds. My company said that he was having network problems and he asked for someone to come and reconnect him."

"So, Mr. Reynolds is expecting you?"

"Yeah, that's right."

"Okay, let me call him and announce that you're here."

"You got it."

What the doorman didn't know was that Reynolds had known that Healy was on his way over. But for a different reason. The doorman dialed Reynolds intercom and waited for the tenant in the top floor to answer.

"Yes, Mr. Reynolds, it's Ian downstairs. I have a computer repairman here saying that you are expecting him? Yes, sir. Yes. I'll send him right up, sir. Thank you." Ian the doorman hung up the intercom phone and smiled at Healy. "You can go right up. It's the second elevator on the left."

"Thanks," Healy said. He followed the instructions to the correct elevator and headed upstairs.

The ride up took a few minutes, but when he reached the top floor of the prominent apartment building on Pavonia Avenue, looking out over the Hudson River at the skyline of the New York Financial District, Healy was met by Reynolds. The disguise startled Reynolds for a moment before he realized why it was needed.

"I've got my wife packing. I told her that a friend of mine had passed away and that we were going to visit their family in Florida," Reynolds told him immediately.

"Fine," Healy said, "Let's get back inside." He had noticed the camera in the hall that was recording everything. Reynolds led him back inside and his wife met them in the living room, carrying two overnight bags.

"Is this your driver?" she asked, eyeing Healy.

"Yes, his name is Mike."

Healy was inside and in close quarters now. It was the perfect opportunity to do what he needed to. With a quickness and the precision of a striking snake, Gerald Healy yanked the silencer-attached gun from the back of his waist and placed two close shots into the center mass of Mark Reynolds' wife. Her body jolted back and collapsed onto the couch that she was standing in front of. Reynolds cried out in shock and Healy grabbed his wrist. He tried placing the gun in Mark's hand but he had clenched both into fists.

"Open your fist or I will kill you slowly."

Mark Reynolds looked into Healy's eyes and saw that the man in front of him would not hesitate to do so. Mark opened his left hand and Healy placed the gun in it. He squeezed Reynolds' fingers tight against the gun's grip. Reynolds' prints were now clearly on it. One more detail needed to take care of. He raised Reynolds' left arm up and aimed the gun at his wife once more. Being careful, he tucked his hand under Mark's and pressed his trigger finger tight to let off another shot into the woman's already dead body. There, he thought, the gun shot residue was now on Mark Reynolds' hand.

"W-w-why?" Mark stuttered.

Healy yanked the gun from Reynolds' hand and dropped it on the couch. He then gripped Mark's arms at their biceps. Squeezing tight, he looked Reynolds in the eyes and smiled at him.

"Because you're a moron." Before Reynolds could debate the response, Healy rushed forward, pushing Mark Reynolds backwards. Reynolds howled like a nervous seal, unsure what Healy had planned for him. He turned his head to see what Healy was pushing him towards and realized what the hired killer had planned for him.

Reynolds and Healy were headed toward the balcony of Reynolds' apartment. And at the speed that they were moving, Reynolds knew that he would not be able to stop in time. In a matter of seconds, Mark Reynolds went from standing in his living room in shock to twisting heels over head over the balcony railing and plummeting down to the ground far below.

Healy watched in pleasure as the lawyer fell like a stone and broke like a dropped egg once his body hit the ground. He smiled and was proud of the scene that he had created. The police could not doubt what they found. Healy quietly left the apartment and snuck out of the building through a side exit used for maintenance workers in the building. He would be long gone by the time the police arrived on the scene. And what a scene they would arrive to, he laughed.

81

Brett had returned to the precinct to go over what Melvin had found in the fingerprint at Doug Martin's apartment. Brett asked the crime lab tech to run the same analysis on the palm print that they had pulled off the weapon that was used to murder Peter Rogers. As he did, Brett tried calling Josh to give him the news. He received Josh's voice mail. Knowing that Josh would not listen to it tonight, he left a message anyway. He explained that the fingerprints were faked and that they were closing in on proving Craig Waterford innocent. But the identity of the real killer still eluded them.

Next Brett called Chief Black at home. He risked pissing her off by the call but the news was too good to wait until tomorrow. Christine Black answered on the third ring.

"This better be good, Foster," she answered.

"Sorry for the bother, Chief but I have good news. Craig Waterford is innocent after all." Brett went on to explain what Melvin had earlier. Black listened intently and took in all the information that Brett gave.

"Okay, that is good news. But we need to find out who this real killer is and what Martin's boss has to do with it if he even does have some involvement."

"I'm already working on it."

"Keep me updated if you find anything tonight." Black hung up and Brett checked up on Melvin who was still running the test on the shiv that killed Peter Rogers in Stevens Park. He stopped and realized that the incident in the park had occurred a few days ago yet seemed like it had been a month.

Thinking that it would take somewhat longer, he sat back in one of the chairs and ran over the clues once more in his head. But before he could make sense of anything, Mac walked into the lab.

"Hey Foster, I've got some news that you might be interested in."

"And what's that?"

"Your suspect, Mark Reynolds? He just pulled a Humpty Dumpty."

"It just gets better and better, doesn't it?" Brett sighed.

82

Raghetti sat in the Whiskey Bar, nursing the first drink he had since the Doug Martin case had graced his desk a week ago. The week had been draining on him and the fact that he was back here again in the same rut that he was when the murder occurred was not disappointing. He had tried so hard throughout the week to be the better man that Angie deserved. And for what? So that she could sleep with Brett instead?

"Life is a cruel blue balling bitch," he muttered to no one.

"You say something?" the bartender asked.

"No, nevermind." Josh poured the rest of his drink down his throat in one gulp. Wiping the tiny bit that splashed on his lip, he dropped the glass on the bar without the care that it may shatter.

"You want another one?" the bartender asked, scooping up the glass and examining it for cracks. Josh debated the choice before him. He wanted another one. He wanted to drown the pain and humility coursing through him. But he wanted to prove Angie wrong. He wanted to show her that he could be a good father to Tamara the most of all. And another drink would lead to two more, then three more. And in the end, he would be staggering out of the bar and wind up in an alley, vomiting like some piece of garbage that he would be throwing in the drunk tank overnight.

"No, thanks. I have to go." Josh pushed his stool away from the bar and got up. He walked out of the bar and headed over to Angie's home. He found it amusing how it had once been their home, but now it was solely hers.

He stepped up to the front door and knocked. The bell next to the door was lit but he knew that Tamara would be sleeping by now. He waited a minute before knocking once more. The second knock had been heard and Angie soon appeared at the door. She saw Josh and knew right away that Brett had told him about the night previously. She was a good judge of character and could read his face no matter how hard he tried to hide it.

"Hey," she said, opening the door a little wider.

"Hi," Josh said quietly, "Do you have a few minutes?"

"Sure I do." She stepped out and proceeded to sit down on the steps next to where he was standing. "It's cooled down out here. It's nice."

"How's Tamara?" Josh asked, sitting down next to her.

"She's doing good. She just fell asleep and my mother's inside so she can keep an ear out for her."

"Good," he replied. He was unsure of what to say and how to say it. The moment turned awkward in the silence of the cool night. He tried to form a suitable sentence but failed to speak it. Angie decided to take control of the situation.

"Brett told you?"

"Yeah, he did."

"You kicked his ass didn't you?"

"Yeah, I did."

"Don't blame him, Josh. It was all me. I came on to him. You know how lonely he was. And we both know what a good friend he's been to you all these years. Don't let it end here."

"It hurts, Angie. I still care about you."

"I know and I still care about you too. But it would never work out with us. We both know it. It would just be a waste of life for the both of us. And Tamara is getting to be that age where she's beginning to understand everything. I couldn't bear to raise her in the middle of that. We have to think about her too."

"I want to be a good father for her. I do. But I don't have the first notion of how to do that."

"You love her unconditionally, Josh. That's all. Be patient and guide her."

"Okay." Josh rubbed his hands together thinking about how to resolve the fight between him and Brett.

"And as for Brett, apologize to him. He feels like crap for coming in-between us but I wanted to see if there was something there."

"Is there?"

"Not at first, but the more I spend time with him, the more I find myself falling for him. He does remind me of you at times. You two and your dedication to the job. This time, I've had experience so I'm prepared."

"Well, at least he's not some oiled up, slick haired joke with a couple of chains around his neck."

"Please, give me some credit. I married you, didn't you?" Angie said. It made Josh smile. He looked over at her and patted her knee.

"Thank you for understanding. And for putting up with me all this time."

"I would never change anything if I had the chance to." Angie leaned over and hugged him. He wrapped his arms around her and hugged back. It felt good. He held her as long as he could, remembering all the good times that they had had before things went bad. "Are you going to be okay?" she asked him at last.

"Yeah," he said, "It'll take some time but I believe I will."

"Good, because I don't want to have to worry about you any more than I already do."

Josh sat there with her and they enjoyed each other's company until Josh received Brett's voice mail. He looked at his phone, staring at the name on the lit screen. Angie noticed the name as well.

"You going to answer that?"

"It's already gone to voicemail."

"Still, he is still your partner. What if he needs your help?"

"You're right." Josh tapped a few buttons and listened to the voicemail and the good news regarding the fingerprints.

"It's good news," he told Angie, "We just got a break in the case we're working on."

"Good. See? It's not so bad."

Josh smiled and was going to respond but was interrupted by the phone again. He looked at it and saw that Brett had followed up with a text message. It read: REYNOLDS IS DEAD.

"Actually, I think you may have spoken too soon."

83

"Hi Dean!" Connor shouted as he plowed into the hospital room where Dean Williams was resting. Kristie rushed in after her son, trying to quiet him down as quickly as possible. Connor suddenly stopped short when he saw that Dean was still attached to a few machines and had an IV running into his right hand. The young boy's mouth dropped open and he whirled around back to his mother for comfort.

"Connor, this is a hospital. You have to be quiet."

"Mom, is Dean going to live?"

"Yes, sweetie. The doctors said that he will recover just fine, it will just take a little while for his body to heal up."

"Like Wolverine's?"

"Well, yes, like Wolverine, just not as fast. Dean's not a mutant."

"It would be cool if he was, wouldn't it?"

"I guess so." Kristie slowly walked over to Dean's bedside and saw his eyes open. He saw her and she smiled. Dean's hand moved over and placed it over her own.

"What a nice view to wake up to," he whispered.

"You play your cards right and you can wake up like this every day."

"Hey Dean, I made this for you," Connor said, excited. He held up a get well card with a picture of the X-men on it.

"Hi little man. How are you?"

"I'm good. Mom said I listened to you perfectly."

"It's good to see he's okay. I was worried," Dean said to Kristie, "No one would tell me anything."

"He's fine. He did exactly as we planned it. I owe you big time for taking care of him."

"I'd give my life to save Connor. And you."

"Good, because the cult I joined needs a sacrifice for our ritual next Sunday," she joked.

"I'll try to make it but don't get mad if I'm late."

Kristie smiled. She was glad to hear from the doctors that Dean had been lucky with the gunshots. The shot to the gut had missed any vital organs and the bullet to the head never pierced his skull. From the distance that the killer shot at, he only grazed Dean's temple. No internal injuries or brain damage had been caused.

"Mom said that when you get out of the hospital, we can all go to a baseball game. Right, Mom?"

"As long as Dean is up for it."

"I wouldn't miss it for the world," Dean replied, "And I wanted to ask you something."

"What?" Kristie asked.

"I wanted to ask you to move in with me."

"Move in? Wow," Kristie said. She couldn't believe he had said that. She was enjoying their relationship and was extremely happy that Connor was accepting Dean as well as she had hoped. "Well, I'd have to see if Connor would like to. Connor, would like to move and live with Dean?"

"That would be awesome! Can we?"

"I guess that makes it unanimous," Kristie said. Life was turning around for the better and she couldn't be happier.

84

It was a scene that Brett never expected to see in his career. The mess a body made when dropped from twenty-five floors was massive. It was so bad that they needed two forensic examiners at the scene in order to find any and every piece of the once big-time lawyer. One of the examiners began handing out shoe covers, in the event that anyone inside the police cordon accidentally stepped on a piece.

His jaw and side still hurt like the devil. But the thing that hurt the most was his dignity. Brett had done wrong to his partner and that was something a cop never did. He had to rely on his partner in times of trouble and here he was alone and investigating solo. He stood out like a sore thumb around the uniformed police and forensic workers.

When he had first gotten there, the uniformed were running the yellow tape around the area so he went upstairs to look around. In the lobby, the doorman was still recovering from finding the body outside. A uniform was interviewing him and taking notes. The doorman gave a description of the computer tech that had arrived shortly before Reynolds flew off the balcony. Brett ignored the description. He knew who had done this and that the description would be only a disguise.

Upstairs was the decoy, Brett thought. He looked around and saw Reynolds' wife dead on the couch, three gunshots to the chest. The gun was found on the floor near the window to the balcony. It was guaranteed that the examiners would find gun shot residue on Reynolds' hands, or what was left of them. He walked over and looked down. The height was mesmerizing and he wondered then what Reynolds thought when he was falling.

Brett was showing the forensic examiner what areas he believed should be dusted for fingerprints even though he knew they would find only those of Reynolds and his wife. As he was pointing out areas in the hall, the elevator doors opened and out stepped Raghetti. The sullen look on his face made Brett secretly cringe. He was responsible for that.

"It's a pretty gory scene down there," Josh said.

"Yeah," Brett replied, "But you and I know this is a waste of time."

"It was Martin's killer, wasn't it?"

"It appears to look like a murder/suicide. Wife is over there shot three times and then Reynolds takes a header. But this reeks of set-up."

Josh knew that they had assigned Reynolds to death when they came to the law firm to question him. The hired killer must have found out about it and took out Reynolds to cover his own tracks.

"So then the only piece left to this case is finding the guy who did all this?"

"Guess so. Still doesn't answer the question of why Reynolds had Doug Martin killed in the first place."

"Or why they even framed Craig Waterford," Josh added.

"Maybe Waterford's lawyer is having better luck with that?"

"We'll have to see if he's found anything after this," Josh said. He looked around the well-to-do apartment and said, "Boy, is Judge Irwin going to be broken up. I think she had her lips stitched to his ass."

"Hey about, you know."

"I had a long talk with Angie. I'm over it. Sorry about the jaw. Looks swollen."

"Don't worry, the punch to the kidneys hurt more."

"Look, if you want to see her, I'm fine with it. At least she didn't upgrade after me."

"Fuck you, Raghetti."

"Fuck you twice, Foster."

"Too late, Angie already did," Brett smiled, satisfied with the burn.

"That was low, man."

85

Craig opened the door to find Jacob and Robin standing there. He and Jackie had been expecting them. Jacob called twenty minutes before asking if he could stop by and talk to the couple about the things they had found about the case, in hopes that either of them could shed some light on anything and help them further in closing the case. Craig welcomed them in and Jackie offered coffee and tea.

"None for me, thank you," Jacob said.

"I'll have a cup of coffee please," Robin asked. Jackie headed into the kitchen to pour her a cup. Jacob sat down next to Craig and placed the folder on Craig's case on the coffee table in front of him.

"Craig, do you know a Maurice Devito?"

Craig looked over at Jacob, frowning, "No, I've never heard of him."

"You don't know anyone who's albino?"

"No, never."

Jacob threw Robin a look. He was hitting a wall again. Jackie returned from the kitchen and handed Robin her cup. Robin thanked her and Jacob noticed Craig's wife sit down next to him. A thought popped into his head.

"Jackie, have you ever met any one albino or named Maurice Devito?"

Jackie thought for a minute and then she shook her head, "No, I don't remember anyone like that."

"Why ask Jackie?"

"Well, maybe this isn't about you after all," Jacob offered, "Maybe Jackie's been the target all along?'

"I don't get it," Craig said, "Then why frame me?"

"To get to her. Think, her husband gets framed for murder. Jackie, how did you feel when you heard that?"

"I was crushed. I know Craig could never do something like that."

"You were hurt," Jacob continued, "And then her face shows up in the picture with Doug. Again, it's an attack on her and her faithfulness to Craig. You were insulted when the police asked you if you had an affair with Doug, right?"

"Well, yes. I love Craig and I would never do anything like that to him."

"Exactly. Let me ask you, then. Did you know a Mark Reynolds?"

"No," she said, "I've never met him either."

Jacob's mind flashed back to the conversation he had with Reynolds about Doug's murder. There was nothing in the office that stood out and the words that Reynolds used, didn't reveal anything either.

"I'm missing something. I've got all these pieces and nothing to connect them all. It's like the piece in the center is hiding."

"Maybe some fresh eyes to look at the fragments is what you need?" Craig suggested.

"He could help us," Robin agreed.

"Okay," Jacob said. He took the folder on the table and opened it up. Inside were documents and photos of everything that Jacob had noted and involved in the case of Doug Martin's murder. Craig picked up one of the pages and looked it over.

Jacob explained everything that had happened in the last 48 hours. He told them about the attack on Kristie's family. He went into detail over the audio clip that Doug had hidden and finally skimmed through the case of Maurice Devito. Jacob made sure not to leave anything out in hopes that something may click in either Craig's or Jackie's head.

"Wow, this is bigger than I thought," Craig tried joking. Yet no one at the time found it funny. Time was running out and the lawyer was stumped as to where to look next.

"We don't even know where this ends yet, do we? I mean there's a few questions left unanswered," Robin added.

"All of which Reynolds knows," Jacob said, "How we get the information out of him is beyond me. He's too good at what he does."

"Is there some way to get through to him? Is there something he treasures or covets? Maybe he has some dark secret that you can unearth?" Jackie wondered.

"I doubt it, but even if he did, he'd work hard at keeping it buried."

Robin reached over for one of the photos on the table and Jacob felt a buzz on his waist. It was his phone ringing. He looked down and saw that it was Brett Foster.

"Hang on, Detective Foster is calling," he said to Craig. Answering the phone he soon wished he didn't. Robin watched his facial features going from having some hope to having no hope whatsoever.

"Hey Detective, any good news?"

"Where are you?" Brett asked him.

"I'm with the Waterfords, hoping that they might have some insight on the case that we missed. Anything on your end?"

"Yes and no," Brett reported grimly.

"What's going on?"

"The good news is that our crime lab tech found tiny pieces of latex flesh on the fingerprints we took off Doug Martin's briefcase and the knife that was used to kill Peter Rogers. This proves that Craig did not murder them."

"That's great news! So what's the bad?"

"I'm at Mark Reynolds' home. Looks like our murderous friend paid him a visit. He's dead."

"What? Are you sure?" Jacob wondered what made him ask that. As if Detective Foster may have been wrong with his observation.

"Trust me, there's no coming back for him."

"Thank you for letting me know. I'll call you if we come across anything that may help the case." Jacob hung up. He looked at everyone, one by one. His face showed defeat. Another dead end that may be the end for his client.

"What is it?" Robin asked, "What happened?"

"They just found Reynolds dead."

Craig Waterford felt his future slip away at that moment.

86

After escaping Reynolds' apartment building, Healy returned to his hotel room and took a long shower. He washed away all the evidence down the drain and cleansed himself of the sin that he had committed. Once he was done, he walked into the bedroom, naked. Feeling the cool air-conditioned air on his bare skin felt exhilarating. Healy opened the drawer of the hotel dresser and pulled out a new set of clothes.

The job was improving now that Reynolds was dead. He celebrated by ordering a bottle of Krug Clos du Mesnil champagne from room service and then, on his own cell phone, dialed the main number that he was given.

"Yes?" said the voice on the other line.

"Reynolds is no longer part of the interview process," Healy reported in code.

"Good," said the voice, "I guess you were right from the beginning. I should have never involved him in this. He only made matters worse. I take it you're done then?"

"There is one more thing I would like to take care of personally," Healy told the caller. He knew it may be costly but he refused to let Waterford's lawyer and his bitches get away.

"Sounds good. Thank you for the effort. The funds will be placed into the account like before."

"Good doing business with you."

"Likewise." The caller hung up in time for the room service to knock on the door to Healy's room. Healy opened the door and tipped the server who had delivered the champagne. Then closing the door behind him, he popped open the champagne and poured himself a glass. Tipping the glass to his lips, Gerald Healy celebrated his win before the last dance took place.

87

W hat happened?" Craig asked.

"I don't know. Foster didn't tell me. All he said was that Reynolds was definitely dead."

"So now what?" Jackie asked.

"Foster did tell me first that their crime lab found that latex flesh was used to place your fingerprints at the scenes of the crimes."

"That clears me, doesn't it?"

"Yes, it does. But we're still clueless as to why you were framed for it in the first place."

"But does it matter?"

"Well it wouldn't hurt to know and add that to your defense."

"Okay, so what is next then?"

"Hopefully, the police can get a search warrant into Reynolds' office to see if they can find evidence behind the case?" Robin asked.

"They would need to find a judge willing to allow it. Reynolds was friends with lots of local judges. Their friendship would prevent them from allowing the police to make Mark look bad to the media."

"You could look in there, couldn't you?" Craig asked Jacob.

"I could but I'd be breaking the rules of the firm. And then it wouldn't be admissible in the trial."

"So who can?"

"Neither of us," Jacob said, "Maybe Hoffman?" he asked Robin.

"He does talk to you," she smiled, "Which is more than the others in the firm get from him. You might be able to get him to help."

"But then what are we looking for?"

"That's a good question," Robin said, returning to the papers on the table, "There should be something in here that may lead us elsewhere."

"I have a question," Craig posed.

"What's that?"

"You said that the case that your friend, Doug, was put on is the one mentioned in the conversation that he taped in Reynolds' office.

"Yeah so?"

"Well, what if it wasn't?"

"I don't understand what you're getting at?" Jacob said, confused.

"What if this albino case isn't the one that they were talking about? What if the case they were talking about was the one he was taken off of?"

THREE

THE CASE

88

"H oly shit, why didn't I think that?" Those words rang through Jacob's head the following morning as he pulled into the parking lot across from the building that housed the Reynolds and Hoffman law firm. Robin sat next to him in his car as he parked. Taking the key out of the ignition, Jacob wondered about the conversation that brought him here and what he was about to do.

"Are you going to be okay with this?" Robin asked him.

"This goes against everything I've worked for."

"Yes but it's the right thing. You know this will not only help Craig, it'll answer all the questions that the police have."

"But this will never be allowed into the trial because of what we're doing."

"I'm sure you'll find a way to get it admitted. You always come through for your clients. That's what makes you such a wonderful man. And I'm here to help, alright?"

Jacob flashed back to the night before when Craig raised the question that Jacob may have been looking down the wrong path. The conversation quickly changed course into how they would find out about the case. There was one major problem with the new revelation.

"Who took the case?" Jacob asked.

"Delgado told you about Doug being taken off the case, maybe he would know?" Robin said.

Jacob took out his cell phone from his coat and dialed Delgado's number. He waited for an answer and received one.

"Hello?"

"Chris, it's Jacob."

"What is it now, Scott?"

"Do you remember telling me that Doug Martin was taken off a case and put on the Rosenvelt robbery one?"

"It wasn't that long ago, if you're implying I forget things." Jacob shook his head.

"No, I didn't mean it that way. I was hoping that you knew what happened to the case that Doug was taken off of."

"I don't know. Ask Reynolds. He would have assigned it to someone else."

"I can't, he's dead," Jacob said before he realized what he was saying.

"What? Reynolds? No he isn't. I just spoke to him earlier this evening."

"The police just found him and his wife dead at his home an hour ago."

"Are you serious? What happened?"

"I don't know. They wouldn't tell me anything."

"Do you think this is related to Doug's murder? Should I be worried?"

"Yes, I think it's related but I don't think you have anything to worry about. I think it may be related to this case that Doug was taken off of."

"I don't know anything about it," Delgado said, "Doug only mentioned it in passing. Did you ask his assistant? That Kristie woman?"

"No, but that's a good idea. I'll try her. Thanks Chris."

"Hey, you would tell me if I were in danger of being next, right? I got a wife and daughter."

"Chris, I believe you're safe from this. But I would keep it to yourself until this blows over."

"Thanks Scott. Like my aunt would say, you're a good egg." Jacob was surprised to hear a compliment coming from Chris Delgado. But he wasn't going to toss it to the side.

"Thanks for the help, Chris. You're not so bad yourself." Jacob hung up and told the other three that Delgado did not know anything. Then he called Kristie's cell phone. Kristie answered.

"Hey, Kristie, Jacob here. I need your help." Jacob placed the cell phone on speaker so the others could hear both sides of the call.

"Hey, I just put Connor to bed, what's going on?" Jacob caught Kristie up on everything since he last saw her. He explained about Reynolds and the conversation they had just had.

"Do you know about that case?" Jacob asked her, hoping that they could finally get some answers. He needed an uplifting end to the day.

"There was a case that I remember Doug working on right before he was handed the Rosenvelt case. But he was keeping it to himself mostly. I do remember overhearing him talk about a rape case. But he never asked me to help him with it."

"Do you remember who took it after Reynolds handed him the Rosenvelt case?"

"No, he never really talked about it. But he did seem like he was happy to take the Rosenvelt one over it."

"We think that's the case that he was talking to Reynolds about on the iPod."

"It would make sense, seeing how he acted a little strange about it when I would try and ask him anything on it."

Jacob never remembered Doug talking about a rape case, nor did he remember anyone else talking about it. He figured if Reynolds knew about it and Doug was being quiet about being assigned to it, then perhaps it was someone Reynolds knew that was being accused of rape. But who? And what did the conversation have to do with it?

"We need to find this case," Jacob told them all, "And I'm afraid of what we're going to need to do in order to find out the truth."

Jacob explained to them that he would need to get into the system and find out the name of the case and who was assigned to it. And if Reynolds wanted it kept quiet, the notes for it would most likely have been kept in Reynolds' office. His office was now off limits and locked. That was the problem that Jacob was worried about. He wondered if Reynolds was involved in a cover-up, was Hoffman involved too?

"Come on," Robin reassured him, "Remember, you're part of the firm and if it's in there, you are allowed access to it."

"I guess you're right," he replied, "Well, let's go save the day." He got out of the car and they approached the building.

89

The building inside was as quiet as a tomb, except for the security guard in the lobby, reading what looked to be a fantasy romance novel, called Breath of Fire. Jacob raised his eyebrows but decided not to judge the large, muscular bald man in the security uniform with the night stick and taser on his belt. He and Robin signed in and then they headed upstairs to the law firm.

When the elevator doors opened to the floor, the silence was frightening. He was never alone on the floor, even when he was working late. The new clerks and lawyers were always putting in 60 hour work weeks. But the ambiance of the firm when no one was there was haunting.

"Am I the only one that finds this place creepy on the weekends?" he joked.

"Shush, you'll only make me hear things that aren't there."

"Do you think Reynolds would come back to haunt the firm?"

"That would be really sad."

"You know, now would be a perfect time to show each other on how we feel," Jacob said. Robin stopped short and threw him a look. Jacob raised his hands in surrender. "It was just a joke."

"We'll see who has the last laugh," Robin said, "when you're left high and dry."

"You wouldn't."

"Try me, defense boy." She smirked back at him.

They walked across the main floor and over to the door that led to Reynolds' office. Jacob tried the door and found it locked. He sighed and looked at the knob. It was a standard key lock. He had never jimmied a lock before and didn't know the first thing about doing so.

"Know anything about lock picking?"

"No, nor do I want to."

He looked at the door frame and saw that the lock could be slid open with the old credit card trick he had seen in dozens of old movies. Jacob took out his wallet and checked through it to see if he had anything he could use to open the door with.

"What are you doing?"

"Just checking. Here we are." Jacob pulled out an old video store card. It was laminated in a plastic coating and thick enough to use without breaking.

"A video store card? Do you plan on renting a lock picking video?"

"Sarcasm is not pretty on you," he replied.

"Is that why I catch you looking at my backside from time to time?"

"I don't know what you're talking about." Jacob took the card and pried it into the thin space between the door frame and the door itself. He wiggled it up and down to get it through and once he was able to get so far, he pushed the card in. At first the card slid upward and around the deadlatch. He cursed and tried it again. After two more tries, he got the card to slide back the deadlatch and the door popped open.

"Look out Penn and Teller." Jacob waved his hand in the air and allowed Robin into the office first. Robin took the offer and entered. The corner office had a haunting feel to it as well. Robin thought it was because of her knowing of Reynolds' horrible demise the night before. She felt as if he were behind her, watching her invade his personal space and she hoped that he forgave her for it.

Jacob walked over to Reynolds desk and tried the drawers. Luckily, they were not locked as well. The middle drawer held nothing but pens and a yellow pad. He then went for the side drawers on the left side. They held a pair of sweats and sneakers. Even at the age of 57, Reynolds found a regular regime of exercise four times a week to keep him healthy. He closed the drawers and headed over to the right side of the desk. Opening the bottom drawer, Jacob paused and looked at the gun he had found. He had never knew that Reynolds owned a gun, let alone kept it in his office. He went to reach for it when Robin shouted in a whisper tone.

"I found some files!" Jacob jolted up like a child caught with his hand in the cookie jar. Robin looked at him, puzzled. "What are you doing?"

"I found something," he told her, "A gun."

"What? Why does he have a gun here?"

"Maybe he knew that he was in danger?"

"This is starting to scare me."

"Listen," Jacob said, rubbing her arms slowly, "If you want to back off from this, it's okay. I'll understand. But I have to do this. For Craig and Doug."

Robin thought about taking him up on the offer. A month ago, she would have said yes. She would have taken time off and gone to see family. But things had changed in the past week. She felt closer to Jacob. She had begun missing him when she left at the end of the day. She wasn't sure if it was the danger that made her attracted to him or if it was her feelings finally coming to the surface. Whatever it was, though, she didn't want it to stop.

"No, I'm with you on this now." The answer made Jacob smile. He had hoped she'd stay. He wanted it to be her choice but he had hoped she stuck through it to the end at his side.

"Good," he said. Then he walked over to the small filing cabinet and looked into the top drawer. There were over a dozen file folders there. Each one was labeled with the case name. None seemed familiar to Jacob as he looked over the names.

"Okay, let's get this over with, I'll start from the back, you start from the front and point out the ones that deal with the charge of rape," Jacob said.

Suddenly, the couple halted when they heard the sound of a click outside of the office. The sound was similar to that of a closing door. Jacob's head twisted towards the entrance of the office. There was no one in the doorway and the outside of the office once again fell silent.

"What was that?" Robin questioned, her words dripping with fear.

"I don't know. I'll go check it out. Maybe someone is here, other than us."

"Please be careful."

"I will. Stay here and go through them. I'll be right back." Jacob walked out of the office and glanced around. He saw no one else on the main floor. And none of the doors to the offices were open. Slowly, he crept out and around the office doors. He checked each one and found them all locked. Jacob stopped at each and listened in for any other sounds. Every time he moved to the next office, the eerie feeling of someone jumping out at him increased. Once he was sure that there was no one in the office, he moved on to the next one. He was five offices away from Hoffman's office when Robin called him from Reynolds' office.

"Jacob, I found one. It's the only one with a rape charge."

Jacob raced back over to her and she handed him the folder. Without looking at it, he tucked the folder under his shirt and went back into Reynolds' office.

"Did you find anyone?" she asked as he began cleaning up their visit to the partner's office.

"No, but I don't feel safe here right now. Let's just clean up and get out of here." Robin helped him close all the drawers and wipe the handles with a tissue from the top of Reynolds' desk. Once everything was back to the way it was, Jacob led Robin out and closed the door behind them. The deadlatch clicked back into place and once again the floor was deadly silent.

"Let's get back to my place and we'll go over this," he said to Robin, patting his chest, now covered with the folder that was snug under his old Pearl Jam t-shirt. Robin followed him to the elevator and back out of the building.

90

He was glad that Jacob never got to check all of the offices. Hiding in one of the last ones, the other visitor to the law firm of Reynolds and Hoffman, emerged from his hiding spot. He had seen Jacob Scott and Robin Masters enter the building and he had followed them in and up to the law firm, curious about the reason why they had come there early on a Saturday morning. The visitor had an inkling of why they were there but he wanted to see what they had planned.

The visitor smiled as he watched Jacob break into Mark Reynolds. He didn't know that the lawyer had it in him. What a bad boy, he thought. Once they had gotten in, he was curious what they were doing inside. He could hear drawers opening and closing.

What were they looking for, he thought of asking himself. But he knew. He knew at that moment why the couple had shown up at the law firm. It surprised him that they had gotten that close to answers so soon. It would only be a matter of hours before they figured it all out. And then the secret that others had worked so hard to hide would be revealed out into the open for the media vultures to feed off of.

He opened the door of the office to sneak out and get a closer look. But he forgot that the door would close behind him. The click of the latch was deafening in the silence of the floor. As quickly as he could he quietly opened the door and ducked back inside before Jacob caught sight of him sneaking.

The visitor almost sighed out loud when Masters diverted Scott from searching the offices. She had found the folder for him. He smiled, watching them rush to the elevator with the folder that answered everything. They had saved him the trouble of finding it himself.

91

Brett and Josh walked into the precinct with one thing in mind, solving the Doug Martin case. They sat down at their desks and laid out the case in front of them. Josh handed Brett the cup of coffee he bought him and still felt ashamed about the yellowing bruise on Brett's chin. He had promised Angie that he would not make this awkward. Although to him, it was.

"Reynolds is dead," Brett said, "So where does that leave us?"

"Depends on if he was the one behind it. Do we know for sure that he was?" Josh looked down at the paperwork, looking for an answer to the questions that the case posed. Brett slapped a hand down on the desk. He was getting frustrated.

"What the hell are we missing?" he said, "We've got an innocent guy being framed, we've got a killer covering his tracks, and we've got two lawyers dead because of something. What's the link?"

"Hang on," Josh said. He rummaged through some papers and looked for something that was on the tip of his tongue, "What if Waterford was not so innocent for something else?"

"Then why kill Martin?"

"Okay, work with me on this for a minute. You've got dead lawyer #1. He's the start of this. Doug finds something bad on a case he's working that Reynolds denies. Reynolds is afraid that it'll get out so he hires Killer guy to keep Doug quiet. Then, to really make sure that he is not suspected, he gets Killer guy to frame Waterford. And he frames Waterford because he's getting back at him for something Craig screwed him over with in the past."

"So we need a link between Reynolds and Craig. I'll see if there's anyone in the courthouse today. Try giving Waterford a call and see if he did a round of jury duty when Reynolds was trying a case." Brett went to pick up his desk phone and his cell phone began buzzing. He checked the screen and saw it was Jacob Scott.

"Good morning, Mr. Scott," he answered.

"Detective, I believe we have the answer to why Doug Martin was killed. Can you meet me at my home?" Jacob's voice had a tone of stress and Brett could hear that he was in a car on his cell phone.

"Yeah, I can be there in about fifteen minutes," Brett said. Jacob gave the detective his home address and thanked him. Then Brett hung up and looked over at Josh.

"That was Jacob Scott, he says he knows why Doug Martin was killed. I'm going to go find out what he has. I need you to keep looking into Craig's involvement in this."

"I'll call Waterford now and then check the courthouse. Maybe I'll even give good ol' Judge Irwin a call. She'll be happy to hear from me," Josh smiled.

"Thanks partner," Brett said.

"You're welcome. And if you ever get all sentimental or cheesy on me, I'll kick your ass again."

"Duly noted," Brett replied before he left to see Jacob.

92

Robin read the case file as Jacob spoke to Brett Foster on the phone. She took note of the names involved and the story behind the trial. Jacob looked over as he was driving and noticed that Robin was deep in thought as she made her way through the folder.

"Anything of interest?" he asked her.

"Yes, but I'm trying to find what Doug had found with the evidence. Whatever it was, it was well hidden. We're going to have to go over everything in order to truly understand what this is all about."

"Detective Foster is going to meet us at the house."

Three minutes later, Jacob pulled up to his house. Approaching the door, Jacob felt the need to open it slowly and look inside before going in. Robin followed him in and also looked behind her as she closed the door. He had now realized what trouble they had entered into when he accepted Craig's case.

Heading into the dining room, he dropped the case folder on the table and opened it. The first thing he saw was the evidence photos the police had taken of the rape victim. Robin covered her mouth at the sight of the wounds and massive bruises on the young woman's body. The head shots of the woman looked like something from a horror movie. The entire right side of her face was swollen and purple. Her right eye had swollen shut and her bottom lip was puffy, as if someone had overdosed it with Botox. From the left side, Jacob could tell this woman was once beautiful. But that was no longer the case. The next photo that Jacob saw was of the woman's chest. Cigarette burns had spotted her collarbone and breasts. The following photo was of her flat belly. It, too, had been bruised by punches. A close-up showed a distinct symbol embedded in the bruise. It appeared like the outline of a ring. The last photo was of the woman's pubic area. Robin was forced to turn and walk away from the table. She closed her eyes, trying to remove the sight from her mind and being unable to.

"Jesus," Jacob whispered. He turned the photos over and began reading aloud the evidence list. There were the photos, the rape kit, nail scrapings and the ring that matched the shape on the belly bruise. "We need to get Craig in on this too," he told Robin.

"Do you think he'd be able to help at this point?"

"He has to know something that he's unaware of." Jacob grabbed his home phone and dialed Craig's home number. He reached Craig's voice mail and hung up. He dialed the deli's main number and asked for Craig. After being put on hold for a few minutes, Craig answered. "Craig, it's Jacob. Can you leave for an hour? I've got something here that I want you to look at. I'm hoping you might recognize something. Okay. See you then." He hung up again and continued looking at the file. There was another photo in the middle of the folder of a set of hands. The knuckles seemed red and bruised. There were no pictures of the suspect's face. Only the name of Carl Hartford of Alpine, New Jersey gave the suspect an identity. He had not heard of the name before, nor of this case.

He continued going over the paperwork in the folder for the next ten minutes until a knock on the door told him that Brett Foster had finally arrived. Robin went and opened the door for him. As she was letting Foster into the house, she also saw Craig headed on foot towards the house. She waited until he was also inside before she closed and locked the door again.

"What is it that you found?" Brett asked. Jacob showed him the case folder that he had found in Reynolds' office. He explained what he and Robin had found out through Delgado.

"This was never mentioned to anyone else in the firm but I can tell that Doug was involved in this case. These notes on the side of this page are in his writing. I'd know that writing style anywhere," Jacob explained. He gave the two men a quick rundown on the story behind it and the evidence collected.

"Craig, thanks for coming," he continued, "I was hoping that you may known either the suspect or the victim. I thought that maybe you would have some link to them which would explain your involvement in all this."

"I'll try but I don't know anyone who was recently raped or accused of it."

"You never know," Brett added, "You may have known them from years back."

Jacob warned Craig of the photo he was about to show him. Craig braced himself and Jacob held out the photo of the woman's head shot. Craig cringed at first from the sight of the woman's face. Then he looked closer at the side that was not disfigured.

"She doesn't look familiar," he said, "Sorry."

"Okay, it was worth a try," Jacob said, "What about the name Carl Hartford? Have you ever known a Carl Hartford?"

Brett gasped out loud at the moment Jacob spoke the name of Carl Hartford. It surprised Jacob and Craig. Robin stood up quickly from behind the dining table they had huddled around.

"What?"

"Did you just say Carl Hartford?"

"Yeah, why, do you know him?"

"Carl Hartford is the son of Thomas Hartford," Brett explained.

Jacob didn't know Carl Hartford, but he definitely knew of Thomas Hartford. And it was not a good thing.

93

Thomas Hartford was the current governor of the state of New Jersey. He had been known for two things: his successful cut back on state taxes and the disgrace known as his son. Hartford had been voted into office three years before and was working hard on giving the public a reason for a second term. The previous year was good enough reason when he rolled out his respectful changes in the state budget, lowering the state tax by a full percent. The local news had promoted it as a step in the right direction and talk shows had pointed out that the president could learn a thing or two from Hartford.

That's what Hartford had been hoping for. He had announced another benefiting plan for the state but he would not be able to put it into effect for another two years, after the first term was over. So he used it to campaign for his second term. His public relations manager was excited and had confidence that he was a shoe-in. And then his son stepped into the limelight.

Using his father's fame, Carl Hartford had begun to enjoy life to the fullest. The numerous DUIs and speeding tickets were just the beginning. After a night of partying in Hoboken with some friends, Carl Hartford was later accused of beating and then raping twenty-seven year old Jennifer Tomasi who refused him several times that night. Her sister had later found her in the alley behind the club an hour later as she was returning home. Two months later, Jennifer still had not fully recovered physically.

"So Carl Hartford is behind all this?" Robin wondered.

"No," Brett said, "Carl comes across as too much of a brawler and less of a planner."

"Then maybe that's where Reynolds comes in," Jacob tried to play it out, "Both Reynolds and Hoffman are good friends with Tom Hartford. So Carl goes to Reynolds for help on getting off. Reynolds knows that it would get him in with Tom and takes it on to help. He alters the evidence slightly in Carl's favor and Doug catches wind of it. Doug was a bit of a boy scout. He must have found the altered evidence and refused to go along with it."

"And Reynolds gets some one to shut Doug's mouth?" Robin questioned, "I'm sorry Jacob, but that doesn't sound like Mark Reynolds."

"Maybe Carl hired the killer and Reynolds figured out that he did after the fact. Then Carl sicced the killer on him to cover all the bases."

"Something doesn't fit right, though," Brett added, "If Carl altered the evidence, then why would he involve Craig in all this? Craig, do you know Carl Hartford or Jennifer Tomasi?"

"No, I'm never heard of them before. I've heard of Tom Hartford but I've never met him personally."

"What about jury duty? Were you ever involved in a trial?"

"I've had jury duty twice in my life. The first time I was called into a trial. It was about a man accused of molesting his neighbor's daughter. The evidence was insubstantial and the case was thrown out. But I thought the guy did it. It was me and one woman who believed the guy did it. The others thought he was innocent."

"So what happened?" Jacob asked.

"The group went over it for 2 days and finally they convinced the other woman and I that he was innocent. Then it was over."

"Do you remember the man's name?"

"Um, it was unique. Something Harrison. Artie? No, it was Arnold. Arnold Harrison."

"What about the second time at jury duty?"

"I was never picked for a case. I sat there for a week and then was dismissed."

"Jacob, can you look into that case and see who was involved?" Brett asked him.

"It'll take an hour or so, but I can."

"Go for it. Detective Raghetti is at the precinct. I'm going to call him and see if he can look into the case from our end. Maybe this Arnold Harrison was accused of it more than once."

Craig stepped back and waited while Brett and Jacob made calls. He tried to keep a blank look on his face. He didn't want to show his emotions on his face. Detective Foster didn't notice anything odd yet. But he may if Craig gave his thoughts away. He was racking his mind trying to remember that one thing that was just out of reach in his mind. He had heard the name Carl Hartford before. But for the life of him, he just couldn't remember from where. Once he did, he would confront the man on his own and find out why Carl Hartford wanted Craig to pay for something he did not do.

94

I'll get right on it now," Raghetti told Brett over the phone. He hung up and pulled the keyboard closer to him. Tapping the keys furiously, he put the name Arnold Harrison into the search field. Hitting Enter, the cursor turned to an hourglass and Josh waited for the results.

As he waited he thought of what he was planning for Tamara this evening. Angie had agreed to allow him to take her for the rest of the weekend as long as he had her back Sunday night before her bedtime. He knew that Chuck E. Cheese was her favorite place to go. He could take her there for dinner and games. After, if she still had some energy left, there was a new kids' movie playing in Secaucus. It was a 3D movie and he figured she would enjoy the animation jumping out at her.

Seconds later, he had two hits. He checked the first one which was the arrest of Harrison when the neighbor had reported him. The charge was later dropped after the trial. Josh checked the second hit and found that the neighbor had taken things into his own hands. Arnold Harrison had been shot dead from multiple gunshot wounds one week after the trial ended. The neighbor had confessed when police arrived on the scene. The neighbor had also dragged out evidence from Harrison's hidden basement compartment of the pictures that Harrison had taken of the children he molested. Josh shook his head at the case.

He reached for the phone to let Brett know about the dead end and stopped himself. He had another idea about looking up Craig's past and checking for anything there but Brett had distracted him with the call. Raghetti typed Craig's name into the system and hit Enter. The one hit came up and he looked into it further by clicking on the link below the information. A new screen appeared on the monitor and Josh read all the details that popped up. As he read on, things began making sense and then a name appeared within the details that brought it all together.

"Ah crap," Raghetti said, shaking his head slowly. He sighed loudly, knowing that the information on his screen just made things a whole lot worse. He picked up the phone as if it weighed twenty pounds and punched the numbers to Brett's cell phone.

95

This is it," Jacob said to Robin and Brett. He tapped his finger on the piece of paper that he had been reading.

"What is it?"

"This is what Doug had found. The doctors at Hoboken University Medical examined Jennifer Tomasi and listed all fibers and DNA evidence they pulled off her. Here's their list," he handed the page to Brett. Robin stood next to him and read the page as well. "Now, later, the police, for their own records, re-inventoried the evidence. Here's their list." Jacob handed him another page. Brett held the pages side by side and went through the lists. He matched each item together until there was one left.

"This hair follicle?" Brett asked.

"Exactly. From the time that Tomasi was examined by the doctor to the time that police went through the evidence that hair follicle suddenly appeared in the evidence bag. Then, the police crime lab tested the hair follicle for DNA. It turns out, it's from a blond male. Carl Hartford, of course, has red hair. Thus the defense jumps on this piece of evidence, trying to prove that Carl never touched her. With the way DNA is being accepted in trials, it's turned the trial in favor of the defense."

"And Reynolds let this go?" Robin asked him, "That seems unlike him."

"It does but the audio clip proves that he did." Jacob knew Robin had a point. Mark Reynolds did not seem like the type to commit crimes. He had built a strong reputation in Hudson County and to let it all slip for one case was definitely the opposite of what he portrayed at the firm. But everyone has their deep dark secrets. Jacob's mind wondered, though, how deep and dark did this go?

"So we need to find Carl Hartford and get some answers," Brett said.

"He lives in his father's mansion in Alpine. That's about 45 minutes from here. Shall I drive?" Jacob smiled and held his keys up in the air for Brett to see.

"Guess again, Mr. Defense. This is for the professionals."

The conversation stopped when the doorbell rang. Jacob looked at Robin who looked at Foster who looked back at her. Jacob went to the door and looked through the small window at the top of the door. He held his thumb up in a sign of safety. He then opened the door to let Kristie in.

"Sorry I'm late, I had a little trouble getting my sister to watch Connor. Have I missed anything?" Jacob caught Kristie up on everything they had found at the office and in the case file. As he did, Brett checked his messages and Robin sat looking around. She then realized that Craig was not in the room. She stood and walked over into the back of the house where the bathroom and bedroom was. The bathroom door was wide open and there was no one in the bedroom. The kitchen was empty as well. She returned to the living room where they had all gathered. She walked up to Jacob as he was finishing the story with Kristie and asked him, "Jacob, where's Craig?"

Jacob stopped talking and looked around. He, too, finally noticed that Craig was no where to be found. Brett looked up from his phone and quickly walked to the front door. He threw it open in time to see Craig Waterford driving past the house. Foster's stomach dropped to his feet when he caught the look on Craig's face as it past the house. There was determination and anger blended into one emotion all over it. The look scared Brett. He knew what it meant, knowing Craig Waterford from dealing with him the whole week. It meant one thing.

"Damn," Brett sighed.

"What?" Kristie asked, "Is he gone?"

"Yeah, and I know exactly where he's headed."

96

H e's headed for Hartford's home, isn't he?" Jacob wondered aloud. It made perfect sense. Jacob knew that put in Craig's situation, he would have probably done the same. After the week of hell that Craig had been put through and still not know the answer as to why, he didn't blame him for sneaking out to get what his lawyer and the police had been unable to figure out yet.

"That's what I'm afraid of," Brett replied, "We have to stop him before he gets there."

"I'll go with you," Jacob volunteered. It was the least he could do for his client. Craig was innocent right now and he didn't want that to change in an act of anger.

"Please be careful," Robin told him, giving him a kiss before he ran off doing what he did best.

"I will," he said, "Love you." Then he turned back to Foster and the two men headed out of the house and into Brett's car.

"You know your client better than I do," Brett said, "Does he have it in him to actually kill someone?"

"A week ago, I would have said no. But the nightmare he's been through. From what I've seen in my line of work, it's possible now."

"Yeah, that's what I thought." Brett retrieved the flashing light from under his driver seat and placed it on the dashboard. Flipping the switch on he pulled out of the parking spot and sped off towards the Hartford home.

Robin and Kristie watched them leave and Robin smiled to herself. Kristie looked over at her and was puzzled.

"Why are you smiling?"

"I'm sorry. It's not the situation. I just caught him tell me that he loves me and it sounded so normal to him."

"You really care about him, don't you?"

"I do." Robin pulled herself out of the dreamy state that she was in and looked over at Kristie.

"I'm so happy for you. And I have to say he fits into that suit pretty good, huh?"

"Oh yes," Robin laughed, "Very yummy."

Healy sat in the rental car several houses back from Jacob Scott's place. He had followed the lawyer and his eye candy from the law firm and back here. He was planning to strike until the pig cop showed up. He didn't need any trouble with the hit that, to him, was now personal. Waiting patiently for the cop to leave, he was disappointed to see the lawyer leave with him when he did. But the sight of the two women who had caused him pain standing on the front steps alone filled him with adrenaline. It was as if fate had stepped in to give him a gift for his hard work.

Gerald breathed deeply, taking in the scent of excitement and opened the car door. He stepped out, taking his bag of toys off the passenger seat with him and walked to the front of the house. The women had returned inside already and closed the door. He casually approached the house as if he had been expected there. He did not want any neighbors in the area noticing him as being strange.

Each step he took to the door made him more powerful than the last. The sense of accomplishment surging through his veins. Once he had gotten to the front door, he paused. Opening his bag slightly, Healy rummaged for his .45 automatic with attached silencer and took it out. He kept it tucked to his side, so not to be obvious to anyone walking by. Then with his free hand, he knocked on the door.

He knew that the women would have their guard down and not think of him at this moment. But the shock on their faces when they saw him, almost made him laugh out loud. He composed himself quickly when the knob of the door jiggled. The door opened and he saw the blonde eye candy standing there with the bitch that smashed the coffee pot into his face standing a few feet behind her. The blonde's mouth dropped open at the sight of Healy at the door. Then he propped his foot against the door to keep her from slamming it in his face.

"Good afternoon, ladies," he said sticking the gun into Robin's rib cage. She looked down at the gun and her body went stiff with fear. Healy smiled and said, "Got any coffee?"

97

Revenge was not the immediate feeling that Craig felt. He just wanted answers. Answers to the nightmare that his life had become in the past week. He needed to know what his involvement was in all this. He needed to know why it was him that was chosen and not some other regular joe that was picked to be framed for the murder of a man he had never met.

Driving through Fort Lee and heading north, he thought of calling Jackie to tell her he loved her and their baby in the event that something happened once he got there. The realization of what he was doing was beginning to sink in. But the need for answers overpowered the creeping fear.

His cell phone rang again. He didn't need to look to see who it was but he did anyway. Jacob's name appeared on the call display screen again. He ignored the ringing because he knew that his old friend was only going to try and talk him out of it. But he was adamant that this was something that he needed to do.

Who was Carl Hartford and why did he want Craig to pay for something that he planned? Did he really know the man? The name did sound familiar but he still couldn't remember from where. The answer was foggy in his mind and he couldn't wait for the fog to clear. He needed this over and the true answer lay in Alpine. It was waiting for him.

*   *   *

Josh cursed to himself when Brett's cell phone went to voice mail once again. He couldn't understand why his partner had turned his phone off. The thought of him in trouble flashed in his head. He pictured the vision of the killer waiting for them at Jacob Scott's home. The image scared him. He should have gone with Brett to Scott's home and been backup.

He grabbed the sheet of information that he had found in the system and folded it into his pocket. He threw his windbreaker on and headed for the door. As he was walking through the parking lot to his car, Lyndsay pulled up in her own. She parked next to Josh and rolled down her window. Josh stuck his head in and smiled as best he could.

"What's going on?" she asked him, noticing the look on his face and began growing worried.

"I think Brett may be in trouble. Are you armed?"

"Of course," she replied.

"Good. Can you join me in going to Jacob Scott's house?"

"The lawyer? Yes, what's happening?"

"I just figured out what Craig Waterford's involvement is in all this." Josh took the paper out of his pocket and explained it all to Lyndsay. She was surprised to hear the news. But yet, it made sense.

"You think Doug Martin's killer is at Jacob's house to cover their tracks?"

"He would be answering his phone if he wasn't in trouble. I just hope I'm not too late."

"You won't," Lyndsay told him, "Hang on, Raghetti. We'll be there in two minutes." Lyndsay turned on the dashboard light and sped up to Washington Street to Jacob Scott's house.

98

Kristie dropped her glass of water at hearing the voice that had haunted her dreams since the first time she heard it at Doug's home. Then she watched Robin slowly raise her hands as she backed away from the front door. Gerald Healy appeared from behind her and smiled at Kristie. The smile sent shivers down her back. She couldn't believe he was here.

"Good to see you too," he said to her. Then the gun with the attached silencer appeared and he motioned her over with it. Kristie raised her hands also and stepped away from the dining room table. He slowly walked over to Robin and stood next to her as Healy watched.

"I'm sorry about the coffee pot," she said to the man.

"I highly doubt it, but it was a good strike. I'm a bit impressed by it. I'll have you know that broken glass to the face hurts like a mother." Healy walked over, keeping the gun trained on them the entire time, and picked up a piece of the glass that Kristie dropped. He slowly approached the women with it held up for them to see. He turned it and let the sunlight coming in through the windows glint off the sharp points.

"Please," Robin said.

"Oh, don't worry. This will take some time but not too much." He brought the piece of glass to Kristie's cheek and dug a sharp edge into her skin until she flinched from the dot of blood that appeared. He smiled.

"Why did you do this?" Robin asked Healy. Healy was confused by the question. His face frowned at her.

"Because it's what I do. Because I was paid well to."

"By Carl Hartford?"

Healy laughed at the accusation. "Carl Hartford? You think that pile of moronic testosterone shit plotted this all out? You must be truly blonde then."

"If it wasn't Carl then who?"

"I know," Kristie spoke up.

"I knew you were the smarter one," Healy smiled, "You are the formidable opponent."

"So you did this all for money?"

"It's what I do. It's what I'm good at."

"Yet I managed to smash your face with a coffee pot," Kristie instigated.

"You got lucky, bitch. And you two are going to pay for it now." The comment from Kristie angered him and he grabbed her by the hair and pulled her towards him. He placed the barrel of the gun under her chin. "What now? Shall we see if your inner beauty is as lovely as your outer beauty? What do you say?"

Robin noticed that Healy's focus had moved away from her. She turned to her right slowly. Looking over her right shoulder, she saw the tacky vase that Jacob had decorated his coffee table with. It's thick porcelain base would be the perfect club to hit the killer with. She turned her attention back to Healy who was digging the piece of glass into Kristie's other cheek. The piece was now drawing blood. A thin line of red ran down her friend's left cheek. Kristie was cringing from the pain that Healy was causing her. It was now or never, Robin thought.

She tucked her hand back and gripped the neck of the vase. Taking a step forward, Robin brought the vase up in an uppercut swing. The base of the vase made contact with Healy's jaw. His head jolted back and his grip on both the glass and the gun was lost. Both items clattered to the wood floor. Kristie collapsed as well holding her cheek in pain. Healy staggered backwards from the hit. He shook off the shock and looked back at Robin. She became scared by his stare. Pure anger and fury took over in him and he lunged forward, knocking the vase from her hands. Healy wrapped his hands around Robin throat and pushed her to the floor. He squeezed as he straddled her waist, blocking the air from entering her lungs.

Robin tried to fight back, clawing at his hands and face. She tried everything she could to get him to let up on her throat, but it did not help. Her lungs began to burn from the lack of oxygen it was used to. Healy's grip refused to loosen and she could feel her body lose all it's energy. Not now, she thought. She was finally happy with her job and with Jacob. She couldn't die now. Through all the pain, she felt the tear from her eye trickle down and she closed her eyes, feeling the blackness begin to cover her world.

And suddenly a noise broke the silence and the air rushed into her lungs. She opened her eyes and saw the shock and surprise in the killer's eyes. His hands let go of her throat and they reached around his back as if he were trying to reach something that he couldn't. Then he leaned over to the side and fell to the floor next to her. Robin tried sitting and rubbed her neck. She saw Kristie standing with Healy's gun in her hands. The gun's barrel released a puff of smoke from the bullet that exploded out of it.

"Are you okay?" Kristie dropped the gun to the floor and rushed over to check on Robin. She checked her neck and saw that it was just red. Robin was getting her breath back and her color was returning.

"How did you learn to shoot a gun?" Robin asked.

"My father took me hunting as a kid. He figured that if I was going to make it in the world, I'd need to make sure I could defend myself."

"Can you teach me?"

"Yeah, sure." Kristie looked over at Healy who had remained slump over. She slowly reached over to check his wrist for a pulse. She could not find one.

"Is he....dead?"

"Yes. We're safe."

The room was interrupted by the sound of a phone buzzing. Kristie stood up and walked over to the table. There she found Detective Foster's phone. Realizing that he rushed out of Jacob's house without it, she picked it up and answered it.

"Hello?"

"Who is this? Where's Detective Foster?" the man on the other line asked.

"He's headed to Alpine. This is Kristie Marks."

"Miss Marks, this is Detective Raghetti. Did you say he's headed to Alpine?"

"Yes, Detective. He rushed out of the house without his phone. Can you please come here, we have the killer."

"What? Are you okay?"

"Yes, he's dead."

"I'm pulling up outside, can you please open the door?" Kristie walked to the front door and opened it seeing Detective Moskin and Detective

Sean Lennon

Raghetti getting out of the car double parked in front of the house. Raghetti rushed around the side of the car with his hand on his gun holster in case there was something waiting for him inside the house. Lyndsay Moskin followed him in the same way. Kristie held her hands up to show that she was unarmed. Robin was still sitting on the floor catching her breath. Lyndsay rushed over to check on Robin and Josh walked over to Kristie, looking at Healy's dead body on the floor.

"You do this?" he asked Kristie. She nodded and he smirked, "Nice shot."

99

Pulling up to the gate that led to the Hartford's mansion, Craig looked at it and took a breath. He collected all his courage and stepped out of the car. The estate of Thomas Hartford looked the way he imagined it. There was a eight foot wall bordering the estate with a wide iron gate blocking the entrance. Walking up to the gate, next to him, there was also a call box with one button and a speaker. He looked through the gate and noticed the paved path that led to the huge home. He could only see bits of the house through the trees that spotted the land. But he could tell the home was spacious.

Your tax dollars at work, Craig thought jokingly. He reached over and pressed the button on the call box. He waited a minute or two before someone responded.

"Can I help you?"

"Yes, I'm here to see Carl Hartford."

"I'm sorry but Carl is not here. Are you one of his friends?"

"No, my name is Craig Waterford and I was hoping to talk to him. Do you know where he can be reached?"

After that, there was no reply from the other side of the intercom.

Thomas Hartford stepped back from the intercom speaker. He almost expected Craig Waterford to jump through the intercom at him. Gripping the kitchen counter behind him, he tried to figure out how Waterford connected everything to him. Then Hartford realized that he was asking for Carl not him. Perhaps Craig believed that Carl was behind it. The thought almost made him laugh out loud. The idea that his disappointment of a son plotted out the entire thing was ludicrous. Carl was the reason this had all happened.

Tom walked around the island in the center of his kitchen, thinking of what to do. If he pointed the finger at Carl, the spotlight would not be so bright on him but it may still hurt his chances at the end result of what he had worked so hard for. He wished at that moment that his wife had aborted the fetus that he would later call his son. The fear in him soon turned to anger as he thought about Carl. He had done everything for him when he was growing up and now that he was a man, he was the opposite of what he had hoped for.

The intercom buzzed once again, bringing Tom back to reality. Craig was still at the gate. Tom knew he would not be going anywhere. It was now or never. Thinking quickly, he pressed the button on the intercom.

"There he is," Jacob said, pointing to the figure next to the gate. Brett breathed a sigh of relief, knowing that he had gotten there in time. He flicked the switch off on the police light and slowed down. Pulling up next to Craig's car, Jacob jumped out before Brett could place the car in park. Jacob ran over to Craig and placed his hand on his client's shoulder.

"Craig, you can't do this the way you want to," he said to him, "You have to obey the law in order to remain innocent."

"I wasn't going to hurt or kill him," Craig explained, "I just wanted answers. But Carl Hartford isn't even here."

"No one's home?" Brett asked.

"Someone's there. I was just talking to him. But when I asked where I could find Carl, the person just stopped responding."

"I'll get Josh to put out a BOLO for Carl." Brett reached to his side to call Raghetti to send out a Be on the Lookout report to all neighboring counties for Carl Hartford and realized that his cell phone was not on him. "Damn, I must have left it on your table back at the house. Can I use you phone?" Jacob reached into his back pocket and handed over his cell phone to Brett. As he and Craig talked, Brett dialed Josh's number.

"Raghetti," Josh answered.

"Josh, it's Brett."

"Where are you?"

"At the Hartford estate in Alpine."

"So you know about the link between Waterford and Hartford?" Brett wondered what his partner was talking about.

"What link?'

Josh explained the link that he had found while running the background on Craig back at the precinct. As he told his partner all that he had found, Brett was shocked to hear that the case was finally coming full circle.

"No kidding?"

"No, that's the piece we've been missing the whole time. Oh and we've got the killer."

"Wow, you've been a busy boy."

"Well, it wasn't me, it was Marks and Masters. After you and Scott left, the killer must have been sitting in wait and went in after them. Luckily, Marks was a trained shot when she was a kid. She got the gun away from him and shot him dead. Lyndsay and I found a W Hotel key in his bag of tricks and we're about to head over there to see what we find."

"Hopefully you'll find something worthwhile."

"I have a feeling we will."

"Okay then, I'm going to be a while here. Thanks for the update, it'll help when interrogating Hartford." Brett said goodbye and hung up. He walked over, handed the cell phone back to Jacob and pressed the intercom buzzer button.

"What are you doing? Carl Hartford's not home," Craig said.

"I don't need Carl Hartford to get a confession," Brett said. He looked into the estate through the iron gate, waiting for a response. Seconds later he got one. The gate clicked and slowly began to open.

"It's show time, councilor," Brett said.

100

Josh and Lyndsay walked up to the front desk and flashed his badge to the woman behind it. The woman, dressed in a navy blue dress with suit jacket, looked up with a smile from her computer and glanced at the badge. Seeing it, her smile slowly drained from her face.

"Hello officer, is there something I can help you with?" she asked.

"Yes, I would like to get access to the room that this card key is for. Can you please tell me what room number?"

"May I ask what this is in regards to? Did you find that card key outside this hotel?"

"Listen," Josh said curtly, "The guy we found this on is dead. He was a suspect in a series of murders and we believe some evidence in those murders may be in the hotel room he paid for here. Now if you want to give me a hard time, fine. I'll involved the press and return with a search warrant. And then you can explain to your boss why you gave two local cops a hard time."

"I'm very sorry, Detective. I was only thinking of our guests' privacy," she said taking the card off the counter and scanning it into the computerized box to her left. She glanced down at the box's display and handed it back to him. "It's for room 815. Would you like more information on the guest?"

"Yeah, what's the name the room is under?"

"I'm showing here that," she tapped some keys and looked down at her screen, "the room is signed under a Gerald Healy. The elevator to the eighth floor is down the hall there on the left side. Would you like someone to accompany you?"

"No thanks, we'll only be a few minutes."

"Um, there's no, er, need for the press anymore, is there?"

"No. Thank you for your assistance." Josh walked away and Lyndsay smiled at the woman behind the counter.

"Nice threat, Raghetti."

"I've got plans this afternoon. I don't have time to play games with some snobby woman who thinks she's better than me 'cause she has a degree on her wall."

Upstairs, they found the room and dipped the card into the electronic lock on the door that read 815. The green light flashed and Josh turned the knob. The door opened and the two detectives walked into the spacious room. There was one king-sized bed in the middle of the far wall with a table and cushioned chair towards the back by the long window. To the left wall was a modern dresser with a 47" flat screen TV sitting on top of it.

Josh immediately noticed the opened case on the bed that had not been made. He walked over and saw what appeared to be strips of flesh. He took out his pen and scooped it up onto it. Bringing it to his face, he looked closer.

"What the hell is that?" Lyndsay asked.

"I think it's that latex flesh that Melvin found on the fingerprints at Doug Martin's place. Do you have a baggie on you?"

"No but I have it in the trunk?"

"I think you're going to need to grab your bag. It looks like we're going to be here for a while."

Lyndsay headed back downstairs for her crime scene kit and Josh continued looking around. He opened the small closet and found tattered clothes. He picked at them and found that it was the outfit that the homeless man who killed Peter Rogers in Stevens Park had worn that day.

"Jackpot," Raghetti said to himself. He left the closet door open and turned around to the bathroom door. He pushed it open gently and reached in to turn on the light switch. The light turned on and saw the bathroom counter covered in tools and black dust. He walked in and looked into the shower first. He wasn't sure that the killer worked alone and wanted to make sure that he was safe before examining the counter. Once he found that there was no one in the bathroom with him, he looked at the dust on the counter. He immediately recognized it as fingerprint dust. Then he saw the coffee cup that had been covered in the dust.

It all made sense now. The coffee cup looked like the ones that were used at Anthony's Deli that Craig had owned and worked. That was how the prints were placed at the crime scenes.

Lyndsay returned to the room and Josh showed her what he had found. She looked at the coffee cup and then back at him with a confused look.

"Yeah so you found the killer drank coffee, big deal."

"No, that is the same coffee cup that Waterford uses at the deli he owns. Get it? The killer goes to the deli, gets Waterford to pour him up some coffee and then uses Waterford's prints that are on there to make the latex flesh prints and attach them to his own fingers. Wow, this guy's good."

"So, then, let's get started." Lyndsay pulled some gloves on and opened her crime scene kit. Josh paused for a minute and dialed Lucky's home number. Lucky answered with a frustrated tone in his voice.

"Raghetti, what can I do for you?"

"Lucky, I need you to come down to the W Hotel and help out with a crime scene."

"Are you kidding? I just got the chance to start playing the new Call of Duty I picked up last week!"

"Sorry buddy but we've got a big one here and need all the help we can get." He heard Lucky sigh in between the screams and gunshots from the TV in the background.

"Fine, what room number?"

"815. See you when you get here." Josh hung up and joined Lyndsay in the start of it all.

101

B e cautious," Foster said, "We don't know what we're walking into here."

The gate had opened when Brett pressed the button but he could not see any video cameras near the entrance. But that did not mean there wasn't one watching them. Brett drove in and Crain with Jacob followed him in with Craig's car. They slowly pulled up to the front door of the house and got out. Brett surveyed the area. He was nervous and hated not knowing what to expect.

"Now what?" Jacob asked him.

"You've got me."

At that moment, the front door opened and a tiny older woman stepped out. She carried her purse and waved to them.

"Good afternoon gentlemen. Mr. Hartford is awaiting you in his study. I can bring you to him."

"Yes please," Brett said.

The three men followed the woman inside and through the house. Craig looked around him as he walked with the others. He was amazed at how big the house seemed from the inside. The giant chandelier in the entrance was bigger than his desk in the deli. He couldn't help but look at all the expensive decorations around him.

"What could anyone want with all this stuff?" he wondered.

"To show off," Brett told him.

"Mr. Hartford rather enjoys the simple things in life," the woman said.

"Is that why his house is bigger than the entire Hoboken Police Plaza?"

"I'm sorry? I don't hear too well anymore," she said.

"Nothing," Brett said.

Finally, the woman opened a door and motioned for the men to enter. Brett went in first and found what he was looking for. Behind a desk straight ahead sat Governor Thomas Hartford. He sat casually but straight. It was an easy business pose that he had sat in before whenever in front of a news camera. Brett saw the look on his face turn from professional to confusion when he noticed that Craig was not alone. The others followed Brett in and stood at his sides.

"Good afternoon, gentlemen," Hartford said, "Can I have Helen get you something to drink?"

"No thanks. You know why we are here, right?"

"Yes I do. Thank you Helen, that will be all."

"Just let me know if you need anything before lunch, Mr. Hartford." Helen left and closed the door to the study, leaving the four men alone.

"Please sit," Hartford offered. Jacob and Craig sat down but Brett remained standing. Tom held his hand out, offering one of the other two chairs available.

"I prefer to stand."

"Well, suit yourself, Detective."

"Where's your son, Carl?" Craig asked forwardly.

"Carl is down in Point Pleasant, doing what he does best. And that's being a complete asshole. The man is 41 years old and still acts like a snot nosed teenager. Not much for a man like me to pass the legacy on to."

"Were you ever planning on doing that?" Jacob asked.

"When he was born, I did. The fact that I now had a son to raise like myself gave me such high hopes."

"Ended up being the total opposite, didn't he?"

"Of course he did. I never did half the things he has in my lifetime. And I never could figure out what it was that I did wrong to make him grow to be such an incompetent slug. Did you know when I first came up with the idea of lowering the taxes successfully for the state that my assistant thought I was drunk?"

"We're not here to listen to you rattle on about your political career," Brett said in a low tone. Tom looked at the detective in the eyes and saw what he was afraid of.

"You know, don't you?" he asked the homicide detective. Brett didn't speak. He only nodded a response. Jacob was a little confused before but it clicked in his head at that moment. Craig, on the other hand, did not understand what was going on.

"We know that Carl hired someone to murder Doug Martin to cover up for the tampered evidence found in his rape trial," Craig said, "Now if you can just give us an address to find him and get some answers, we will be out of your hair, Governor."

Tom threw Craig a puzzled look and then looked back at Brett.

"You haven't told him yet?"

"Told me what?" Craig questioned the detective.

"Carl Hartford isn't responsible for all this," Jacob said.

"Then will someone please tell me who is?"

Tom Hartford leaned forward in his large office chair and placed his hands on the top of the desk straight out. "I'm the one responsible for your trouble, Craig."

102

W hat?" Craig said, now standing up. He looked at Brett and then at Jacob. Jacob lowered his head at the revelation and couldn't believe that it was coming to this. He had never expected the end of this case to wind up the way it was now.

"Detective, would you like to explain it all?" Hartford offered him.

"No, I'd rather he hear it from you."

"Fine." Hartford picked up the small glass of liquor and poured half the liquid down his throat. The alcohol burned nicely as it went down and Hartford reveled in one of the things that he would not be allowed any time soon. He wanted to get up and walk around but knew that Detective Foster would unholster his weapon if he stepped from behind the desk. So he remained seated.

"Carl is the reason this all happened. His disregard for anything his mother and I had done for him was the reason why three people are dead and you, Craig, had entered the nightmare life that you have for the past week.

"You must understand one thing first. I never wanted anyone dead when this first began. You must believe that. It's very important to understand it before I continue." Brett stayed silent and Jacob felt it wasn't his place to say anything. Tom Hartford sighed and started again.

"It began with Jennifer Tomasi. She noticed him at one of the bars in Hoboken a few months ago when he was out drinking with his friends. She flirted like any woman would to someone who's linked to power and money. But she didn't know Carl like the others did. Carl can be very aggressive after drinking. And at that point in the night, he had had a lot of alcohol. One thing led to another and when he tried to grope her in the back alleys, she pushed him away. That's when he punched her in the face and beat her near death. She would have died if her friend had not found her shortly after. In my opinion I believe she no longer speaks to her friend for that same reason. I don't blame her. I'd rather die than live the rest of my days looking the way she does now.

"The doctors got their hands on her and it was all over at that point. I even managed to sneak in there to try and talk her out of it. I, the governor of the state, tried to pay off the woman who was beaten and raped by his own son. But she didn't want to have any of it. She wanted him to be stopped. She wanted to make sure that no other woman ever had to go through what she had to that night. Do you know what the press never got word of? Jennifer told me this when I spoke to her. When Carl was done with her, he stomped his foot onto her head to make sure she would die. I shutter every time I think of that. My flesh and blood carelessly taking a life like that.

"But I digress. Once Jennifer told me that she wasn't going to keep quiet, there was only one other thing I could think of. I had to change the evidence that the doctors had taken off of her to make it seem like it wasn't Carl after all. So I followed the officer that picked up the evidence and diverted him while he was on route so I could make it appear that it was a case of mistaken identity."

"But if you are so disappointed in Carl, why not just let him go to jail?" Craig asked.

"He couldn't," Brett spoke finally.

"No I couldn't," Tom explained, "Because if he had gone to jail, then his criminal record would have ruined my political career. Who's going to vote me back into office? And then there was the presidency I was dreaming of in my future."

"Fat chance of that ever happening now," Brett added.

"No I guess not. But it is my bed that I've made and now I have no choice but to lie in it."

"But where did Reynolds come into all this? I mean why even involve him?" Jacob piped up.

"Mark was an old friend and he had faith in me. He knew that I could do great things for this country. I just had to convince everyone else. For my own sake, he chose to help me get the case thrown out. But he made a mistake. He let in that other lawyer he had working for him for help. But he was a boy scout. He noticed what we did right away. Reynolds tried to convince him otherwise but that guy wouldn't have it. He had to out the evidence. That's when I involved someone to kill him. It was a dumb thing to do but by this point there was no turning back. So I hired someone by the name of Healy to get rid of him and make it look like something else."

"And it was your choice to frame Craig."

"Of course."

"But why? Why did you do this to me?" Craig asked taking a step towards the desk that Tom hid behind. Hartford leaned back in his chair, afraid that Craig was going to jump over the desk and hit him over and over. Brett moved in and grabbed Craig's shoulder, holding him back from attacking. Craig stopped but still waited for an answer. Hartford felt the need to let him know the reason behind it all.

"Craig, you don't remember me, do you?"

103

I've never met you before in my life," Craig told him.

"You may not remember me but you would remember Kim."

The name made Craig want to run and hide in the deepest and darkest place in Earth. There had been only one Kim he'd ever know and he wished that he hadn't. He sat back in his chair and placed his head in his hands. Jacob looked over and remembered the story that Craig had once told him years ago. It had all come back full circle.

"Kimberly O'Neil was my niece. I was there at the scene that night and saw you there talking to the police. The mistake that you had made was showing all over your face that night. And I hated you with a passion all those years later. She had such potential for doing good. She had wanted to be a doctor, did you know that? No, you didn't. Because you wanted to bury it away inside you and never speak or think of it again. And you know what? When I became governor, I wanted to use my power to reopen the case and nail you to the wall for what you did."

"It was an accident!" Craig yelled back, "I had nothing to drink. The breathalyzer that I took proved it. It was late and I fell asleep at the wheel for a second. You don't think that she doesn't haunt my dreams still? I've tried to move on for so long but her body lying there on the street is still as vivid in my mind like it happened this morning. I never meant to ever hurt anyone. I'm forever sorry that I hit her!"

"Craig, it's ok," Jacob tried to console him. But Hartford had gotten to him.

"And you know what? I almost believed you were a few months ago.

My assistant taught me to forgive and forget. Yet, you looked fine to me weeks ago when I walked into your deli. All smiles with your wife and co-workers. That was the day you received the award from the Hoboken Better Business Bureau. You were very proud. And my fury came back. So I had the man I hired to kill that lawyer make it so you would be the main suspect. And from what I've been reading, he did a fine job. But I didn't expect Mr. Scott here to be such a help to you. Well done councilor." Hartford began to clap slowly.

"You're quite the big man, aren't you, Governor?" Jacob said, loudly, "You obviously don't think that you were going to get away with it, were you?"

"At first, I was hoping to. But my relying on your boss was my mistake. That was my falling asleep at the wheel. I knew it was too late then but that man, Healy, needed to cover his tracks. He had a reputation to uphold. I couldn't stop him if I wanted to try. It was his choice to kill Peter Rogers but I'll admit that it was my idea to get rid of Doug Martin and Mark Reynolds. He was a moron. And he had to pay for the mistakes he made."

"And it was up to you to make him pay? What makes you above everyone?" Brett couldn't help but get involved.

"I'm the Governor of New Jersey. Haven't you heard what I've done for the state? I was praised by our President for Christ's sake! I had such a future ahead of me. And now that demon spawn I call a son has done me in."

"No," Jacob interrupted, "You did yourself in."

"I guess so." Hartford calmed down and finished off the liquor in the glass next to his hand. "To err is human. To forgive is divine. Craig, can you find it within yourself to forgive me? I wasn't thinking straight. And I am truly and deeply sorry for what I put you and your wife through."

"I don't think I can forgive you, Governor. The things you did to me this past week were beyond revenge. It was cruel and unusual punishment."

"I understand, my boy. Well then Detective, what next? I mean you've learned the truth. You've caught the bad guy and got your confession."

Jacob stood up and handed Brett something that he had been holding in his hand since they entered the study of Thomas Hartford. Tom leaned forward, trying to get a good look at what it was. Brett held it up and showed Hartford that thanks to Robin's new iPod, he had gotten the whole confession on video recording. Brett smiled and placed the iPod in his pocket for later.

"Bravo, gentlemen," Hartford clapped, "Well done. I do have one request before you haul me away as they say. Jacob, being the civil one of the group, would you please relay a message to my wife? Would you please let her know I'm sorry for all this and that I do love her with all my heart."

"Don't worry," Brett told him, "You can tell her yourself from behind bars." He stepped towards the desk with his handcuffs open. But he was unaware of Hartford's quickness as an older man. Before he knew what was going on, Hartford had threw open the top drawer in his desk, plunged his hand into it and pulled out something that glinted in the slants of sunlight peeking into the room.

Brett dropped the handcuffs and his hand went for his holstered weapon. As he did that, he shouted to the others, "Gun!"

104

Hartford pulled another surprise move by raising the gun and placing it under his chin. He held his free hand out, hoping to stop Brett Foster in his tracks. Craig saw the gun dug deep into Tom's throat. The barrel dug into his flesh. He turned away, not wanting to see what was about to occur.

"Put the gun down, Thomas," Brett said to the governor, "This isn't the way to end it. Have some dignity."

"If I go to jail, all my dignity goes out the window. I choose the way of the Feudal Japan. That was where if you brought dishonor upon yourself, the way out was to kill yourself and save your family honor instead."

"Put the gun down, Tom."

Hartford looked over to Jacob who was mesmerized by the scene before him and looked him in the eye. With a stern tone, Hartford said, "Make sure my piece of shit son gets nailed to the wall." Jacob could do nothing but nod.

Then Hartford pulled the trigger of his gun. The boom echoed off the back wall and the bullet would later be proved by the examiner to have travelled upward in a straight direction through the center mass of Hartford's brain and out the upper back of his skull. The majority of his brain would be found to have followed the bullet out and onto the back wall behind the desk.

Craig gagged and tried to hold back any vomiting that his body wanted to purge. Jacob closed his eyes and silently said a prayer on behalf of the governor. He was exhausted and his shoulders slumped forward.

Jacob's hands were placed on his knees to stabilize himself. Brett lowered his gun and his head in shame for not being able to stop Hartford from committing suicide. He felt the need for Angie right then and there. He needed some emotion, some life in the room with him to prove that he was still alive, even though Thomas Hartford was not.

The case was now closed. What had started with one death ended with another. But Brett didn't feel the sense of accomplishment as he did when closing other cases. And then a saying that his mentor had always told him popped into his head.

"You can't win them all."

FOUR MONTHS LATER

Jacob Scott strolled down Washington Street in the thin blanket of snow that had fallen that morning. The town was now celebrating the coming of Christmas and the main street of Hoboken had been decorated as such. Banners of Christmas images hung from the street lamps and most store windows were either painted with symbols of the holidays or they were outlined in Christmas lights. Passer-bys smiled staring at the decorations while carrying large bags of gifts.

Holding his hand and walking beside him was Robin. A smile on her face, she tightened her grip on his hand to let him know that she was here for him. Jacob had been nervous about doing what they were about to. It had been a few months since he had been by the deli due to the rearranging of the Reynolds and Hoffman law firm.

Hoffman had stepped in after that weekend and made some changes as he had been wanting to but Reynolds had held him back. Hoffman took Jacob and Chris Delgado into his office the following Monday morning to speak personally to them.

"Gentlemen, I have something I feel the need to tell you. Both of you are exceptional lawyers and I am proud to have you both here representing this firm." Hoffman stood up from behind his desk and walked around it, sitting on the corner in front of them, "You obviously know about Mark and what he was doing at the firm here, correct?"

Jacob nodded and Chris replied, "Yes, sir."

"Good. I hate to bad mouth a friend and a co-worker but I had known about what he was doing for the past two months. The Carl Hartford case was not the first one he altered. But I trust you two in not letting this out of this office. The problem was catching him in the act which was tough for a crotchety old man like me. Then I saw you, Jacob, with that assistant of yours figure it out on your own and I was glad to see that Doug Martin wasn't the only boy scout here. I was even here the day you found the case file for Carl Hartford. It was very impressive."

"You mean that was you we heard in the office?" Jacob asked.

"It was but I didn't want to reveal myself in case you were armed. Anyway, what I saw that day made me realize the force I have here at this law firm. And as you know I have to assign a new partner to the firm. But before I do, I want you to know, Jacob, that I consider you my Golden Boy. You have a lot of potential and can help bring this law firm to the forefront of Hudson County. That's why I want to keep you in the trenches for now. You're the best one here to lead the soldiers out in the field. Delgado, I'm offering you the position of partner if you'll have it."

"I'd be honored sir."

"Good. And don't forget, Jacob, I won't be doing this forever. If you stay on I can guarantee you'll be first in line to take over for me. Besides, I need you to keep Judge Irwin in line. She's a hard ass."

"I wouldn't think of leaving, sir," Jacob smiled.

"Oh and one more thing, don't worry about the relationship you're hiding with Ms. Masters. She's a feisty one and not one to let slip away. She's also an asset to the firm. Just don't let me find you two in the broom closet, hear?"

"I promise."

Jacob and Robin had talked about their feelings over a romantic dinner in New York City. He had told her that she was everything he looked for in a woman and wanted to see where their relationship took them into the future. She agreed as long as he agreed to get rid of the tacky vase in his living room. He did so and a couple of months later she began to leave things at Jacob's home for those late nights and even later mornings.

"Are you going to be okay with this?" Robin asked him as they reached the front of Anthony's Deli. He looked in and saw the busy crowd inside. Each person was waiting to place their order of Christmas entertainment trays and sliced meats. He saw Craig behind the register and was glad that the smile on his face had returned.

Craig had a hard time coping after the incident in Thomas Hartford's study. Jacob didn't blame him. That was not the way he thought the case would end. But with the video clip that Jacob had recorded on Robin's iPod Craig's case had been thrown out of court and he had been freed on all charges that following Tuesday. Even though Guy was disappointed in not winning the case, he was thoroughly happy with the win he had in the Carl Hartford trial.

With the release of the video from Hartford's study, no defense lawyer would dare take the case for Carl. So Carl decided to defend himself. And Guy jumped at the chance to be prosecutor on the trial. The trial was listed as the biggest joke in the history of courtrooms along the East Coast. Carl was found guilty of the rape and battery assault on Jennifer Tomasi. While the trial was going on, three other women found the courage to come forward and take the stand against him. Germaine Irwin sentenced Carl to a minimum of ten years in a maximum security prison, six years for the rape and battery and another four years for tampering with evidence. Jacob had heard recently that Carl Hartford was learning how it felt to be Jennifer Tomasi in the prison.

"Yeah, I can do it. Let's go say hi." Jacob followed Robin into the deli and swam their way over to the ticket feeder. He pulled out a ticket reading 135 and looked up at the digital reader that was showing ticket number 125 was currently being served.

"We could be here a while," Robin said, looking at the number on his ticket.

"That's okay, I know some people who can get me the good stuff without the wait," he smiled at her. Grabbing her hand, he nudged his way through the crowd again and over to the register where Craig served each customer with happiness. He was in the middle of ringing up number 124 that he didn't notice Jacob and Robin reach the counter. Jacob waved at Craig and he jolted up in surprise.

"Hey!" Craig said.

" 'ey," Jacob said in his best Italian voice, "Youse know where I could get some fresh mozzerel?"

"That is the worst Italian accent I've ever heard," Craig laughed.

"You think that's bad, you should hear his Irish one," Robin joked along.

"How are you guys doing?"

"We're good. Where's the mother to be?"

"She's in the back putting together an order for next week. We're swamped with tray orders."

"So the deli is running fantastic huh?"

"We've hired an extra two hands for the holiday rush. Business is booming."

"That's great. I'm really glad things are working out for you two."

"Hey, I owe it all to you, Jacob. You believed in me when no one else did. This is all because of you. Listen, before Jackie gets a hold of you, please say you'll stop over next week for dinner? My parents are in Florida enjoying their retirement and we'll kind of be alone other than our work family. She'd love to have you visit."

"I'll tell her we'd love to," Robin told him.

"Thank you. Did you need anything?"

"No, we were just stopping by to say hello and to deliver a little pre-birthday gift." Jacob held up the medium-sized box that he had gift wrapped for Craig and Jackie's baby.

"Yeah, just go on into the back and say hi."

Robin followed Jacob into the back of the deli where the supplies and walk-in fridge was located. They found Jackie in the fridge with a pen and clipboard. Jacob was surprised to see the growth of her belly since he had last seen her months before. He almost thought she was ready to deliver yet she still had four months to go till the end of term.

"There's the woman who's smuggling the Christmas ham, officer," he joked. Jackie turned around and smiled big. She waddled forward and gave Robin a hug.

"How are you two? It's been so long."

"You look great," Robin told her.

"Please, you don't have to lie. I have an inflatable beach ball in my stomach who is gearing up to be a future UFC fighter," Jackie replied.

"Well for someone like that, you look good."

"Thank you."

"Okay," Jacob said, "Robin and I have a debate going. I say girl, she says boy. Who's right?"

"He's still getting the hang of this relationship thing, isn't he?" Jackie asked Robin.

"Not yet, but I'm hoping that you can help set him right."

"Jacob, you have to remember. From now on, Robin is going to be right. And in this debate she is."

"Well, it's a good thing the gift is multi-gendered," he smiled. He handed her the gift and she opened it there in front of them. Inside was a little tanned stuffed dog with a name tag that read: MURRAY.

"That's so cute, thank you." Jackie gave them hugs again. "You two must come over for dinner next week."

"Craig already begged us and we would love to."

"That's great. And what about Kristie? How's she doing?"

Jacob explained to her that Dean had made a full recovery and he decided to move into Kristie's home with her so that Connor could continue going to the same schools and she could work at passing the bar as Hoffman had promised her Doug's office at the law firm. Dean had helped raise Connor like his own during her schooling. She was getting nervous as the holidays rolled by seeing how her first chance at the bar was coming up in January.

"That's great," Jackie said, "Please tell her that she's invited too."

"We will."

"Do you have a name for the baby yet?"

"We've decided on Alexander."

"He's going to grow up to be great, you know," Jacob joked. Jackie looked over at Robin and Robin shrugged.

"What can I say? I'm a sucker for a cheesy guy."

Outside, Josh and Tamara were returning from visiting Santa at the nearby Newport Center Mall. He chose to stop at the deli for some hot chocolate for her and a hot cup of coffee for him. Then they were going to return to his new apartment and decorate his bachelor-like Christmas tree. Tomorrow, the two of them were going to go skating in Central Park with Angie and Brett.

His ex-wife and his partner were taking things slow for Tamara's sake. She had wanted to prevent Tamara from rebelling when she got older. So far Tamara was happy to still have both Josh and Angie in her life, even if Brett was becoming part of their group now. Their first test, Thanksgiving dinner, went over with flying colors.

"Here we go," Josh said. They approached the door to the deli with the bustling crowd beyond it when a car pulled up to the curb behind them. The car horn gave out two quick beeps and Josh turned to look at the origin of the noise. He saw Brett and Angie wave to him.

"Oh look, Mommy and Brett are here to join us," he said to his daughter. He walked over to the car and Brett stepped out of the car.

"Sorry to cut your quality time short but Valentine and O'Sullivan just called me. They need help with a drug deal gone sour."

"What? But that's their department," Josh complained.

"Yeah but seven men went into the meeting place and only one came out. And O'Sullivan said something about an interesting surprise to it."

"What surprise?"

Brett shrugged his cold shoulders, "He wouldn't say."

Josh looked down at Tamara and pondered what he should do. Then he looked back at the crowd at the deli and finally back to Brett.

"Okay fine but I'm getting some coffee and hot chocolate first. You two want anything?" Tamara looked up at her father and smiled.

Acknowledgements

Thank Yous go to the following:

- Ray Victor, for teaching me the ways of the Force and for being a brother like no other.

- Christopher Diaz, for your help in the legal matters in this book. Always ready to assist at a minute's notice.

- Audrey Welch and the crew at Authorhouse, for the help in making my dream of publishing this book easier than it looked.

- Lucky Revilleza, for his help in making the cover pretty kick ass.

- Christie Dietrich, for the mysterious and cool photo that makes me look professional.

- To my personal fan club cheerleaders, Christine Mendoza, Eric and Maura Valentin, Jacqueline Kociniak, Kristie "Winchester" Mahieux and Jacob Smith. Your egging on and support did not go unnoticed.

- My mother, Phyllis, for believing in my talents.

- My son, Alex, who taught me that all work and no play makes Dad boring.

- And most of all, my wife, Lisa, who kept me on track and pushed me to be better in every way.

CPSIA information can be obtained at www.ICGtesting.com
Printed in the USA
LVOW110112031111

253250LV00001B/37/P